Nine Lords of the Night

To my mother Fannie Lee Gibson who taught me how to read and encouraged me to write

Helotes, Texas

March 3, 2008

Nine Lords of the Night

E. C. Gibson

Embella, Inc.
Elgin, Texas

 ISBN # 1-890184-16-0

Published by Embella, Inc., Attn: Deborah A. Kaufman, 704 N Main St, Ste 100, Elgin Texas 78621-1630, 512-285-3440 or 866-505-3400.

Note: Embella, Inc. was previously publishing under the name Gothic Publishing, Inc.

Printed and bound in the United States of America.

I

"I sensed that the world was a labyrinth, from which it is impossible to flee."
Jorge Luis Borges, "Death and the Compass"

1 Death and the Compass

On the day she vanished only two people were left in camp. The August afternoon passed sluggishly as stagnant heat rose off the rain forest. A tropical storm gathered over Belize and Guatemala to the east. All day long jagged black clouds had piled up and now a massive wall of dark, swollen thunderheads dominated the eastern sky. To the west the sky was clear, but over the camp the clouds were low and ragged. The humidity was oppressive and left a film of moisture on grass, leaves, and skin. Even the insects moved slowly in the thickening air of lowland Chiapas, Mexico.

Two graduate students stayed behind to look after the camp and the archaeological field collections. The rest of the crew drove the Land Rovers into San Javier to pick up supplies and have dinner. Jesse Salazar was in the field laboratory cleaning a skull. Kathryn Haden was walking out to the ceremonial plaza of the ancient Maya settlement looking for her compass.

Kathryn was anxious to find it because of its' sentimental value. An old friend had given it to her some years ago and she carried it on projects in Europe, Hawaii, and Central America, never losing it until that morning. She would have to admit that she considered it her "lucky" compass, something like a talisman. Most archaeologists had similar beliefs in luck. In fact, almost everyone she had ever known believed in it to some extent. They were a superstitious bunch.

Kathryn wondered if the archaeologists who had discovered the site, and classified it as a "minor ceremonial center" almost fifty years ago, had been superstitious. They had named the site Chanul Tzuk which meant "conjured spirit" in Maya, as part of a reconnaissance project for the

1

Carnegie Institute. In 1946 they had spent a week doing some preliminary mapping and surveying and then moved to Bonampak to the north, where some spectacularly violent and well-preserved murals had been discovered. No further work had been done until 1993 when Chandler Bennett of the University of Oregon had started his project.

As she approached the partially cleared pyramids in the center of the site, thunder broke and rolled over the lagoon. The clouds seemed to have a greenish hue and opened in torrents, as if cut open, drenching her in seconds. She ran to the nearest excavation trench, covered by long blue plastic tarps to protect the work in progress, climbed down a ladder and took shelter at the main pyramid.

A flash of blue-white lightning lit up the plaza and the thunderclap was so loud and close, that stones fell out of the excavation walls. Kathryn thought about Dennis Puleston, a young professor from the University of Minnesota, who had been killed by lightning at Chichen Itza's highest temple back in the 1970s. She sat with her back against the sidewall of the excavation trench hoping to present a smaller target to the lightning. At least I'm out of the rain, she thought. The storm seemed to hit all at once, as if a switch had been turned on. The temperature had dropped at least ten degrees and now the rain was pouring down hard.

Kathryn huddled in the trench against a back corner. She felt trapped and hoped the rain would let up soon. Water was starting to pool in depressions in the tarp, causing it to droop. It would not hold the rain off indefinitely. She watched the tarp sag and the lines to the poles and stakes tighten. The end of the tarp was like a waterfall. She thought about the pavement of limestone underneath her. People long dead had placed it there three thousand years ago and now here she was waiting out a major storm, the first person to use the temple for protection since 900 BC. The rain fell in sheets as the wind blew sideways. She began to worry. What if the storm went on for hours? She could be trapped here for a long time, and she was at least three miles from the camp. Actually, Kathryn hated to admit to herself, but she was starting to feel a little claustrophobic and apprehensive. She also felt a presence, as if something out in the jungle waited, was aware of her . . . was watching.

"Jungle fever." Kathryn said out loud, just to hear her voice over the roar of the storm. "The jungle's getting to me. My nerves. Happens to everyone eventually. Maybe I should just go ahead, get soaked and head back in." She looked out at the ancient plaza. The rain was blowing almost parallel to the ground. No way was she going out in that. At least the tarp was still holding up and keeping the water out of the trench. "I wish I'd brought something to read."

She could not see the men in the jungle running along the trail. They wore backpacks and carried picks and shovels. Their rain-soaked clothing clung to their bodies and glistened in the lightning flashes as they ran, ignoring the storm.

Kathryn thought she heard something on the other side of the trench. Was something moving around out there in the rain? She stood up on her tiptoes but the excavation walls were over 6 feet, just barely too high for her to see out. A stake gave way at the top of the pyramid and one corner of the tarp flapped up with a loud rip, startling her, and exposing her to the rain. She moved to the dry area on the other side of the trench. The winds were getting stronger and she worried would the tarp hold?

Two of the up-slope stakes came out and the tarp was flapping up and down in the wind. Rain stung Kathryn's face, as she tried to get away from the opening. Some more loose rubble from the core of the pyramid fell, as the east wall slumped and caved in. It occurred to her that all of the walls might collapse and she could be buried if she stayed there much longer.

Looks like it's time to go, she thought.

At Penn, she played intramural basketball and she was in good shape. Good enough to run all the way back to camp. She steeled herself for running, when the last two stakes pulled out and the tarpaulin blew up, floated down, and engulfed her.

As she struggled to free herself, a man leaped from the edge of the trench. Two more quickly followed. The first man grabbed her and she screamed. He silenced her when he threw her down hard to the limestone pavement. Kathryn weakly tried to pull off the tarp but he grabbed her, picked her up, and rammed her head into the rock wall. Blood ruptured from her forehead. She was passing out. But she tried to fight it off.

The tarp fell off her head.

Kathryn looked up in pain, dazedly blinking back the rain and her blood, and recognized one of her attackers. She tried to scream again but could not. Another man raised his shovel and struck her in the face. He hit her again, but she ducked and the next blow struck the top of her head. She clawed at his wrist and tried to get loose from the tarp, which had twisted around her legs. He hit her again harder, and she heard her skull crack. A blinding flash of pain. Blackness. She stopped thrashing. The thunder crashed down and the wind whipped up - blowing the tarp off of her and taking it somewhere in the direction of Guatemala.

* * * * * * * * *

In the camp, Jesse stopped cleaning the skull as water blew in through the window of mosquito netting. He turned off Radio Belize, which was playing "Oh a storm is threatening, our very lives today. If I don't get some shelter, oh yeah I'm going to fade away." Nice sense of humor he thought, as he went about the lab securing the netting before he made a quick dash for his hut. It was pointless. He ran as fast as he could but was soaked instantly. When he got inside, he stripped out of his clothes and toweled off. He hung his towel on a nail and ruefully looked down at the lime dust sticking to his wet feet. "Ah yes," he said to himself "the romance of archaeology." A rudimentary examination of his stomach and arms showed half a dozen new swellings from the biting flies and mosquitoes.

Lightning struck nearby in the jungle accompanied by a blast of thunder. A tree limb cracked nearby, and Jesse winced and ducked instinctively. Kathryn was out there, in the ceremonial plaza.

I hope she's okay, he worried. She should be getting back now.

He lit a small, thin cigar, not because he enjoyed them, but because he had been told the smoke discouraged mosquitoes and flies. After pulling on a fresh pair of GI surplus fatigues, he sprayed his chest with insect repellent, then his neck, back, legs, and feet.

A loud detonation of thunder and a blazing white flash caused him to flinch and close his eyes. When he looked out toward the main plaza, boiling clouds obscured the tops of the pyramids. The storm was right on top of them.

He decided that he should go out and look for Kathryn. She had been gone for over two hours, and it was a three-mile walk out to the plaza. The storm was intensifying, water was pooling up in the low spots and it showed no signs of stopping any time soon. I'd better go out there now, he thought. Something might have happened. He pulled on an old cut off sweatshirt and looked for his rain poncho. Jesse dreaded going out and knew he would get soaked, but he loved Kathryn more than she knew. He had to go see if she was all right. She would have done the same for him. He pulled on his rain poncho, put on his old cowboy hat, picked up his machete, and headed out into the rain.

He made it as far as the tool shed on the east edge of the site, when the storm stopped him. He could not see where he was going. The thunder was almost continuous and the winds were blowing palm fronds, sticks, and leaf litter into his face. He could feel the storm strengthening and hear tree limbs snapping and crashing in the forest. His pants were soaked, flapping in the wind, and he kept falling down, tripping over tree limbs, and rocks. Jesse was getting frustrated. He could not make any headway. From his hut he had gone nearly a mile, and it was starting to get dark enough that he would need a flashlight soon.

He could find no sign of Kathryn; maybe she had made it back to camp by now. At least he hoped so. She had probably reached the same conclusion he had... that it was getting too dangerous to walk around in the storm. Both of them had been left to look after the camp. Now it was completely unguarded. He decided to go back and get a flashlight. Hopefully Kathryn was on her way in, if she wasn't already there.

* * * * * * * *

The storm lasted until just before dawn. No one came back from San Javier. After going repeatedly out into the storm, unable to walk or see, Jesse was exhausted and returned finally to the camp to wait for Kathryn. He spent the night alone, worrying about her and whether the camp could hold up through the storm. The wind and rain lashed his hut, and the thatched roof leaked in a dozen places. The thunder detonated all around, and the echoing sounds played with his imagination. Several times he thought he heard people talking, and hoped it was the crew returning from San Javier. But no one showed up. From exhaustion, Jesse had drifted off a couple of times during the night but he had tried to stay alert. He felt guilty about not helping Kathryn, but she was an experienced archaeologist and had probably figured something out.

When there was enough light to see, he started toward the ceremonial plaza calling for her. The storm had uprooted a lot of trees, ceibas, palms, cohunes and coconuts on the edge of the jungle and by the lagoon. The storage hut was completely flattened and most of the roofs in the camp were damaged. The excavation units were full of water. Not good. The water would cause artifacts to fall out of their context and information would be lost as a result.

So far all of the tarps were gone, blown far away. But maybe the one at the main pyramid was still up. That one would have offered the best protection.

As he approached the ceremonial plaza the sun was starting to break on the horizon and the jungle seemed to wake up. Birds were singing faintly. A flock of green parrots took off from a cohune palm and screeched overhead. The clouds were breaking and it looked like they might burn off. Jesse thought again about what a horrible night Kathy must have had if she was exposed out here in the storm. He just wanted to find her as quickly as possible.

When he entered the plaza, he called out for her again. No response. He rounded the edge of the Classic Period ball court and there was the main pyramid. The excavation trench had collapsed on all sides and it was full of rubble, water and mud. The tarps were gone. He hoped she had not gone here. She might have been buried alive.

Jesse quickly looked around the edges of the slumped trench walls. Not a trace of her. So much damage had been done to the excavation; it would take a team of laborers a week to clear it. Dr. Bennett would not be happy when he got back from San Javier. He tried to calm down and concentrate on systematically searching every meter of the site, if it took all day or until the rest of the crew came back. Kathy had to be somewhere.

* * * * * * * *

Four hours later he still had not found a trace of her anywhere in the plaza, or in the jungle next to it, or on the lagoon shore. He felt like crying as he searched desperately.

At around 11:30 he heard the Land Rovers up on the road and was glad the crew had made it back from San Javier. Jesse hoped that Kathy had gone to the village down the highway where the local Maya Indians lived. She knew many of them because they worked as laborers on the project. That would be the next place to look. Jogging back to camp, he ran by the main pyramid again and saw something blue on the edge of the clearing, in a tree branch. He climbed up the tree and pulled down a University of Pennsylvania baseball cap. It had belonged to Kathryn.

2 Introduction to Anthropology

The zodiac floated on the ceiling. Holmes Hall had been the centerpiece of Harvard Medical School when it was built in 1799 but now it was used for large introductory courses. The medical school had moved across the river to Boston in 1810. The domed ceiling was forty feet above the floor. For reasons that were long forgotten, on its azure blue surface the signs of the zodiac were painted in gold and accurately rendered, as they would appear in the constellations of the evening sky.

Cordelia Bell was sitting in the last row directly under the balcony overhang, checking Professor Mamett's slides and projectors. They were her responsibility since she was Mamett's head teaching fellow. She placed her coffee cup on the floor, stretched out her long legs and looked up at her own birth sign, Libra, the scales of balance, an air sign floating above her on the ceiling. It was certainly an odd lecture hall but Cordelia liked it because it was strange. She had read that in the 18th and 19th centuries, many of Harvard's benefactors and alumni had been members of various obscure and secretive Masonic orders and the zodiac on the roof had something to do with the masons, but how it all fit together was unclear. Someday when she had the time, she intended to research it a bit, because the zodiac floating above Holmes Hall intrigued her. But that would not happen today-or tomorrow for that matter. Today was

7

Wednesday. She had to be Dr. Mamett's teaching fellow in ANT 120, Introduction to Anthropology, for the morning, and the rest of the day was reserved for the last twenty-four hours before her oral examination for her Ph.D. in archaeology.

The hall had just about filled with sleepy undergraduates and why Mamett insisted on teaching at eight thirty in the morning was a mystery. Since her teaching partner Laurence Eikelmann, had not shown up yet, Cordelia gathered up lecture two's handouts and walked down to the front row passing them out as she went. Mamett walked in and as he reached the front row, he motioned her over.

"Hello Delia, how are you on this fine September morning?"

"Trying to wake up Dr. Mamett." She handed him his obligatory cup of water, which he would sip from during the lecture.

"Well, I am happy to see you here in light of your imminent rite of passage. Some graduate students on the eve of their orals have been known to call in sick and use every remaining moment to prepare. Of course for some students like Ward, yesterday… well, it was really too bad." He waved his hand dismissively and handed her another slide carousel. "Your assistance under such stressful conditions is greatly appreciated."

Like many professors Mamett liked to talk - to the point of being long-winded. His comment about Phil Ward annoyed her. For one thing, a professor should not gossip about students with other students. It wasn't proper. For another, Ward was a close friend, who after failing the exam yesterday afternoon, had simply disappeared. Ward would receive a "terminal" master's degree for his five years at Harvard, a permanent stigma. Many of his fellow graduate students had written him off.

"I don't think there is any more room in my brain. I am as ready as I will ever be."

"I am sure you will do fine. I predict total success."

It was good to hear him say that since he represented one fourth of the examination committee. "Oh. Would you like one of these handouts?"

"Why? I wrote it. I think I know what's on it."

Mamett walked up the stairs to the podium. He was barely six feet tall and a little pudgy. His black hair was curly and unruly and he needed a haircut, Cordelia thought. He straightened his tie, smoothed his beard and began to lecture. Mamett's approach to intro to anthropology was unique, but it was a difficult course to teach. Trying to cover all of the sub fields of anthropology and their respective contributions to social science in one semester was almost impossible to do well. Mamett was unorthodox, and did not even try to provide such coverage. Instead, he presented his "greatest hits of anthropology" and engaged the student's interest from the start.

Today's lecture was the third of the new semester, since the undergraduates were still shopping courses it was designed to lure them in and keep them. The initial segment titled "Magic, Science and Religion," would occupy coverage for the first three weeks. During their organizational meeting Delia, Mamett and Eikelmann, had met to plan the strategy of the course. Mamett offered his view on how teaching such courses would help him obtain tenure.

"First, no one recognizes how important these big introductory-level courses are. This is where we snag the undecided majors. I mean, how many students enter college saying they are going to major in anthropology? Not too damned many. You see it's our mission to win them over and convert them to majors. Then with enrollments up, the administration increases funds to the department. More research gets done. More graduate research money is available. Everyone prospers. All because we take on the courses no one else wants to teach and make them an asset."

Implicit in Mamett's plan was the prospect that he would create his own following - a good source of free research labor and a good way to build up popular support within the department's student community. By coupling this plan with his ongoing archaeological projects in Chiapas and Belize, Mamett averaged ten to twelve published manuscripts a year. Next year when he came up for review, he would be a strong tenure candidate. His plan seemed to be working, because enrollments were up and the number of anthropology majors had increased. Of course what all of these

B.A.s in anthropology were going to do after graduation was not clear. The graduate students knew it was not exactly a growth field.

Having quickly dispensed with explaining the course requirements, textbooks and grading system, Mamett launched into the lecture.

"Magic. Science. Religion." Three very different topics at first glance, but are they really? They are all systems of belief. They are all ideologies. Yes, even science is ideological… talk to any devotee of Charles Darwin. Everyone on the planet today believes in at least one or more of these systems and this is true of every civilization that has ever existed.

"Belief. How many of you believe in the supernatural?" About ten hands went up, scattered across the hall.

"I count approximately nine or ten people who are willing to admit they believe in the supernatural. Keep your hands up. No one else?" Heads turned in the seats to see who was foolish enough to put up their hands.

"Okay. So the rest of you do not believe in God? Correct? Because you know, God is a supernatural being. Our Judaeo-Christian God or any other god. You can't see Him. You can't analyze Him scientifically. He works in mysterious ways. He's supernatural. He is the foundation of all religions, creator of heaven and earth and apparently not all that popular in this class."

This brought subdued laughter from the students.

"So even God has a tough time at Harvard." Now almost everyone was laughing as Mamett paused for effect. "Let us reconsider the question. How many of you believe in the supernatural?"

This time hands went up all over the hall. Mamett smiled to himself.

"Good. Because you see, this part of the course is all about belief. The nature of belief and the belief in nature. Why do all of the world's religions show striking similarities to each other? Who is your God? Or who are your gods? In the first part, we will explore the relationships between belief systems and their respective roles in the evolution of civilization. Magic, religion, art, science and politics were fused together in the early states and rooted in shamanism. Take for example, the pyramids of the ancient Maya.

"As you will see in the slides I'm going to show, they built them to represent the other world, as sacred mountains erected on the back of a mythic turtle floating in a primordial ocean. These beliefs are ancient, back to a time when Maya religion was shamanistic. The plazas and courtyards represented valleys and the ball court symbolized a crack in the earth leading to the underworld. Royalty lived nearby in palaces built to glorify the rulers and their lineages.

"Maya kings were thought to have supernatural powers gained by birth and maintained by the use of drugs and sacrifice. They would sacrifice their own blood, the blood of others, animals, art objects. These sacrifices occurred at public ceremonies held in front of the pyramids. The combination of blood loss, acute pain and drugs induced hallucinatory visions in the royal practitioners of these mystic rituals. This is how the rulers transformed the landscape into sacred places of spirituality. These visions are depicted in the mythic art and architecture of the Maya."

"Blood magic. Ritual sacrifice. It was all part of their religion - as were the pyramids and the monumental art of the stelae. These monuments clearly show the supernatural bridge that the Maya lords provided to the heavens above, the underworld below, and the world of humans in the middle. Highly evolved shamanism. It's all woven together and documented in the hieroglyphics, or as archaeologists prefer to say, the glyphs."

The lights in the hall dimmed and the slide show began.

3 Were-Jaguar

I'm breaking one of diving's taboos Jesse thought, as he unhooked his scuba gear and waded out to the white limestone rim of the cenote. The sun was beginning to sink into the jungle canopy and diving any longer would be too risky. Hell, diving alone is dangerous enough, I've been trained never to do it and that damned hole in the ground gives me the creeps. Damned good place to get trapped.

11

He started carrying the tanks and gear to the battered old pick-up. It was a '69 GMC with a million miles on it. None of the gauges worked, it ran when it wanted to and the passenger's door was missing. Jesse had paid the owner of the local tienda one hundred US dollars to use it and a one-room pensione for a month. Hell of a deal, Jesse thought, wondering if it would start this time without priming the carburetor. He walked up the rain-carved gully that served as a road for the truck, brushing aside overgrowth as he went. This time it started right up and blasted blue smoke into the jungle evening as he started up the hill to the main road to San Javier.

Driving down the gravel road, his mind turned to the last afternoon he and Kathryn had been together…how she thought she might be pregnant. From the start of the project there was an attraction between them, and they had fallen in love quickly. She was intensely private and wanted to keep it secret. Now she had disappeared.

Over and over he asked himself, where else can I look that I haven't looked? What am I missing? He thought about how he had overheard the other students speculating about his "poor judgment" in leaving Kathryn alone on the site during the storm. Why didn't he go after her? They had no way of knowing how blinding the storm had been. God only knows what they think of me, he thought, and no matter how you look at it she was my responsibility. I've got to find out what happened.

The shimmering lagoon was coming up on his right. On this side of the site a field of cattails and saw grass swayed in the evening breeze. Kathryn had disappeared out there somewhere. He had looked for almost three weeks now, and had only found her hat. Jesse decided that he would stay in Chiapas until he figured it out. "No matter how long it takes." He said out loud, and drove on to San Javier in the dark.

* * * * * * * * * *

By the next morning, the drizzle that had been falling all night ceased. As Jesse neared the lagoon he saw a new track going off to the left, towards the north shore. He hit his brakes and looked at it. Someone had driven a heavy vehicle down the slope, flattening the thick palmetto, and churning up two wide muddy ruts. Two sets of tracks going in and coming out.

12

That definitely wasn't there yesterday, he thought. Whoever did it went in last night…in the rain.

He turned to the left and started down the muddy track. Something very large and heavy had driven off the road. Jesse followed the deep muddy ruts for about seven miles until they went into a water filled ditch, where they widened out before continuing through the saw grass. Whatever the vehicle was, it had skidded and bogged down here before continuing. Jesse was sure that the GMC would never make it through the hole. He grabbed his field pack and machete and got out of the truck.

In the middle of the tall grass it was humid and sweltering, with no trace of a breeze. He walked around the trough and followed the trail. He could see that the tires were wide, and the tread marks were deep and thick.

Looks like a tractor pulling a trailer maybe, he thought. Probing one of the ruts with his machete, he pried up a red fragment of Late Classic pottery. So I'm near another site? Or maybe Chanul Tzuk extends this far to the east. We never surveyed this area; the ground cover is way too dense.

The trail curved around a swampy area of brackish water to his right. It smelled of rotting plants. Part of the lagoon system? How far am I from the lagoon? At least a couple of miles, and over seven miles from the road…probably a swamp that drains into the lagoon. His shirt was sticking to his back, and he stopped to drink from his water bottle before continuing. The grass was thicker now, and the trail was narrower. Suddenly he felt afraid. He stopped in his tracks, the glaring sun the rotting black water, the smell; it was getting to him. He slowed his pace and squared his shoulders before pressing on.

Can't believe I'm getting spooked out here in broad daylight. I don't get panic attacks! What the hell is wrong with me?

He shrugged to adjust his backpack, and followed the twisting path back to the left. The vegetation was changing, stubby palmettos, and ceiba saplings, with their distinctive spiked trunks, were mixed in with the saw grass. He came to a place where all the vegetation was flattened into a large oval shape, and the ruts were deeper. It looked like the vehicle had turned around in here, and churned up a lot of mud.

13

A narrow trail had been cut off to the left. There was a ridge that way. He could see a cleared milpa, an empty cornfield up ahead. Through the morning haze, he could make out treetops in the distance, a couple of miles off to the north. He started down the narrow trail.

The smell of something rotting was changing, pungently getting sweeter and stronger. He was feeling anxious again. He plunged forward into the brush, swinging his machete lightly to widen out the path. It just felt good to have it in his hand. Sweat soaked through his shirt, and rolled off his nose. He stopped, took off his hat, and wiped his forehead with a bandanna before continuing. Breathing hard, he tried to catch his breath, but the air was really putrid now, and he nearly gagged on it. The sickening sweet stench permeated everything.

He heard something. What the hell is it? He chopped some more towards the noise, heard a flapping sound, and a large black shape flew up from the brush a few feet ahead. Scaring the hell out of him, he raised his machete to fend it off…a vulture.

Another vulture flew up. He found himself in a clearing right in front of a low ridge. In the center, someone had erected a cross. The cleared area around it was almost covered in vultures. This was where the foul smell was coming from. There was a litter of rum bottles all around, some spent cartridges, pieces of meat, scattered bones, and a puddle of blood, covered in flies. They were swimming in it, some were stuck.

A few vultures took to the air, slowly. Others sat on the ground. Bloated. Staring at him. They were unnerving, and disgusting, just sitting there looking at him.

Jesse picked up a rock and threw it at a fat one on the ground. It hissed and took off. He yelled, and charged the ones clumped together under the wooden cross, swinging his machete at them. They took off too. He had cleared them out. Above him about a dozen vultures were flapping their wings silently as they struggled to gain altitude. Now he could see what was lying under the cross.

A partially burned and gutted animal carcass sprawled in the dirt, reeking of putrefied flesh and gore. Jesse covered his nose with his bandanna, and tried to identify it. A long slender skull with rows of dagger teeth,

14

apparently a crocodile, was mixed in with tapered legs, ending in hooves…a deer. Everything was covered in flies, hundreds of thousands of flies.

Someone came out last night and killed a crocodile and a deer in the dark and the rain? The carcasses appeared to be jumbled together. It all made him uneasy.

Jesse wiped the flies away from his face, and saw another trail heading toward the ridge. Feeling like he was being watched, he started down the trail. He sure didn't want to stay where he was.

He was covered in sweat and felt clammy. Climbing slowly up the ridge, he noticed the loose square masonry stones, fragments of red pottery, and a very recent cigarette butt. He examined a monochrome pottery fragment. It was of the Chicanel type and dated from the Late Preclassic, around 300 BC. He was standing on the edge of a large structure. It was a long low, platform mound, probably a Late Preclassic plazuela group. The path bisected the mound near the center, and wound between clumps of cohune palms. He turned to look back the way he had come, and saw the vultures dropping back down to feed.

In among the trees it was gloomy, and the insects were thicker, flies, gnats and mosquitoes competed for his skin, incessantly humming. Sweat was streaming off of him, as his eyes adjusted to the shadows. Ahead was a wet earth path leading further into the center of the platform and a large pile of back dirt to the right of the trail. Someone had been digging here recently.

Next to the back dirt was a large hole, eight meters in diameter and about three meters deep. He could make out partially uncovered masonry steps, leading down to a block of limestone carved in the shape of an altar. It was thousands of years old and had been recently excavated. Mud was still sticking to it. Poles had been cut from the underbrush and were lying by the sides of the pit. Someone had obviously tried to pry it out of the ground. The altar had to weigh at least three thousand pounds. He knew that looters had done it, yet it did not look at all like a typical looter's pit. The excavation technique, the square hole, and straight walls suggested professional training. It occurred to him that whoever had dug the hole could be coming back at any time to haul the altar off. He looked around to see if anyone was nearby, and then climbed down into the pit, his excitement building in spite of his anxiety.

He knelt down beside the altar and saw that it had elements of Maya and Olmec designs carved in it. This was an incredibly important discovery. The face carved in the center of the altar had large extended fangs; a feline nose blended with human features - a were-jaguar, the classic Olmec icon. It was framed by Maya hieroglyphics that looked like calendrical dates. Jesse wished he knew Maya epigraphy better, but there was no question that this was from the very dawn of Central American civilization, and showed connections between two of the most evolved cultures in the region. Jesse had to somehow salvage it before the looters came back. Then he noticed that the table area of the altar had a sticky substance in the center, surrounded by puddles of wax, and melted down votive candles. He touched it with his finger. Blood.

4 Resignation

In some essential ways Harvard would never change. Carl Prefontaine, holder of the McNay Chair of American Archaeology, was in his office reading an undergraduate's diary, written in 1692. A graduate student had found it in the archives and brought it over to Carl. As part of his study of the archaeology of the college, Carl was attempting to understand how the early architecture influenced the student's cognitive experience and perceptions. What did they think of the place basically? How did it affect them? This particular student in the portion of the diary that Carl had read thus far thought his professors were quite ill tempered, the food was bad, and the workload was too harsh. Carl smiled and thought of the timelessness…three centuries of certain features of the Harvard experience. The phone ringing on his private line disturbed him. Only friends and close colleagues had that number.

"Yes?"

"Carl?" It was his first Ph.D. student, Chandler Bennett.

"Chandler. How are you?"

"I've been better Carl. This whole thing has me at the end of my rope. It's not enough, the agony I feel over what happened to Kathryn. I think about it constantly. Yet now…" His voice wavered.

"Chan. I've known you for over thirty years. You can tell me anything."

"They're investigating me Carl. My own department investigating me…for negligence! Plus, the Haden family is suing me and the University of Oregon." He took a deep breath. "I'm going to need to call in character references. Can you believe that?"

"We live in a litigious age Chan. Too many attorneys with too little to do, I guess. I would be honored to testify to your character, if you think I could help."

"Thanks. It might come to that, but…" His voice trailed off. Carl, I've decided to retire. No matter how the investigation turns out, at the end of this academic year I'm retiring."

"Well, I can see how it looks bad right now, but give it some thought. From what I've heard you didn't do anything wrong."

"I have thought about it Carl. You know, even before this tragedy happened, the whole field experience was getting tiresome, and it has been for years. I'm tired of fieldwork, publishing preliminary reports, attending academic circle jerks, writing research proposals, competing for grants…publishing for the sake of publishing. It hasn't been fun for some time. Hell. The truth is I hate my job. I didn't look forward to going to Chiapas last summer." He took a deep breath. "I dreaded it, and if I hadn't gone, Kathryn Haden would still be alive."

"You don't know for sure that she's . . . not alive."

"Carl, half the Mexican Army, and all of the local police, turned Chiapas upside down looking for her. They searched for two weeks. She's vanished. It is likely that she is dead." His voice cracked.

Both paused for a few seconds, and then Carl asked. "When did you get back?"

"About two weeks ago."

"How is everyone doing out there at Oregon?" Carl was almost afraid to ask.

"Well to my face, everyone's very solicitous, but clearly everyone also feels the cloud created by Kathryn's disappearance. So far, no one has wanted to talk to me directly about it. But of course they're all talking behind my back, and that's to be expected."

"I can only imagine how you must feel Chandler." He paused before asking. "What really happened out there?"

"Do you know you are the first one to ask me that point blank, since I've come back? My wife won't even ask me, although I know she wants to." He cleared his throat again. "Where do I start?"

"Tell me about the young woman." Carl said, gently.

"Kathryn Haden. She had applied for the ceramics position late, before the deadline, from Penn. Highly recommended by Ray Burgess, her advisor. You remember Carl? We were at Harvard together, back in the mid 60s?"

"I remember. You and Ray were my teaching fellows. Hard to believe it's been thirty years."

"Well anyway, Ray was right about her. She was very smart, well read, and knew Maya ceramics as well as anyone, and a hard worker. She took excellent notes."

"So what happened?"

"Our field schedule was ten hour days, Monday through Friday. On Saturday's we worked mornings, and in the afternoons we went into San Javier to resupply and do a little personal shopping, drop things off at the post office, you know. . . That Saturday it was Kathryn and Jesse's turn to take care of the camp."

"Now who's he?"

18

"Jesse Salazar is my graduate student, from San Antonio. He's Tex-Mex, a big guy, about six feet three, two hundred and fifty pounds, I figured if anything happened, that he could handle it. He has a lot of field experience. As an undergrad he played football, defense, for A&M - second string, but he saw some action. He was on a lot of digs in Texas for A&M, worked in the underwater archaeology program, a certified scuba instructor as well. He has a very impressive resume."

"So he and the girl were left to watch the camp."

"Right. It was August 23rd, two weeks before the end of the project. The forecast was that a tropical storm would hit Belize and Guatemala, but Chiapas would only get rain late that evening. So I figured we'd get back from town in plenty of time. But we didn't. The storm came in fast with seventy-five mile an hour winds, and gusts of over one hundred miles an hour and it rained like you wouldn't believe. It hit with the force of a hurricane, at about four in the afternoon. We were stranded in San Javier that night. I put the crew up in a hotel."

"When did you get back to the camp?"

"At about 10:30 the next morning. The roads were full of water, so it took a long time to get through. The camp was empty, not a sign of Jesse, or Kathryn. Then Jesse came jogging up and told me Kathryn was missing. He had been searching for her all morning. She had been out at the main plaza when the storm came in, and was apparently stranded out there all night!"

"So he was the last person to see her alive?"

"Yes. She went out to the plaza just before the storm hit. Jesse stayed behind to watch the camp and do some lab work. The storm came in while she was out on the site . . . Now he's been devastated by all of this Carl, he won't come back, and he may quit archaeology altogether. He took the semester off and stayed down in Mexico. That's where he is now."

"His story checks out? No holes in it?"

"Yes. Of course. He's one hundred percent trustworthy. He called me from Chiapas a few days ago. He's still looking around for her. In vain. I told him he needs to come back to school."

"Did anything unusual happen that week? In camp, or at the site? Any unusual visitors?"

"Nothing out of the ordinary. Every season, we get a lot of visitors. A number of graduate students from various departments including Harvard visited the site off and on, all summer. Of course the usual amount of Mexican archaeologists and government officials came by several times. Nothing unusual there."

"Who came down from Harvard?"

"Laurence Eikelmann came by for a couple of days."

"Ah yes, I saw him last week at the museum. So how was it going at the site?"

"Everything was going fine, until the storm tore up our excavation units - very badly. At the main pyramid, the entire trench caved in. You know, I thought we were about to hit a royal tomb, or vault, but after we cleaned out, and re-excavated the trench, there was no time to expand it. We were afraid we would find Kathryn in there, but all we found was a pick someone had left out. Nothing else."

"She wasn't romantically involved with anyone? No one had a motive?"

"No. There was nothing like that going on." Chandler seemed offended by the question.

"Predators then. Is it jaguar country, did you have crocodiles in the lagoon, Chan?"

"Caimans in the lagoon, but they're not big enough to do much damage. The crocodiles I think have been almost hunted out. Jaguars are in the area, but they are very rare, actually endangered. Of course the most likely and deadly predators would be the snakes, a fer-de-lance perhaps. But a predator would have left something for the vultures. She disappeared without a trace Carl."

"You think she's in the lagoon?"

"Well it's pretty shallow, eight feet at its maximum depth. We even had Jesse, and the Mexican police divers check it and the cenote. Jesse's been checking out the lagoon and cenote for the past couple of weeks. Paying for it out of his own pocket too."

"So he's not given up yet?"

"No. Far from it, he's almost obsessed with trying to find her."

"And they weren't involved?'

"Honestly, I don't know for sure. If they were, neither of them ever showed the slightest sign. I seriously doubt it. Someone on the project would have known, and said something. You know how small a field camp is, when it comes to something like that."

"Is the cenote there like others I've seen? A big sinkhole? Is it very deep at Chanul Tzuk?"

"The divers say it's over a hundred feet deep, and it's fed by an underground river that empties into the lagoon. The police did some testing by dropping a deer carcass into the cenote. It was never found. If she fell into it, then her body might never turn up. Sometimes I think that could have happened, yet still, she wouldn't have fallen into it Carl. She knew the site well. She had been on the mapping crew the first three weeks of the project. I just don't see that happening."

They paused. Carl looked out his window. The sun was starting to set over the rooftops and spires of Cambridge. A raven preened and walked back and forth on the windowsill. Carl looked at his desk clock. He was due at Leakey's colloquium in about ten minutes.

Chandler resumed. "Unfortunately, we may never know what happened to Kathryn Haden, and despite how the investigation turns out, I've had enough. Ultimately, she was my responsibility, and I'm the one to blame.

I'm leaving at the end of the spring semester. I should serve out my contract, and then that's it."

"Have you told your chairman?"

"No I haven't told Merrifield yet, haven't told anyone, other than you. I want to ask you a favor too, which is why I called in the first place. I want to turn over Chanul Tzuk to Pat Mamett, and I want you to see if he's interested. I don't know him all that well, but I admire the work he did at Ubala, and Montebello. He knows the regional archaeology as well as anyone, and has great relations with the government, and the local Maya."

Carl was stunned. Bennett had built the program at Chanul Tzuk up from nothing. Clearly, he was serious about retiring. "Of course I'll talk to Pat. But don't you want a little more time to consider this?"

"No. I'm done Carl. I want to wrap it up properly. I'll call back later this week. Take care."

"Goodbye Chandler. Call me if you need anything."

As he hung up the phone, Carl felt depressed. Instead of all the contributions Chandler had made over the years, the disappearance of one of his students was how everyone would remember him.

5 Shamans

It was an emergency and Laurence Eikelmann needed help. Delia Bell was in her BMW driving fast through Arlington, Massachusetts. Fifteen minutes earlier he had called, barely able to tell her that he was violently ill, and throwing up. Then his voice lapsed into incoherent mumbling. She cleared the rotary on Route 2 at Alewife, at high speed and turned onto Mass Avenue. Delia ran the first red light, made a quick left, and she was in Somerville. Five minutes later she pulled up in front of Eikelmann's apartment building on Mystic River Road. When she got out of the car she flipped her cigarette in the gutter, and ran to the porch.

She took the stairs two at a time, and stopped on the second floor gasping for breath. I really should stop smoking one of these days she thought, as she banged on Laurence's door. The door was unlocked. Not a good idea in this part of Somerville, she thought. She walked into the living room and saw Laurence sprawled on his leather couch in stained boxer shorts. He looked catatonic, and he whispered words that were barely audible, as if he were about to fall asleep at any moment. His swollen eyes were almost closed. The unease she had felt for twenty minutes since getting his phone call, blossomed into full-blown fear, and she immediately called the emergency room at Mount Auburn Hospital. They told her an ambulance was on the way.

Laurence's eyes suddenly opened wide. His pupils were huge. He strained to make his words heard. "Funny. It's not like they said. There's no light… it's dark… feels like a whirlpool. I'll never make it." His eyes closed and he said, "God. Delia. I'm so tired."

Delia knew from her Red Cross training that she had to keep him awake until the ambulance arrived.

"What have you done Laurence? Did you take something? What did you take?"

"God…Belinda. She...did not...deserve that. I tried to help her, but…"

"What? What do you mean? What about Belinda?"

"I couldn't…she didn't mean anything. What was she doing there? She wasn't supposed to be there."

Delia was upset but tried to be calm. In Laurence's phone call he had mumbled something about Belinda Boothe, and that something had happened. This surprised her, because she had been looking after Belinda's apartment, watering her plants, and feeding her cat. She had written Delia that she would not be back from Guatemala for another four or five weeks.

Maybe Laurence had overdosed on something. He sure wasn't making any sense. In the five years since they had entered graduate school together, she had known Laurence Eikelmann to be brilliant, and a bit uptight. He was also a computer hacker of the first tier. His laptop computer was open on the coffee table in front of the couch, with a stack of disks, and an empty glass next to it.

She saw Laurence as a little neurotic, but then so was the rest of their class; after all, they were Harvard graduate students. They were supposed to be neurotic. It was part of the program. Laurence's father was a big-time corporate attorney in Connecticut, and his family was very tightly knit. He was aloof and not very friendly to any of the other graduate students. Delia was one of the few exceptions.

Laurence was now on his back staring at the ceiling. "I'm so sorry. I tried to fix it." He whispered.

"What? What about Belinda? She's still in Guatemala. Isn't she?"

Laurence couldn't answer her. He was unconscious. His skin felt clammy and his pulse was slow. She called Mount Auburn again, to check on the ambulance. The emergency room operator assured her it would be there momentarily. Next, she called Belinda.

"Hello. You have reached 494-8290. I can't come to the phone right now. So please leave a message and I will call you back."

"Belinda. This is Delia. Are you back?"

What should she say? That Eikelmann was in a coma? "Listen, Belinda, if you're back . . . Laurence is in trouble. I'm over at his place. He's going to Mount Auburn right now. When did you get back? Is everything all right? I'll call back later . . . sorry if I'm a little incoherent, things are just really weird right now. Sorry."

If Belinda was back from Guatemala, why hadn't she called? What was going on? She looked up and saw red flashing lights reflecting off the brick building across the street. The ambulance had arrived.

The paramedics worked on Laurence where he lay. Delia stayed out of the way, and looked at Laurence's laptop. The screen showed that he had e-faxed something to a number in the 516 area code, which she recognized as Long Island. The paramedics continued to pump out his stomach. A

24

clump of half-digested vegetable material resembling Brussels sprouts came up, no pills or capsules.

They began to ask a lot of questions while they put Eikelmann in the ambulance. Did he have mental health problems? Was he depressed? Delia could not answer them. She had been busy preparing for her oral exam for the past several weeks, and had seen Laurence only once during that time. She had spent the month of July in Ohio, visiting her parents and studying. Laurence was very reclusive and secretive by nature and not being around for three or four weeks at a time was common for him. He did not have any close friends in the department. Delia was probably closer to him than anyone else, and she couldn't say she knew him very well.

The paramedics asked if she would come over to Mount Auburn right away and give a statement. This was a standard request they made in all cases involving attempted suicide, if that's what it turned out to be. Delia agreed to drop by, but first she had to drive over to Belinda Boothe's apartment to see what Laurence was talking about.

As the ambulance drove off, Delia stood by her car and lit a cigarette. In spite of the commotion the street was deserted. This part of Somerville would need more than an ambulance to bring people outside after midnight. Too strange, she thought, what the hell is going on? Laurence was not prone to emergencies, of any sort. The incident had all the indications of a drug overdose, but it did not track. This kind of thing did not happen in their circle of friends, and certainly not to Laurence Eikelmann.

She thought she saw her cigarette glow reflected in a hallway across the street. Then it moved, and she realized someone was watching her. So the ambulance attracted one curious onlooker it seemed. Well, it was time to get over to Belinda's anyway. She flicked her cigarette in the street and got in her car. As she pulled out, she looked again, over toward the hallway. No one was there, just a large stray cat licking himself.

"The show's over." She said as she drove away.

Belinda's loft apartment was above a boutique on Eliot Street down from Harvard Square. Delia took the elevator up to the third floor, walked down the hall, and knocked on the door. She heard Belinda's cat jump down on the floor inside. She knocked a second time, without a response. Then she unlocked the door and went in. The living room looked the same as it had on Monday the last time Delia had watered the plants. Belinda was not home. The apartment was absolutely silent. Her cat Ziggy, a massive Russian Blue stared at her from the kitchen doorway with narrow yellow green eyes. Ziggy had to weigh at least fifteen pounds, and any time Delia got within three feet of him; he bared his fangs and hissed. She always left several bowls of dry food in the kitchen to keep him at bay. Delia was not a cat person. Ziggy was not a personable cat.

"Hey Zig. Seen Belinda?" Delia looked around the room. Ziggy stretched and went into the kitchen. The roll-top desk looked different. Some new books were stacked there, and several American Antiquity journals had been removed from the bookcase. The new books were *The Archaeology of Shamans, Rituals, and Magic, Artifacts of Altar de Sacrificios*, and *The Cult of the Feline*. A receipt was next to them. They had all been bought that day at Oxford Books, one of the best-used bookstores in Harvard Square. Delia and Belinda had shopped there often.

She picked up the copy of *The Archaeology of Shamans, Rituals, and Magic*, saw that it had a bookmark and read it:

"Shamanism, one of the obsessions of anthropology, is the most ancient form of consciousness in the world. Many researchers have made a compelling case that the traditions of New World shamanism emerged from a Siberian-Altaic complex more than 100,000 years ago. Others claim that it is the progenitor of all religious systems. In all cultures the shaman is believed to be able to have visions, cure ailments, and use animals to assist him. These animals are called "familiars." In some tribes the shaman is believed to be able to shape-shift and transform himself into these animal forms. The ability to conduct dream travel of the shaman's soul to the dreams and minds of other people is another widespread belief, and animal familiars can facilitate this ability. In modern Mexico and Central America, shamans depending on context and background are called *Curanderos*, *Brujos* and other terms. Use of animal familiars is quite common."

"Ziggy are you trying to be familiar, or a familiar?" Delia put down the book, surprised to have the cat rub against her legs. As she entered the bedroom, she knocked on the door. Yes, Belinda was back. A battered leather suitcase and a nylon duffel bag were placed by the foot of the bed. Mystery solved. What had Laurence been talking about then? He was probably just out of it, for whatever reason. Everything was in order. Belinda had returned a couple of weeks early without telling Delia, which was her prerogative, and not surprising at all. She had been to Oxford Books, but she hadn't unpacked yet. The apartment was clean, the plants were watered, the cat was mean, and everything was normal.

The only room she had not checked was the kitchen, so she went in and was surprised to see Ziggy's food bowls flipped over, and empty. Why hadn't Belinda fed him or picked up the bowls? She had probably gone to the market. The refrigerator had been empty for four months, yet it was like her to buy books before she bought food. She took the cat food down from the top of the refrigerator, and was putting a bowl down for Ziggy, when she noticed the light blinking on the answering machine.

I wonder if she got my message. Delia thought about playing her message back just to see how incoherent she sounded, before deleting it - when the phone rang. It made her jump, and she stepped back and broke a cat bowl, as the answering message began. She was picking up the pieces, when she heard Phil Ward's Kentucky drawl in Belinda's kitchen.

"Hey Belinda. You're probably not back. I don't know if I'd be ready to talk to you if you were, but... you'll soon hear how I was..."

She picked up the phone. "Phil this is Delia. How are you?"

"Delia? Did I dial the wrong . . . oh yeah? You're taking care of her place. How the hell are you?" From his jocular tone, Phil sounded like he had been drinking.

"Phil it's been a weird night. I'm supposed to be getting ready for the orals tomorrow, when out of the blue Laurence calls me, something happened to

27

him. I don't know what, but I think he might have overdosed on something."

"Come on. Laurence doesn't mess around with drugs. You know that."

"Yeah. You're right Phil. So there must be some other reason why he's in the ER at Mount Auburn Hospital right now." Delia sat on the floor. She was worn out.

"You're serious? Okay tell me what happened." All the jocularity was gone.

"I don't know what happened. He practically went into a coma right in front of me. I think they pumped his stomach out in time. Maybe he combined the wrong medicine with alcohol or something like that. I tell you, he looked like a corpse by the time I got there." She watched the cat eat. He acted like he was starved.

"Delia, now you know Eikelmann. If he did anything, it was accidental."

Delia smiled; she enjoyed talking to Phil again. "Why did you take off like that Phil? People were worried."

"Yeah? Like who?"

"Well, me. I was." Delia felt awkward.

"Well I'm sorry Cordelia darling, but I had to get! I don't handle failure very well."

"Okay Phil. How much have you had to drink? And where are you anyway?"

"I haven't had nearly enough to drink honey, let me tell you. I need several more drinks yet. Do you know how bad it got? They asked me how many mortuary vessels were found in Burial 166, in the North Acropolis at Tikal. I mean what are we playing? You know? Trivial Archaeological Pursuits or something? This was my career that got screwed. Of course if I had known the material a little better, I mean, maybe I wasn't ready…"

"Eighteen."

"What?"

"That's how many pots were in Burial 166."

"Ah come on Delia. You make me feel really stupid as usual. How did you know that?"

"I don't Phil. I was joking." Nevertheless, she did know the answer, and she knew she had inadvertently made him feel worse. It was just that Delia knew the tombs at Tikal almost as well as if she had excavated them herself.

"Well you got me. Anyway, it seemed like they just kept probing anywhere they could, until I got rattled, and I couldn't think straight at the end. I knew they were going to fail me."

"Don't remind me Phil. I'm facing it at one o'clock tomorrow."

"I know. They won't fail you Delia. You know the material better than they do. Certainly better than I did. They like you too, and that helps." His voice trailed off. Delia paused and decided that as much as she wanted to talk to Phil, it was time to go home and go to bed. He was acting vulnerable and she didn't like hearing him that way. It was totally out of character.

"Phil, I'm sorry but I really need to go home. It looks like you just missed Belinda. She's probably at the market. I think she got back this afternoon. I haven't seen her yet."

Phil let out a long sigh. "I thought she... Oh well, if you see her; tell her I need to talk to her. Tell her I miss her."

"Tell her yourself, and try not to be so maudlin." Phil was starting to exasperate Delia, but she felt sorry for him too. "Just call back in an hour or so."

29

"No can do. I'm going up into the hills, a place where there are no phones, just the forest and me, Kentucky. I've got some things to sort out. I need to simplify my life."

"Phil. Please call me again soon. If you need anything..."

"Delia I need a lot. But nobody can help me get what I need but me."

* * * * * * * * *

After talking to Phil, Delia put more food out for Ziggy, and looked around the apartment checking for clues to where Belinda went. A scrap of paper on the floor by the couch caught her attention. It was a receipt from the Belize City airport duty-free shop, one bottle of scotch, and one bottle of rum. Delia smiled. Belinda never missed the opportunity to get a bargain. Maybe they could get together for a drink, and Belinda could tell her about her trip. She was an excellent storyteller, and Delia looked forward to hearing about her experiences. She hated to admit it but she was a little envious of Belinda, who always seemed to be having more success, and a better time than Delia. Partly that was attributable to Belinda's outgoing personality. She had a beautiful smile and was a very friendly, happy person, more socially at ease than Delia. Still, she was her best friend, and Delia had missed her. She realized she was hanging around the apartment hoping Belinda would show. Delia wanted to know what she would make of the Eikelmann incident.

"Where are you anyway?" She said out loud and walked to the bay window that overlooked the curve of Eliot Street. Someone had gone into the apartment building across the street, and a Volvo was backing in to a space by the bicycle shop. A few pigeons protested and moved out of the way.

No sign of Belinda. Delia picked up her purse and left. On her way down the stairs, Delia decided she would call Belinda's aunt tomorrow, early in the morning, which should be a good time to catch somebody at home. She could definitely reach Madeline at her office. Madeline would know where she was.

As she drove away, she did not notice the Toyota Camry pull out from behind the Volvo and follow her down Eliot Street.

6 A Really Bad Day

After he failed his Ph.D. exam, Phil Ward went straight back to his apartment, packed his bags, left a check for his landlord to cover the bills, and headed west on the Mass Turnpike. Outside Pittsfield, Massachusetts he bought a six pack of beer that lasted only as far as Albany. He stopped there, and in a lounge at a Holiday Inn he had a double bourbon. That was when everything hit him at once. He had been numb until then.

What a complete disaster. This was a seminal moment in his life and the latest disaster in a long string that reached back to the summer of 1969 when he graduated from high school in Winchester, Kentucky to enlist in the Marine Corps and then Camp Pendleton, Oceanside, California. Next, on to Viet Nam, and all that shit with the good old Third Division. When his third tour ended in 1982, he had enrolled at the University of Kentucky to study archaeology. He was on GI Bill money for a few years, took whatever courses interested him, and went out with a lot of women. Gradually the pain of Viet Nam subsided a bit. Finally, in 1987 he got his BA in anthropology at the "mature" age of thirty-five. On to graduate school at U.K., and after a couple of years in Central America he had worked his way up from shovel-bum to archaeological project director. It had taken over ten years to get into Harvard, and one hour and thirty minutes in one morning to kick him right out. Forty-two years old now, unemployed, and overeducated he had no idea of what to do next, except have another drink.

After his second bourbon Phil started thinking about Mamett. They hadn't got along very well since Montebello, Guatemala back in 1990, when Phil had seen Mamett lose it out in the jungle. He had simply unraveled.

It was the kind of thing that had to be kept confidential. It all started when Mamett allegedly had an affair with a student from UCLA, and after she left for another project, he came unglued. Mamett yelled at everyone, stayed in his tent for hours, and became ever more remote from the rest of the staff. It was mild stuff compared to what Ward had seen on a regular basis in Viet Nam.

Phil never understood what had set him off, but as Mamett's assistant director, it was his responsibility to control the situation, and keep the project running. He had driven Mamett over the border to San Ignacio in Belize, checked him into a hotel, and hired someone to be Mamett's gopher and look after him. It had taken some doing, but Phil had kept things quiet and under control for another week until a calmed and heavily sedated Mamett returned to close out the project a week early. His wife had come to join him at the end, and they went to Cancun for a week. Just like nothing had ever happened, which was fine with Phil. Mamett thanked Phil profusely for handling everything and keeping it all under wraps. They both knew that such an incident could ruin a non-tenured professor's career. But a problem seemed to simmer beneath the surface. Although outwardly he appeared to have forgotten all about it, Mamett had probably felt indignant and embarrassed about it ever since. At least it seemed that way to Phil, as Mamett became aloof.

Eventually, Phil decided to request another professor with Maya expertise to serve as his advisor instead of Mamett. The only one available was Carl Prefontaine, who was really a New England historical-era archaeologist. When he asked Mamett if he would mind, he seemed grateful to be relieved of his responsibilities to Phil.

Prefontaine had worked in the Maya lowlands at the beginning of his career back in the late 50s, and was probably the most decent fellow in the department, with Samuel Thomas a close second. He was the kind of guy everyone wanted on their committee, because he never asked any difficult questions, and was always ready to adjourn.

Prefontaine had been consumed with one project for the past fifteen years, the historical archaeology of Harvard College itself. In his office and lab were enormous boxes of files, maps, artifacts, letters, and notes amassed over two decades. Many a research assistant had been frustrated by the futility of trying to impose order on the Prefontaine collection. Phil had been the most recent R.A. to take it on, and had made some progress until yesterday.

It only takes one, Phil thought, one really bad day and everything goes to hell.

7 Oral Examination

At the appointed hour Delia walked into the Bowditch Room at the Peabody Museum and took her Ph.D. oral exams. Two hours and forty-five minutes later, the four professors of her examination committee, Prefontaine, Mamett, Ken Zucker, and Samuel Thomas, dismissed Delia, and told her to wait in the hall. It was well known among the graduate students, that the longer you waited, the worse your chances were of passing. If deliberations lasted longer than fifteen minutes, you might as well hang it up. Fortunately, for Delia, she waited only five minutes before the door opened and Mamett led the other three out to congratulate her.

Mamett assumed a tone of professorial condescension, "Delia, as your advisor I must say I expected you to acquit yourself well, and not discredit me, but actually you far exceeded my rather high expectations. You did a superior job, just superior."

Thomas and Zucker both gave their "warmest regards" and muttered several other academic clichés. Carl Prefontaine extended his hand and said, "Good job Cordelia, can I buy you a drink?" This of course was the best offer she had heard in days.

Prefontaine, Mamett and Delia headed for the Boathouse Pub; a bar dedicated to such Ivy League pursuits as rowing, and darts. After two pitchers of beer, Mamett excused himself to leave for a dinner at Adams House, and left Prefontaine and Delia alone at their table. Happy hour was getting underway. The waiter came over and Prefontaine said, "If it's okay with my younger colleague I believe we will have two Glen Livets on the rocks with a splash of water."

Delia nodded her assent. The silence between them stretched out. They watched more patrons stream in as twilight came on, turning the late September light a deep amber outside.

"Dr. Prefontaine, I was wondering . . ."

"Delia, why don't you call me Carl? We've known each other over four years; you just passed your orals. Frankly this unwarranted formality is starting to get on my nerves."

Delia sipped her scotch not exactly sure what she should say. She was a product of prep schools, Yale, and Harvard, eighteen years worth. The formal ways of doing things were second nature to her. Prefontaine was old enough to be her grandfather, and she basically had a lot of respect and affection for him.

"Dr. Prefontaine," she said feeling the booze now, "respectfully, I must decline, I mean, I just cannot call you Carl. I'm not exactly sure why. I mean I could call Mamett, Patrick, without any problem, because he's not that much older than me. However, when it comes to you..."

"Delia, call me Carl, and be done with it. Treat me the same as Patrick."

"Actually I like Patrick a lot."

"Yes. He's a decent fellow, hell of a scholar, and one of the best fund-raisers I've ever seen. He plays the game exceptionally well." Simultaneously, they reached for their drinks. "You know Cordelia; you are only the sixth woman to specialize in Maya archaeology that I've worked with. Most of the women that come through this program work in North America or Europe. Very few have made it in your area, at least as far as you have."

"Well Belinda Boothe has made it further." Delia observed.

"I'm including her. You have to admit your female representatives are scant, compared to other areas."

"Why do you suppose that is?" Delia had her own opinion, but she wanted to hear what Prefontaine thought.

"I think it's that whole "mystique of the Maya" you know? Remote jungle setting, arduous conditions, it's a place for manly men." He chuckled, and then added, "I'm only half-joking Delia."

"So the old-boy archaeologists think it's too hard for women?" Delia was starting to get annoyed because she knew many male archaeologists old and young who held such beliefs. She was constantly fighting outdated attitudes it seemed.

34

"Something like that. Say I'm not being politically incorrect am I? You know I'm old enough to remember when the words "feminist" and "sexist" did not exist."

"Please." Delia held up her hand. "Dr. Prefontaine, my definition of feminism is simply that women should be treated like human beings. It's really kind of basic, and no, don't worry about offending me. A woman who stays in archaeology long enough grows a pretty thick skin. Either that or she gets out."

"Even so Delia, you will at least concede that it's not easy to work in Central America, with the unstable governments, occasional revolutions, strange tropical diseases, and parasites."

"I don't think it's that tough anymore. I mean not like it used to be. And I think the men who controlled access to it exaggerated the hazards to begin with."

"Well you have to admit it's still dangerous at times. Yesterday, I was talking to Chandler Bennett. He was one of my students you know, here in the mid-60s."

Prefontaine took a drink. "It was his project in Chiapas where that young woman disappeared last month. Devastating. I mean Delia, death is rare, but it does happen."

"They haven't found her body, have they?" Delia interrupted. She remembered how upset her mother had been when she told Delia about it, after seeing it on CNN.

"Not a trace."

"At first they thought an excavation unit collapsed on her, right?"

"God. Yes." He took a large drink. "I had a trench cave in once in Vicksburg, Mississippi, was almost buried alive." Prefontaine frowned at the memory.

"So what did Bennett think happened? You know, I met her once, Kathy Haden, at a conference in Mexico. She was a very pleasant, very friendly person."

"Chandler doesn't know what happened. The local government and the military searched the region for ten days. Nothing."

"No word? Messages home? No ransom notes?"

"Nothing. It's as if the storm consumed her, or Chanul Tzuk absorbed her somehow."

8 Axis Mundi

Jesse drove the GMC as fast as he could up the gravel road cutting through the forested hills leading to San Javier. Gravel dust billowed in plumes behind him, and blinded the oncoming traffic. But he didn't care. He had to get to the Institute before the regional archaeologist Sergio Avendano, left for lunch. In true Latin American tradition, lunch for Avendano usually took two hours. Jesse wanted to get the government's official representative out to the altar before the looters came back. Thinking about Avendano, Jesse wondered how he would react when he saw the sculpture. They had become friends in the weeks following Kathryn's disappearance. Jesse had been invited to Institute functions hosted by Avendano, and they had talked shop on a number of occasions. Avendano was one of the most knowledgeable Mayanists that Jesse had ever met, and was the Latin definition of a gentleman and a scholar.

He passed through the constantly expanding shanty towns, the slums that ringed San Javier along the valley's edge. Everyday it seemed that more and more Maya; Tzeltal, Tzotzil, and Chol, were giving up on farming their exhausted land, leaving their ejidos, and moving into the slums. Many of them still wore their traditional clothing; hats decorated with multicolored ribbons, white trousers, woolen ponchos, but others wore faded T-shirts and patched jeans. It always saddened Jesse to see them, and their despair, the last surviving remnants of the Maya civilization. It made him want to think about something else, because there was nothing

36

that he could do for them. They were the poorest people he had ever seen. They really had nothing.

He thought again about the crocodile and deer, the body parts that had been intermingled in the clearing in front of the looter's pit. The combination of these two animals suggested something to him, but it was just on the edge of his memory. He could not quite get to it.

Now he was driving down the cobble stone streets of the town, and getting close to the institute. He pulled into the parking lot, and honked as he saw Avendano about to climb into his vintage Mercedes 280 SL. Jesse stopped next to it.

"Buenos Dias, Jesse." Avendano nodded, holding the door handle in his left hand, his briefcase in his right.

"Buenos Dias, Professor." Jesse got out of the GMC, and noticed that he was covered in dust, so he slapped his pants and shirt, and brushed off his face.

"Where have you come from in such haste?" Avendano asked.

"I have found an important sculpture, an altar actually, with Olmec and Maya iconography, in a looter's hole near Chanul Tzuk!"

Avendano stiffened, then walked around to the space between the vehicles, and whispered to Jesse. "How far from here?"

"It will take about an hour to drive and another hour to walk in. It's in a rough area. I think they drove a tractor in there last night."

"What if we take the institute's Bronco?"

"We could probably make it." The old '77 Bronco was well maintained and seriously rigged for off-road work. Jesse remembered it from the search party.

"Then let's go."

* * * * * * * *

They were in the Bronco, bouncing down the track to the looter's pit. Hitting the watery area at fifty miles an hour, and throwing up a muddy plume, they skidded hard to the left, and fishtailed back to the right, before the tires crunched in to the rocky sand on the other side. Speeding down the trail, saplings and shrubs whipped under the brush guard. Jesse hoped that Sergio would slow down before they crashed into a boulder or tree stump. The radio handset kept bouncing out of its bracket, and hitting Jesse in the knees. He gave up on putting it back and just held it in his hand.

A vulture flew up about three hundred meters ahead of them, and Jesse pointed toward it.

"Over there. We're almost to it."

Avendano nodded.

They stopped directly in front of the cross, as the vultures took off again, almost resentfully, Jesse thought. They got out and Sergio went around to the back of the Bronco, while Jesse walked over to the brush to relieve himself.

Sergio waited for him in front of the cross. He cradled a pump-action shot gun in each arm. "Can you use one of these Jesse?"

"Looks like a pair of matching Mossberg 590s. Twelve gauge repeating shotguns. The magazine holds seven rounds, modified choke barrel; maximum effective range is 50 yards."

Sergio extended one to him. "I guess you answered my question."

Jesse took the safety off, and chambered a round with the pump. "Yeah, my dad keeps a couple of them at his bar in San Antonio. I grew up around firearms. Plus, we had weapons training when I was in the corps at A & M. Military issue?"

Sergio nodded "US Marine Corps surplus."

"Expecting some trouble?"

"Some of these looters are refugees from Guatemala. They don't give a damn about anything. If you know what I mean."

"Displaced Maya?"

"Many of them, yes. Chol and Tzeltal Maya to be precise, from the highlands. Some of them are bad hombres. Look here, cigar butts, and liquor bottles. Looks like they were drinking aguardiente, sugarcane brandy." He motioned at the open space in front of the cross, and knelt down next to the crocodile carcass. The stench had abated and a strong breeze dispersed the odor. A green and red stream of leaf cutter ants meandered through the dirt.

"So they partied while they looted." Jesse observed.

"Actually no. Cigars and libations are part of many Maya religious rituals. Inebriation is thought to bring one closer to the gods. To them it is like Holy Communion."

"What makes you think this wasn't a barbecue?"

Avendano stood up. "Several things. The cross in this context is not Christian. It symbolizes the foliated cross that is found throughout classic Maya iconography. It is the world tree that connects the underworld, the earth in the middle, and the upper world of the spirits. It is in fact the axis mundi."

Jesse looked closely at the cross; it was made from two freshly cut saplings, and was roped together in the middle. Maybe it was supposed to represent the world tree. He had to agree with Sergio, the place sure didn't have any Christian aspect to it. Actually, it felt quite alien to him.

Avendano knelt beside the crocodile's head and dug something out of the ground. Flies whirled all around him. He held the object out in front of him and squinted at it.

"Looks like the ear of a deer."

"What is it about deer and crocodile symbolism? It struck my memory when I was out here earlier. Do you know what it means?" Jesse asked.

"I know exactly what it means." Avendano's eyes narrowed as he looked at the trail leading to the platform. "It's the cosmic monster of the classic Maya. It's often depicted as a crocodile or dragon-image. Crocodile head, deer ears and hooves, and it always marks the path between the natural and supernatural worlds, as it exists on the edge of the cosmos. Anchor to the Milky Way, the Cosmic Serpent. Very powerful imagery."

Jesse knew Avendano was right and felt a chill as he remembered.

"Interesting. I interpret this to mean that someone was attempting to open the portal to the supernatural last night. The whole set up was probably more intact before the vultures got to it." He paused, thinking out loud. "Of course Lord Kisin, the vulture god, god of death, is one of the most powerful lords of the Maya underworld." Avendano looked up at the circling vultures overhead, and then started down the trail. "Someone has opened the gateway between the natural and supernatural worlds, and has religiously followed ancient Maya symbolism."

"Señor." Jesse followed him down the path. "You almost sound like you believe it yourself."

Avendano did not reply.

9 Red River Gorge

"Said I woke up this morning and I got myself a beer."

Phil tipped back a lukewarm Heineken, and sang along with dead Jim Morrison on the truck's radio.

"The future's uncertain and the end is always near."

The Red River Gorge was beginning to show autumn colors in the higher elevations of the winding narrow roads. It was a warm September morning, with a little bit of summer still left in the air. He had driven all day and half the night to get there, and not stopped except to get food, gas, and relieve himself, until last night when he called Belinda, and got Delia.

"My luck to have this great speech rehearsed for Belinda, and I get Delia Bell instead."

Delia was a great friend, very pretty, petite, a brunette with startling blue eyes. Phil had always liked her. She was a bit green in the ways of the world, but still she was only twenty-six; when Phil was twenty-six, he had been to Viet Nam twice, and spent nine years in the marines. His interest in archaeology had started then, when he was a guard at the American embassy in Guatemala City. If he had not gone to Tikal back then, his life would have been different. "If, if, if!" He took another drink, and said to the truck, "What was it Kipling said?"

"If you can keep your head while those about you are losing theirs and blaming it on you; If you can trust yourself when all men doubt you..."

"And if bullfrogs had wings they wouldn't bump their ass on the ground…me talking to me again, uh-huh, well so be it." He drove along listening to the music, and taking in the beauty of the gorge on a spectacular morning. Even though his world had caved in and he had no idea of what he was going to do next, he had to admit it was good to be here. "Hell. It's just good to be alive." From the moment he realized that somehow he had survived Quang Tri, he savored every day, because he had not expected to make it out alive. He had accepted and expected annihilation, not too many people knew what that was like. This was bad, but he had seen much worse. Men are bloodthirsty animals at their core, he thought. Once you understand that, life is a bit more bearable.

After the disaster at Harvard, the first thing he thought of was to go back to the rock shelter, the one where he had met Belinda back in 1988. Harvard had just accepted him into its graduate program at the time, much to his amazement, and he was an assistant director of a field school at Copperhead Rock Shelter. It was the first year that the University of Kentucky had offered a graduate-level field school, and about a dozen students from other colleges and universities, were taking it. Belinda Boothe had been one of them.

He was eating breakfast at the camp on the first morning, when a youngish looking woman of about twenty-two, drove up in a Jeep Wrangler, way too fast, and sent a cloud of dust across the camp. The girl climbed out of the Wrangler, and pushed over the seat to get her bags out. At that random moment, Phil saw her bend over, and as the baggy shorts stretched taut across her butt, he thought: "I must get to know this one."

The way she was dressed in crisp khaki clothes that looked brand new from Banana Republic, right down to the safari hat with a blue scarf, suggested to Phil that she had never been in the field before. This turned out to be true. The other truth about Belinda was that she nearly ignored him for the first week of the course. She would not accept any of his invitations to have a drink. She would not allow herself to be left alone with him, and only talked to him when he initiated it. She was not in the least bit interested in him. Of course this only served to inflame his desire to pursue her.

One afternoon during the second week of field school he had decided that it was time to teach archaeological reconnaissance methods in the valley of the Red River, and he arranged it so that Belinda was on his team. After they had found a site on a ridge late in the afternoon, Phil had sent the other two students to get the vehicle, while he and Belinda finished mapping the site. She held the compass and the end of the tape, while he measured artifacts in off her bearing. Aiming the compass, with her right hand she lined him in on the bearing with her left hand.

Following her directions, he suddenly found himself backing over the ridge and falling down a slope covered in loose fragments of sandstone. He fell about thirty meters on his butt before coming to rest against a large boulder. "Wow! Look at you." Belinda was bent over, hands on her knees, laughing at him. Phil dusted himself off, and started up the slope in silence. About fifteen feet away he stopped and looked at her. She was beautiful, her long brown hair was hanging in wild tangles, the sun behind her gave it a halo effect, her hair flew around her face and here eyes were alternately hidden and revealed by the gusting breeze coming off the ridge. Her lips were pulled back and symmetrical, and laughter was cascading out. She clutched her sides, pushing up her breasts that moved freely inside her loose yellow blouse that was coming out of her khaki shorts. Now five years later, Phil held her image clear; he would always remember her that way.

"Don't you want to know if I'm all right Belinda?" He asked trying to be stern and professional, wanting to laugh.

"Well I didn't think a big tough ex-marine like you would be hurt by a little fall like that."

"Are you making fun of me?"

"I give up, am I?" She was looking at him with one hand on her hip, defiantly sexy.

"I think so Belinda. I think you meant to direct me off the ridge, and now you are adding insult to injury." He knocked the dust off his pants, trying to hide his smile.

"Maybe I did and maybe I didn't." She said picking up the compass.

"Well either way it's okay. Never let it be said that I can't take a joke." With that he smiled back into her beautiful green eyes.

That fall down the slope had been the icebreaker between them. Later on, lying in his arms in bed, she told Phil that she stayed away from him at first because the things she heard from the other graduate students had turned her off. It pained him to learn that behind his back his younger colleagues thought him to be an arrogant womanizer, a loner, and a half-crazed hard drinking Viet Nam vet, who had somehow talked his way into Harvard's graduate program.

Trying to make light of these comments he had said to Belinda, "Oh? And what did you do to get accepted?"

"It was easy for me Phil. I went there as an undergraduate, plus my father is an alum, and my aunt, is a professor in the Biology Department. Harvard is like any other university, except it's Harvard. You'll find out."

Phil realized how far apart their worlds were. He was the first person on either side of his family, to go to college…period. This girl was some kind of Ivy League aristocrat. His experience told him there was no way that it could ever last.

****

The night wore on in Copperhead Rock Shelter and Phil continued to drink Wild Turkey straight from the bottle. He listened to a whipper will in an oak tree above the ledge. Calm, and more or less at peace, he stretched out on his sleeping bag and went to sleep. The fire crackled, and sparks flew aloft against a rock roof, blackened by ancient camps, as Phil began to dream.

He dreamed he was in a vast forest, but it was not the Red River Gorge. In his dream it was highly detailed, the woods of northern New Hampshire. Big, fat, moist snowflakes were falling through the stark interlocking branches. They were the size of quarters. Phil was trying to catch them on his tongue like he used to do when he was a kid. He strolled through the silent woods with his tongue out, happily.

From far away he heard Andean flutes playing softly, and he smelled something familiar, yet exotic and spicy. Sandalwood incense? Belinda was that Belinda up ahead? There. He saw her. She was spying on him from behind a tree, the way a little girl would, like they were playing hide-and-seek. She wore a black wool cap and her hair fell to her shoulders. A purple scarf hid her face like an Arabian veil, but her blue-green eyes were unmistakable. Her long black cape was embossed with gold oak leaves. Her beauty was clear and distinct in the white world.

"Help me." She said so softly, Phil could barely hear her. It was like the forest was swallowing her words, the sounds were muffled. "Help me. I need you."

The forest darkened suddenly as if the light had been turned down. He started toward her, but fell, floundering in a snow drift. The flutes stopped playing. In the twilight, she started to levitate, and float a few inches above the snow.

She floated up…up, until she was a few feet above the interlocking branches of the forest. She extended her hand to him, holding it out.

Against the black wool of her sleeve, her hand was white, like delicately articulated ivory. She reached closer. At the moment their fingers met, a tattoo of a vine began to grow along her wrist, and up her arm. Rosebuds slowly blossomed on the vine, and bloomed…red roses, a green vine, tan skin, and a dazzling light.

He fell back in the snow bank, and did not want to look at her face. Something was wrong. The forest felt sinister, menacing.

He woke up next to the campfire, completely disoriented. I'd better call her; in the morning and see if she's okay. The he realized where he was. He had come here to get away from phones and civilization. He found himself praying out loud. "God I haven't asked for much lately, and you know I could have used some help, but please don't let anything happen to Belinda."

10 Wooden Sky

Avendano propped his shotgun against the side of the altar, and touched the sculpted face of the were-jaguar. He looked up at Jesse who was standing by the edge of the pit.

"Jesse this is extraordinary. This is clearly an Olmec design. The mouth is in the shape of a jaguar; almond-shaped eyes and the rest of the features are humanoid. On each side there are Maya calendrical glyphs. I make them out to read 297 BC."

"About the time that the Olmec were fading and the Maya were ascending. Did you see that blood on top of it?"

Avendano examined the blood with his index finger. "Right. Could be anything, certainly not a large amount." He knelt down next to the altar. "And look, there are smaller glyphs here on the side."

"But blood on an altar?"

Avendano shrugged. As excited as he was, he began to carefully pull the dried mud clumps off the right side of the altar. He continued to talk and remove the mud. "The calendrical style is similar to the stelae found at Tres Zapotes. But Olmec finds are extremely rare in Chiapas, as you know." He grinned, stopping for a second to catch his breath, and wipe the sweat off his forehead, as he studied the glyphs he had just exposed. "I cannot identify the first two glyphs. I have never seen anything like them before. The third one here is a noble, with his eyes closed, and a bloated tongue, coming out of taut, thin lips. Obviously a dead noble. This glyph next to it seems to incorporate a stingray spine with an abstract tooth and eye; possibly it's a bloodletting glyph. This is amazing; I'm going back to the vehicle to get my camera. Can you clean off the glyphs on the left side of the altar?"

Before Jesse could reply, Avendano was out of the pit and headed down the trail. Jesse leaned his shotgun against a ceiba tree and jumped down into the pit. The place still gave him the creeps. Even in broad daylight, with someone with him, and both of them armed with shotguns. Yet the altar was so unique, and mysterious. He pulled his trowel out of his backpack and started digging along the edge of the altar that was still buried in the mud, trying to determine how much of it remained to be exposed. Midway down the edge, the trowel went into a cavity, the mud fell back and a fist-sized hole appeared next to the edge of the altar. He widened it out and looked inside, but it was to dark to see anything.

"What have you found?" Avendano was on the edge of the pit taking pictures.

"There seems to be a space behind this edge of the altar. But I can't make anything out."

"I have a small flashlight here in my camera bag." Sergio jumped down in the pit next to Jesse. In seconds he had his flashlight out and was peering in to the cavity. "Looks like a small plaster and limestone vault. I can make out a cache of two bowls, one inverted on top of the other, red monochromes, there's some object behind them covered in lime dust, and I can't tell what it is." Sergio paused to get out his camera and flash unit and set them up on a small tripod. He started taking pictures of the inside of the cavity, and Jesse climbed out of the pit to give him more room.

46

Jesse noticed a cleared area directly behind the pit that he hadn't seen before. A thatched structure of leafy green saplings had been erected. Walking toward it, he noticed that a bunch of gourds were hanging from the roof of the structure and there was a straw mat directly underneath the gourds. A stone pot filled with some amber liquid was centrally placed on the mat. Flanking it on either side were two plates containing a dark gummy material, and an empty bowl. Everything looked carefully arranged. He heard Avendano climbing out of the pit behind him.

"Señor. Take a look at this." Jesse wiped his forehead with the back of his hand.

"What is it?"

Avendano stood beside him. "This is a ka'an te' - thirteen gourds, under an arch of saplings, tied together." He whispered and seemed apprehensive. "It seems that someone, or more likely some shaman is at work here. The gourds are centered. The arch represents the Milky Way, the Cosmic Serpent. The thirteen gourds symbolize the constellations of the Maya zodiac. Those are religious offerings on the mat, copal incense, and balche liquor made from honey and bark, all very traditional..." He stopped talking and started photographing it from different perspectives with a wide-angle lens. He continued talking and took pictures. "Roughly translated, ka'an te' means "wooden sky" and it is used to reproduce the cosmos. Jesse, this is a gateway constructed to the supernatural world through which a shaman can pass. I wonder if it is linked to the foliated cross back there in the clearing. This altar would be worth a lot of money on the black market, but that's not what they are after here. Something other than money, I think, some kind of power perhaps."

They heard a diesel engine revving up not far off. Avendano jumped down in the pit and retrieved his shotgun. He motioned for Jesse to do the same. He started to climb out, but then turned back and pressed mud back over the exposed cavity, until it was completely covered up. When he was finished, he raised his right hand to Jesse, for a quicker climb out of the pit.

"Later Jesse. We have company coming!" He started jogging down the path, as Jesse followed him. The diesel was getting closer.

11 Ethnobotany

Delia called Mount Auburn Hospital to see how Laurence was doing, but they had released him the night before. The twenty-four-hour observation period had ended, and he had wanted to go home, so they let him. As she pulled on her blue jeans, she cradled the phone against her shoulder, and listened to Laurence's phone ring. No answer. She was a little groggy from drinking with Carl the night before, and moving so slowly this morning, that she had no time to put on her makeup. Delia had thirty minutes to get to Madeline's class, so she pulled her hair back in a ponytail, applied a little lipstick, grabbed her purse and book bag, and at the last minute tried to call Belinda one more time. No answer there either. She was probably still asleep or out somewhere. Hopefully, by now, Madeline had heard from her.

* * * * * * * *

Delia caught Madeline at the end of her course, *Introduction to Ethnobotany*, which met at the ungodly hour of 7:30 on Mondays, Wednesdays and Fridays in the Science Annex. She waited out in the hall and listened to the close of Madeline's lecture.

"To summarize then, the tropical rainforest is home to approximately 70 percent of the million or so species of complex plants that inhabit the earth. After two hundred years botanists can name about 250,000 of these species.

"Shamans in cultures like the Yanamamo of Brazil, and the Maya of highland Chiapas in Mexico, use thousands of these species of plants in their daily medical and quote "magical" practices. We are just beginning to understand how much more our native indigenous cultures know about plants and their properties than we do.

"So to answer the annoying question from Wednesday, that's why ethnobotany matters, and that's why I became an ethnobotanist."

Delia waited for the room to clear out, before walking down to see Madeline. "What annoying question from last Wednesday? You seemed a little pissed off there at the end. Although I can understand you being a little bitchy at this ridiculous hour. And also a little preachy, trying to save the rainforests again?"

"Hello Delia." Madeline smiled, as she gathered up her lecture notes. "Was I? Oh, you know how some of these undergraduate pricks are; they want you to prove your course is relevant. But ultimately, what is really relevant is that they all expect to get A's." Madeline shrugged, and picked up her purse. "Students can be so tiresome. I probably overreacted. I don't think the little shit that asked me was even here today. So, how are you?"

"I'm okay Professor Scott, but you sound like you could use a vacation."

"Good idea Delia. Too bad I just came back from one. If only I could have stayed in Santa Fe. Maybe I could get a job at Saint John's. So what's new? Have you heard from Belinda?"

"That's funny."

"What's that?" Asked Madeline, as she put all of her papers into her briefcase.

"I was about to ask you the same question."

"Yes? So?"

"Well her luggage is in her apartment. So I assume she's back. You haven't heard from her?"

"It's been at least a month. She's not expected back for a few weeks yet either. Are you sure?" They started up the stairs toward the exit. "Because maybe she dropped it off before heading out to somewhere else. You know Belinda."

"Without calling either one of us?"

Madeline paused before answering. "She's got a new boy friend?"

49

"So you're not worried?"

"Of course not. She's a big girl. She can take care of herself. She always has."

"Well let's call each other as soon as we hear from her. Okay?" They stopped in the foyer of the Science Building Annex.

"Sure. You want to eat breakfast? We could go to the faculty club."

"No. I have to go TF for Mamett."

"I'll see if I can track down my niece." Madeline started toward her office, shouldering her purse and briefcase.

12 The Living Force

"We have determined that most of you actually do believe in the supernatural, at least to the extent that you recognize that God is a supernatural being." Mamett paused and straightened his tie. "Yet you sit before me in this lecture hall, at one of the top universities in the world, and your overall socioeconomic status is predominantly upper class, upper middle class, with a strong representation of talented scholarship students from politically correct ethnic backgrounds."

Easy. Delia thought, you are hitting too close to home for some of these students, Dr. Mamett, and your attitude is moving past challenging, and closer toward patronizing.

"So one would hardly think that this is the kind of group that would believe in the supernatural. I mean after all, here we are in the late stages of the twentieth century, the end of the second millennium, at Harvard University. Not some Tea Room in New Orleans, but an institution of higher learning, and yet we find this belief in the supernatural.

"Is it because your professor tricked you with his statement that to believe in God is to believe in the supernatural? Is that why? Does anyone care to challenge this premise? Hmmmm?" No one challenged him. Mamett had them. They were no longer half-asleep. In the pause, Holmes Hall was silent, no papers rustling, no whispering, and not even a cough. Mamett went on. Delia had to admit that he was the best lecturer she had ever seen

"Okay. Let's review it for those of you who weren't here Wednesday. To believe in God is to believe in the supernatural. Because God is an unseen being with limitless power, and he lives in an unseen world, known as heaven. Thus, God is the supreme supernatural being." He placed a large volume on top of the lectern.

"If you don't believe me, let's check Webster's Collegiate Dictionary for the word God." He opened the dictionary at the lectern, and put on reading glasses. "I quote; 'God: the supreme or ultimate reality . . . a being believed to have more than natural attributes or powers.'" He closed the dictionary, took off his glasses, gestured with them, and said softly, "More than natural powers."

"Is it not interesting, that the "ultimate reality" is by definition supernatural? Transcending the laws of nature? This means that the ultimate reality or "God" cannot be studied in most of the academic departments established at this or any other liberal arts university, except at the Divinity School. And even there your belief or disbelief in God, the ultimate reality, is entirely a matter of faith. God defies our abilities to study Him. And maybe that's why He's God."

"How many Catholics in the room? Let's see your hands." Hands shot up around the room. She smiled thinking about good old parochial school programming, and its influence on the undergraduates.

Delia suddenly had a vivid memory of being a young girl in rural Ohio. She had sat on her bicycle one summer evening when she was about nine, and watched a fundamentalist tent revival meeting. It was riveting, and a little frightening, watching the mercurial preacher work a crowd of Baptist farmers, talking about hellfire and damnation, and being washed in the blood of the lamb. Mamett was like a revival preacher. He was talking about believing.

"About a third of this class is Catholic, as am I." He raised his right hand, and put his left hand on the lectern, and quoted from the Apostolic Prayer.

51

"We believe in one holy Catholic apostolic church." He stopped and looked sharply around the room. "What else do we believe in? The Father, Son, and Holy Spirit, is that supernatural enough for you? How about the Blessed Virgin Mary, the virgin birth? I find that a little on the supernatural side. Don't you? Ever take Holy Communion?" Heads nodded around the hall. Delia thought she felt a vague uneasy feeling moving through the students. Mamett was examining aspects of their life that many had taken for granted until now.

"What happens when you take Holy Communion? What does it symbolize? Take this, and drink, eat. Blood of my blood. Flesh of my flesh. The Holy Spirit of Jesus Christ comes into the church. Did you ever consider the ritual cannibalistic symbolism of it? Kind of supernatural isn't it?" He paused and sipped from the cup of water on the lectern.

"Still, have you ever noticed, or more importantly, have you ever experienced the actual transcendent power the ritual of Holy Communion offers? Because it does have power for people who truly believe in it. They feel close to God. They attain a state of grace. They are at peace when they return to their pews and kneel down. Rituals have power."

Mamett softened his voice and walked from behind the lectern to the edge of the stage. "Why do I belabor this? To understand other cultures, try making sense of your own culture first. Maybe my next example will provide you with a clue.

"The Classic Maya believed in a basic principle of reciprocity. The gods of the Maya could not exist without ritualized offerings.

"They conceived *ch'ulel*, an idea that is still viable among the Chol, Tzeltals, Tzotzils, and other Maya in Chiapas. Ch'ulel is the living force that pervades existence." He paused for effect and said, "Yes. I know, and if it helps, you can think of it as 'the force is with you.'" This caused some laughter. "Everything has life force, living energy… rocks, rivers, sculptures, and temples. Human blood interacts with the life force of the gods, and human blood is where ch'ulel lives.

"All human blood was sacred, the reservoir of the life force. To offer human blood was to give your essence to the gods. They in return would give back, rain, and assistance. Rituals were centered on blood sacrifice.

52

Men would slice their penises. Women would pierce their tongues. This is how the life force was actually provided to the gods."

Groans were heard around the hall, as Mamett took another sip of water.

"Yes. How Freudian." Mamett nodded. "Sounds most unpleasant, and was certainly quite painful, but they believed in it. Now, think about the sheer power of belief today, from Belfast to Bosnia. Ideology has great power, it always has and it will continue.

"In our own world, belief in the supernatural is rampant in every day life, look in the paper, it takes on every form; new-age channelers, tarot readers, Neo-Druids. You know, every belief system that has ever existed in human history still exists today in some form or another. Guess what? They can't all be right."

* * * * * * * *

After the lecture Mamett and Delia met with the students who lingered, waiting to ask questions. He had really stirred them up. A young woman worked her way to the front of the group, and stood waiting patiently next to Mamett, when her chance came she raised her hand.

"Professor Mamett, may I ask you a personal question?"

Mamett was trying to leave for a brunch meeting at the faculty club, but paused. "Sure. Go ahead."

"From the way you talked about communion, I was wondering, are you religious?"

"Yes, very much so. Why do you ask?"

"Well I'm thinking of becoming an anthropologist, and I was curious about whether anthropology, ever gets in the way of your own religious beliefs."

Mamett smiled, and said, "Yes. That is a personal question. And as I will explain in a future lecture, evolutionary theory, and Darwinism, caused me a great deal of difficulty when I was your age."

"Really?" Delia exclaimed, not meaning to interrupt, but this was a side of Mamett, she had never seen before.

"Oh most definitely. You see before I went into archaeology, I almost joined the priesthood. I even went to a seminary for a year." He picked up his briefcase, and started toward the exit. "Now if you'll excuse me, I prefer not to be late to my meeting."

Delia thought, so why did he leave the seminary? There was a story there no doubt. She started up the aisle toward the east door but slowed down when she saw a man in the shadows of the west doorway, much too old to be an undergraduate. Although he hovered in the gloom, and she could not see him well, she thought he looked kind of Indian. He reminded her of a predator, a feline, and strangely it made her feel uncomfortable. With a quick movement; he turned and seemed to glide through the shadows in the corridor.

Now who was that, and why did I pick up those weird vibes from him?

It was starting to drizzle, and she wished she'd brought an umbrella. As Delia walked by the Science Annex, she saw her friend Janice Helms, another archaeology graduate student, walking out of the revolving door, waving her over. The rain was a steady cold mist.

"Hi Delia. Here. Take part of my umbrella." Janice pushed it open, and they walked along together. "Congratulations. I heard you aced the orals that's wonderful!"

"Thanks. It's a major relief to have it over."

"How long did they make you wait in the hall?"

"About five minutes."

"Wow. You must have really done well. Of course we all knew you would pass. I mean you are so committed and all. What did Mamett say?"

"He said," Delia paused and smiled, tucked her chin in and said in a deep voice, "As your advisor I must say," she had to clear her throat, and then continued. "I must say, I expected you to acquit yourself well, and not disgrace me, but actually you far exceeded my great expectations. You did a superior job, just superior."

She laughed, and added, "Or words to that effect."

Janice was laughing, and patted Delia on the back. "God. Do they know how pompous they sound sometimes?"

Delia shook her head, "I don't think so . . . and you know it's funny now that you mention it. Professors are a very intelligent, self-aware bunch, but when it comes to being aware of their own arrogance, most of them are clueless."

"Yes. It's funny how once some guys get into Harvard, they really start to believe that they are "the best and the brightest." It's a fairly common affliction even known to affect some professors."

"Ah yes. Janice, I think we will call it the "Halberstam Syndrome.""

"Characterized by?"

"An affinity for Harvard ties, scarves…"

"Harvard coffee mugs." Janice added.

"Blue Blazers, button down oxford shirts, penny loafers..."

"With no socks, khaki pants. Drinks scotch, but willfully mispronounces it as "skatch" through his nose." Delia was chuckling.

"Wait a minute. Did you say he drinks skatch through his nose?"

"No you nut. He mispronounces it through his nose." Now they were both laughing hard.

"Like he pronounces Harvard, Hahvud."

"He also has an annoying ability to refer to Shakespeare in any given social situation."

"Starts way too many sentences with the words, "One would think . . ."

"As in, "One would think that you should have had your orgasm by now."

"Or, "One would think that three minutes of foreplay should be sufficient."

They cracked up, people scurrying by looked at the two of them laughing in the rain. They stopped in front of William James Hall, where Janice had her office.

"What else?" asked Delia.

"Drinks sherry, at Hahvud functions."

"And pretends he likes it."

"Drives a BMW."

"Wait a minute Janice. I drive a BMW."

"Does it make you feel self-important?"

"Of course."

* * * * * * * * *

Mamett walked rapidly trying not to be late for the meeting. The Faculty Club was on Quincy Street, one block down from the Sackler Art Museum. As Mamett walked past the museum, he spotted Thomas, and Prefontaine, on the opposite side of the street. They motioned him over, and they walked the rest of the way together through the rain that was starting to fall harder.

In the foyer, Mamett waited while Carl and Samuel checked their raincoats. They were seated immediately by the Maitre D' who had known Carl for over twenty years, and placed him at his favorite table, in the back left corner. From there, they could observe the entire room.

They ordered coffee, and read the brunch menu. Carl started the discussion. He looked toward the door, then at his watch.

"Well I guess Zucker is not coming, he said he might not be able to make it. Pat, Sam, since the three of us represent most of the New World section of the archaeology wing, I wanted us to meet informally. We need to talk about a complex, fairly delicate, situation. For reasons that will soon be obvious, the nature of this subject is sensitive enough that we should keep it between ourselves for now." He sipped his coffee.

They nodded, waiting for him to continue.

"We are all aware of the tragedy last month at Chanul Tzuk. Chandler Bennett has called me several times this week, and we've discussed the situation at length."

"What does he think happened to the girl?" Thomas asked.

"He doesn't know. Chandler thinks we may never know what happened to her."

"That's quite possible. It's a missing person case now, and they often go unsolved in Mexico." Mamett observed.

"In any case, Chandler has been deeply affected by what happened down there, feels personally responsible, and has decided to resign his position at Oregon." Carl continued.

"My God." Thomas whispered. "Why Carl? Why? Does he blame himself for it?"

"He shouldn't but I believe he does. However, I also think he was approaching burn out, and this tragedy has simply pushed him over the edge."

"Hell of a career. He was one of the best." Mamett shook his head. "He'll be missed."

"Well it is in Chandler's spirit of sharing that I asked you both here. Patrick, he wants you to take over his project at Chanul Tzuk."

"What? You're not serious Carl!" Mamett spilled his coffee, and missed the saucer with his cup. He blotted the spill with his napkin.

"I am indeed. He asked me to ask you."

"I can't believe it." Mamett gave up on the coffee spill. "Bennett has what? Like five years of NSF grant money left. Plus NGS money. He's exceptionally well funded. Chanul Tzuk's one of the three most significant sites being worked in the Maya area today, the other two being Palenque, and Tikal." Mamett leaned back in his chair, and crossed his hands over his chest. "Carl, why does he want to give it to me? I mean I'm deeply honored but... shocked." He shook his head.

"He likes your work. You're well connected in Mexico, politically. You're well known and respected in the region. These are some of the reasons he mentioned. I think there are other obvious reasons, as well; you're young, energetic, and associated with a relatively prestigious institution."

Thomas smiled, and said, "I suppose the reason that I'm here, is you want my help in selling this idea to that institution. I think it would be good for the program provided it doesn't spread us too thin."

"Indeed it would be, Samuel." Carl nodded, and added, "And it should not be that difficult to sell. The visibility, the research money, the research opportunities speak for themselves."

"So does the missing girl." Thomas observed.

"Yes that will have to be addressed." Carl agreed. "We will have to develop our own site security plan, to assure our people that all project personnel are safe. I'll leave that up to you and Patrick to work on."

"I'll be the one to ask the obvious question." Thomas said. "Patrick, given how much work you have on your plate right now, can we reasonably expect you to take over Chanul Tzuk too?"

"I think so. The work at Kichpanha, in Belize, is at the preliminary stage. It can be mothballed a year or two." He rubbed his beard. "Ubala is close enough to Chanul Tzuk, that if I scaled back that reconnaissance project a bit, put in a caretaker crew, and checked in once a week, I could probably run them both simultaneously. Avendano is my co-director there for the Istituto Nacional. He would gladly take on the overall supervision of it. By the way, he's coming in Saturday and he'll be staying for a week to work on the Ubala material. Now when does the NSF contract start up again at Chanul Tzuk?"

"January first, so we'll have to arrange for you to have the spring semester off." Carl observed. "That should not be a problem."

"Well, I don't go back into Ubala until the end of March, so there's no real conflict there."

"Who among our graduate students would you select to help you run Chanul Tzuk?" Thomas asked.

"That's an easy one. I would try to convince Eikelmann to finish his rewrite, so he could be Dr. Eikelmann, and have the proper credentials to be an assistant director. Mexico is more rigid on credentials than say Belize or Guatemala. He would also be the resident computer jock. For staff ceramicist, Delia Bell, hands down. She knows the material better than I do, plus she's very stable, and reliable. Belinda Boothe would also have a position of responsibility, if it enhanced her thesis research, rather than inhibited it."

"For the sake of continuity, you would retain some of Chandler's people from Oregon wouldn't you?" Thomas asked. "I mean that would only be fair."

"Of course. That goes without saying. Any commitments made by Bennett to his students would be honored." Mamett was excited, thinking about the possibilities.

"Well then. I think you have a deal Patrick." Carl smiled and offered his hand. "I'll relay your acceptance of Chandler's offer within the hour, and set up an introductory call."

13 Kind of Like Archaeology

Delia wanted to check on Laurence, invite him to dinner if he was up for it, and if not, and see if he needed anything. Then she would go home, close the blinds, disconnect the phone, and take a good long nap. The last few days had been hard with the exam, Phil's departure, Laurence's emergency; it had all taken a toll.

She pulled up in front of Laurence's building, a two story, Dutch colonial converted into two upper and lower apartments. She flipped her cigarette in the gutter again, the same place as two nights ago. It seemed a lot longer than that she thought, as she trudged up the stairs to Eikelmann's apartment. Now that I've passed the orals, I'll quit smoking, she thought. Things will settle down.

Delia paused at the top of the stairs, and looked at Eikelmann's paneled oak door. It wasn't only unlocked, this time it was ajar. Anyone could walk in. "Laurence?" she knocked on the door and it opened part way.

"Hello? Laurence? Anyone home?" She pushed the door open all the way, listening for sounds coming from the inside.

Nothing. Dead silence. She felt something was not right. Delia stared into the gloom. It was a small one-bedroom apartment and she had been there often, but it felt alien.

"Laurence?" She could hear her pulse; her heart was starting to pound hard. She was afraid to go inside. People didn't break into apartments in broad daylight, and leave the door open. Did they? Were they still inside? Or had Laurence just forgotten to close his door?

She listened hard, and her hearing ability seemed to have intensified from her anxiety, because she could hear a faucet dripping from somewhere inside, and that was all. Should she leave now and call the police?

Delia decided she needed something. What she wanted was a really big knife, or cleaver, but the kitchen was all the way to the back. Laurence's golf bag was in the corner nearest the door. She grabbed an iron at random and stepped toward the hall. The blinds were drawn, and the living room was dark. She could hear the dripping in the shower clearly now. It was the only sound, except for the muffled sounds of traffic from the street outside. If she needed to call the police, the closest phone was in the bedroom.

"Laurence?" Her voice rasped, and she coughed. "Laurence?" A much better attempt, firmer. The place smelled of dirty clothes, like a locker room, and something else that she could not identify. He was not a fastidious housekeeper.

On the bed was a large conical mound, a pile of laundry; clothes, sheets, blankets, and towels. Out of place. Totally wrong. Although Laurence was not a neatness fanatic, he would not have left his bed like that.

The edge of the mattress was streaked and shiny with dark red blood.

She walked, dropping the golf club, stumbling, toward the blood, and she felt light, like she was leaving her body and watching it from a great distance across the vastness of the room as it staggered toward the bed. The room seemed tilted, like the deck of a boat. Dazed, she touched the sticky clotted blood, like red syrup… A wave of nausea knocked her to her knees and she swallowed hard as she fought it off, gagging.

Delia knelt with her elbows on the edge of the bed, taking short ragged breaths. When she opened her eyes, the room was blurry and foggy; I'm going to faint, she thought. She shook her head. Her vision cleared, and under a pillow she saw Laurence Eikelmann's slashed neck, the dried arterial blood, his mouth, and his perfect, gleaming, white teeth. His dull eyes gaped at her. This time the nausea won, and she vomited beside her dead friend.

* * * * * * * * *

Delia sat on the porch outside, waiting for the police, too shocked to think. Why Laurence? Why would anyone do such a thing? She tried to breathe properly. It didn't work - neither did the cigarette that she stubbed out after one draw. She was glad to see the police car pull up. Delia stood up as the uniformed officer of the Somerville Police Department came up the sidewalk.

"I'm Cordelia Bell, I reported this . . ."

"Sergeant Palmeri, let's go on up to the apartment." They walked into the entryway of the building. "Has anyone been here since you called?"

"No. No one."

"How long have you been here?"

"Twenty or thirty minutes."

"And you reported this," he glanced at his watch, "what ten minutes ago?"

"That sounds about right." An unmarked car squealed to a stop. Just like on television, she thought.

"Well Somerville homicide has arrived," Palmeri observed.

"Palmeri. What you got?" Another short, Italian-looking fellow asked. He was built like a refrigerator.

"Lieutenant this is Miss Bell. She phoned in. We haven't been upstairs yet."

"You know the victim?" The lieutenant pulled out a Marlboro offered one to Delia and she took it. "Hey where's my manners, I'm Sal Martin," he put out his hand.

"Cordelia Bell." She felt stupid, because Palmeri had just introduced them. Two more cars pulled up and cops started getting out.

Lieutenant Martin held up his hands, and said "Everybody slow down. Before we touch or do anything else, Miss Bell and I are going to go upstairs and she will show me what she found. Then, under my authority the investigation will proceed according to my directions. You men keep everyone out until I come back. Miss Bell. Would you accompany me please?"

As they walked up the stairs, Martin talked, "Miss Bell. When we get up there, if it's comfortable with you, I want you to look around and give me your impressions, anything that comes to mind, please share it with me. Can you do that ma'am?"

"I'll try."

"Understand please that anything you notice, anything you think of, it might seem insignificant to you but it could have great importance to us. Okay?"

"Okay."

She didn't realize that she had left the door ajar. As Martin opened the door, he turned to her and said, "Please don't touch anything, and please try to remember and tell me what you have already touched."

"Kind of like archaeology." She said.

"Excuse me?" Martin asked politely.

"When we first encounter something, we think could be important in an archaeological excavation, we don't touch it, and we document it first." Delia said feeling slightly embarrassed for bringing it up.

"So you are an archaeologist?

"I'm studying to become one. I'm in graduate school... at Harvard." She felt embarrassed again, and she didn't know why.

"Harvard huh? You must be pretty smart. I always thought that that would be fascinating. Tombs, pyramids. *Indiana Jones*. It's not really like that is it?" Martin looked around at the dark room.

"No. Not really."

"Yeah. I know. Being a cop ain't like being Colombo either."

They surveyed the living room, from the doorway. Martin was very patient. He would have been a good archaeologist. He looked at her and said, "Let's put out our cigarettes outside before we go any further."

Martin asked, "So how did you know the victim?"

"He's a friend of mine. Was a friend of mine? We knew each other from school."

"He an archaeologist too?"

Delia nodded.

"Okay. Let's go in and turn on the lights."

They went upstairs, Martin opened the door, flipped the wall switch, and the living room was illuminated. There was the couch she had found Laurence on two nights ago. The empty glass was still on the coffee table. Where was the laptop computer? It had been there two nights ago. Delia looked around the room.

"You notice something?" Martin asked.

"Two nights ago, Laurence had his laptop out here on the coffee table."

"Very good Miss Bell. That's the kind of insight only you could provide."

They were in the bedroom now. She could smell the vomit she had left on the floor, and felt her nausea swimming back. She wished she had cleaned it up. Martin squatted by the edge of the bed and looked at Eikelmann's corpse.

"I would say a large and very sharp knife. He's been cut to the cervical vertebrae. Damned near decapitated. Imagine that death was instantaneous." He massaged his forehead. "You know, there ought to be more blood than this."

Martin stood up and looked at her. "What is it Miss Bell? The vomit? Don't feel bad; sometimes it even gets to us. You okay?"

"Yes. No. It was what you said."

"What? You mean being sick? Don't worry about it."

"No. The decapitation. The cervical vertebrae. That's how the Maya, Aztecs, the Sumerians of Mesopotamia, sacrificed their victims. They did other things too, but decapitation is a common method of sacrifice."

"Good job Miss Bell. That's something I would not have known."

"And the pile of laundry? That's like a burial mound." Delia began to feel strangely detached. "Someone sacrificed him and buried him."

Martin looked at her, frowning, "You sure about that? Or are you doing like I asked… just saying what comes to your mind?"

"Well, it struck me. Why else bury him? I mean it's symbolic…"

"Like the murderer is saying, I'm an archaeologist. I sacrificed this man?" Martin asked.

"Either that, or…"

"Or it's somebody who is not an archaeologist, but who wants to frame somebody who is." Martin said matter-of-factly.

"Or maybe whoever killed him was an archaeologist, but an insane one." Delia added.

"Why do you think the killer is insane?" Martin asked.

"Look what he did Lieutenant? Is this the act of a well-adjusted personality?" Delia shuddered, and fought off another wave of nausea.

Martin smiled. "Well technically, let me contribute something from my own field. First of all this looks organized and planned. The killer seems to have personalized the crime scene. Other than serial murders, most people kill for what they think are good reasons. I think most serial killers are quite insane, messed up sexually you know. But actually they can

65

mask themselves in our society. Go about their business, look like normal people - never giving themselves away." He walked to the bathroom, and looked in. "Looks like the perpetrator took a shower before he left. He's a cool one. Organized. Look. See the blood on that towel?

"Anyway these sociopaths get away with it for a while. Sometimes for a long while. Like the Boston Strangler or Ted Bundy." Four men knocking at the doorway interrupted him. "Crime Scene Investigator," was stenciled on their windbreakers. They had briefcases, cameras, and tripods.

"Excuse me Miss Bell. I'm going to huddle with the team for a few minutes. Could you wait in the living room for me?"

Martin got too busy to get back to Delia, so she left her number and went home. All the way back she felt sick and worn out and didn't want to think about it. She could not even begin to absorb everything that had happened.

* * * * * * *

"I'm in denial, disassembling." Delia said to herself as she trudged up to her apartment. "Exhausted too."

She checked her mailbox. Nothing. No email on her computer either. Far too early to hear anything more from Phil Ward. She wished he hadn't left. He had always been so steady. "I'm disassembling. Need to get a grip."

I'll just lie down and rest for a minute, she thought.

14 Shotguns and Pistols

The tractor's engine was getting louder and they could smell the diesel fumes as it approached. Sergio stopped running and crouched down on the platform slope behind an old masonry retaining wall. He motioned Jesse to get down next to him. From this spot they had a good view of the clearing. The tractor emerged from the brush, pulling a flatbed trailer with six men riding on blocks, chains and cable spools. It stopped next to the Bronco.

66

The tractor driver seemed to be in charge and he directed two of the men who had shotguns, over to the Bronco, and sent the rest down the path towards the looters hole. Jesse saw Sergio check the safety on his shotgun making sure it was released. He looked over at Jesse and smiled grimly. Jesse nodded back after releasing his own safety. "This is an interesting situation is it not?"

"Any ideas?" Jesse asked.

"Let's watch a while."

The two men opened the doors to the Bronco and looked around inside. They looked in the back, talking and gesturing to each other. One of them pulled something out of his pocket that glinted in the sunlight, and then knelt down beside the front tire. "Problem." Sergio whispered.

The man straightened up and walked around to the other side of the Bronco, and knelt down again.

"We won't be driving the Bronco out." Sergio pointed as the tires slowly deflated, and the front end of the Bronco sank down. They could hear the men laughing. Apparently satisfied, the men headed down the path towards the pit. They were quickly out of sight. "Feel like taking a little walk Jesse? I don't think our diplomatic skills will get us very far."

"It's at least nine miles to the road." Jesse said getting to his feet. "We'd better get started now; it will be dark in a few hours. Then it's another twenty miles to town."

They jogged softly into the tall grass that was starting to billow as the breeze from the lagoon intensified. Jesse cradled his shotgun in the crook of his right arm, and swung the machete with his left hand. Sergio ran right behind him.

A voice called out something that Jesse couldn't make out. A pistol shot went off. Jesse ran harder, thinking about when he played special teams at A & M. Hell of a time to think about football. Need to move now!

He heard another shot and simultaneously heard a buzzing sound in front of him. He had hunted enough to know the sound of a bullet. He tossed the machete aside, and gripping the shotgun with both hands made a hard right and dove into the grass clumps, rolling over and coming to rest propped up on his elbows. He looked back and saw Sergio crouched low, bringing up his shotgun, and aiming it at three men running down the slope of the mound. They were at least a hundred yards away, well out of range, when Sergio fired. They took cover in the undergrowth of the slope and one of them fired his pistol again. The bullet hissed by overhead.

Sergio looked back at Jesse and pointed toward the other side of the mound where a half dozen other men were crouching low, trying to flank them. Sergio fired toward them, but they too were out of range. He yelled to Jesse, "Go back to the right and try to intercept them, I'll hold here for a few minutes, then I'll catch up with you."

"Right. In that tall grass we might have a better chance." Jesse yelled back and ran deeper into the billowing grass. More shots went off, pistols and shotguns. He ran like an animal on pure adrenaline…scared and worried. What the hell have we got ourselves into? Doesn't matter, keep running. He ran as hard as he could, wildly, holding out the shotgun in front of him to knock down the grass. He ran into a recently cleared cornfield, and felt exposed. He circled back to his left and ran into another field of saw grass. He kept running, extending his legs, really moving now.

Suddenly he broke through the grass and slipped on mud, almost falling down and used the shotgun stock to break his fall. He recognized the place. The churned up deep ruts, stagnant water, he had come to the track the vehicles had made going in to the mound. It was as good as place as any to wait for Avendano. He needed to calm down.

The only sound was the grass rustling in the wind, and his lungs heaving. He waited a few minutes, and then decided to walk down the track toward the road. He hoped Sergio would catch up with him soon.

* * * * * * * *

Jesse made it to the main highway by sunset. He heard no more from the looters or Avendano. Carrying a shotgun along the road at night would make it hard to catch a ride, so he went into the saw grass and hid it. He tied his bandana to a rock to mark the place, and walked back to the road to wait for a ride, hoping that Avendano would show up soon. The nocturnal insects began their incessant chirping and clicking. It was a clear night, the Milky Way emerged from a black sky, the wind whispered through the grass, and Jesse felt isolated in the middle of the universe, lost and worried. He tried to think about other things, but he could not.

After about a half an hour he heard the now familiar sound of the diesel tractor coming through the fields. As it neared the road Jesse went back into the grass, picked up the shotgun, and waited.

The tractor emerged from the field and Jesse saw that the men on the trailer were now sitting on a large block covered in a blue tarp. They had the altar. The tractor and trailer turned left, heading away from San Javier.

Jesse waited a few minutes, and warily crept back to the highway, again leaving the shotgun behind. He decided to walk towards town and hope that someone would stop and give him a ride.

Not one vehicle came down the road.

After almost two hours, a flashing red light appeared down the road, a jeep rapidly approached him. Three soldiers were inside armed with M-16s. The jeep stopped next to him.

"Who are you?" The driver asked.

"Jesse Salazar. I need help." He stretched out his hands to show he was unarmed.

"Were you with the professor?"

Jesse nodded and they motioned for him to get into the jeep. As he climbed into the back, he asked the soldiers, "How do you know about the professor?"

"He radioed us about an hour ago."

"Is he all right?"

"He was an hour ago."

"Did he tell you about the looters? Because they just left, they went south down the road."

"We will help the professor first, and then we will deal with the looters."

They drove quickly back to the turnoff. As they bounced down the track, Jesse noticed that the soldiers seemed tense, and fidgeted with their M-16s.

The Bronco's taillights reflected the Jeeps high beams. They pulled up behind it and turned off the engine. Something seemed wrong, and Jesse recognized it immediately, the insects were silent. All he could hear was the wind blowing through the grass and underbrush.

From above them on the platform, Avendano called out. "Jesse is that you? Are you all right?"

"Señor! Yes. And you?"

"I am fine. Although, it's been a little hectic around here these past few hours."

Avendano emerged from the undergrowth, and walked down to them. He pointed his shotgun toward the ground. "I suppose you know they have the altar."

"I saw them go by a couple of hours ago."

"With that much of a head start it will be impossible to find them tonight. We may as well go back to town. I could use a drink."

"Uno momento." The driver said and walked back to the Jeep he dug around in a field pack and produced a bottle of tequila. He handed it to Avendano.

"Gracias." He held it up to look at the label. "Ah. Sousa Anejo. Bueno." He took a long drink, and handed the bottle to Jesse, who followed suit.

They made room in the back of the Jeep for Avendano and started back to town. "I'll send someone out tomorrow and retrieve the Bronco." He said to Jesse. "There are a number of things we need to discuss."

"The rituals…?"

"These are not your average looters. They have a special agenda of some kind."

15 Mystic River Road

The phone was ringing in Delia's dream. For some reason she could not find it in her house. In her dream a flock of ravens surrounded the phone and covered her dresser, hopping around on it. Then she realized as she woke up that it really was ringing. She groped for the portable receiver by her bed.

"Hello."

"Miss Bell?"

"Yes."

"This is Lieutenant Martin."

Christ. Delia thought what now? The light on her VCR said 4:30. Was it a.m. or p.m.? God, I'm groggy.

"There are a couple of things over here at the victim's apartment that strikes me as kind of odd. I wonder if I could get you to come over here in a little while and offer me your opinion."

"What sort of things are they Lieutenant Martin?"

"Let's say they might support one of the interpretations you offered earlier."

"Which interpretation was that?" Delia yawned. "Please excuse me if I seem disoriented. I am. I was asleep."

"Oh, I'm sorry. It's just that this is pretty important stuff, if you don't mind." Martin sounded genuinely sincere in his apology.

She took a deep breath.

"Miss Bell, I know this murder has shocked you, and I wouldn't call you if I didn't need your help."

She sighed. "Could you please tell me what it is?"

"Let's say that I think you may be right on two counts. The killer may have been an archaeologist, and your friend Mr. Eikelmann was sacrificed."

Delia was stunned, but managed to gasp, "I'm on my way."

* * * * * * * *

Mystic River Road was choked with cars and vans. Police, Coroner's, Eyewitness News, Channel 7, NBC, CNN, it was a media feeding frenzy. Delia ran into Palmeri a block away from Eikelmann's apartment building.

"Where should I park?"

Palmeri gestured. "Everyone else is double parked. You might as well too."

She parked next to a patrol car. A block up the street a white Camry pulled in to a space but no door opened.

Delia closed her door and walked over to Palmeri who was watching a News team set up. He turned to Delia.

"You see? This is great stuff for the media types. The timing is perfect. They'll be able to broadcast live at 6:30. Ain't the first amendment wonderful?"

"Sergeant, you seem to be cynic."

"I am when it comes to these vultures. Local news is the worst of a bad bunch."

"Lieutenant Martin said he needed me to come back."

"Well why are we standing here then? I'll take you to him."

They walked through the crowds of neighbors, and law officers to the front of Eikelmann's apartment, and found Martin taking a cigarette break on the front porch. Martin looked as tired as Delia felt.

"Thanks for getting here so quickly." He took a deep draw on his cigarette, and offered one to Delia, which she accepted.

"Okay." He pushed back his thinning hair. "In spite of everybody wanting to get their licks in, I was able to conduct, what I believe is a thorough and controlled investigation of the crime scene. We videotaped everything. We took each piece of the mound of laundry off the victim, one piece at a time. Then we bagged it, tagged it, and took a picture of how it looked after they removed each piece, just like archaeology. Right?"

"Exactly right Lieutenant."

"There are a lot of finger prints all over the apartment, and we got all of them It'll take a while to sort it all out."

"What about what you told me on the phone?"

"I'm coming to that. While we were taking apart the mound, I started to see it as a mound. I'm convinced the murderer selected things that would give it that kind of structure." He paused, and stubbed out his cigarette.

"Okay. Still, I haven't told you just how right you are about this." He paused and looked hard into Delia's eyes, he was probing. "You see Miss Bell, after we uncovered the body completely; we found something that was deliberately left with the body. Not to mention how the body itself was arranged. Then there are the artifacts."

"What do you mean?"

"I'll show you. Come over to the truck with me?" He gestured toward a van parked in the middle of the street.

"We've removed everything including the body, and the body parts we found..."

"Oh my God. What body parts? You don't mean he was mutilated too?"

"I'll explain it all in a minute. I want you to identify some things for me first." He opened the back of the van and pulled a long cardboard box from the back. He fished around in some plastic bags and pulled out one with a ceramic bowl in it.

"Can you identify this? Don't take it out of the bag, please."

Delia took it, and turned it over. "This is a basal-flange ceramic bowl, probably from the central Peten region of Guatemala. It dates to the Early Classic, from about 300-500 AD." She handed it back to Martin. "Where did you find this?"

"In a panel, in the ceiling above his bathroom. This and another one like it. So this is Maya, Aztec...?"

"Maya. It's Classic Maya. It's the real thing. It has been in the ground awhile. See these root tracks down the side? Was it in a box; were there any notes with it?"

"No. It was wrapped in a pillow case."

Martin was digging in the box again, and fished out a smaller bag. Inside was a thin, smoky glass needle.

"What is this, Miss Bell?"

"An obsidian...needle" Delia looked at it glinting through the bag in Martin's hand. "I have never seen a better example."

"Obsidian? What's that?"

"It's volcanic glass. It's formed in volcanic vents, from lava that cools quickly. It's very sharp. Sharper than surgical steel. This is an obsidian bloodletting tool rendered in the shape of a stingray spine. It's one of the longest and thinnest ones I have ever seen."

"A blood letter?"

"In many Maya rituals, priests, and other dignitaries, would cut themselves; sacrifice their own blood to the gods, usually at the height, at the climax of a ceremony. They would open up their veins with a needle like this. Sometimes they would use a knife, or even an actual sting ray spine."

"We found the obsidian needle in the victim."

"In?"

"Yes Miss Bell. In. The obsidian needle. It was stuck in the victim's penis."

"What?" Delia stared at Martin's bloodshot eyes.

"I'm sorry Miss Bell. That's not the worst of it. Whoever killed him removed the victim's heart, and he took it. It's nowhere to be found at the scene."

* * * * * * * *

A brief rainstorm made them take shelter in the front seats of the van. Martin was explaining to Delia the many aspects of the murder that baffled him.

"You know, usually we don't have that many clues to go on. Usually they're rare, or we have none. Here we have a glut of them. He's very controlled, very sure of himself; either doesn't care, or is so arrogant he doesn't believe we'll catch him. A couple of other elements stand out. One, the person or persons who did this, had knowledge of anatomy. The medical examiner said the heart, and sternum were almost surgically

75

removed. Like he had done it before. Two, whoever did it, had access to ancient Mayan artifacts. That narrows it down considerably; they almost had to be someone you know at Harvard."

"Not necessarily." Delia said defensively.

"Why not necessarily?"

"Well. The artifacts may have come from Laurence's own fieldwork. Alternatively, art collectors, antiquarians, archaeology buffs, museums, and looters could have them. These are just some of the people who could have access to such artifacts."

"You don't want to believe it's someone in your department."

"No. I don't want to believe it. I don't want to believe any of this. Can I go home now?" Delia suddenly felt tired. She felt like she had been with Martin all day.

Martin gave her a sympathetic look. "Sure, you've helped me a lot today. Another question for you to take with you. In my experience, there are generally three reasons why people kill, greed, jealousy, or revenge. Try and think if your friend knew anyone that would want to kill him for these reasons. Okay?"

"Well Lieutenant Martin, we can rule out greed right off, and as far as jealousy goes, I don't think Laurence dated anyone. I think he has an ex girlfriend back in New York. Still, he's not the kind of person to be involved in some bizarre love triangle. What was the other one? Revenge? That seems unlikely as well." Delia started to open the door to leave.

"Could you elaborate for a minute before you go…why you think this? Take the greed motive for example."

"Well. The only thing we know that is missing from his apartment is his laptop. Whoever killed him didn't do it to steal that."

"How do we know? There could have been something stored in the computer that implicated the killer somehow."

76

"There's that possibility." Delia admitted. "But what about the artifacts? Each of those bowls is worth thousands of dollars on the antiquities market. The blood letter too, probably. I don't keep track of that stuff. But still, there's a reason why looters loot. Greed. Leaving those pots behind doesn't make sense. They're worth a lot of money. Unless…"

"Unless what?"

"I was going to say unless they didn't know they were there, or they had access to more and better ones. A big supply." She thought of the antiquities trade, the black market. Impossible. There was no way Eikelmann could have been mixed up in anything like that.

"Miss Bell, I want you to keep your knowledge of these bowls between you and me for now. I'm going to hold this back from the press, okay?"

"Okay."

"Now the only place I know around here that would have a large amount of this stuff, would be the Peabody Museum, would it not?" Martin asked.

"Well yes, a very large amount, try thousands, hundred of thousands of artifacts from all over the world. However, they are all kept in storage collections, with very restricted access that would make it very difficult for someone to smuggle out one, much less two ceramic bowls. Besides there was no trace of accession numbers on the vessel you showed me."

Martin nodded.

"Look. There's something I almost told you this morning, but I forgot in the midst of all of this pandemonium, Lieutenant."

"What's that?"

"The other night when I came over here. I came because Laurence had a medical emergency of some kind. He wound up in the ER at Mount Auburn. They let him out last night."

"It would have been nice to have known this a little earlier Miss Bell."

"I'm sorry. It's been hard for me to concentrate on everything. I'm tired and…"

"That's okay. Just tell me what happened."

Delia began describing the events of Wednesday night. She left out the strange reference Laurence had made about Belinda, but told Martin everything else. She made a mental note to go back by Belinda's when she could. After she finished, Martin closed his notebook and looked over at Delia.

"That's it then? You leave anything else out?"

"That I still wonder what happened to Laurence that night. What was in his system? Mount Auburn might still turn something up I guess."

"Don't worry, I'll find out, I'm going over there next." Martin opened the door; the rain was letting up. "Before you go, I want you to know something. I feel like I should warn you. Right now as far as I'm concerned, everyone in your department, every teacher, every student, every janitor, every secretary, is a suspect in this homicide investigation, with only one exception."

"Who's that?"

"You, Miss Bell. I would stake my eighteen years of police experience on you. You strike me as an honest woman and a decent one. I don't think you could have killed your friend."

"Thanks Lieutenant, I guess."

"Excuse me Miss Bell? I'm the one who should be thanking you. You stayed here and helped me when you were still in shock this morning. After that, you probably went home, passed out from emotional exhaustion, I wake you up and now you've been helping me again." He squeezed her shoulder. "These days most people don't want to help the police, or if they do they want their attorney present, you know?"

"It never occurred to me. I hope you catch the bastard that did this, and soon."

"We will Miss Bell. This person thinks he's awful smart, but I think you're right. He's crazy as hell."

"Well thanks Lieutenant, I'm going to go now."

"Be careful Miss Bell. I think the killer is someone known to you."

"God I hope not."

"Well if he is, he may reveal himself somehow. So stay alert and call me if you need anything. You got my card, my home phone number, and my pager. Be extra careful Miss Bell."

16 Raxabe

Jesse drove aimlessly past Chanul Tzuk thinking about how he had met Avendano for breakfast at El Milagrito, a restaurant off the main plaza in San Javier. They ate outside under a large blue umbrella emblazoned with the Corona cerveza logo. Jesse was starved, sleepy, and needed a lot of coffee, and a huge breakfast. Avendano had sat down across from him, and discreetly placed his camera bag on the table. He then carefully removed one tissue wrapped object and then another one. He unwrapped two long, thin oval shaped jade plaques, which were incised with Maya hieroglyphics.

"These are what I pulled out of that cavity behind the altar last night."

Jesse was too stunned to reply. In all of his experience, he had only seen one other example like the two specimens in front of him, and that was the famous Leyden Plaque, dated to 320 AD. It had turned up in a museum collection in the '30s and had no known excavated context, because it had been looted, and smuggled out of Central America. The glyphs on the Leyden plaque were in the Central Peten Early Classic style, and probably from Tikal, and that was the best placement that could be provided for it. These two plaques on the table were not only earlier; they were from a known excavated context.

Avendano went on to explain how important the plaques and altar were, when taken together. They provided the strongest evidence yet of a Late Preclassic Maya group in Chiapas that was closely tied to the Olmec "Mother Culture" or cultura madre. Probably it was a large burial mound, and in any case the Instituto would begin salvage operations there as soon as he could arrange for funding. That would have to wait until he returned from his trip to Harvard next week. It was also critical that they recover the altar quickly, before it was moved out of the local area.

Avendano had the military and the federal police looking for the looters. He explained that after they had exchanged shots with them, and he had become separated from Jesse, he hid deep in the grass, next to the swamp and waited for sunset. Sneaking back to the edge of the platform, he listened and watched as the looters extracted the altar with a winch, and block and tackle.

He had heard enough to know that they were Tzotzil Maya, and that they were reverential in the respect they held for the altar. They did not behave at all like typical looters. They were conscious of not damaging the altar and they seemed genuinely happy to have it in their possession. Avendano speculated that they might not be looting it for export or money at all, but rather seemed almost intent on keeping it for themselves, for whatever reason.

Jesse took a left at the fork to San Juan Chamula, realizing that he had been aimlessly driving for over an hour, and now was in an isolated valley he had only seen once before. The project team had driven past it on his way up to San Javier back in June, when Chanul Tzuk had first started up. It seemed like a lifetime ago, so much had happened since then. Kathy had disappeared, and now looters were active near Chanul Tzuk, was it all connected? He looked off to his left and saw some Maya farmers furrowing their milpa cornfields with mule-drawn wooden plows, next to a muddy road with two deep ruts. Something about the ruts made him stop and back up.

He couldn't believe it but it looked like the looter's trailer had made them. He wanted to be sure before he alerted Avendano, so he turned off the highway and drove slowly down the dirt road.

The road led past a large murky lake with white egrets standing in the shallows. Just beyond that was a field of mottled white cattle, and more egrets. The trail was in danger of disappearing altogether and wound down a ravine, which had recently flooded and washed out. Off to the right the ruts scarred the edge of a low ridge covered in vines. Jesse gunned the engine and hoped he would make it up the steep slope. He barely made it over the top, and found himself in a narrow valley with thatched huts clinging to steep eroded gullies stretching off to the east and west. In front of the nearest hut a sign had been erected. It consisted of a weathered plank with the word "Raxabe" spray painted in red across it.

"Raxabe." Jesse said out loud. He remembered the name from the *Popol Vuh*, which was the Quiche Mayan book of the dawn of life and the glories of gods and kings. Raxabe meant "The Green Road" and it was the place where all of the sacred roads crossed.

He turned off the engine and slowly got out of the truck. He knew he was being watched, although the huts seemed deserted. There was no one outside, nobody moving anywhere that he could see. He looked in front of the truck; the ground had changed to hardscrabble gravel and flat lime stones. The trail was getting much harder to follow, but it looked like it continued further to the east. He looked back at the nearest hut. He thought he had seen something glide out of the shadows.

"Estése quieto, no se mueva." He felt a gun barrel in the small of his back.

17 Harvard Square

Delia drove to see Madeline Scott again, and thought about how often she and Belinda had dined at Madeline's house in Beacon Hill. They were all good friends, and although Madeline was in her mid 40s, and held an endowed chair, she did not act older. Belinda said Madeline had always been more of an older sister to her, rather than an aunt. To Delia, Madeline seemed very down-to-earth and youthful. Madeline claimed that three divorces in twenty years had kept her young. Right now she considered herself "resting up between marriages."

Belinda, Madeline, and Delia often went out together to music clubs in Boston, and to plays at the Cambridge Repertory Theater. They enjoyed scouting out potential suitors for each other. Lately, the pickings had been pretty slim, Delia thought. When she called Madeline thirty minutes earlier at her lab and explained her continuing concerns about Belinda, Madeline had simply said, "Come over here right now."

Delia entered the lab, and saw that Madeline had draped her white coat over a chair. She was eating yogurt while she watched her computer screen display one graph after another. She turned and smiled at Delia.

"I see you wasted no time in getting here."

"Traffic is pretty light at this hour on a Sunday."

"Now explain to me why you are so worried about Belinda. It's been what? Two days since we last talked." Madeline had a penchant for getting to the point.

"Well you know about the murder."

"Yes. It's very tragic, and quite grisly. Hard to believe something like this could happen at Harvard. Although I vaguely remember reading about some professor at the Medical School, back in the 1890s that chopped up one of his students, and was caught stuffing various arms, legs, and other body parts into an incinerator in the basement of Holmes Hall. How does this graduate student murder concern Belinda?"

"Belinda and I know the victim. Two nights ago under very strange circumstances, he said something about her. I found it disturbing." Delia went on to recount Eikelmann's trip to Mount Auburn, and her trips to Belinda's apartment.

"Okay. So she returns a couple of weeks early without telling anyone. That's fairly typical of Belinda. You know how she is, secretive, full of intrigue. She's probably with a man and they went away for a few days." Madeline was exiting her computer files while she talked. "Belinda does have her appetites."

"Still, what about him saying she didn't "deserve" that."

"Delia. You just told me he was incoherent."

"I know. I just have this feeling. Do you think we could go over to her apartment, and check it out together? I really need to know what you think."

"Well… I needed a break anyway. It's a pleasant walk from here. Let's go."

* * * * * * * *

Walking together down Divinity Avenue, Madeline said, "Maybe she went somewhere with Phil. I always hoped they would get back together."

Delia listened to their heels clicking against the brick sidewalk. Red and orange leaves drifted down from the sugar maples in the early afternoon light. Undergraduates hurried past, heading to some reception, blue blazers, and crimson neckties swinging in the light wind.

"That much I do know the answer to. They terminated Phil after his orals Tuesday. He's left town to do God knows what."

"What? How? He's been studying for months. That's why Belinda wouldn't let him come with her to Guatemala. At least that's part of her story."

"What do you mean?" asked Delia.

Madeline took a deep breath. "You know how independent she is. He wanted to postpone his exams, and help her with her research this summer. He didn't want her traveling by herself down there for six or seven months. Nor did I for that matter. For reasons that escape me, Belinda said he was "clinging" too much, and was becoming too dependent on her."

"Yes. I've heard her say that."

"Well that's what she says. Whether she actually believes it is another matter. Anyway, they argued a lot about it. It's a tossup which of them is the most stubborn, but as you know, all of it led to her breaking up with him before she left."

"I thought she wanted to date other men. She told me that was what it was about."

"Oh I'm sure that's possible. Belinda, God love her, requires constant affirmation. You know how she is at any social situation. If there are any men present, she wants to be the focal point, the most admired. She's been that way since she was little. It's really sad."

"What do you mean?" Delia had never heard Madeline talk about Belinda this way before.

"Well can't you tell? Behind that worldly, cultured facade of hers is an insecure little girl. We're a very self-absorbed family, and more than a little neurotic. So you see, in spite of everything, she has very low self-esteem. This is why she jumps from man to man, and never has a lasting relationship." Madeline frowned, and said, "Of course, I must be some kind of expert with my three divorces. The whole thing is probably genetic. Probably on the X chromosome."

"She was with Phil for quite a while."

Madeline nodded. "Longer than anyone else. That's because Phil wouldn't put up with her bullshit, and he placed limits on her self-indulgences. He was older, more mature, self-contained and confident. All of the things she lacked, and do you know what else? The poor idiot really loved her."

Delia nodded. "Yet then she found him to be "clinging" to her."

"That's right. That's what she says. I doubt she believes it in her heart. The women in my family tend to get what we want eventually, and when we do, we reject it. Case in point. Me." They stopped talking as they jaywalked across Massachusetts Avenue. A flock of pigeons jumped into the air and then landed behind them on the cobblestones. As they turned down Eliot Street Madeline said, "So they broke up when? Early May? How come you didn't um, you know?"

"Go out with him? Madeline he never once asked me."

"Still, aren't you a liberated woman? Were your fingers broken? You couldn't call him?" Madeline was smiling at her, teasingly.

Delia blushed, and said, "Maybe I would have if I didn't know that he still was in love with my best friend. Can we please talk about something else? By the way he's closer to your age anyway!"

Madeline laughed. "I believe I hit a nerve! True. Still, I don't think he goes for us older types, not that I wouldn't mind . . . Delia; you know you are a good friend. A good girl scout. Very responsible and ethical. I wonder if Belinda would have done the same for you." They stopped in front of the boutique. "Well look. Here we are. You have the key? Let's go up and look around."

As they entered Belinda's apartment, Ziggy dashed from the hall straight to Madeline, who scooped him up in her arms. "Well hello to you to Ziggy. You don't look like you've missed too many meals. So Delia, I see you've been taking good care of him."

"Yes but we're not exactly the best of friends. He's always hissing at me. That is when he's not demanding to be fed. Frankly, I prefer dogs."

"Well Zig has been in a bad mood ever since he was neutered. Isn't that right Zigger?" She put the cat down and said. "So Belinda came back on what? Wednesday? Four days ago."

"Yes those books on her desk are new, but they haven't moved since then. Her bags are in the bedroom." They looked at the room.

"Well she hasn't slept here for a while. It's too neat," observed Madeline, looking around the bedroom. "Do you know she's had that leather suitcase since she was in boarding school?" Madeline started unzipping the suitcase, "Let's see if we can find any clues shall we Miss Marple?"

Delia sat next to her on the bed and they neatly unpacked clothes, socks, underwear, books, and manuscripts. "My God she's crammed a lot in here. Oh look, a newspaper from Merida, Mexico, *Novedades de Yucatán*." Madeline handed it to Delia. "You can read Spanish." It was dated August 24. She saw Kathryn Haden's picture on the front page, and read part of the story.

"It's about Kathy Haden, the woman from Penn. The one who disappeared in the tropical storm." Madeline didn't answer. She was going through the contents of a Manila folder. She handed an envelope from it to Delia.

"Looks like she never got around to mailing it. She comes from a family of impressive procrastinators."

"No stamps. She probably never got around to buying any stamps. Should I read it?"

"Your name's on it. Why not?"

"Okay here goes." Delia opened the letter and read it out loud. "It's dated August 24th, a little over five weeks ago. Dear Delia:

"Greetings from Tikal. I've left my place on Calle Orellano de Salazar in Guatemala City for a few days. I live there in a little pensione, about two blocks from the National Museum, and four blocks from the American Embassy in the event any "difficulties" arise. Did you know that before Phil got into archaeology, he was a Marine Corps guard at this very same embassy?"

"They stationed Phil here after he came back from Viet Nam in the late 70s. I wonder what he was like as a Marine. Phil is just so kind and generous, and he rarely talks about the Marines, much less Viet Nam. He's not exactly your stereotypical, media-inspired, psycho killer. Phil is just a big teddy bear. Probably the least neurotic of anyone I know."

"I've been thinking about him ever since I left. The fact is I should have let him come with me, I wish he was here right now. I can't even tell you why I was so mean to him. I guess it had something to do with wanting some time away from him for a while to figure things out, but I went about it in a totally wrong way. Now I miss him more than I can tell you."

"I miss you too and Madeline, and my cat. I guess now that I've been gone almost five months I'm starting to get homesick."

Madeline interrupted again. "Just listen to that. How many times does she use the word "I"? Oh no. She's not too self-centered." Madeline shook her head. "Poor thing. She still cares about Phil, but I bet you she didn't tell him. She's not going to admit to him that she made a mistake. Not Belinda."

Delia continued. "Some weird stories are coming out of the Peten and Chiapas these days. They are looting a lot of sites up by the Belizean border very effectively, and very systematically. I've visited some sites and someone is digging straight, professional looking trenches right into the hearts of the temples. They are looting many tombs. God only knows what they have destroyed. Hector Obregon, a Guatemalan archaeologist from the museum, took me up to Topoxte last weekend and the devastation was unbelievable. We counted eighteen different trenches in nine different mounds. I wondered about it. Why nine mounds? As you know, nine is a sacred Maya number, as in the Nine Lords of the Underworld, The Nine Lords of the Night. Did the looters know that? They must have. The rumor mill down here says that a gringo, who's leading a team of experienced local boys, is doing it, and quite successfully. They are smuggling the artifacts out and selling them on the antiquities market. Last year some jade masks and polychrome vessels from Rio Azul turned up in a New York art gallery down in Soho. The emblem glyphs on the masks confirmed they were from Rio Azul. Hector says that Rio Azul was one of the first sites they hit. At Topoxte I took some pictures, made some sketch maps, and we bagged some artifacts that were hanging out of the sidewall. Most of the stuff we recovered was from the Early Classic. You know how rarely that is found."

"It ends there, I think she meant to write more don't you, it's kind of left hanging isn't it?"

"What's an emblem glyph?" Madeline asked.

"It's a hieroglyphic symbol that represents a Maya capital's name. They are very distinctive."

Delia folded the letter and put it in her purse. Madeline was repacking the suitcase. "Was there anything else in there?" Delia asked.

"Just some blank post cards from Guatemala City and Tikal. Why don't you dump out the duffel bag?"

Delia untied the duffel bag and dumped out the contents. A strong odor of mildew escaped into the air. "Ugh. Looks like she forgot to do her laundry. These clothes are filthy and damp."

"She must have left on impulse," observed Madeline. "I think that my niece has better hygiene than to do this under most circumstances. Here, let's put them back in the bag. I'll come by on the way home this afternoon, and take them to my house to be washed."

"Okay. So Madeline what do you think?" asked Delia.

"You know, I still think she's off somewhere having fun. Yet, I think that she would have at least dropped this duffel bag off at the laundry, or at my house. Unless for some reason she was in a big hurry. Yeah, I know it may seem strange to you, but these damp dirty clothes are not typical, and they worry me."

"So?"

"So since her parents are still in China, I guess it's up to me. If we don't hear from her by tomorrow night, I'll go to the Cambridge Police."

"And do what"

"File a Missing Person's report."

18 Ninth Precinct

The Ninth Precinct of the Somerville Police, Homicide Division, was in a new, four-story, nondescript brick building in the Winterhill section of Somerville. Martin was in his office on the fourth floor looking over the materials on Eikelmann he had obtained from Mount Auburn Hospital.

Strychnine? Moderately high levels of strychnine had been found in his blood. They had not identified the specific toxin until the day after he had checked himself out of the hospital. He had gone home in a cab, the receptionist told Martin, and he was due in for the outpatient follow up treatment on Sunday.

"Today." Martin said. "Not going to make it. He's in the morgue."

They had released Eikelmann at 6:30 P.M. Thursday night. He was found at 11:30 A.M. the following morning. The medical examiner had determined the time of death at 12:00 A.M. to 2:00 A.M. Friday morning. No one in the apartment building had seen or heard anything because his downstairs neighbors had been out until 3:00 at a party.

Martin was baffled. He was wondering if the archaeological clues, the clothes mound, the needle, maybe even the heart removal were a smoke screen, contrived to throw the investigation off in a direction away from the killer. Or killers? Possibly but most unlikely, it could be someone who was crazy enough to believe he really was sacrificing the victim, trying to replicate some ancient Maya ritual. Unless they stole the ceramic bowls, then they might be sending a message to someone in the smuggling profession. He had known Colombian drug dealers to kill a traitor in the cartel, and then dump an ounce of cocaine on his head. It was a strong message.

The other thing was that a little over twenty-four hours before they killed him; he had ingested enough strychnine to put him in the Emergency Room. How had he been poisoned? Had he tried to kill himself? You don't go around eating poison by accident, unless someone's trying to poison you.

The young man had pierced his nipples, which Martin thought was a bit odd, and, the other thing was that sometime in the past week or so, he apparently had shaved his body of all body hair. Martin asked himself, what kind of men shave bodies besides swimmers and transvestites?

Face it. You have no understanding of this case at all.

His intercom buzzed, it was the departmental receptionist, "Lieutenant Martin, there's a man on line two who wants to speak to you about the Harvard murder. He says he knew the deceased student."

89

"Okay I'll take it." This makes five hundred and twenty-five calls in six hours he thought, and picked up the phone. "Lieutenant Martin, homicide."

"Good morning. You are the officer investigating Larry Eikelmann's murder?" It was a soft-spoken voice, sounded like a middle-aged man. He was the first person to call him Larry, as far as Martin knew.

"Yes, I am. Did you know him?" Martin reached for his notebook.

"We used to have a couple of drinks together. I saw him around. He was a friend."

"Who am I talking to?"

"I wish to be anonymous."

"Okay. So where did you and Mr. Eikelmann have drinks together?"

"At the Living Room Club."

"I see." The Living Room Club was a yuppie gay bar in Boston, Martin recalled.

"Do you Lieutenant? I wonder."

"What do you mean?"

"You probably jumped to the conclusion that Larry was gay. Didn't you?"

"Well no, not really sir. I try to keep an open mind. You tell me. Was he?"

"I think he was, but I think he was just coming to terms...he had problems with his identity. He was very young and conflicted. This is all so tragic. He'll be twenty-three forever." There was a long pause.

"Yes it is tragic. When did you see him last?" asked Martin.

"Early Wednesday evening at a happy hour, about 7:30 at the L.R.C., that's what we call it."

"Was he alone?" This felt like a genuine lead. Martin was alert.

"Well that's why I called. He was with someone, I don't know his name but he is a professor in the Harvard Anthropology department. He's tall, and if you squint your eyes; he looks a bit like a young Richard Chamberlain, very urbane . . ."

"Any idea what they were talking about?"

"No, I couldn't hear what they were saying."

"You're sure this man is in the Harvard Anthropology department, not over at Boston University, which is closer to the L.R.C?"

"I'm pretty sure he's at Harvard. You'll recognize him when you see him. Look I have to get back to work. I'm not saying this man is the murderer, he probably isn't. I just thought you should know." The caller hung up.

Martin thought about what Delia Bell had said the day before that Laurence didn't date anyone. He was supposed to have a girlfriend in New York, and he wasn't the kind of person to be involved in a triangle.

Well, he thought, you sure know more about archaeology than you do about your friend Laurence Eikelmann.

19 EZLN

Raxabe was quiet. It was siesta time, and Jesse guessed that most people were asleep, although he hadn't seen but three or four men since he had been captured. Most of them were young, in their early twenties, with big-time macho attitudes. No one explained why he was being detained, or what was going on. He had been pushed around and shoved into a hut. They dumped everything out of his backpack, took his Walkman, his cassettes, his camera, energy bars, pocketknife and compass, some of his clothes. He had spent the night with an armed guard sitting outside.

At about midnight another guard had taken over and stayed there until dawn. Sometime after that he had heard a lot of vehicles arrive and leave, including his truck; that scared him, because it was connected to him. There had been a lot of activity for an hour after that, and then everything had become very quiet. Jesse was starving and thirsty, all they had given him so far was a cup of water.

The guards were dressed in paramilitary clothing, camouflage shirts and pants, Viet Nam style jungle boots and floppy hats. Their uniforms were mismatched, and bore no insignia. They all had M-16s, and did not seem in the mood for conversation.

From his doorway he could see a well with buckets and chains, and two skinny dogs sleeping in the shade of a large cohune palm. A table and two chairs were lying on their sides, next to some broken dishes, strewn clothing and scattered debris. He could smell a trash fire not far away, but could not see it from his hut. The hut nearest to him looked as if a graffiti battle had taken place on its walls. Someone had spray painted "PRI" on it. That had been painted out and "EZLN" had been painted next to it. Then that had been painted over and "PRI" had been painted back.

Jesse knew what PRI meant, that was the political party that had ruled Mexico since the 1910 revolution. He had never heard of the EZLN, but small political factions popped up in Mexico all the time.

All in all Raxabe seemed deserted. Jesse wondered where everyone had gone and whether these paramilitary types had run them off. There was little he could do but wait, and hope that no one would shoot him.

* * * * * * * * *

He awoke to gunfire. One loud rifle shot echoed across the hills. His guard and other M-16s responded, followed by another volley. Jesse threw himself prone on the dirt floor of his hut. He heard motors start up, and vehicles leave, as the gunfire tapered off.

After that it was very quiet. Only the palm branches rustling in the breeze broke the stillness. Even the constant buzz of insects was silenced. He carefully rose and looked out the doorway. A blue haze of gun smoke and cordite drifted under the palm trees. The dogs had disappeared. He heard a metallic clanking, and heavy footsteps. Several armed men seemed to materialize in the clearing. They were an eclectic group. Some wore military clothes; others were in jeans and brown shirts. They were armed with shotguns, rifles, machetes, and a few of them had M-16s and AK-47s. All of them wore black ski masks, or had black bandanas tied across their faces. A short and skinny young man appeared in the doorway, and pointed a machete at Jesse's chest.

"Quién es?" A youthful voice asked.

"I'm Jesse Salazar." He raised his hands slowly. "I'm an American."

Another man stepped up and the short one moved back. This fellow loosely held an AK-47 in the crook of his arm. He seemed to be a leader of some sort. He carried himself like El Jefe.

"An American?" He asked in perfect English. "Whereabouts?" He could have been from California his accent was that clear. Jesse knew that his own accent was thicker, moderately Tex-Mex.

"San Antonio."

"Tejas. Home of the Alamo, a famous symbol of independence." He chuckled lightly to himself, and said, "I went to grad school at UCLA, and you?"

"A and M, and Oregon."

"The ducks! My Pac-10 brother. Ha. Actually you are an aggie slash duck. A very strange creature. Of course so am I, I went to UNAM as an undergraduate. You are a very long way from home. What the hell are you doing down here?"

"It's a very long story."

"Well why don't you tell me? We have plenty of time." He sat down Indian style across from Jesse, and set the safety on his AK-47.

"You see, back in August a tropical storm came in…"

II

"Maybe this world is another planet's hell."
Aldous Huxley

20 Eulogy

Laurence Eikelmann's eulogy was scheduled to begin at 4:00 p.m. at Holmes Hall. The media representatives started arriving after lunch around one o'clock. By the time Delia was walking toward the steps at 3:30, a large cluster of curious undergraduates, and other gawkers, had formed a crowd to struggle through. Harvard Police were trying to move the onlookers away and impose some semblance of crowd control. Cindy Norwich of Channel Nine spotted Delia and said, "She's the one who found the body!" Like a herd of goats the crowd surged toward her.

Patrick Mamett appeared from the crowd, grabbed Delia's elbow, and propelled her up the stairs while fending the reporters off with his right arm.

"Let us pass please. Show some respect." He said firmly. It was not a request. In the foyer, piles of electronic cables formed a web that snaked across the entrance to the women's room. Madeline Scott was carefully stepping over them as she came toward Delia and Mamett. "Can't something be done about these vultures Patrick?" she asked.

"Madeline, I'm afraid they took us all by surprise. Although when you think about it, we should have expected something like this." Mamett gestured at a clump of photographers crowded against the back of the lecture hall. Then he added, "Are you all right, Delia?"

"I'm fine . . . Thanks for helping me get up the stairs."

"You're quite welcome. I guess this story has become national now."

"I spoke to Samuel Thomas a minute ago," Madeline observed. "He said that "Inside Edition," and "Hard Copy" are here asking questions about that young woman from Penn, and whether Laurence knew her. Can you believe that?"

Mamett shook his head.

"He did." said Delia.

"What?" Mamett and Madeline asked simultaneously.

"Last year we were all down at that conference in Mexico, the one in Merida. Remember Dr. Mamett?"

Mamett rubbed his beard and nodded. "Yes. The International Conference for Maya Studies. A year ago last May. She was there? Did I meet her?"

"I think it was at that party that Penn hosted. The next to last night we were there. She was very interested in your work at Ubala."

"Was she the kind of tall one? About five, eight, athletic… brownish blonde hair?"

"That was Kathryn. She talked to Laurence several times about his computer models of royal Maya precincts."

"Right. I remember her. She and you, Belinda, Salazar, Ward, and Laurence roamed around together at the conference for a couple of days. I didn't realize it was the same woman."

"Mmm Hmm. She and Laurence had many similar interests."

Lieutenant Martin had picked his way through the crowd of photographers. "Hello Miss Bell." He nodded at Madeline and Mamett.

"Lieutenant Martin, this is Professor Scott and this is Professor Mamett." They all shook hands.

"Sorry to interrupt but could I speak with you for a moment Miss Bell?"

"Certainly Lieutenant . . ."

"Excuse me," interjected Mamett. "Delia before you go, I want to ask you a favor."

"Yes?"

"Could you say a few words at the Eulogy? Speaking for the graduate students? You and Belinda probably knew Laurence best."

The request took Delia off-balance, but she managed to stammer. "Sure. I guess I could."

"Thank you."

Martin and Delia left Madeline and Mamett talking in the foyer. They walked down to the front row and Martin looked around before saying.

"Tell me which one of these guys is Philip Ward."

"Excuse me?"

"Who is Ward?"

"He's an ex-graduate student. They terminated him last week, and he's not here anymore. Why do you ask?" Something about Martin's tone worried her.

Martin pushed back his hair and looked around before answering. "We just might have a lead that could implicate him. Do you know how I can get in touch with him?"

"No, not really. I haven't heard from him in days. What kind of lead?"

"Well, I guess I could tell you. You seem able to keep a confidence, since no word has leaked out about those bowls we found in the ceiling yet, right?"

Delia nodded and smiled, and tried not to think about how she had discussed it with Prefontaine when she was drinking.

Martin pulled a notepad out of his back pocket. "According to Harvard University Police, on September 13th Ward checked those two pots out of the Kichpanha collections."

"I knew I'd seen them somewhere before, in the Museum reports . . ." Delia mumbled.

"What?"

"I thought at the time they looked familiar. Never mind. So how did pots that Phil checked out wind up in Laurence's ceiling?"

"How indeed?"

"Someone could have removed them from Phil's lab cabinet. Did you check his cabinet in the Maler lab?"

"The Harvard Police did."

"Did they find anything?" Delia refused to believe that Phil had anything to do with Laurence. He could barely tolerate him. They had never really gotten along.

"Only his passport, some receipts, lab notes, and some papers he had written, and a radio with dead batteries. It looks like he left in a hurry." He read from his notepad, and closed it. "That's about it. There was no evidence that anyone had tampered with the lock."

"Well Lieutenant, I know from experience that anyone could pick those locks, with a plastic credit card… or… did you say he left his passport? Was it current?"

"I think so. I'm going over there this evening to look at this stuff myself."

"I can't believe he would leave without his passport. He must have forgotten where he put it."

"Miss Bell. You don't seem to think this fellow Ward is involved, I take it?"

"No, I don't."

"Want to explain to me why?"

"I know him well. He would not do anything, umm, irregular with the museum collections. He had a respect for artifacts, if you ever saw…"

"Maybe you mistook respect for obsession. Maybe he…"

"I think you are reaching. Sorry but…"

Music started, it was from Chopin, Sonata Number 2, signaling everyone to be quiet. The room had nearly filled while they were talking. The eulogy was beginning. Martin noticed a tall fellow, who from the side resembled Richard Chamberlain, sitting in the front row. "Who is that sitting down next to your Professor Mamett?" he asked.

"What? Oh that's Professor Thomas, Samuel Thomas, he works in the Caribbean."

"So that's why he has such a nice tan." Martin whispered, and stood up to allow Madeline Scott, and Janice Helms pass by and sit next to Delia. "Ladies." He nodded at them.

The archaeology faculty sat together in the center of the front row, Thomas, Prefontaine, Mamett, and Zucker and the rest. The hall held about eight hundred people on the first floor, with room for six hundred on the two upper balconies. It was packed to capacity. "Just fourteen hundred of Laurence Eikelmann's closest friends." Madeline whispered to Delia, who shrugged in agreement, thinking about how he had been cremated earlier that morning, how he was gone and how no one would ever see him again.

Carl Prefontaine walked up the stairs as the music faded. Flashes fired from the back of the hall as he walked to the lectern.

"First I want you photographers to cease taking pictures from this point on until the eulogy concludes." He glared fiercely at them. Delia had never seen Carl so imposing, and was impressed. The camera shutters fell silent. "Thank you."

"This is a sad day for me. Laurence Eikelmann was one of my students. I remember him from when he first interviewed to come here six years ago. He was young, quite brilliant. He graduated Magna Cum laude from Columbia when he was seventeen with a double major. Anthropology and Mathematics, a rather unusual combination. Before that he had set standards of excellence at Andover. In the interview he was like a meteor. He talked fast, as if the words from his mouth could barely keep up with the thoughts from his brain. My first impression was this young man needs to switch to decaf." Prefontaine smiled.

The crowd laughed quietly.

"Nevertheless, that's the way Laurence was. A quick study, articulate, and yet… although he probably was a genius, he was not arrogant. Rather retiring and shy, you would not notice him in most social situations; he was low-keyed unless someone asked him a question that stimulated his intellect. Then it was off to the races."

"I remember the Society for American Archaeology meetings in Pittsburgh two years ago. Laurence presented a paper on computer models of Maya settlements that eventually became his doctoral dissertation. His presentation was almost like performance art, multimedia, illustrated with slides, video, and computer graphics. The sheer excellence of it stunned me. The poor fellow who had to give the next paper said 'Now I know what it would have been like to go on after the Beatles'."

"And that is how I will always remember Laurence, standing there on that stage at the William Penn Hotel in Pittsburgh, absolutely astonishing the crowd, and as many of you know it was a tough crowd. Not easily astonished. We will miss him. Thank you." Carl walked off the stage to warm applause.

As Prefontaine sat down Patrick Mamett stood up to take his place at the podium. He held a Bible in his hands. "This is the first eulogy I have ever attended for a student of mine. I hope there is never a need for another one." He paused, and looked to Delia like he was lost for a second. He quickly seemed to regain his composure. "First, I would like to thank Carl Prefontaine for those kind words. Laurence's family sends their regrets for not being able to attend, but we know they are here in spirit." He stopped and took a sip of water.

"Let me begin with Ecclesiastes, Chapter 3, verses 17 to 22, I read from the King James' version: 'For there is a time for every purpose and every work. For that which befalleth the sons of men befalleth the beast... as the one dieth, so dieth the other; yea, they have all one breath; so that a man hath no preeminence above a beast: for all is vanity. All go unto one place; all are of dust, and all turn to dust again... Wherefore I perceive that there is nothing better, than that a man should rejoice in his own works, for that is his portion: for who shall bring him to see what shall be after him?'' He paused and looked at the pages a moment longer, before closing the Bible. "I had prepared some remarks," Mamett patted his suit pocket. "Still, I don't know, I don't think so. This is a time for words straight from the heart." He paused and surveyed Holmes Hall.

"Just a couple of weeks ago I stood here in this very hall, for the first class of Introduction to Anthropology. Laurence was one of my teaching fellows, along with Cordelia Bell, who will speak after me." He nodded at Delia. "Laurence sat back there in the last row. I can see him as plain as I see you all now. Eight thirty, Monday morning, a large cup of coffee in one hand, a copy of the *Harvard Crimson* in the other." Mamett put both hands on top of his head, and pushed his hair back. His voice quavered. "Excuse me for a moment."

He leaned down on the lectern with both elbows and covered his face with his hands. "Just a minute..." After a few seconds Mamett pulled his hands down and looked at the audience in anguish.

"You know, I had a little speech, and I'm a pretty good lecturer when I want to be, but words fail me right now. Laurence Eikelmann was a good young man; he had so much to offer, and now he's gone." Mamett fought to compose himself. "Please bear with me..." He walked from behind the lectern, clasped his hands together, and looked up at the ceiling. "Somewhere Laurence is watching us right now. I believe that. And he knows how much we will miss him. How much I miss him. That's all I have to say. Thank you." Mamett walked off the stage to a silent hall.

Delia was stunned. She had never seen Mamett so emotional. Madeline elbowed her and whispered, "Delia you're supposed to go up there now." Delia put her purse down and started toward the stage. She felt butterflies in her stomach and could hear whispering, rustling and coughing as she walked to the lectern.

"Professor Mamett asked me to represent the graduate students, Laurence Eikelmann's friends. I don't really know where to begin. He was a quiet guy, very studious." Delia looked at Carl in the front row; he seemed to be nodding encouragement. "Laurence would spend hours at the computer, on the Internet, writing programs and macros, emailing people, faxing things. It was like an extension of his body. He carried that laptop of his just about everywhere. Call him what you want, computer jock, cyberpunk, techno cowboy, whatever. He was very good at it." She paused and flipped her hair back.

"And I have a confession to make to my advisor." She looked at Mamett, and saw that his head was bowed. "Dr. Mamett as you know, and as my Graduate Record Exam shows, I am, shall we say… mathematically challenged? And as many of you know, one of our graduate requirements is a yearlong course at MIT called Statistics and Computers in Archaeology. I lived in fear of it. I expected it would be my demise. If Laurence Eikelmann had not taken that course with me, I don't know how I would have fared. Yet I will say this, he knew more about that subject than the professor who taught it did. And because he essentially tutored me, I got an "A." Who knows? He probably saved my career."

"He just seemed to know when I needed help and he was a good friend. A good friend who is gone." Delia paused and looked up at the balconies and the zodiac on the ceiling. "If he were here, I wonder what he would say about all of this." She gestured at the photographers in the back. "He was such an introvert. He didn't seem to need a lot of attention. Yet look at it all . . . You know he'd probably just ask you to leave him alone. He liked being alone. Once I asked him about it, because I'm just the opposite. I hate being alone. And he said, "Delia I am alone a lot, but I'm never lonely." But now he's gone for good, and we're left alone without him. Goodbye Laurence. Thanks for being my friend."

* * * * * * * *

After the eulogy, Martin, Delia, Thomas, and Prefontaine stood together in the foyer, waiting for the crowd to thin out. The reporters and photographers were a gauntlet to pass through, and they had already taken Mamett by surprise. Delia and Madeline watched him try to navigate his way through cameras, microphones in his face, and questions shouted at him as he stepped over the cables.

"Do you think they sacrificed him?"

"No comment."

"Is Harvard intensifying security for its archaeology graduate students?"

"No comment." Mamett had reached the doorway, and was looking frantically for an escape route.

"Is it true? He was gay?"

"What? What did you say?" Mamett swung around, and the media mob surrounded him as he went down the stairs. Delia and the others lost sight of him.

"God. Delia, we're not leaving that way. You're not going to be exposed to that. They'll eat you alive." Madeline looked around trying to think of another way out.

"What audacity." Delia shook her head. "Why did they ask if he was gay?"

"Miss Bell, we've heard similar comments from the gay community." Martin interjected. "It's getting to be a very complex case. Do any of you know where he might have kept that laptop of his? Also, does anyone know anything about his sexual orientation?" He looked directly at Samuel Thomas.

"Are you talking to me? Excuse me. You are?" Thomas assumed an imperious stance.

"Lieutenant Salvatore Martin, Somerville Police, homicide. Look. I'm just asking if any of you people heard or knew whether the victim was gay. I'm just asking…"

"After all, is his sexual orientation relevant?" Thomas interrupted, "Wouldn't it be just as relevant to ask us if he was heterosexual, bisexual, or asexual, I mean really. I fail to see how…"

"Actually, no it doesn't matter at all. It does not matter in the least, but we are required to investigate his contacts, and it is likely nothing will come of that. Still, you never know where you might get a lead." He pulled out his notepad. "Like this whole issue of sacrifice. You know this weekend I went to the library and I saw these paintings from some place called Bonampak. Is that how you pronounce it?" He looked at Delia, and she nodded. "These men looked like they were captives, had their hands tied behind their backs, and their captors were cutting their heads off. That's very similar to how the victim was killed. You know?"

"Now that at least does seem relevant," Thomas said.

"Then there's the strychnine Miss Bell. The night he called you and went to the ER, he had very high levels of strychnine in his bloodstream. I have to wonder, how did that happen?"

"Strychnine?" Prefontaine asked. "Was it organic or synthetic?"

"I would have to check. I'm not sure."

"Because there are organic alkaloids present in peyote that are nearly identical in structure and action to strychnine." Carl rubbed his jaw. "Delia, I have been meaning to ask you, you said that the material they pumped from his stomach looked like Brussels sprouts, could it have been cactus?"

"God Carl. I have no idea. They were green and gummy. I guess it could have been."

"When you found him were his pupils dilated? Was he drowsy? Low blood pressure?" asked Madeline.

"Well yes. Yes he was. He was almost catatonic."

"I'll bet you it was peyote," Madeline said firmly. "The alkaloids in peyote that most closely resemble strychnine are lophophorine and pellotine."

"Could you spell those please?" Martin had his notepad out.

"I am impressed Madeline," said Carl. "I didn't know you had a background in pharmacology, I thought you were a botanist."

"Ethnobotany, actually Carl. Lieutenant, there are more than fifty alkaloids and related compounds in the peyote cactus. Many of them exist in sufficient quantity to alter human physiology. The best-known is mescaline."

"This of course is a powerful hallucinogen. Used by many Indian tribes in Mexico and North America for sacred vision quests. It is part of their religion, central to their belief systems." Carl spoke to Martin, who was busily writing in his notepad.

"So you think it's possible, Eikelmann was taking this the night he went to Mount Auburn?" Asked Martin.

"It's entirely possible." said Carl. "He could have been on a quest like Aldous Huxley who wrote *The Doors of Perception*. And he sure wouldn't be the first anthropologist or field scientist to take peyote; Wasson, Harner, Davis, Schultes, among others did, and I do know that Laurence had a research interest in it."

"Like what? Enough to experiment with hallucinogenic drugs?" asked Martin.

"Perhaps. One thing I have learned in over thirty years as a university professor is that the actions of my students can no longer shock me. Besides, in his first year seminar with me he wrote an excellent paper about peyote use among the Huichol Indian shamans of northwestern Mexico."

"Please excuse me, but what is a shaman?"

"In our popular culture we commonly call them "witch doctors" but in twenty-five words or less, a shaman is a healer, and a medium that has magical powers. They have animal spirit helpers, and claim to be able to become these animals through a process of shape shifting. A rich body of folklore is associated with these people, and they have great power and status among tribal cultures, particularly the Huichols.""

"So he was interested in that area too?" asked Martin.

"Well I don't know how interested, but enough to do a bang-up job on the paper. He researched it extensively. In fact, a version of it was published in *American Anthropologist* last year."

"What was so great about it?"

"Laurence theorized that there were certain structures in the brain, actual physiological loci, like a synapse, or specific glial cells, 'like sectors on a computer disk' is how he put it. Anyway, he maintained that hallucinogens activated these sectors and that because they had similar physical structure in all humans, that they thus produced similar hallucinogenic patterns and imagery in diverse cultures."

"Like the geometric patterns seen in the art of many formative cultures, symbols seen in Persian rugs, the way images flow together, other things that I can't remember." Carl shrugged. "His point was that these physical properties and shared hallucinatory visions accounted for the similarities seen in the great shamanic, formative religious art styles of the Americas such as the Olmec, and Maya. It was very original, conceptually."

"So you think he might have tested his own theory on himself by taking peyote?" asked Martin. "Like Dr. Jekyll and Mr. Hyde?"

"I wouldn't put it exactly that way. Yet it's possible."

"I wonder if the lab at Mount Auburn even looked for mescaline traces, or misread the data?" Madeline asked Carl, who shrugged in response.

"What other symptoms are there associated with peyote?" asked Martin.

Madeline rubbed her forehead and said. "Let's see. Excessive dilation of the pupils. Inability to walk steady. Umm. What else? Heavy perspiration."

"He was really sweaty that night," offered Delia. "He was only wearing boxer shorts."

"Nausea, increased urinary excretion, often a strong desire to defecate. That's all I can think of right now." said Madeline.

"Geez. It doesn't sound like a lot of fun." Said Martin.

"Well eventually most of the adverse side effects pass, and they say feelings of euphoria replace these negative aspects. Reports of heightened and intense awareness, closeness to the divine are common." Madeline shrugged. "However, if you got a bad cactus, one with high levels of lophophorine, and pellotine, it could send you right into toxic shock. What the hippies in my day used to call a bad trip."

"So where would he have got peyote around here? If it turns out that that's what happened?" Asked Martin.

"It grows in the deserts of Sonora and Nuevo Leon in Mexico, also southwest Texas. Basically on both sides of the Rio Grande." said Carl. "I have no idea how one would acquire it in Cambridge. Still, our graduate students are well traveled. They know people all over the world."

"Well I'll look into it." said Martin. "Thank you for your help. Look you guys. Why don't I pull my car over to the freight entrance, and give you a ride through the reporters, and over to your cars? Where are you parked Miss Bell?"

"On Kirkland Street by the Science Annex."

"Legally I hope?"

"No. Not really." They all laughed.

"I've got to get back to my office, so I will decline your offer Lieutenant. I don't think I'm too important to the media. See you later." Thomas left through the side exit.

"Okay, I'll meet you guys by the freight entrance." Martin left to get his car.

"Madeline," Carl said, "I remember reading a paper about the ethno pharmacology of the peyote cactus many years ago. It produced remarkable somatic and psychic effects among those who had used it."

"Which were?"

"People who take it fall into two categories. Some who believe it is divine and others who feel it is a tool of the devil."

21 Political Economy

After Jesse finished his story, El Jefe introduced himself. "You may call me Professor Garcia." He extended his hand. "My name is not Garcia, but I really am a Professor."

"Of?" Jesse asked, and shook hands.

"Political economy."

"And this is what?" Jesse gestured at the armed men lounging outside the hut. "A politically economical field trip?"

"Yes." Garcia started laughing. "Yes it most definitely is that." He laughed again. "That is a very accurate description."

Jesse decided to play along, since Garcia seemed to have a good sense of humor. "And your current institutional affiliation?"

"The U. of the EZLN." He became serious.

"EZLN? What is that?"

"Ejército Zapatista de Liberación Nacional."

"I saw the graffiti." Jesse pointed towards the hut outside. "That was the first time I had ever heard of it."

"You will hear much more, believe me."

A man came up and reported to Garcia. "Professor. We had no casualties in the attack."

"Bueno. How about our enemies?"

"We have found no bodies."

"How about that? A truly bloodless victory, just the way I like them."

22 Hacker

Phil Ward woke up early Tuesday morning at his sister's house in Fort Lauderdale. Her guest bedroom looked out on the backyard, which was beside the New River. Tied up at the dock was Patty's latest sailboat, *Hera's Song...* a sleek forty two-foot Island Packet Yacht built for ocean sailing. The technology was so advanced that one person could operate it entirely alone. Patty was very proud of it, and she was glad to have Phil there to help her learn more about the onboard computer systems.

Patty Bernhard was one of the top yacht brokers in Fort Lauderdale, a city with about five hundred such brokers, and internationally recognized as the boat capital of the world. Patty sailed as often as she could, and had taken her little brother out with her, every summer since he was eight; a continuous span that was finally ended by the Viet Nam War.

She was eight years older than Phil was, but they had always been close. In many ways she had been more like a mother to him, since she had been left in charge whenever his parents were out socializing, which was often.

Patty had married a yacht broker, John Bernhard when she was nineteen. He was twenty years older, and it had been his third marriage. It lasted six years, during which she had learned the business better than her husband.

Dappled sunlight reflected off a small swimming pool between the house and the river, and on the ceiling in the bedroom. Phil had slept with the windows open, the sounds of the river lapping against the dock pilings, and the palm fronds rustling in the breeze had lulled him to sleep for the past three nights.

Stretching to get up he thought, well I made one good decision. This was definitely the place to go. He felt more relaxed just being there. Most of the anxieties of the past few days seemed less pressing except the big one. What are you going to do with the rest of your life? He shrugged. Well, that was a tough one, but something would come to him. Something always did. Today, Patty had found him a job rewiring a catamaran. It would take at least all of this week and part of the next. His sister did not believe in idle hands, or feeling sorry for yourself.

Probably Belinda was okay too. All of his anxiety and stress had been manifested in troubled and strange dreams these past few nights. He had been playing phone tag that was all. Belinda had always been hard to catch at home. He decided to get up and try her number again.

On the kitchen table was a note from his sister.

Phil: Went to show a big old ugly Broward to a client from Toronto. Be back around three. Don't forget the cat in River Bend Marina. They expect you there at nine. Want to sail tomorrow? See you later.

P.S. Nice to have you back.

Sailing *Hera's Song* was a great idea, he thought, and warmed up a cup of coffee in the microwave. Patty had said that maybe they could take a trip down to the Exumas. The coffee was very strong, just what he needed to clean out the cobwebs. He sat his coffee mug down, and dialed Belinda's number.

"Hello. You have reached…" Phil waited for the beep.

"Hey you. This is Phil. Again. We keep missing each other. I hope all is well with you. I'll leave my number again, here at my sister's, 305-796-7467. The place is pretty much like it was when you were here last Christmas. But now she's got a new sailing yacht that's absolutely beautiful. You should come down if you get the chance. Call me when you get back in. I miss you."

After he hung up, he thought, God. Why did I say that stuff? It's over between us. Maybe I should leave another message. No. I'll call Delia. Maybe she's seen her.

He dialed Delia's number. It rang four times before she answered. "Hello?"

"Dr. Bell, I presume?"

"Phil! I was hoping you would call. Where are you?"

It was nice to hear her voice, and Phil realized that he missed her too. "I'm at my sister's place in Fort Lauderdale."

"That's like the yacht capital of the world isn't it?"

"Yes. Have you seen Belinda yet?"

"No. Neither Madeline nor I have heard from her. Yesterday afternoon, Madeline filed a missing person's report with the Cambridge police."

"What? What the hell is going on Delia?"

"I don't know. I still have the keys to her place, and since . . . when did you and I last talk? Wednesday?"

"The night Eikelmann was sick…"

"You don't know about the murder then?"

"What murder?"

111

"Someone killed Laurence. I found him in his apartment. Don't they have newspapers in Fort Lauderdale?"

"Patty doesn't subscribe, and we haven't turned on the television since I got here, been too busy catching up with each other. What happened to Eikelmann?" He sat down, stunned.

"Phil. It was horrible." She started sobbing.

"Delia. Delia?" He spoke softly. "Calm down. You have to tell me what happened."

"Oh Phil. It was . . . It was . . . They almost cut his head off." Delia took a deep breath. "Just give me a minute Phil. Just a minute."

"Of course. I'm sorry if I pressed you. Just tell me whatever you want. However you want to do it, I can wait. God. I hope he didn't suffer."

Delia rushed through the story of Eikelmann's murder and finished with Prefontaine's speculation that Laurence experimented with peyote, when Phil interrupted.

"Hold on. Get a rope on it honey. Laurence Eikelmann on peyote?"

Delia smiled in spite of herself. "I know what you mean Phil, and to some extent I'm inclined to agree with you. Still, you know how reclusive he was. Who really knew him?"

"No one. Yeah. He did keep to himself a lot."

"Right. He just wouldn't be around for weeks at a time. Remember? When he finally did show up, and you would ask him where he'd been he'd say "oh just home working." He was very noncommittal."

"Even so, I have a hard time picturing Eikelmann as a drug-crazed hippie."

"Me too. Even if he had been experimenting with peyote, how would that figure in his murder?"

"Delia, it's not really apparent to me. But hell, I hardly knew him. There's probably not a lot of money in peyote buttons . . ."

"But what about Maya polychromes? We both know there's a lot of money in those."

"Yeah. So? What about them?" Phil felt like she was holding something back.

"Two exquisite polychrome bowls were found in his ceiling. They were from our Kichpanha collections and their accession numbers had been removed."

"That is unbelievable. They would be worth thousands…"

"That's not all that's unbelievable. Those bowls are checked out on your ID, Phil."

"What? That's impossible . . . When?"

"The day before you took your exams. By the way, have you seen your passport lately?"

"Oh hell. I went off and left that in the lab. You know I left in such a hurry…"

"Well, brace yourself Phil. The Somerville and Harvard police want to talk to you about those pots, and they have your passport."

"I have no problem with that. I didn't check them out. As for my passport, I have no travel plans in my immediate future. For one thing, I'm just about out of money."

"So did you loan your ID card to someone else?"

"Nope."

"Do you have it with you? Why don't you check?"

"Okay. Hold on for a minute. My wallets in the bedroom. You know something? I did look at those Kichpanha pots when I was working on the Montebello Project. One of them has Kin Balaam, the jaguar god in the center. The other is mostly geometric, with a bunch of vultures dancing around the rim. Underworld imagery. Am I right?"

"That's them."

He walked back to the bedroom, and pulled his jeans off the back of the door where he had hung them. He pulled out his wallet. "Okay. What have we got? Maxed out Visa card, Kentucky driver's license, graduate student I.D. Here it is."

"So Phil, how did those pots get checked out to you?"

"I have no idea." He sat on the edge of the bed. "Let's consider the possibilities. One. Someone took my card, without me knowing about it, and then replaced it, also without me knowing about it."

"Not very likely." Observed Delia.

"Nope, I would say damned near impossible. Okay. What else? Someone was able to duplicate my card, right down to the proper access code..."

"This also, could only be obtained by copying your card, which means someone would have had to borrow it. Have you loaned it to anyone, ever?"

"Never. Not even once. Goes against my military training."

"Then how else could someone have acquired your I.D. access code?"

"Only other place they record those that I can think of, other than our cards is the museum's main frame..."

"So if someone could hack their way into that system..."

"Only one guy I know who could possibly hack the Peabody's security system. Only one fellow smart enough to even attempt that."

"You mean Laurence."

"Exactly." Both of them paused and thought about it. Delia responded first.

"So what does it mean? That he was involved in the antiquities trade? Smuggling pots out of the museum? That he used your access code as a precaution in case he ever got caught?"

"Hell I don't know. I'm making this up as we go along, just like you. It could be he's been doing it for some time, with the backup plan of framing me in the event he ever got caught. I find it very hard to believe though. Tell the Harvard police to pull up everything ever charged out to me, and I'll compare that against what I know I checked out. That should clarify the situation somewhat."

"Well right now the Harvard police think you took those pots, and that ties you into the murder as far as they are concerned. The Somerville cops want to talk to you too."

"Yeah. That does present a problem. How do I prove to them that he may have compromised their security system? Damn. I'm going to have to think about this, give me a day or two will you?"

"Okay. But Phil. What would have been his motive? Why would Laurence do such a thing?"

"Hackers don't need a motive. They break into systems, write viruses, and mess with records, simply because they can. We are assuming a lot here though; we don't know that he did it. As far as selling stolen antiquities goes, the cops will check his personal finances. He would have left a money trail. You can be sure of that… except for the fact that he was rich, wasn't he?"

"Well he always gave that impression, but without flaunting it."

"Anyway, the police will soon know all about his financial situation. So we'll leave that to them."

115

"True. The other thing is what do we do about Belinda? What happened to her? I'm really worried."

"You know, I've been worried about her for several days." Phil hated to admit it.

"Why? I didn't tell you she was missing until a few minutes ago..."

"Yeah. Still, I knew something was wrong way before you told me. You're going to think I'm a little strange..."

"Phil. Everyone knows that."

Phil laughed; it felt good considering the current situation. "Okay. Look. I've been obsessing about her. I haven't been able to reach her at all. Gradually, I've become apprehensive about Belinda... see. I told you I was strange."

"It makes sense to me. My subconscious has been telling me for days that something's wrong with Belinda."

"What are the police doing about it?"

"Not much. Not nearly enough, with the exception of Lieutenant Martin, who is with the Somerville police. He told me late last night, that so far the Cambridge police have checked the airlines. No records. Her return ticket has not been used."

"But she checked her luggage? Picked it up at Logan?"

"Apparently so. I mean her bags were home Wednesday night. She'd been to Oxford Books."

"But did anyone ever see her?"

"No one's turned up yet. The police are talking to people in her building."

"Have you called Hector Obregon at the museum in Guatemala City? He might know something."

"I tried but he's out in the field for another week. I will try him again when he gets back."

"Delia, if you or Madeline have any pull with the police, have them find her, okay?"

"Okay. I'm sure it will all be cleared up soon. At least I hope so." Talking to Phil made her feel better. She was glad that he called and didn't want to hang up. "Well, you sound like you're doing all right Phil."

"Honey. I'm pretty damned far from all right. But I'm getting there. I've seen worse than this. Much worse. How are you doing? Do you need me to come back?"

"And do what? The department screwed you over. The police want to talk to you. They're under a lot of pressure. Do you want me to give them your number?"

Phil thought about it before he answered. "Only if they ask for it. Don't lie to them Delia. Not for me. Not for anybody. It's a bad idea. If it turns out that there's anything I can do to help, just call me." He paused before adding, "By the way, it wasn't the department that screwed me over, if I had been better prepared, I could have passed no matter what they threw at me. So, ultimately the responsibility is mine."

"Don't be so hard on yourself. And thanks for offering to come up anyway. Call me again tomorrow. Or I'll call you. Okay?"

"Okay. You take care of yourself, all right?"

"I will. Please keep in touch."

"Belinda. God, please let her be all right." Phil said and stared into the river without seeing it.

23 Tikal

On the same day that Kathryn Haden disappeared, Monday, August twenty third, Belinda Boothe left Guatemala City at dawn, to do research at Tikal. All day long she worried about the water pump on her rented Land Rover. She took the long, scenic route with the good roads, the Motagua Valley way.

By midmorning she reached Zacapa, and noticed the Rover was using a lot of water and coolant. At a small service station outside of town she bought extra jugs of water and antifreeze. She drove on to Lago Izabal, watching the temperature gauge creep slowly upward. The trip to Lago Izabal took more than four gallons of water. Belinda decided to stop and find someone to fix the water pump before she went any further.

That night she stayed at the Hotel Nuevo Mi Amor in Modesto Sanchez, where the road turned to gravel. The owner's son seemed to know his way around Land Rovers, and worked on the water pump that evening. Belinda sat out on the patio, enjoying the night breeze, and watched him take it apart, as the "working girls" in their bright cotton dresses promenaded for the truck drivers in front of the hotel, which also functioned as a bordello. They were still working when she went to bed, dreading the bone jarring part of the trip that was still ahead of her.

The next morning the Rover was fixed and she headed out on the road to Flores. She crossed the Sarstun River and could see Belize downstream. The road was appalling, and the scenery was worse. The ridges had been deforested of all trees, ceibas, mahoganies and zapotes, and scraped down to rock and clay.

Part of Guatemala's advance to prosperity, she thought.

Belinda left at eight, and by noon she had only made it as far as Machaquila, about 60 miles, when the rain started. A massive tropical storm was blowing itself out, and sheets of rain swept across the road for the next eighty miles. It washed out the gravel, and arroyos, and slowed her down. The road was a river of sloppy mud and rock. She could drive around the smaller puddles, but some of them she was forced to drive through slowly. Late that afternoon she reached Flores, where she had hoped to meet Hector Obregon at the Itza Cafe, but he failed to show. The rain was lifting, so she pushed on for Tikal on the good paved road, which was a relief after what she had been driving on all day.

Unfortunately, she drove the Rover too hard, and by the time she got to Tikal the water pump blew up, and she coasted into the gravel parking lot of the Jaguar Inn, with the engine smoking. The inn consisted of about fifteen thatched-roof bungalows, and a dining hall, with grounds landscaped in banana plants, purple bougainvillea, and coconut palms. It was one of Belinda's favorite places in all of Central America. She was glad she had made it at least this far.

She propped the hood up, checked out the damage, and decided it looked hopeless. While she stood there thinking about how long it would take the agency in Guatemala City to get a replacement Rover up to her, another Land Rover pulled up, the horn honked, and Laurence Eikelmann of all people, hopped out.

"What are you doing here?" Belinda was surprised but happy to see him.

"Alex and I have been doing some recon work for the institute." Laurence dusted himself off, and cleaned his glasses on his shirttail, while a short man came around from the other side and extended his hand; Belinda shook it, and introduced herself.

"Alejandro Sanchez. Mucho gusto" He reeked of strong body odor.

She turned to Laurence; "I didn't know you were coming down here this season."

"I didn't either, but an opportunity came up so here I am. I'm just down for a couple of weeks. I'm heading back in a few days. Having problems with your Rover?" Laurence asked.

It seemed to Belinda that he had lost a lot of weight. He had always been kind of skinny, but now he looked gaunt, as if he had been ill. Also, she thought, he needed to lose his scraggly beard.

"The water pump seems to be shot. It's been giving me trouble all day."

"Alex can fix it. He knows engines inside and out."

They unloaded their luggage, with Laurence taking special care with his ever-present laptop computer. Belinda was glad to see him, and couldn't wait to get caught up on what had been happening back in Cambridge. She wanted to tell him about the looting problem in the Peten, get his ideas on it, and she also wanted to give him some letters to take back to Cambridge. Trouble was she was going to have to write them first.

* * * * * * * *

After her shower, Belinda wrapped herself in a beach towel and sat down to write a letter to Phil, to put her feelings into words. After several failed attempts she started writing a letter to Delia instead. She was almost finished when there was a knock on the door and she heard Laurence asking. "Belinda are you decent?"

"Just a minute." She put on an embroidered blue Maya cotton dress, and let him into the room. He was carrying a bottle of rum in one hand and a bag of ice and limes in the other.

"Buy you a drink?" He had showered and shaved, and put on a clean pair of khakis and a white knit shirt. Even though he was clean, he still looked sickly.

"Sure. I can even contribute some orange juice; let me get it out of my bags. By the way Laurence, you look like you've lost a lot of weight. Too much weight even."

"I guess I have. I picked up some kind of bug when I was in Mexico. It tore me up for a few days." He put the limes on the bamboo desk, and started slicing them up.

"Where were you in Mexico?" Belinda asked and handed him a can of orange juice.

"Oh I went by Vallejo's project at Palenque. Made the rounds, the usual stuff you know." He shrugged. "He's field testing my precinct model. As if it needed testing."

"Well, I thought it was still theoretical Laurence. I can see why Vallejo would be interested though. He's always been such a tomb-hunter."

"That's where the funding has always been, my dear, nothing is more important. Tombs. Loot. Jade. Gold. The National Geographic Society." His sarcastic wit bordered on cynicism, it seemed to Belinda. "The Mystique of the Maya," he added and tipped back his drink. Something in his attitude made her feel a little uneasy, but Laurence had always been a bit high strung.

"You seem unusually cynical tonight Laurence."

"Do I? Oh sorry then, I've been among the proletariat for too long I guess. I had better get that out of my system before I go back to El Norte. Don't want to cause a stir in polite society. Particularly not at fair Harvard."

"What do you mean Laurence? You are not exactly my idea of a working-class hero."

"Hardly." He took another drink, put on his glasses, pulled a dog-eared, muddy pamphlet out of his back pocket, and opened it. "You know Belinda you're right about me, but let me read you a poem by Luis Munoz Marin, it really makes you think, and oddly enough, it's called *Proletarios*:

A donkey ascending a mountain, slowly, vibrating under the weight of the saddlebags (His optimist ears slant toward the summit.).
A bricklayer setting brick upon brick, (His humming is monotonous, interminable.)
God, hard at work with the stars. (His silence is profound.)"

He took another large drink and looked at her through the bottom of his glass. "So what do you think of that?"

"I like it, but I see several different meanings..." He cut her off.

121

"I only get one meaning. Hope is absurd at any time and any place. Just baseless self-delusion." He took another large drink, smacked his lips, and thumbed through the little book. "Well how about this one? It's very straightforward, it's called *Panfleto*:"

"I have drowned my dreams in order to glut the dreams that sleep for me in the veins of men who sweated and wept and raged to season my coffee...The dream that sleeps in breasts stifled by tuberculosis (A little air, a little sunshine!)..."

His voice cracked and his eyes teared. He took another drink and wiped his eyes before finishing.

"I am the pamphleteer of God, God's agitator, and I go with the mob of stars and hungry men toward the great dawn..."

Neither of them said anything, for a moment they just sat there and listened to the evening sounds of Tikal, a howler monkey, birds fluttering in the thatched roof, raindrops dripping on tile, a distant radio playing a Spanish love ballad. In the background was the constant buzz of a trillion insects.

Laurence finished his drink and stood up. "Sorry about getting emotional on you Belinda. Here you can have this one." He placed the pamphlet on the table. "I have another one." He stretched his arms, and yawned. "I'm going to take a little nap. Want to have dinner with me and Alex at about eight?"

"Sure. You okay Laurence?"

"Yeah. I'm fine. Just a little strung out from all the driving we've been doing. See you in a bit then. I'm really glad I ran into you Belinda. What a coincidence, huh?" He opened the door to leave.

"Down here Laurence it really is a small world. It's good to see you too." As he walked away, she looked at the pamphlet title, *Poemas para El EZLN*. Now where did he find this? She wondered.

24 A Glock, Nine Millimeter

Delia caught up with Madeline as she was leaving her classroom. They had an appointment to meet Lieutenant Martin at his office in Somerville after stopping for a drink on the way.

Delia climbed into Madeline's Pathfinder and they pulled out of the faculty parking lot next to the Law School, and right onto Massachusetts Avenue just as the rush hour began. In her rear view mirror Madeline noticed a white Toyota Camry pull out two spaces behind her.

"That's funny." She said.

"What's that?" Asked Delia.

"Look in your mirror. You see that white Camry back there?"

"Yeah."

"Now I'm not sure, but when we left the eulogy yesterday in Martin's car, I thought I saw a Camry like that stay behind us until we got over to your car. Then when we jumped out and went the opposite direction, we lost it. I thought he was probably a reporter."

"Madeline, maybe he is. Or maybe it's a different Camry."

"Maybe. But let's just see if he really wants to try to keep up with me. Tighten your seatbelt dear."

Delia did as she told her. Madeline punched the accelerator to the floor and the Pathfinder took off, with Madeline weaving between cars, and scaring the hell out of Delia.

"Jesus Christ Madeline!"

"Hang on!"

Madeline took a sharp right on Roseland Street and headed toward Porter Square. The Camry turned right behind them.

"It would appear Delia that he is following us." Madeline said through clenched teeth.

"Why?" Delia looked back to see the Camry closing on them. Fast.

"He's not very discrete either."

They hit Porter Square, and the rear end of the Pathfinder fishtailed, as they skidded sideways narrowly missing a garbage truck. Delia closed her eyes.

"Get his license number?"

"There's no front plate."

Madeline straightened it out and weaved right, then left, and headed straight to Mossland Street. Then she made a hard left on Holland. The Camry stayed right with her.

"Hell. He must have a six cylinder in that thing. Let's see if he can keep up with this."

She took a sharp left, with the tires squealing, in front of oncoming traffic that narrowly missed them. They were on College Street, heading back toward Mass Ave. The Camry was falling back a bit. Madeline whipped it left again on Mass Ave. and floored it. Delia looked at the speedometer. They were going seventy-five miles an hour.

"Professor Scott I think we're a bit in excess of the speed limit."

Madeline never took her eyes off the traffic as she said, "You think?" And kept the accelerator floored.

Delia looked in the rear view mirror and saw the Camry about a block back. "Punch it Madeline, I think we can lose him."

The engine revved higher. She looked over and could see that Madeline was smiling. Miraculously, there were no cars in front of them on the tree-lined avenue. They were approaching Harvard Square at eighty miles an hour when they flashed past Lesley College.

Madeline downshifted, grinding gears, and turned in front of oncoming traffic again. She left skid marks across Mass Ave. They jumped the curb between Jarvis Street and the Law School. Delia bumped her head on the roof when they bounced over the curb, and squeezed though a narrow gap between two fences. The Pathfinder was slithering on the lawn, going about fifty miles an hour. Clouds of leaves and dust blew up behind them. A flock of pigeons took off, and law students jumped and scurried out of the way.

"Hey Delia," Madeline was laughing. "How many points do I get for law students?"

Delia did not reply and closed her eyes as they weaved in and out through the elm trees. They went past the graduate school apartments, crossed Oxford Street, and pulled up in front of the Peabody Museum where Madeline decided to stop.

"I'll bet that did it. It finally came to me that I should use the Pathfinder's advantage, and go off the road." Madeline was laughing and looked over at Delia. "You okay?"

"Professor Scott I think you enjoyed that. You're a frustrated stunt driver. You think you know somebody…" She shook her head, and in spite of herself, Delia laughed.

"Maybe I am. Do you see the Camry anywhere?"

Delia looked at the leaves and dust settling between the elms and all the people staring at them, and laughed again. "No, it looks like you lost him."

"Good. That was my intention. Now let's go have that drink at a more dignified rate of speed."

* * * * * * * * * *

O'Brien's was off Porter Square in Somerville. It was a rather typical Irish pub, Delia thought; probably a thousand like it in the Boston metropolitan area. As they entered, Delia saw that it was very dark, with a massive oak

125

bar dominating a long narrow room. Some regulars were playing darts in the back. Madeline selected a booth near the door.

"Madeline. I know you like to come here, but what's the attraction?"

"Oh that's right. You've never been here before. Well two reasons. One, I never see anyone from Harvard, and two; they have Pilsner Urquell on tap. It's sublime."

"Okay. I'll try it. Your stunt driving left me in need of sedation. Do you think we have time for a small pitcher?"

"I think so. We have an appointment but he'll probably be busy. Besides if we're a little late, what's he going to do? Arrest us?"

"So who was following us Madeline?"

"I have no idea. A reporter? I wish it was, instead of the more sinister alternative, but I kind of doubt it."

"Laurence's killer?"

"Or someone involved in whatever is going on?"

"That of course seems likely, but why follow us? What does he think we know? I mean we're virtually clueless. At least I am." Delia reached for a glass as the pitcher arrived.

"Maybe he thinks we know more than we do… or maybe?"

"What?"

"Maybe we haven't discovered what it is he thinks we know? Maybe he doesn't know that we don't know, what he thinks we know?" Madeline laughed. "Delia, did you follow that string of logic? I think I'd better have a drink." Madeline stared into her beer. "Seriously though, maybe we haven't put it together yet, and he thinks we have. That would mean that whatever is going on is understandable. Perhaps we should try harder to figure this all out. If so, we better do it quickly." Madeline frowned into her beer glass and took a large drink.

126

"You flushed him out rather easily. It's like he really didn't care that we knew he was following us. Which means... what?"

"He's trying to scare us?"

"Or worse?" Delia sipped her beer. "I think it's safe to say he's trying to send some kind of message, that's for sure."

"Maybe you should stay with me and Ziggy for a while. Starting tonight. That way we can watch each other's back. If he gets too close, I always have this." She opened her purse under the table so Delia could see the butt of a pistol, in the inside pocket. Delia's eyebrows went up.

"What kind of gun is that?" Madeline was full of surprises it seemed.

"A Glock, nine millimeter. Don't leave home without it." Madeline smiled grimly.

"How long have you had it?"

"It belonged to Mark, spouse number two. I started carrying it again last January, when there were all those rapes in Beacon Hill."

"Have you ever fired it?"

"Mmmm. Hmmm."

"Are you any good?"

"Not bad. But then, it's an automatic. I don't have to be that good. I just have to be within fifty feet, and a rapist would look like Swiss cheese."

"Isn't it illegal to carry it that way?"

"Yes. But it just gives me peace of mind in this turbulent world of ours."

"Do you think you could actually use it on someone?"

"Don't know for sure. Hope I never have to find out."

* * * * * * * *

They arrived at Martin's office five minutes late. He had them come right in. "Sit down ladies, please." He pulled up a chair for Madeline. "We have a lot to go over."

"There's been a development for us Lieutenant. Someone tried to follow us about an hour ago, and he was not very subtle."

Martin sat and said, "Did you get his license number? Come on talk to me."

"He had no front plate." Madeline recounted the incident.

"You drove like that through Somerville and Cambridge, at rush hour without getting a ticket? That's amazing. I wonder where our traffic cops were." Martin laughed. "You're quite a woman Dr. Scott."

"We're just lucky I guess." Madeline shrugged.

Martin was busy taking notes. "It sounds like a rental car. What did the driver look like?"

"A male, maybe Hispanic, dark hair, bulky, not very tall. Maybe a thin mustache? That's about all I could see of him unfortunately." Said Delia.

Martin frowned. "Well that's something at least. I'll have someone check it out. I agree with you Dr. Scott, I doubt it was a reporter. Speaking of reporters, did you see this afternoon's *Boston Herald*?" He handed the paper to Madeline.

The headline read "Curse of the Mayan Archaeologists?" Half-page pictures of Kathryn Haden, Laurence Eikelmann, and Belinda Boothe, were underneath it. Under that the caption was, "Two Are Missing: One was sacrificed." Madeline looked at Martin and Delia, and said, "That's the picture I gave the Cambridge police yesterday. How did it get in the Herald so quickly?"

"Cambridge cops love to play to the papers, Dr. Scott, I should have warned you. I'm now coordinating the investigation with the Harvard and

128

Cambridge police, because the activities of Mr. Eikelmann and whoever killed him happened in three jurisdictions. Before it's all over, we'll probably have the Boston police in it too."

"Do you think my niece's disappearance is somehow connected to Eikelmann's murder?" Madeline pointed at the newspaper.

"It's too early to tell. Possibly Belinda will turn up today. She might be in hiding, protecting herself, or…" Martin's voice trailed off.

"Well I think something has happened to her. She's been in town a week and hasn't called me. The fact that it happened the same week that Laurence was killed strikes me as more than coincidental." Madeline paused and looked over at Delia. "It's all a bit scary isn't it?"

Delia nodded. "I just wish I knew what was going on. Is it really possible that all of this is connected?" she asked, as she picked up the newspaper.

Martin loosened his tie and said, "Let me review it with the understanding that you will tell no one, that it goes no further than this room."

Delia and Madeline nodded their assent.

"The Cambridge Police haven't found anyone who remembers seeing Belinda Boothe, in and around her apartment building. They've interviewed about eight people so far." He paused, and read from another legal pad.

"Next, Eikelmann's laptop computer is still unaccounted for. In his trash, we found marijuana seeds and stems. The M. E. verifies the marijuana use, traces of THC were found in his system, enough to suggest casual usage. No conclusive traces of peyote. I don't know how relevant or irrelevant any of that is. Marijuana use is common among college students these days. I'm more interested in the laptop. Delia, can you think of where we might look for it?"

"Not right off. But I'll think about it."

"Neither do I. Maybe you can turn something up online? Nobody in my department surfs the Net, so we're farming this out to the computer fraud section. We appreciate your ideas too." Martin shrugged, and continued. "Now, according to the Harvard police, the pots found in Eikelmann's ceiling were originally checked out to Philip C. Ward. The Peabody Museum computer records bear this out. Someone has removed the accession numbers but traces are still microscopically detectable. His fingerprints are all over the pots. Confirmed by the Department of Defense, U.S. Marine Corps records. Miss Bell you didn't tell me he was a Marine."

"Yes, he's an ex-Marine. Viet Nam veteran too."

"Once a Marine always a Marine. There are no "ex-Marines" only older and younger ones. I was over there too. We were both in the Third Division, and according to his service record, we were over there at the same time in 69 and 70." Martin looked down at the file. "Ward picked up a few more decorations than I did; Navy Cross with oak leaf cluster, Silver Star, two Purple Hearts, various citations for valor, distinguished service, volunteered for S.O.G. or Special Operations Group, and that part of his record is still classified by the way. After Nam he was an embassy guard, in Guatemala City. Only the cream of the crop gets to be embassy guards, honorable men with squeaky-clean service records. Did you know all of this?"

"I didn't know about the decorations or the special operations."

"Winning the Navy Cross once, much less twice… well it's tough. Reading these reports opened up some old memories. I think I remember hearing about this guy. The action he saw in Quang Tri Province… He probably should have got the Congressional Medal of Honor. Let me read you one of his Navy Cross citations:

'In connection with combat operations against an armed enemy in the Republic of Viet Nam, on 4 March 1969, Company C, Second Battalion, Ninth Marines, Third Marine Division was dispatched to the area of Vandegrift Combat Base in Quang Tri Province to assist another company which had become heavily engaged with a well-entrenched enemy battalion. While moving through dense jungle undergrowth, Corporal Ward's squad was brought under extremely intense small arms and automatic weapons fire. The platoon reacted swiftly, getting on line as best they could in the thick terrain. Advancing through heavy enemy fire,

Corporal Ward personally neutralized one enemy position, and though wounded, he calmly led an assault against the main point of the hostile emplacements. Upon encountering a North Vietnamese Army officer, he overwhelmed him in fierce hand-to-hand combat. Observing three other soldiers firing on his comrades from behind a bunker, Corporal Ward ignored the enemy fire, and racing across the hazardous area dived into their position, where he neutralized them. His bold initiative, intrepid fighting spirit, and unwavering devotion to duty in the face of almost certain death undoubtedly saved his comrades from further injury or possible death, and reflected great credit upon himself, the Marine Corps, and the United States Naval Service. Signed Richard M. Nixon.'"

"Neutralized them?" Delia asked.

"It means what you think it means." Martin paused and stared at the citations. His mind was miles and years away, in Quang Tri Province, 1969. Then he broke his reverie. "This Philip C. Ward is one tough S.O.B. I admire and respect what he did over there. He's the kind of Marine…" He paused, walked to the window, and looked out at the sun setting, without seeing it. "The rest of his Viet Nam file is classified. He joined the Special Operations Group, and conducted several covert missions. All classified. My corps experience tells me he can't be Eikelmann's killer." Martin leaned on the windowsill, and massaged his forehead before resuming. "Still, the evidence, such as it is, is accumulating around him. Hell. He's almost the only suspect we have right now." Martin paused and thought about his only other suspect, Samuel Thomas, and the fact that the bartender at the Living Room Club had identified him with Laurence on the evening of the murder. He would be talking to Professor Thomas tomorrow. That should be interesting, Martin thought. "Have you spoken to Ward lately?"

"He called me the other night." Delia whispered.

Martin smiled at Delia. "I know you don't believe he's mixed up in any of this, but do you happen to know where he called from, or where he was going?"

"He was on his way to Kentucky. I don't remember if he said exactly where he was, but he was trying to reach Belinda."

"Why?"

"They had terminated him the day before, and I guess he just wanted to talk to her. They had been very close at one time."

"How close?"

"Lovers." Delia blushed. Madeline squeezed her hand.

"You haven't heard from him since then?" Martin looked up from his legal pad. He saw that Delia was fidgeting, swinging her foot nervously, and looking very ill at ease. She didn't respond right away, so he asked her, "Hey. You feel okay?"

"I'm fine. No, I haven't heard from him since that night."

"You're doing it again. You're holding something back. I thought we had an understanding?"

"We do. It's just that I think you're on the wrong track. Phil has nothing to do with any of this." Delia said firmly.

"Well... I'm willing to consider that possibility. His service record describes a man of honor and integrity. The kind of man I know well. There aren't that many left." Martin paused and thought, also a man who did his share of killing in combat, special ops guys killed quietly and with knives, garrotes, whatever was handy... He looked up from the file and continued. "Still, we have to take these issues one at a time, and deal with them. For example, we have evidence that Ward went to Mexico recently. Do you know what he was doing down there?"

Delia shook her head. She was too surprised to speak.

Martin opened his drawer, and placed another manila file folder on the desk. As he opened it he said, "Here are some receipts. He stayed three days at the Fiesta Americana in Merida, and a week at the Krystal Hotel in Cancun. Did anyone know that he was down there? Did anyone go with him?" Martin leaned back in his chair and clasped his hands behind his neck. "Now the problem this raises is that he was in Mexico when Haden disappeared, he was in Cambridge very close to the time that Eikelmann was killed, and now his ex-girlfriend is missing."

Delia was busy writing it all down in her notepad, and took a deep breath before she said; "I didn't see anyone in July because I was home in Ohio visiting my folks. Still, I never heard that Phil had gone to Mexico. I was under the impression he spent the whole summer in Cambridge, studying for his orals."

"No. He spent a month down there in Mexico but we don't know what he was doing. I would like to talk to him. Clear up any misconceptions that we could form."

"Such as?" Asked Delia.

"Such as how come he keeps popping up in all the wrong places? We have an awful lot of coincidences swarming around Mr. Ward. Like Dr. Scott, I don't believe in coincidences. Ward is someone I really need to talk to." He put his hands down on the desk top. "By the way, do either of you carry any…protection? For self defense?"

"I have something." Madeline shrugged.

"What is it?" Martin asked.

"A Glock, nine millimeter."

"Can you hit anything with it?"

"I haven't practiced in awhile." Martin noticed she looked embarrassed.

"You might want to practice a little. Just in case."

25 The Savior's Field Manual

Jesse had been traveling with Garcia and the EZLN for six days. He was not being held against his will, and he was free to leave at any time. Being with them offered him an opportunity to get under the surface of what was going on in Chiapas, and maybe find out what had happened to Kathryn. He was the only one who was unarmed, and although they treated him well enough, they also kept their distance. There was no question they considered him an outsider, and probably some of them questioned the Professor's decision to allow him to travel with them, but no one voiced their opposition. They had stopped wearing their masks, as they became more accustomed to Jesse. But by traveling with them, the Professor made it clear that Jesse was taking some dangerous risks. The right-wing paramilitaries they had run out of Raxabe could return at any time. Garcia's EZLN groups were all Tzeltales, Maya Indians native to the region. They were committed to ending discrimination against all Indians, and political land reform. Garcia recognized that this was an impossible task, but he was fond of quoting Cervantes.

None of them knew anything about the missing altar, or Kathryn Haden, but Garcia indicated he had ways of finding things out. When he spoke to the Maya, he spoke Maya, when he spoke to Jesse he spoke English. It seemed he liked things compartmentalized; he rarely used Spanish, because he said everyone understood it. "You see I have other channels of knowledge besides the obvious ones, Jesse." He said, while they were hiking over a ridge and into a deeply forested valley.

"Such as?"

"Other ones. Let's leave it like that for now, and appreciate the view. Look at this valley, it has never been logged; virgin rain forest. Not very much of it left."

"What can you tell me about Chanul Tzuk then?"

"Leave it alone. We've already been over that. I will tell you this for now, some dark forces have been at work there, and they are not done yet."

"Professor. Could you possibly try being less circumspect? This is very important to me."

"As Cervantes said in Don Quixote: 'To withdraw is not to run away and to stay is no wise action, when there's more reason to fear than to hope.'"

Jesse countered with one of his favorite quotes. "Montaigne would reply: "Let us not be ashamed to speak what we shame not to think.""

"Touché. Bravo. I like having another scholar around, I must admit."

"Please understand that this is all very important to me."

"I understand that, but you need to understand my priorities. Democracy. Human rights you know Jesse; you might consider the fact that you are the only anthropologist to witness the first post-communist, post-modern, revolution in Latin America. Why not make the most of it?"

"This is a revolution? It looks more like we're just a bunch of guys wandering around in the wilderness."

"Don't all saviors have to spend some time wandering in the wilderness? Haven't you read the savior's field manual?" The Professor laughed, much amused by his own joke.

26 Cowboys of Anthropology

Martin walked in toward the end of Mamett's lecture, and unable to find Delia, took a seat in the back row. Holmes Hall was dark. Slides continuously flashed on the screen next to the podium.

"This is the lower Usumacinta drainage. This river system divides the Peten region of Guatemala, and Chiapas in Mexico, but in ancient times it unified the Maya highlands and lowlands. The drainage includes the Pasion, Lacantum and Salinas rivers. This river system links Altar de Sacrificios, Yaxchilan, Piedras Negras, Bonampak, and Chanul Tzuk to name only a few ancient Maya capitals. The geological base is a limestone plateau that rivers and rain have channeled into classic karst topography. Underground drainages, rivers, and lakes occur throughout the region. Deeply hidden caverns and tunnels are abundant. There are sinkholes, called "cenotes" by the Maya, and deep gullies, all of which are associated with the dissolution and collapse of the carbonate limestone. In essence, water has been hollowing out and dissolving the limestone for millennia."

"Even in the worst droughts these underground water sources were available to the Maya, which probably has something to do with the sacred symbolism that became associated with them. The caves and cenotes are some of the most sacred spots in all of Maya religion and ideology. They saw these underground chambers as the actual passages between the world of humans, and the gods and spirits that dwelled in the underworld. Other gods and spirits lived in the sky, but the underworld was central in Maya ideology. They were obsessed with it."

"The underworld was called Xibalba, and the Nine Lords of the Night inhabited it. Each lord ruled a particular day in the 9-day Maya weekly calendar. Quiche and Lacandon Maya entities like Lord Kisin, Skull Scepter, Sukunkyum, Blood Gatherer, Blood Woman, Hachakyum and Crunching Jaguar. Like all the Maya gods they had multiple manifestations, facets and forms. These gods and spirits of Xibalba were very real to the Maya. They believed one could actually encounter these lords and their ch'ulel energy in trance states, and in caves and cenotes. These places were not accessible to commoners, only to priests and nobility, and only after they conducted the proper sacred rituals. Down in these holy underworld sites the earliest mystical experiences occurred, and Maya religion was born. The entrances to the underworld were sacred. Feared. Respected."

The ten o'clock bells rang and Delia turned the lights back up. "I seem to have overrun my time. Sorry about that. Remember, you will discuss chapter three of Tambiah in teaching section this week." Mamett started gathering his lecture notes, and Martin saw Delia down near the podium, passing out papers with another female graduate student. He walked down to see her. A tall Hispanic man, in an elegant suit approached Mamett, and began talking to him in Spanish. Martin remembered seeing him briefly at the eulogy. Delia saw Martin, and smiled.

"Good morning. Lieutenant, this is Janice Helms; she's the new Teaching Fellow."

"Pleased to meet you. Excuse me. Miss Bell could I talk to you for a minute? We tried to reach you at your apartment last night. Have you moved?"

"I'm staying at Madeline's place in Beacon Hill for now."

"That's probably a good idea. I'll have the Boston Police look after you. What's the address there?"

"1105 Charles Street. Nice, a really charming place. A two-story townhouse, red brick, lots of ivy."

"Right in the heart of Beacon Hill. What about security?"

"Well, it has a wrought iron spiked fence and locked gate in the front and back."

"Nineteenth century security."

"Floodlights outside. It's got a Brinks alarm system, and motion detectors."

"Good. That's better." He put his notepad in his back pocket.

Mamett and his colleague joined them.

"Lieutenant Martin. Good morning. Allow me to introduce my friend Sergio Avendano, of the Instituto Nacional de Antropologia y Historia, in San Javier. He's officially responsible for our research area. Sergio, this is Lieutenant Martin of the Somerville Police Department. He's working on Eikelmann's murder."

They shook hands. Martin noticed that Avendano's grip was firm and dry, like leather. Works with his hands, Martin thought.

"A terrible thing. I knew him well. He worked with me a year ago at Ubala."

"Now where is that?"

Mamett interjected, "In the region I was just lecturing about. The Rio Usumacinta, between Guatemala and Chiapas."

"It looked beautiful in your slides. Pretty wild too. Many people live in the jungle?"

"Just the Maya and the archaeologists." said Mamett.

"Hard to get to?"

"Very." Added Avendano. "Particularly Yaxchilan. On one side is the river, which is very fast there, a lot of white water. A six hundred-foot moat encircles the rest of it. The best way to come is by boat, downstream from Frontera Corozal."

"Sounds pretty exotic. Have you been down there Delia?"

"No I've never been any closer than Palenque, which is about a day overland from Yaxchilan."

"Well that's all about to change Delia." Mamett said and gathered his slides and briefcase. "You are going to be my Assistant Director at Chanul Tzuk. That is if you accept it. Sergio is going to run Ubala without me, but we'll all be going back and forth a lot."

"Congratulations." Janice patted her on the back.

Delia was surprised and excited. "That's wonderful! When do I leave? Can I go tomorrow?"

Everyone laughed. "It would be good to get away from here wouldn't it?" Mamett said. "You'll be going soon. Sometime in December, you and Sergio and some people from Oregon will form the advance party to set things up, oh, and Boothe too, as soon as she turns up."

Martin turned to Mamett. "So you think she's all right?"

"Well she did this same scenario last Christmas break." Mamett sighed. "She and her boyfriend went to the Bahamas, and didn't tell anyone. She called me from down there and told me she would be a little late getting back to grade papers."

"Who was the boyfriend?"

"Phil Ward."

"Has anyone called him to see if she's with him?"

"I don't know."

Delia changed the subject. "Is Professor Bennett going to be at Chanul Tzuk?"

"Probably not Delia. He's retiring, and has turned Chanul Tzuk over to me. I'm still a bit shocked by it all." Mamett held the door open for everyone.

"So who will be coming down from Oregon?"

"We're still working that out. Probably Salazar, if he ever checks his mail, and a couple of others."

"I know Jesse. He's a good guy."

"He's been down in Mexico this semester. Apparently he was deeply affected by the disappearance of Kathryn Haden. Sergio says he's still looking for her."

Avendano nodded. "Yes. I saw him just last week. We had a rather intense experience with some looters."

Martin stopped, and everyone paused with him. "That's right this is the same place. Aren't all of you worried about security down there, in light of what happened?"

Avendano placed his arm around Delia. "We're making plans to insure everyone's safety and security. I can assure you that nothing like that will ever happen again. If I have to get the army to protect us. Whatever it takes."

"Anyone know where I might find Eikelmann's computer?" Martin asked.

"You checked his cabinet in the Maler lab, and his study drawer in the Tozzer Library, I assume?" Mamett responded.

"Yes, thoroughly catalogued, and inventoried. The only computer related materials were some blank disks in the library drawer and some printed sheets with Internet addresses on them that we found in the trash behind his house. I gave copies of the Internet stuff to Delia to find out whatever she could. That's it so far."

"I think he had a locker in the alumni gym. He swam there a lot. Also, he might have one at the Harvard Club downtown." Mamett suggested. "I can't think of anywhere else he might keep things that you haven't already checked out."

"Well these are places we haven't looked yet. So I appreciate you thinking of them professor."

Mamett shrugged. "Hopefully it will turn up. Would any of you like to join Sergio and me for coffee in my office?"

"I'm going to meet Madeline." Said Delia. "We're going to get a few more things from my apartment, and then we're going over to her place. I'll use her computer to check out those sites Lieutenant. See you all later."

"I've got to take off too." Said Janice. "Remember to call me later Delia."

As they walked away, Mamett turned to Martin. "Well Lieutenant, would you like to join us?"

"Don't mind if I do. I could use a cup of coffee."

* * * * * * * *

Martin liked Mamett's office; it looked like it belonged to a Harvard professor. The dark mahogany wall panels were nearly covered with citations, diplomas, awards and photographs. Martin particularly liked a watercolor of a jaguar on a jungle trail, centered on the wall behind the desk. The massive mahogany desk repeated the panel pattern. The brass banker's lamp with the green glass shade added a good scholarly touch.

Mamett was busy preparing the coffee that Avendano had brought him from the highlands of Chiapas. Avendano was laying out maps and papers on a long table by the window. Martin decided to get things rolling; he had a lot of people to talk to today.

"So Professor Mamett, according to the statement you gave us two days ago, you had not seen Eikelmann for several days, not since your Monday morning class. That was the last time you saw or heard from him?"

"Yes. However, it wasn't that unusual. He didn't show up Wednesday for class, so I assumed he was sick."

"Right. He was killed early Friday morning. Had anyone talked to him during this time? Anyone say anything to you?"

"Only Delia as far as I know." Mamett passed the coffee out to Martin and Avendano. "Can either of you think of who would want to kill Eikelmann?" Martin asked.

Mamett answered first. "I've thought about it extensively, and I can't think of anyone."

Avendano added. "He did not strike me as the kind of fellow who attracts much attention. To kill him the way they killed him, someone must have hated him. Still, I cannot think of who that could be."

"How about romantic relationships? Involvements?"

"He was very self-contained in the field, a bit introverted. I remember he got along well with the Tzeltales, and our other Maya laborers. He spoke their language better than I do. I liked him very much. He was very hardworking but not very healthy, so the labor took a lot out of him. Other than that?" Avendano shrugged.

Martin made notes, looked up and asked, "Ever hear any rumors?"

"Are you referring to the rumor floating around that he was gay?" Mamett asked, surprising Martin with his candor.

"It falls under that category." Martin nodded.

141

"He could have been for all I know. So what?" Mamett shrugged. "If so... he wasn't obvious about it. I don't really know, nor do I particularly care, if he was or if he or wasn't. But if he was, he kept it to himself. He kept a lot to himself apparently."

"Of course that is understandable given the nature of our profession Lieutenant." Avendano pointed out.

"What do you mean by that?" Martin sipped the excellent coffee.

"Well think about it. They often call us archaeologists the "cowboys of anthropology, and it is not exactly a compliment." Avendano smiled. "In Mexico particularly it is kind of macho, much more so than it is up here. Down there, most field projects have very few women, or none at all involved. Many of us in my generation still do not think that women should be allowed to do fieldwork...although we must keep that opinion to ourselves." He laughed. "So it is primarily men who are cooped up together for weeks or months at a time, in often very remote areas. Such tendencies, if one has them, well I think they need to be repressed. Suffice it to say, that in Mexico if word got out that one was gay, well..." He shrugged.

"Would he be an outcast?" Martin asked, drawing from his own military experience, he could tell that Avendano was being straightforward.

"Regrettably, he would perhaps... not be invited back. It just depends on the crew and the circumstances. Now if it was a British project, it would not matter at all. They are a bit more enlightened than we are in Mexico." Avendano chuckled.

Mamett interjected. "Now Sergio, don't get started. Lieutenant Martin, my colleague has a thing about the British. But as anthropologists, we are all of course very well-versed in cultural relativism. Let's face it, American Anthropology invented it, going back to the days of Franz Boas, the idea that no culture is better than another, and that our own cultural beliefs and prejudices cannot be used to judge different cultures; instead we should study them from within their own cultural context and perspective. So homosexuality *per se*, is not even remotely an issue, from an anthropological standpoint. A rich and extensive gay culture is out there, and obviously it has every right to exist on its own terms. The days of persecution should have long passed, and I in fact, believe those days are over, and thank God, even among "the cowboys of archaeology" in Mexico. However, like Sergio says, it could potentially be a problem on some random archaeological field projects, but it wouldn't necessarily have to be. Still, if in fact Laurence was dealing with such issues by himself, my heart goes out to him…the conflicted feelings he might have faced, and well I just wish I could have helped him somehow." Mamett sipped his coffee. "And perhaps that is why he was so introverted? God. Excuse me. I'm still in my lecture mode Sometimes it's hard to switch it off." Mamett shrugged.

"I understand. What if word got out that say, a professor, or a director was gay?" There was a pause, and looks were exchanged Martin noticed, before Avendano responded.

"Well, I do not know. I mean in Mexico, if he were a field archaeologist, some people would possibly not work with him, or they might think that people might draw the wrong conclusion about one's own sexuality, if one did. Although, I think that this attitude is starting to change frankly. Speaking just for myself, I do not care. My one rule is if you can contribute to the project, I do not care what you do on your own time…" Avendano sipped his coffee and continued. "Some of our best theoreticians on the other hand are openly gay. But they avoid fieldwork. In some circles, it kind of enhances their carefully cultivated "avant garde" image, if you know what I mean." Avendano smiled. "And many theoreticians regardless of their sexual orientation look down on field archaeologists."

"Are you speaking of someone local? Someone in the area?" Martin asked.

"No. I was thinking of Miguel Lobo at the University of Texas, in Austin." Avendano responded.

"Well are there any openly gay archaeologists on any departments, in the Boston area?" Martin asked.

"Not that I know of. Not openly gay. What does that even have to do with Laurence? Is this an investigation or an obsession with you? I mean, I know you are just doing your job, but I tire of this topic Lieutenant." Mamett frowned and looked bored.

"How about in the closet?" Martin asked and immediately regretted it.

Mamett smiled and said, "If they are still in the closet, how would anyone know?"

27 A Renegade Archaeologist

Dinner was strained. Laurence spoke very little, and his friend Alex hardly at all. Alex was totally focused on eating and drinking. Especially the latter. He drank methodically, like a machine. His English was minimal, and although Belinda was fluent in Spanish, he only responded in monosyllables to her attempts at conversation. As they continued to drink like their lives depended on it she became concerned, and asked Laurence to slow down.

"Laurence, do you think it's a good idea to drink so much, so soon after being sick?" His eyelids were puffy, and his skin was splotchy. There was a faint red rash around his eyes, and he looked at her, holding his chin in his hands, elbows resting on the tabletop, clearly in his cups.

"Hmm? Oh yes. You're probably right. It has become a habit for us. You see Alex and I are thoroughly infested with beef worms. Getting really drunk is the only way we can get to sleep. The larvae have matured to the point where they are starting to move around in our skin. Hurts like hell, unless you get them drunk and they pass out. Then they stop moving you see." He laughed, and coughed.

"Where did you run into bott flies and beef worms? And how long ago did they lay their larvae in you? They're not around Palenque, the altitude is too high."

"Oh, when we were over near the Usumacinta last week, that's where they ate us alive. Clouds of them. Never saw so many in my life. I hope this last storm cleared them out." He took another drink of rum.

"So you went to Chanul Tzuk?" Belinda assumed he had dropped in on Bennett's project, the site was known for its insect problem, particularly at this time of year during the rainy season. She noticed that Alex looked up sharply at Laurence.

"Nope. Got near it though. Night before last we were at Bonampak. We were there for a week that's where the flies got us."

"I never heard of them being a problem at Bonampak."

"Me either. Someone forgot to tell the flies though." Laurence shook his head.

"Must have been unusually wet this summer, with all of the tropical storms, I guess." She folded her napkin, and put it by her plate. "So if you got that close to Chanul Tzuk, why didn't you drop in on Chandler Bennett, and the Oregon crew?"

"I wanted to. But the storm ruined the roads in that area. Most of them were completely washed out. So I figured we would do better coming east into the Peten. We have a few sites to visit here and in Belize."

"That reminds me Laurence, have you heard about the looting that's been going on around here?"

"Just bits and pieces. I hear it's getting to be kind of organized and semi-professional."

"They hit Topoxte and Rio Azul real hard. The Guatemalan archaeologists say a gringo leads the looters. Whoever it is knows what he's doing. The trenches are straight, stepped and wide, and also systematic, and they go right into tombs and burial vaults. After I visited Topoxte last weekend, I am convinced that whoever is directing it has had some professional training."

"You mean like a renegade archaeologist?" Laurence seemed to wake up a little.

Belinda had piqued his curiosity.

"Yes."

"I wonder if it's anyone we know?"

Belinda put her drink down and looked at him, he was smiling grimly. "You are joking aren't you? What archaeologist would throw his career away, to turn to looting?"

"Hold on Belinda. I didn't mean someone we know personally. It could be someone we know by reputation or possibly it could be one of the local boys, who is light complexioned, could pass for a Norte Americano, someone who might have worked on our projects in the past. Or it might be one of our European colleagues." He shrugged and poured himself another drink.

"Hector said that from all reports it was a gringo."

"Okay. But it could be a lot of potential gringos. Just consider all of the projects that Harvard, Penn, BYU, Texas, Oregon and SMU have run down here. How many well-trained semi-professional archaeologists is that?"

"Hundreds."

"Right. And from this sample population you only need one to go into business for himself."

"But why? I mean, other than money?"

"Don't be naive dear. Money is all the reason anyone needs. Hundreds of thousands of dollars could be made quite quickly if you knew what you were doing."

"But when they get caught?"

"Why should he ever get caught? Is anyone actively looking for him? The police? The army? You know the only people who care about archaeology are archaeologists. No one else gives a damn."

"Yeah. But we care a lot." Belinda realized she was getting a little smashed.

"That's right dear. We do." He laughed, and started coughing.

"Laurence have you seen a doctor?"

"I will. I'll be back in Cambridge in a week or so. I'll get checked out then." He took a big gulp from his drink. "And for now there's always self-medication." He tipped his glass to her. "What about you Belinda? Have you decided what you will do when you finish up? Research? Teaching? Run away and join the circus?"

"The usual. I'll try to get a tenure-track-teaching job. I just wish assistant professors were paid a little better than they are."

"For what? Teaching is the softest job there is. For what professors do, most are overpaid if you ask me. Besides Belinda, you come from a well-off background just like me. You can afford it. Hell. A professor only works what? Three to five hours a day, if he's got a full load, five days a week, nine months out of the year. It's cushy. Why should anyone be well paid for what basically is a part-time job? You want a tough job, try cutting sugar cane." His mood had changed, and his tone had become belligerent.

"I don't think you're serious."

"Oh, but I am. And what about tenure? Once you get tenure, you don't have to work at all for the rest of your life. They can't fire you! It's beyond unbelievable that such an archaic system still flourishes. You don't have to accomplish one single meritorious act after you have tenure. You can spend the rest of your career on automatic pilot like so many of these incompetents do..." He started coughing again, violently this time. The few people that were left in the restaurant were looking uneasily at them.

Alex quickly took the check to the cashier, while Belinda helped Laurence get up and walk outside. His coughing subsided, but he was covered in a cold sweat. There was no question that he was sick. They stood together on the patio listening to the night breeze rustle through the banana leaves.

"Laurence I want you to get on the next airplane back to the states. I'm very worried about your health."

He hugged her, smiled faintly and said something she would never forget. "Don't worry Belinda. There's nothing wrong with me that death won't cure."

With that he turned and walked away slowly, like an old man.

28 Death of an Operating System

Samuel Thomas and Ken Zucker were in the Peabody Museum collections with three graduate students, taking inventory. Thomas left the Latin American collections on the third floor to Zucker and the students, and took the elevator down to the first floor administrative offices.

He sat at the main computer and estimated that within the hour he would have the master inventory finished. His immediate task was to correlate and compare Ward's and Eikelmann's activities, over the last three months. The Harvard Police had requested this run. Thomas figured it was because both students were no longer with the program, but he wondered what they planned to do with this information. The inventory so far had found no anomalies, or missing artifacts, except for the two pots checked out to Ward. He typed in Ward's access code, and then Eikelmann's and then the correlation macro command. Immediately, a list came up on the screen, and as Thomas was about to press the print key, the computer stopped. Thomas frowned; this was a new one. He went into the direct operating system, and tried the DOS directory command. Nothing happened. The computer was frozen.

"What the hell? A nagging suspicion began to form in his mind. He tried several more fundamental DOS commands. None of them worked. The machine was locked up, totally unresponsive. "Okay then, if you're going to be like that we'll just restart you." Thomas said, and turned the computer off. He turned it back on and checked the hard drive directory, which held all of the museum's data. The monitor flickered and displayed a message: "C:\ is not accessible. Drive not ready."

"Bastard." Thomas said softly. He picked up the phone, and called Zucker's extension.

"Zucker here."

"Ken this is Samuel. You had better get down here. We have a real problem."

"What is it? I'm in the middle of something."

"Ken it's kind of important. The main computer is dead."

* * * * * * * *

Martin found Thomas and Zucker in the administrative office working at the computer. The room was white, spacious and well lit. Zucker was putting on his coat when Martin walked in.

"The department secretary said I would find you here Dr. Thomas, did I catch you at a bad time?"

Thomas looked up from the keyboard, his tie was askew, and he looked harried, as he pushed his hair back.

"What? Oh. Hello, Lieutenant. You might say it was a bad time. Someone has fried our main computer with a virus. Destroyed the hard drive." Zucker shook Martin's hand and said, "Please excuse me I have to get to my class." He turned to Thomas and said, "Samuel I think it is time to call Turner over at MIT, if anyone knows how to salvage our data, he does."

"You're right Ken. It's probably time to get a second opinion."

Zucker left, and Martin pulled up a chair at the computer next to Thomas. He noticed the fine suit coat; Thomas had casually draped over a chair, nodded at it. "Nice suit professor. Armani?"

Thomas was surprised. "Yes, in fact it is. You're interested in suits?"

"Italian suits. Yeah. My brother's a tailor in the North End." He pushed a chair back, sat down, and said, "You know, I don't really understand these machines Dr. Thomas, but I'm curious, how did this happen?"

"I was running a simple correlation program, and the computer just froze up. Something triggered a virus that had already been placed in the hard drive. One of the command lines may have started it."

"So someone had previously placed the virus in the computer, like a land mine waiting for someone to trip it?"

"Apparently so. At least something like that. Whoever did it knew his stuff. I have never seen a virus so thorough in its destruction."

"So you are fairly knowledgeable about computers?"

"Somewhat. I guess I'm the department's resident computer nerd."

"What kind of information did you lose? What were you working on when it happened?"

"We were checking on collections access records, by graduate students…" Thomas was about to continue but thought better of it. He switched to the first question. "What did we lose? Only everything. All records, all accession numbers, storage information, and user data."

"You mean you don't have any typed or written documents to back up the computer files?"

"Oh we have those all right, but it will take months to reenter these data. Months. The correlation program I was trying to run will be really difficult to do by hand."

"And the students you were checking when the computer failed were?"

Thomas sighed, and said. "I was checking the use of the collections by Phil Ward, and Laurence Eikelmann."

"So possibly one of them planted the virus?"

Thomas paused, and rubbed his jaw before answering. "Now that you mention it, yes, that is a possibility. Ward is a capable computer jock, but Laurence was exceptional. But, it could have been someone else, because it may have been a timed virus release, which is the most common variety. Possibly the command lines in the disk operating system did not activate it at all. If that was the case, then the program I was running just happened to be up at the wrong time."

"One's missing, and one's dead."

"What's that Lieutenant?"

"I was just saying that now I have a missing computer and a dead one. A pattern very similar to certain archaeologists that I'm investigating."

"Care to elaborate a little?" Thomas gave up and turned the computer off. He sat back and folded his arms over his chest.

"Eikelmann's computer disappeared from his apartment sometime between Wednesday night and early Friday. Now this." Martin gestured at the dead computer.

"Is it possible that Laurence took his computer to a shop to get it serviced?" Thomas asked.

"Now there's a possibility I haven't considered." Martin admitted. "We haven't found any claim checks anywhere. That doesn't necessarily mean..."

"I'm just curious Lieutenant. Why do you attribute so much importance to this computer?"

"A couple of reasons. The fact that many people say it was something that he always had with him, so its absence is probably significant, given these other computer-related incidents. What do you think?"

"I think that if Laurence had any sensitive data on his computer, you can be sure it was password-protected, and fire-walled. I'm skeptical how useful it would be to someone else."

"Who said anything about sensitive data?"

"That's the implication isn't it?"

"Who knows?" Martin shrugged. "Right now it's just another loose end. Did you know him well?"

"As well as any of our students." Thomas shrugged.

"He ever work in the field with you?"

"No. He did visit our project in Florida last Christmas break. He and Belinda dropped by for a couple of days."

"Where was this?"

"Key West. Is this really important Lieutenant?" Thomas was getting flushed, Martin noticed.

"Well since Belinda Boothe is missing. It could be important. Did she leave with Eikelmann?"

"No, she went up to Fort Lauderdale to meet Phil Ward."

"Fort Lauderdale? Is Ward from there?"

"No, but I think he has family there."

"I'll note that. I would like to talk to Mr. Ward." He wrote it down in his notepad. "So what were you working on at Key West?" Martin softened his tone, he wanted Thomas to calm down and talk.

"A beautiful, early eighteenth century light house. Right on the water, just down the street from Earnest Hemingway's house." Thomas started to relax as he talked about his research. "Have you ever been there?"

"No. Never been to Florida. So did Eikelmann help on your project?"

"He volunteered for a few days. Then he flew back to Connecticut for the holidays."

"In your statement you said that you last saw Eikelmann Tuesday afternoon in the graduate student lounge at the Peabody Museum."

"Yes." Thomas was getting a little red in his face again.

"You didn't see him again after Tuesday?"

"Not that I recall." A thin film of sweat was on his forehead.

"What if I told you that the bartender at the Living Room Club, and a customer, recall you and him having a drink together Thursday night at 7:30, just a few hours before he was murdered?"

"I would say Lieutenant, that if this conversation is to continue, I want my attorney to be present." Now his face was crimson, and his pupils were enormous.

"Well Professor I think you should arrange for it this evening, say 5:30, at my office."

29 Orpheus and Eurydice

Delia was connecting to the Internet from Madeline's state of the art computer with its 21-inch color monitor. She had the townhouse to herself. Next to the computer she had the Internet addresses that Martin had given her and notes from their last meeting. As she waited to be connected to the host server, she turned on the speakerphone and called Phil in Fort Lauderdale, something she had wanted to do, but had also dreaded for the last twenty-four hours.

"Hello?"

"Phil. It's Delia."

"Hey! What's up?"

"Why didn't you tell me you went down to Mexico and saw Belinda this summer?"

"What?"

"It's okay. You don't answer to me. What I mean is I'm just a little surprised you kept it from me, what with Belinda missing and everything else." She felt awkward, unable to talk straight.

"Delia. Hold on. Back up. Just what the hell are you talking about?"

"I'm talking about your trip to Merida. I have the information right here. I got it from the police. They got it from your ticket receipts that you left in your locker. You might want to give them a call. They're looking for you now. Let's see… you spent three days at the Fiesta Americana in Merida, and a week at the Krystal Hotel in Cancun. You went to Guatemala on August 23 and into Belize on the 26th. I have it all right here in my notes."

"What are you smoking? Is this a joke?"

"The Somerville Police don't think it's a joke. Lieutenant Martin has your passport and all of the receipts that that you kept in the lab cabinet. He really wants to talk to you about this."

"Fine. Let him. I was in Cambridge the whole summer."

"Phil. Why are you lying to me? I saw those receipts myself."

"I don't care what you saw, or think you saw. They weren't mine."

"Phil I want you to think this over carefully. I'll call you back when you can tell me the truth. Or maybe you should call me. Good bye."

* * * * * * * *

Delia stunned Phil. She really believed he was lying to her. He tried
calling her back, and got her answering machine. He went outside and sat
down in a lawn chair on the patio, staring at a forty-five foot Chris Craft
heading out toward the intracostal canal. What the hell was going on? He
was being set up big time was what. By who? He needed to clear his head
and think. He knew what to do. He went to his duffel bag, and got out his
Bible, and turned to his Psalm, at least he felt David wrote it for him. He
read Psalm thirty-eight out loud:

"O lord, rebuke me not in thy wrath: neither chasten me in thy hot
displeasure.

For thine arrows stick fast in me, and thy hand presseth me sore.

There is no soundness in my flesh because of thine anger; neither is there
any rest in my bones because of my sin.

For mine iniquities are gone over mine head: as a heavy burden they are
too heavy for me…"

In his memory the sounds of mortar rounds, helicopters, and screaming
filled the air. The old cold numbness came flooding back. Now he could
see the Vietnamese soldier rise up from the ground, AK-47 swinging
around. Sweat glistened on his muddy forehead, and his eyes were wide
with fear. He closed the bible and put it away. From a side pocket he got
out his Makarov, a pistol he had carried since getting it from its previous
owner in 1971. He loaded a fresh magazine. As he went to his truck he
whispered, "Whoever's coming for me, I better get ready."

* * * * * * * *

Delia was angry. She would call Phil back when she calmed down, for now, the net would be a wonderful distraction. She typed in the first Universal Resource Locator address.

A web site appeared, black with silver characters. A silver skull with a blonde wig was centered on the page:

Elena Mink's Hideout
Minks Links:

Delia had been around the web enough to know a hacker's page when she saw one. This one was kind of unusual because it consisted of only links to other pages. Trying to detect meaning in a hacker's page could be a pointless venture. She clicked on Lock Picking.

A skull and cross bones, the Jolly Roger floated down as if it were blowing in the breeze, a message formed over it: "Forbidden! Achtung! You don't have the proper access code! I'm going to have to terminate you. Try again when you know what you're doing."

The screen went black, and a message came from her server Massconnect: "Connection Terminated. Reconnect? Cancel?"

She pressed cancel, and stared at Madeline's screen saver, the French realist painting of Orpheus leading Eurydice from the underworld, by Jean-Baptiste-Camille Corot. She felt like Eurydice, lost in the woods with dark figures lurking in the background, only no Orpheus around to rescue her.

"My Orpheus is in Florida, and I can't trust him. So it looks like Eurydice will just have to handle it herself."

30 El Mundo Perdido

Belinda slept horribly, waking up from nightmares of floods, dark caves, and collapsing excavation trenches. Plus, she had to go to the bathroom every two hours from all of the drinking they had done. Rum always had that effect on her. Talking with Laurence had been very disturbing, and she thought about him for hours. She had never known him to be so fatalistic and cynical, yet at the same time, the poems he had read showed an idealistic social consciousness that seemed contradictory to his dark mood. He may have been posturing, but his repudiation of academia seemed genuine enough.

After a long shower, she went to the cafe for coffee and toast. Someone had left a Mexican newspaper from Merida, *Novedades de Yucatán*, on the table next to hers. On the front page was a story about Kathryn Haden missing from Chanul Tzuk. She was concentrating on reading it when Laurence walked in looking very disheveled and sat down next to her. He signaled for some coffee, and sat back with his arms folded across his chest.

"Good morning Belinda. Alex and I are heading to Belize today after we get your Rover fixed." When Belinda did not respond he said, "Have you got the business page there?"

"Laurence, do you remember Kathryn Haden from Penn?"

"Sure." He pushed his hair back and stretched. "Met her last year at that conference in Merida."

"Well she disappeared in that storm a couple of days ago. The Mexican government has the army combing Chiapas, looking for her."

"What? From Chanul Tzuk? What does it say?"

"She just headed out to the main plaza before the storm came in, and never came back."

"What do they think happened to her?"

"No one knows, she just disappeared, all they found was her hat."

"Are you through? Can I read it?"

As Laurence read the story, Belinda thought about Kathryn Haden. She remembered she was slender, athletic-looking, and very outgoing. She had a real down-to-earth quality about her, and Belinda couldn't imagine her getting lost, or into any kind of trouble. She would describe Haden as intelligent and practical. What could possibly have happened?

The waiter brought Laurence his coffee and he put the paper down, and sipped the coffee looking at Belinda, bleary-eyed. Finally he spoke. "It makes no sense. Someone like Haden doesn't just disappear."

"You know what I'm thinking don't you?"

"What?" He arched an eyebrow.

"That I should go help them look for her."

"Belinda. I just came from Chiapas. The roads are really messed up and the Usumacinta is running high and fast. It took us three days to get here from Tenosique, which is the closest bridge. And we drove night and day. By now the roads might be impassable. I don't know. It would take a few days, of real hard driving just to get there."

"Well I'm going anyway. I could get a canoe ride to Frontera Corozal and from there it should be easy. I know any archaeologist in this area would do the same for me."

"You've got a point there." He smiled and took another drink of coffee. "Okay. I'm in."

"Laurence you're not well enough to go."

"Who says? When did you get your MD? It'll only delay me a few days. Until then I've still got plenty of rum. Besides, no way I'm letting you go alone. It's too dangerous." He finished his coffee and said, "Let's just take our Rover and leave yours here."

"Do you think that's a good idea? If we have one break down, we could at least continue in the other."

"Tell you what Belinda. Alex is working on your vehicle right now; if he thinks it can make it we'll give it a try."

They left the cafe and went to the parking lot. Alex was just getting started on the engine, Laurence was going to assist, so she decided to take a walk on the path to the ruins, and see what the new excavations at El Mundo Perdido had uncovered. It was a beautiful morning, the sky was clear, and birds were singing. The trees arched into a green tunnel over the path and many flowers were blooming. A flock of toucans bobbed around in the upper forest canopy and screeched at her.

After finishing her walk, she started jogging back to the parking lot. When she stopped to catch her breath, she noticed she had lost an earring, part of a set that Phil had given her in the Bahamas. They were her favorites, turquoise, black coral, and shell, and she spent almost an hour backtracking her trail looking for it, with no luck.

When she returned to the parking lot, Laurence and Alex were arguing about something, but they stopped when she came into view. Laurence was in the middle of repacking their gear into the back of their Rover. Alex was putting the air cleaner back on Belinda's Land Rover. She noticed Laurence had already bought more gas and filled up her water cans too.

"So what's our plan?" She asked Laurence.

"We'll take both vehicles; it will probably make it easier for all concerned. I'll ride with you. I think Alex and I are getting on each other's nerves."

"What's up?"

"Oh. Nothing. He's not entirely in favor of the trip. But he isn't paying for the vehicle so…" Laurence shrugged his shoulders.

"Well he doesn't have to come with us Laurence, not if it's going to be a problem." Actually, Belinda hoped Alex would not come with them. There was something about him she just did not like.

"Dissension is part of his discrete charm. At least he's a good mechanic. He fixed your vehicle, so I'd rather have him along than not."

Within the hour they were on the road to Chanul Tzuk.

31 Elena Mink

Delia walked up the stairs to the Peabody Museum, and ran into Samuel Thomas, coming out the door. He looked tense, as he held the door open for her. "Good evening Professor Thomas."

"Evening Delia. Our Lieutenant Martin has been stirring things up today."

"Oh?"

"He's been going over the statements we gave last week to the Somerville Police. You know, I do not have an alibi for the night Eikelmann was killed. I was working on my boat that whole week, in Revere at the marina. Simply because I was by myself, doesn't give them the right to grill me. I talked to him this afternoon, and he was very unpleasant. The Lieutenant has been with Zucker for over an hour now. You know. It's really hard to get any work done with all this turmoil."

"Anything I can do?"

"Do you know how to fix a fried mainframe? Never mind. I have to get going."

Delia watched him walk quickly toward the faculty parking lot. He seemed very detached, and miserable. What was that all about? She walked through the Hall of North American Indians, and took the rear elevator up to the Maler Laboratory. As she walked down the hall, she heard voices coming from inside. Prefontaine and Mamett were talking about the main computer.

"So Patrick have they completely knocked the computer out?"

"We're not sure. Salvaging some data may be possible."

"How does that affect our inventory project?"

Delia knocked lightly on the open door and walked in. "The computer is fried?" She asked.

"Most definitely, someone dropped a major virus into it." Mamett replied. "I don't know why."

Delia thought about her conversation with Phil, and the hacker pages she had seen a few hours ago. "Hackers don't always need a reason. They do things because they can, but this hacker had a reason."

"You sound like you have an idea who did this." Carl said.

"I do, it was Laurence Eikelmann, and he did it to cover his tracks. He probably figured the security system would catch up with him eventually, so he planted it…"

"Or possibly Ward." Mamett observed. "He was good with computers."

"Patrick. You're not exactly objective in matters concerning Phil Ward." Prefontaine added. "I also think this speculation serves no useful purpose, for any of us. We will find out who did this in due time. I have to get back to my office now. I have a student appointment." He paused and turned to Delia. "Have you heard from Belinda yet?"

Delia shook her head. "But I think the fact that she's missing is connected to Laurence's murder, and whatever he was involved in. That other matter that I discussed with you is also relevant."

"You mean the two pots in the ceiling? You can speak freely about that. It's widely known now." Prefontaine nodded at Mamett.

"Well yes that, and other things. Things that Laurence said to me. I only hope it means that Belinda is hiding somewhere and that she'll contact us when she feels safe."

Delia went over to her desk in the lab; she had seen that name Elena Mink here in the lab somewhere, if she remembered correctly.

"I hope that turns out to be the case." Prefontaine said and turned to leave. "Let me know if you hear anything from her. Call me later, when you get home."

Mamett paused too, before leaving. "Delia. Seriously, if you want to take some time off, if you need a break, don't hesitate. Take as much time as you like. Go home to Chillicothie. Whatever you want. We can cover your work here."

"I appreciate that. I might take you up on it later, but I'm okay for now. Plus, I really want to find out what is going on. Do you know what I mean?"

"Yes. I think so, whatever is going on is putting a severe strain on us all, and it needs to be resolved."

"I saw Dr. Thomas on the way in. He didn't look so good."

"Samuel bless him, is taking this whole thing as a personal affront, but it's tough on everyone." He picked up some maps and said, "Well, I'll be in my office, for a while longer if you need me."

"Thanks, but I'm going to meet Madeline at her lab in a bit."

"Well if you need me. I'm just down the hall. See you tomorrow."

The Maler lab was a long room with eight large rectangular tables dividing it up like a maze. Each table had locked cabinets underneath, and these contained storage racks for artifacts. The counters under the windows were covered with trays of stone tools from Kichpanha and Ubala excavation units. Big stone axes, long flint knives, granite grinding stones, and obsidian spear points and blades, covered all the available counter space. Apparently Avendano and Mamett had gotten some analysis in this afternoon she thought, as she opened a window. The lab smelled of old dirt, bone dust, and a trace of mildew. She really wanted a cigarette, but resisted the urge, as she looked down on the courtyard between the museum and the library in the fading twilight. Her favorite time of day.

Suddenly, a sparrow flew into the lab, almost hitting her in the face. She jumped back and watched it strike the wall and ceiling, flapping and fluttering. She opened every window in the lab hoping it would find its way out. The panicking bird made her anxious. Growing up in rural Ohio, she remembered a bird inside the house was considered a bad omen. It meant someone was going to die soon.

"God I'm in a morbid mood. Superstitious too."

Finally, the bird landed on top of a bookshelf in the corner, it looked exhausted. Delia went over to try to catch it, but as she reached toward the bird it flew out through the open window like an arrow. Something about the way the bird behaved reminded her somehow of a shaman's animal familiar, an animal spirit. The bird gave her the creeps.

She went to the corner to close a window, and glanced down at the desk pad on the counter. In the margin of a sheet covered in notes, doodles, phone numbers and cartoons, Eikelmann had written the name Elena Mink with a magic marker and under it an Internet URL address. Delia was excited, she knew she had seen that name in the lab somewhere, and here it was, in Laurence's hand writing.

She went to the lab computer, pulled the plastic dust cover off, got on the net and typed in the address. The screen filled with a large oak tree superimposed on a white field. The text was in large Gothic Script:

Elena Mink, 1993
Links:
Archaeology
Prophecy
Stalking
Dreaming

She went to the archaeology link: A page came up. "More on Child Sacrifice and Ritual Cannibalism at Montebello: Structure Nine."

"In the east end we found two children's graves that indicate elaborate burial rituals. Here the Maya had dug a large pit. In it we found the extended headless body of an infant wrapped in the remains of a basket. Next a large pot was placed over the body. The head, a few cervical vertebrae and a string of beads, in a bowl covered by another bowl, were placed near the shoulders of the decapitated body. They partially filled the pit with animal bones (particularly birds of prey) and a second headless body was placed in it. They wrapped this body in a mat and they bound the legs inside it. A large ceramic plate was over the chest and nine smaller vessels were placed below the knees. Another skull was placed in the pit near the right shoulder. Prior to burial, the skull was scraped to remove the flesh. The occipital bones were broken (post mortem). The skull was then burned or baked - perhaps so the brains would be more appetizing."

"Such are the origins of Maya ritual from the Middle Preclassic."

The lights dimmed and the computer flickered. The power went off.

In the lab it was completely dark. Delia had to feel along the edge of the desk, to find her away around it. All of the lights were out in the courtyard and the Tozzer Library as well. She hated to admit it to herself, but the darkness bothered her, she wanted to leave as quickly as possible, and tried to feel her way toward the door, waiting for her eyes to adjust to the darkness.

Delia heard the door open, but could only make out a shadowy form standing in the entrance.

"Who is it? Who's there?"

"¿Dónde está?" He whispered.

"¿Dónde está que?" She slipped into Spanish without thinking, the reply in English; where is what? Who are you? "¿Quién es?"

"¿Dónde está?" The voice was threatening and not familiar.

"¿Dónde está que?" She pleaded, heart pounding. She could not see him clearly, but heard the metallic click of a round being chambered into a gun. She instinctively reached for one of the round hammer stones, and threw it straight at the figure in the doorway. She missed him, and heard it crash into a glass display case in the hallway.

164

"Oiya. Estas muerta." He giggled. She barely heard him glide to the side of the room. His accent was common rural Mexican. "Me voy a dar gusto." He laughed again.

* * * * * * * *

Carl's appointment did not show, and this allowed him more time to work on deciphering a map from 1777, showing the location of the Continental army's garrison on the Harvard campus. Somewhere was their garbage dump, which would be rich in dietary and material culture information. Prevailing winds were generally from the north and east, so the place to look would obviously be south and west. But how far away from the main camp? He started with a radius of one hundred meters out and delineated areas that had been disturbed by construction activities, this area of campus had seen extensive growth in the subsequent two centuries.

As he plotted the map points, he thought about the day's events. The computer virus was very disturbing. The fact that a member of their own community could do something like this, and the probability that it was directly connected to Laurence's death haunted him. Besides, it would take a long time to rebuild what had been lost, and he wondered now if their reliance on the computer needed to be corrected, after all, the museum had functioned well without one for well over a hundred years.

The other thing was Lieutenant Martin, in his zeal to investigate had seriously disrupted the day to day functions of the department and the museum. Carl's own account of where he had been Thursday night and early Friday morning had been gone over repeatedly. He remembered how he and Delia had stayed too long at the Boathouse, until they were both fairly inebriated, and how he had simply walked the two blocks home, and gone to bed. Thus, he did not have anyone to verify his whereabouts from midnight onward. Not that the Lieutenant considered Carl a suspect, it was just unnerving and a bit humiliating, to have to account for one's actions in such detail.

Everyone had been checked out thoroughly. Patrick Mamett had been to a dinner, and play at Adams House, and he and his wife had got home at about 1:00 a.m. Samuel Thomas had virtually no alibi, and had seemed extremely upset after his meeting with Martin, refusing to discuss it at all. On top of everything else the Lieutenant wanted to have a face-to-face meeting with Phil Ward, whose whereabouts were apparently unknown. The longer this goes on the worse it gets, he thought.

The lights flickered, and went out.

* * * * * * *

Delia froze. She heard him behind one of the lab tables to her left, closing off the door access. If she went out the window, it was three floors to the ground, and she was trapped at least thirty feet from the doorway.

"La estado vigilanto. Está usted muy sexual." He giggled like a girl. It made her skin crawl.

As Delia's eyes adjusted to the gloom, she could make out the vague outlines of the tables, and the doorway. She could not see the intruder, but could hear a shuffling sound in the darkness to her right. She crouched lower next to the table, ran her hands along the table edge and grabbed the first two artifacts that she touched.

Delia yelled and threw a hammer stone and axe at where she thought the intruder was. She heard them hit the floor. Missed. Now she didn't know where he was. She crawled a few feet along the floor and stopped, listening carefully, but couldn't hear anything at first, then she heard someone coming through the exhibition hall.

* * * * * * * * *

Carl put his pencil and ruler down, and looked out the windows. A power failure affecting all of the nearby buildings, he thought, the Agassiz Labs, the Tozzer Library and the Peabody Museum were all blacked out. He felt for his sports coat on the chair, and put it on. He slowly made his way to the door. As he left his office, he heard a loud explosion of glass breaking. It came from down the hallway in the direction of the lab.

He headed that way.

* * * * * * * * * *

Delia wanted to scream but she was so terrified that no sound would come. Her throat was parched and it felt like it was lined with cactus. She also didn't want to make any more sounds that might give away her position. Someone was coming through the hall, hopefully the police. This bastard wanted to rape her, and then kill her, and she needed to elude him until she could get to the door, or until the police came, or the lights came back on. He was moving toward her slowly, she could feel it, but he was very quiet, and seemed to be enjoying himself.

The footsteps stopped just outside the lab. Carl Prefontaine was in the doorway.

"Delia. Are you in there? Are you all right?"

"Carl don't come in!"

Carl walked slowly into the entryway, and the intruder leaped on him like a cat, and pistol-whipped him, striking him several times. The blows were so fast, it sounded like they were slashing the air, whistling, and thudding. Carl fell, and hit the floor. The lab was silent, except for Delia's rapid breathing. She got a whiff of him as he moved back to the right, and it was repulsive. This fellow doesn't bathe very often, she thought.

He was quietly laughing, whispered "Muerta," and chuckled again. He was crawling along the floor on the other side of the long counter in the center of the room, breathing hard, excited. His meaty smell was overpowering, a combination of dirt, sweat, and offal.

Because of his strong odor, Delia knew he was close by. Quietly she felt around again on top of the counter. A sharp edge nicked her finger, and she found a long obsidian knife in her right hand. Perfect, she thought, and gripped it tightly. With her left hand she threw another large hammer stone, grapefruit sized, in the direction of where she thought he was, and heard it hit something.

"Pinche Puta!"

167

Heart pounding, she slowly climbed onto the counter top toward the sound of his voice. He rose up suddenly in front of her with the pistol swinging around, and she slashed him across his gun hand. His breath was horrible. It smelled like vomit, and she gagged.

The pistol clanked on the floor.

Delia dove at him with the dagger. He struck her hard in the nose, and she toppled backwards over the other side of the counter, landing hard on her back, and hitting her head against the wall.

Her teeth slammed together. She felt like all the bones in her body were vibrating.

Dazed, in pain, and moving too slowly, she knew she was dead. Nothing she could do about it. He was going to kill her now. Why am I so calm all of a sudden?

That damned soft laughter was all she could hear. God I hate him, she thought.

"Adios amiga."

"Adios yourself bastard."

Several shots splintered the tabletop. The explosions were deafening in the confined lab space, but Delia heard the man hit the floor nearby, and she struggled, trying to get up. She was seriously dazed and sluggish, and moving in slow motion.

Louder shots were fired back toward the door where the woman's voice came from. He's got something bigger than a nine millimeter, Delia thought.

"Delia you okay?" Madeline asked.

"I'm okay." She took a deep breath, trying to regain some composure. Her nose hurt like hell. "Where's our little friend?"

"I think he's moved back toward the back of the lab. Try to get over to me. I'm right outside the door."

"Madeline, please shoot the son of a bitch." Delia crawled toward the doorway. Her head was starting to throb.

Out on Divinity Avenue she could hear police sirens. Oh God please hurry, she prayed.

Gunfire filled the room. Bullets ripped by, and Delia flattened herself on the floor as Madeline returned the fire.

The lights came back on. She looked back, and saw him go out the window, heard another shot from Madeline and the sound of metal straining and squealing, then a loud crash.

Now all she could hear was ringing in her ears, from the resonating gunshots. A thick cloud of blue gun smoke hung in the air.

Delia went to the window, and saw the rain pipe bent down in a horseshoe shape, lying on the ground. No sign of the attacker. Madeline was kneeling over Carl, checking his pulse. The sirens were right outside now, and the strobing blue lights reflected off the red brick walls in the courtyard. Delia went over to Madeline, who had removed Carl's tie and unbuttoned his collar.

"How is he?"

"Not so good. He's out cold, unresponsive. Pulse is weak, and he's bleeding in the back of his head. Occipital. Could be fractured. Get me some clean rags, paper towels. Hurry."

Delia went to the sink where the towels were, and the lights came back on. Two Harvard policemen came in, saw Carl's condition, and radioed for an ambulance.

* * * * * * * *

Delia and Madeline sat in the waiting room at Mount Auburn Hospital listening to the emergency room doctor describe Carl's condition.

169

"He's critical. He has a subarachnoid hemorrhage."

"Could you please explain what that means?" Madeline asked.

"It's an intercranial bleeding into the cerebrospinal fluid-filled space that is located between the arachnoid and pial membranes on the brain's surface. He was hit with extreme force, because the bleeding extends back into the brain. He was unconscious when he came in, now he's passing in and out of a stupor."

"What does that mean?"

"His symptoms of confusion and delirium are typical of severe trauma. We're prepping him for a CAT scan to confirm the intercranial rupture. We will have to do emergency neurosurgery if our diagnosis is confirmed."

"How soon?"

"Within the hour. It's going to be high-risk, particularly for a man his age. Do you know how to contact his immediate family? Is he Catholic?"

"I know who can contact them." Madeline answered. "I don't know whether he's Catholic, do you Delia?"

"No, I don't." She felt tears in her eyes. Carl was just trying to help her.

"I have to get back. If you could find those things out for me? A priest may be needed."

"Right now." Madeline went to the pay phone, leaving Delia to stare unseeing, at the television on the wall. Stunned by it all, Delia quietly wept. Her ears were still ringing, and she had a major headache. She couldn't believe the bastard had gotten away. The police had found blood drops on the sidewalk on the east side of the museum, but he had escaped into the wooded area by the graduate student dorms. "And he's still out there. Still watching." she whispered to herself.

Madeline came back and put her arm around Delia. "You okay?"

170

"Yeah. I'm fine." She wiped her eyes with the back of her hand. "Who did you call?"

"Ken Zucker. He's going over to the department to look in Carl's personal file. He doesn't think any of his family lives in the area. But I promise you, wherever they are, Ken will find them." Madeline sighed and shook her head. "Poor Carl. I remember when his wife died. Now this. What do you want to do?"

"Stick around, until we know if he's going to make it."

* * * * * * * * * *

Carl was taken into the operating room shortly after midnight. At 9:00 a.m. he was placed in the intensive care unit, still in critical condition. A large vessel had ruptured in his brain, and the surgeons had to cut open his occipital bone and lift a portion of it out, the bleeding vessel and veins had been legated and the skull section was replaced. His son and grandchildren in California had been contacted, and now all that could be done was wait out his recovery.

Delia and Madeline left the hospital at midmorning, and drove out to the Route 2 entrance.

"Which way?" Madeline asked, finally aware of being completely exhausted.

"Back to my place or yours?"

"Neither. I need to decompress, could we just drive for a while?"

"Count me in. I'm not ready to face the world yet. Let's just drive."

Soon they were on the Massachusetts Turnpike headed west. The sky was swollen and gray, it looked wintry, like it could snow, Delia thought as she leaned back in her seat. Soon she was asleep.

III

"Who tracks the steps of glory to the grave?"
Lord Byron

32 *Hach U Pixan*

Fog lay across the jungle treetops like a wet wool blanket. It was a soggy morning outside the village of San Felipe, across the Usumacinta River from Guatemala, and the men of the EZLN were just getting their day started. Small groups were clumped around campfires, burning off the morning's chill. Hungry, they were running out of food again.

Jesse studied their appearance as he drank his coffee; the worn brown shirts, thin and patched fatigue pants, and torn tennis shoes. They did not look like much of an army. He felt very aware of his own nearly new blue jeans and T-shirt, the Red Wing hiking boots, and nylon back pack, an appearance that loudly announced him as an American, before he ever opened his mouth. Lately he had been feeling more and more alienated, that it was time to leave. He saw the Professor emerge from the edge of the jungle, zipping up his pants.

"You seem deeply meditative this morning Jesse."

"I've been thinking I should get out of here."

"Well I would like for you to stay a bit longer, I may be able to use your help on a certain problem that seems to be developing."

"I'm also thinking about what happened at Chanul Tzuk, and how I'm never going to find out what happened to Kathy."

"Chanul Tzuk is a place that is central to you. It is part of your *hach u pixan*; your true soul inhabits the land around Chanul Tzuk."

"But why?" Jesse was skeptical of the interpretations that Garcia offered, but intrigued at the same time.

"I would guess that your *hach u pixan* lost something very important to you there."

Jesse thought about the night Kathy Haden disappeared, and how he had lost her forever. Would he ever know what happened to her?

"I am right. She was very important to you, yes?" Garcia softened his words.

"Yes. Very. And now she's gone and it's mostly my fault."

"No it's not your fault. It's the will of the gods, in antiquity he was known as *Yum Chac*, the god of rain. It is significant that she was taken from you in a hurricane. Did you know *hurakan* is the old Yucatecan Maya god of storms?"

"Yes. But I don't believe in your gods."

"And my gods don't believe in you, yet here we are."

33 Las Olas

Firing the pistol was satisfying. He was still a good shot, and it was gratifying to know it. Phil was at the Seminole Gun Club and Firing Range out in west Broward County, among the palmettos and saw grass, for the fourth day in a row, putting in more practice time. Today he was also sighting in his old AK-47, a firearm that he had not picked up in years. Whenever he was seriously stressed, he found that going to the nearest firing range mellowed him right out.

He was now totally focused on finding Belinda. Self-delusion was not something he subscribed to. He knew that a large part of his motivation was the fact that he still didn't know what he was going to do with the rest of his life, but looking for Belinda was more than a diversion. He owed it to her.

Phil knew he could slip in and out of virtually every country in the region, including the United States. His more pressing problem was money, since he figured it would require several thousand dollars to trace Belinda's trail. If he sold his truck to a wholesaler, he would net about seven thousand, and that might be enough. He decided he would try the car dealers on Commercial Avenue.

Phil knew that he was banking a lot on his instincts, but that was how he lived his life, for better or worse. But he knew as surely as he knew anything that Belinda was alive, somewhere in Central America.

* * * * * * * * *

He paid the cabbie the fifteen-dollar fare from Commercial Avenue to Las Olas, and walked down palm-lined Coral Way, carrying his weapons in a gym bag. Selling the truck had been easy, and he was able to get seventy-five hundred for it, about a thousand more than the dealer had wanted to give.

In his baggy white shorts and University of Kentucky tank top he looked like a tourist, he thought. A rented Lincoln Town Car was parked in the driveway behind Patty's 4-Runner, and Phil figured she had a client. He walked between the landscaped bougainvillea, banana trees, and magnolias, and up the flagstone sidewalk looking toward the front room. Was that a familiar voice he heard? It was.

Delia Bell and Madeline Scott were sitting in the living room with Patty, sipping coffee, listening to Thelonius Monk on the stereo. They all smiled at him when he walked in. Delia came over and hugged him.

He placed the gun bag carefully on the hardwood floor with his arm still around Delia, smiled and said, "Good Morning ladies." He pulled up a wicker rocker near Madeline. "Delia, I don't think you have ever surprised me more in all the time I've known you. What are you all doing here?"

"Well, it started out as a drive to get away from the madness in Cambridge. Pretty soon we were in Hartford, Connecticut at Madeline's sister's house. I didn't want to go back yet, and I needed to see you, so we burned some of our frequent flyer miles and came here. God, the weather is so wonderful. And Patty, your house is beautiful."

"Thank you. I think that maybe we'll take the launch out tonight. Show you the town by water. Phil and I appreciate the company."

"Phil, I called but you weren't here, so Patty gave us directions from the airport. I hope you don't mind."

"No. Hell no." He laughed. "I'm glad to see you both. I've got a lot to tell you."

"And I've got a lot to tell you." Delia added, as she sat back down in her chair.

"Well then, you go first."

"The night before last, I was attacked at the museum . . ." Delia began her story.

* * * * * * * * *

Patty's other boat was an open air, twenty-five foot, navy surplus launch; a boat type designated by the Navy and Coast Guard, as an M.S.B. (Motorized Surfboat), and used to transport people back and forth between ships riding at anchor. Patty had restored it, and made a few modifications, new engine, new fiberglass, and new boat cushions for the built-in benches that could seat twelve comfortably. Phil was at the wheel, which was amidships, on the starboard side. Delia sat next to him on the engine cover. Patty and Madeline were forward laying out a dinner they had cooked.

They had left Patty's backyard dock in the Venetian isle section of Fort Lauderdale, and had just about cleared the New River, as the sun went down. Phil headed her out on the Intracostal Waterway. The ocean breeze was out of the east, and added a light chop as they approached the area by the Bahia Mar Yacht Basin, and went under the Seventeenth Street Bridge. The Marina Marriott passed on the starboard side, and tied up in front was

175

a one hundred and fifty-foot motor yacht. Phil nodded toward it, looking at his sister.

"The Sheik of Bahrain's royal yacht, a brand new Fedship. Wish I had sold it, it went for about eighteen million dollars."

"That would have been a nice ten percent commission." He heard a cork pop out of a bottle and saw Patty had broken out her favorite, chilled white Zinfandel. She handed a glass to Delia who in turn offered it to Phil.

"I'm driving. I'll just take a couple of sips from yours?" He took a sip and looked again at Delia's long slender legs, stretched out next to him. "You cold in those shorts? Patty's got a quilt stowed somewhere if you need it."

"No I'm okay for now. I was just thinking."

"About?"

"Your concerns about Belinda. You're still very much in love with her, aren't you? You sold your truck to go after her, and everything." She shrugged.

"I guess that I still am, I wouldn't say "very much" though, maybe a little, but I know that it's over between us. She ended it six months ago. I still think there was something she kept from me. Something she never explained, but it doesn't matter anymore. And even though I know we're finished, I still care about her, and I'm going to try to find her. Plus, I really need to be doing something; I need to get away. I am only afraid that maybe I…"

"What?"

"Nothing. No that's not really true." He looked out at the channel, and took a deep breath before continuing. "Well okay, I'll tell you. It might help me get a bearing on all this stuff I've been turning over inside. Honestly, I'm a little concerned about my judgment. I've made some bad calls in my life. The orals are not the only tests I've ever failed."

"You're being too hard on yourself."

"I have high expectations. It may be that I'm going on this trip to run away from my problems. That's a big part of it I'm sure. But I also know that they'll still be here when I get back. Either that or they'll just follow me."

"What is it that you are afraid of?" She asked softly. Delia had always pictured Phil as very self-assured.

"Failure. Lack of will. Not getting it done. And see, when my career was on the line at Harvard that's exactly what happened. I couldn't cut it."

"Hey. You were never a typical Harvard guy anyway." She tried to lighten his mood.

"Don't I know it? I always thought the admissions office made a mistake." He laughed. "Do you remember the new graduate students reception when we first got to Harvard?"

"I remember they made us go alphabetically, I had to go first. I remember we had to say where we had graduated from, what we were studying, who we were going to study with..."

"You got up and in this ingénue voice..."

"Ingénue?" Delia asked in mock anger.

"And you said; 'Hello, I'm Cordelia Bell, I went to Yale."

"I believe you're mocking me Mr. Ward." Delia socked him in the shoulder.

They both started laughing.

Phil continued. "Belinda went to Harvard, Eikelmann went to Columbia, Janice went to Cornell, I go last, and I'm the oldest one."

"And I remember you introduced yourself and said, 'I went to the University of Kentucky' and you threw out this attitude, like 'want to make something of it?' You reminded me of Robert DeNiro in Taxi Driver.'" She laughed. "Are you talking to me?" She said, in a very bad DeNiro imitation.

177

Phil laughed. "That's not exactly the way I remember it. I remember the look on my colleagues' faces, a look that said 'How did somebody from a state school get in here?'"

"Really?" Delia asked. "I don't remember it that way at all. A lot of us thought you were arrogant in the early days."

"I've heard that, from Belinda too. Well, what do you think now?"

"I've always thought you were a pretty good guy, kind of complicated though..."

Phil shrugged. "I'm not complicated at all. I've always felt like an outsider. I was aloof because I never felt like I belonged, not at all arrogant, more like an alien. It's just my style. And now I really am outside, all the way out."

"You could always go to another graduate program."

"And everyone will always know that I failed at Harvard..."

"You can overcome that too. If you want to."

"And that's the question that I have to answer on this trip, do I want to? I don't even know right now. I think my confidence has been damaged. Hell I know it has. But I'm not going to let anything distract me from finding Belinda. I feel like I owe her that much."

"You know, in this letter that we found in her luggage she seemed to have some regrets. Why am I telling you this?"

"Like what?"

"The main thing she said was she wanted some time to think things out, and went about it in the wrong way."

"I couldn't believe she could be so cold. I still don't think she leveled with me." He shook his head. "So what happened? Did Belinda send her luggage back, book her flight, and change her mind? Is that it? Because I'm convinced she's still in Central America."

"So who went to Oxford Books?" Delia asked.

"Someone who wants everyone to think she's missing in Boston, it's classic misdirection."

"But who?"

"That is one of the sixty four thousand dollar questions."

"And Carl collided with whoever they are…"

"I'm worried about Carl. I'd like to get my hands on the bastard that did that to him." Phil steadied the wheel and reached for the wine Delia extended toward him.

"Well like I said, they think he has a good chance for a full recovery. It will take awhile though."

Patty came over and stood next to them. "So little brother, when do you take off for Central America?"

"As soon as I find a boat that I can crew on, headed in that direction. Since I don't have a passport, she'll have to have a foreign flag, so that the Coast Guard won't board her, and I won't be picked up."

"*Hera's Song* is British-flagged."

"Yes, I know, it's because you have a British Captain's license, and because you registered her that way. So your point?" Patty was smiling at him. "Oh no. Stop now. I'm not taking your pride and joy to Belize, who would watch her, while I was ashore?"

"I would. I know some people in San Pedro on Ambergris Caye. Caye Caulker too. Piece of cake. I've got the itch to take her out, see what she can do on a long haul. Nothing is pressing right now; I have a comfortable financial cushion, for a change. With good winds we could be there in about a week. By the way, the winds are pretty good tonight."

"We're not sailing out of here tonight. I'm not sold on this idea at all."

Madeline came over and said, "What idea?"

"Taking *Hera's Song* to Belize. Phil said, turning the boat to starboard as they rounded the breakwater at Port Everglades, and entered the Atlantic. "It's crazy."

"Why?" Madeline asked.

"Because I don't know how long it will take to find Belinda. You could be waiting a long time Patty. By yourself."

"She wouldn't be by herself if I was with her." Madeline added.

"Great." Patty laughed. "Now I have company. See Phil. It's starting to make sense it's your best bet."

Phil felt the situation getting away from him, and into the hands of the women. Then he realized this was by no means a spontaneous idea. "Have you ladies been discussing this behind my back?"

Madeline and Patty shrugged.

"So you all are trying to put me together. Let me ask a few questions first. Madeline - have you ever sailed before? And don't you have a job?"

"Yes, I have sailed quite a bit. It's been a few years, but husband number one, Reed, kept a sloop up at Rockport. As for my job honey, I hold the Bishop Chair in Ethnobotany. I can make arrangements. And, I'm in the middle of a family emergency. Belinda has to be found."

"Well you all are not going to leave me behind." Said Delia. "I'm coming with you."

"No one is going anywhere yet. There's no way that I'm sailing off to Belize half-cocked with three crazy women." Phil said ruefully, but he sensed that his protests were going to be ignored, and he already had lost control of the situation, since they were laughing at him, and making lists of things to buy.

* * * * * * * *

The wind had stopped and the Atlantic was like glass, Phil shut off the engine as they drifted just south of Port Everglades. The sky was clear and full of stars and the lights of three cruise ships were strung out on the eastern horizon, blazing like casinos. The waves lapped gently against the hull and Phil leaned back in the captain's chair, watching the women put dinner, on the table. It was a beautiful night, and although the future was full of dread, right now life was just fine. He took another sip of wine and looked east toward the cruise ships, then west to the shoreline of Lloyd Beach, with its coconut groves and clumps of ironwood trees.

Delia brought him a plate. "Dinner is served your lordship. Caribbean chicken with pineapple, red beans and rice, a salad. Peach cobbler for dessert." She slipped and braced herself by holding on to his shoulder, and her hand seemed to linger an extra second longer. Phil met her glance and then looked away.

Phil waited until everyone was served before he started eating. They were all quiet, listening to the waves and the occasional ships horn coming north from Port Everglades. The food was excellent, and he started to think seriously about how it would be to sail with these three. His sister's offer of her boat was touching, and he realized it was his best possible way to travel undetected to Belize. But he would have to go ashore alone; the situation could be dangerous. Besides not having a passport, another reason for a covert approach was that he had no idea of what he was heading into, who or what was involved, and who might be watching for him. He felt some old emotions stirring inside, and they needed to be controlled. These women did not need to be exposed to that side of him. He wasn't sure he wanted to release it either, to feel it again after all of these years. Once the adrenaline and instincts started flowing, they were hard to restrain. Also, there were some details from Delia's story that he wanted to go over. The situation required illumination.

"Delia, did they find out how the lights went out that night you were attacked?"

"Someone sabotaged the main circuit breaker in the Agassiz Labs. It controlled the power to the library and the museum as well."

181

"So we can surmise that it was done only to cover the attack?"

"That seems likely."

"Did this Mexican chap with the severe hygiene deficiency have time to get from the basement of the Agassiz, to the third floor of the museum in the interval between the lights going out, and when he showed up in the doorway?"

"No, he was there within one or two minutes after the lights went out. There's no way."

"So he had an assistant, who went over to the Agassiz, and provided the cover of darkness for him."

Delia was silent. Phil was right. How come she hadn't realized it? Partly because she had been trying to repress the entire experience.

"So that means we're up against at least two people, and these are the same people who nearly killed Carl. They probably killed Laurence too. So they are very dangerous, and we need to be dangerous too."

Madeline added, "We also know that one of them is very good with computers, viruses, forging documents, and is trying to set you up. Making it look like you were in Mexico when you weren't, making it look like you took those pots when you didn't. Making it look like Belinda was home when she wasn't. Someone very clever."

"Well after all you've told me, I think that one of those people is dead. Eikelmann. For some reason that we haven't figured out yet they turned on him. Either that, or there's another group of interests at work. There's an awful lot we haven't figured out yet, but we can deduce that until quite recently there were at minimum, three people in the opposing forces. Two at least still remain. For safety's sake we should assume there may be more people involved, who just haven't been flushed out yet." He paused, as everyone watched a hydrofoil come out of the port, throwing up a plume as it accelerated out into the Atlantic. "Delia, what had you been doing the day you were attacked?"

"Well, I called you that afternoon. We already went over that, I'm sorry I didn't believe you."

"Hey." Phil held up his hand. "You apologized. Once is enough. Besides I don't blame you. It's an elaborate frame-up they're attempting, and they're very good at it."

"Are you going to talk to Lieutenant Martin before you leave? You should… because he doesn't want to believe that you're involved."

"I haven't decided yet. So get back to that day, what happened after you talked to me?"

"I was working on some Internet URL's for the Lieutenant, tracking sites that Laurence had been to. That reminds me, when you were working at Montebello, was there someone on the crew named Elena Mink?"

"No. There were only about eight or nine North Americans on that project. No one by that name. Why?"

"I visited two web sites that had her name on them. Laurence was interested in them for some reason. Anyway this Elena Mink person had a description of a child's burial at Montebello that showed evidence of sacrifice and ritual cannibalism."

"Feature 459. I remember it well. It's described in the Montebello reports, in detail."

"She was using it in reference to savagery. I was reading that when the lights went out. I never did get to finish it."

"How much of it do you remember?"

"Something to do with cannibalism."

"So these web sites addressed Maya religion?" asked Madeline.

"It would seem so." Delia answered.

Phil adjusted the rudder. They were getting in close to the beach. "What I'm trying to figure out is how this connects to Montebello's Feature 459... That summer Mamett had the group from Texas, Mangers from Michigan, me and Eikelmann from Harvard, Stackhausen and a couple of others came down from McGill, and that's it."

"Who found 459?" Delia asked.

"John Mangers and Laurence Eikelmann. They were working at Operation 3006, a small pyramid to the east of the main courtyard group. It was an odd structure, isolated by itself, not associated with any plaza." Phil took another drink, and adjusted the rudder. "It turned out to be the oldest known structure at the site. At first we thought they were monkeys in the burial; that's how Eikelmann identified them. It was Cliver who realized they were human infants, ritually sacrificed, a skull scraped and partially cooked. You know, that afternoon my opinion of Maya religion was radically changed."

"How so?" Asked Madeline.

"I realized that Maya religion was rooted in savagery, decadence, it reminded me of Viet Nam." His voice trailed off.

"Now that is not very politically correct of you Phil. What about cultural relativism?" Madeline asked.

"Screw cultural relativism. It's a totally bankrupt concept that anthropology needs to get over. If something is barbaric - and child sacrifice and cannibalism fits the bill in my book, then no amount of intellectual gyrations and posturing in the name of cultural relativism is going to change it. Take the Aztecs for example. They were pre-Columbian Nazis."

"Phil don't get started on the Aztecs, it's a good lecture but I've heard you give it before." Delia said. "What I want to know is how does all this fit together?"

Phil mused, rubbing his jaw, "Well let's see. Barbaric rituals and Maya religion, Laurence Eikelmann. What was that girls name?"

"Elena Mink."

"And how does Elena Mink link?" Phil asked, and cut himself another piece of pie. "Wait a minute. It's an anagram. Who's got a piece of paper and a pen?"

Patty dug into her purse and handed a pad and pen to Phil. "Here."

"Just move the letters around, and Eikelmann turns into Elena Mink. Voila."

Delia stared at the notepad. Something tugged at her memory, it was important, but she could not quite get it. "So those were Laurence's sites on the web! What was he up to?"

"Whatever it was, the thing about the web is that part of it is a kind of electronic pen-pal meeting place. So he has some friends and associates out there." Phil started the engine up. "What these people are up to, and how many of them are out there, we still have to figure out."

34 Damage Control

Samuel Thomas was agitated while he drove down Grove Street on the outer edge of Lexington. Too many aspersions and rumors were being generated by the police investigation. Gossip. It was the last thing he needed; a man in his position. His precarious position.

He pulled in the gravel driveway that led a half-mile back to his secluded carriage house apartment, wanting a stiff drink before calling his attorney back. He slammed the door of the Jaguar, and took the stairs of his two-story flat two at a time. He and his attorney had met with the Lieutenant for four straight days now, just long enough for his life to start to unravel. He had always feared being discovered, and now it was destined to happen. The questions could end his career, depending on how he handled them, and that was what he needed to concentrate on now, damage control. He needed to find a way out of the turmoil his life had become. It probably was way past time to face the demons.

He poured himself a large tumbler of scotch. "I am going to handle this." He said out loud, walking over to his picture window with his drink. It was pitch dark outside and he checked the time, a little after nine thirty. In the last five hours everything had unraveled. The truth was he had no idea how he was going to handle any of it. He walked over to his high-backed leather chair and fell into it. Behind the bookshelf and between the curtains, he had hidden the leather briefcase. He set it on his desk, dialed the combination, and opened it. Laurence's computer was right where he had left it, and it was singularly the most incriminating piece of evidence against him, much worse than the eyewitness accounts from The Living Room Club.

He stared at the computer, wondering how to get rid of it. Why did he have to give it to me?

He heard soft footsteps on his staircase and looked toward the door. It was common for some of his friends to drop by at this hour, and even later. But he had not heard a car pull up. He started to extract himself from the chair, when he heard someone curse in Spanish outside.

It was not a voice he recognized.

Samuel remembered that he had not locked the door.

The door opened fast, and slammed back loudly against the wall. The man in the doorway simply walked right in. He held a pistol in his bandaged right hand.

He was compact and squat, yet powerfully built, and he looked more Indian than Latin, Samuel thought, but there was a hard edge that suggested barely controlled fury. The man was visibly pumped up on something, adrenaline, drugs, and it showed in his rapid eye movement, his sweaty scowl, and the way he strode right up to Samuel, and shoved the pistol against his neck.

He had a foul odor. It made Samuel's eyes water.

"Vámanos." He said through clenched teeth, and shoved Samuel toward the door. The man walked over to the desk and laughed "Aqui está!" He laughed again and picked up the laptop. He pushed Samuel out the door and then gave him a powerful shove down the stairs. Samuel fell and bounced hard down two short flights.

Samuel realized the man intended to kill him.

35 Greater Arcana

Laurence drove Belinda's Land Rover toward their first objective the Usumacinta River. The roads were drying out quickly in the late August sun, and they made good time to El Subin, and then on to Las Cruces. They could see clouds building up again on the horizon, and it looked like it might rain later in the day.

Belinda had never been in this part of the Peten before, and was struck by how much of the tropical forest had been cut down. Charred and ragged stumps, rutted yellow mud and scrap wood, were all you could see for hundreds of acres. They saw no villages, except for a couple of abandoned ones. From the late 70s to mid 80s the Guatemalan army had been conducting "pacification" programs to curtail guerilla activities in the area. All of the native Maya Indians were suspected guerrilla sympathizers, and they had to be "pacified" too. This was accomplished through forced removal, kidnapping, arson and mass murder. Laurence had a grim look on his face. He cleared his throat and spat out the window.

"Pacification." His voice was thick with sarcasm.

"I know."

"Well it worked. The area is very calm and passive now. It's totally devoid of people and trees, monkeys, deer; all of the mammals are gone. Between the army and the lumber companies they have made themselves a nice little, passive, wasteland here."

"It's horrible."

"That it is. You know what else is horrible? No one knows how many Maya Indians the Guatemalan government killed. Thousands. Hundreds of thousands. Thousands more fled to refuge camps across the border in Chiapas. Thousands more are in the ground." He gestured to a swamp they were passing. "The swamp is a good place to dump bodies. I remember Phil talking once about how when he drove down this road in '82, vultures sat on every stump."

It gave her the creeps to think about it. Even in the humid heat she had gooseflesh on her arms and legs, thinking about all the corpses out there. She really wanted to talk about something else. "Was that when you both worked on the Montebello project?"

"It was back in 1990. He is an excellent field archaeologist. The best I have ever seen. Very meticulous, but also very quick. I learned a lot from working with Phil. I envy him, his confidence in the field. We never really hit it off unfortunately."

"He's good. I know. He taught my first field school."

"Copperhead Shelter, in Kentucky, right? Do you know that I applied to go there but it was already filled up?"

"No kidding? It was a great school, and Phil ran it very well. I didn't like him at first." Belinda thought back to the first time they met.

"Neither did I. And I don't think he likes me, but it's probably because I have very poor social skills. Phil's all right once you get to know him." He laughed. "I guess you know that though. When are you guys getting married?"

She felt herself blushing. "Never. Not now."

"What happened? You were together for quite awhile. I guess I haven't been keeping up. Sorry."

"We were together almost three years. I don't know Laurence; I kind of messed it up. Can we please talk about something else?"

"Sure. I'm sorry. I didn't know."

"It's okay. Really."

188

They drove in silence for some time after that, finally getting out of the logging area and back into solid jungle and swamps on both sides of the road. She thought about Phil and how much she had hurt him, the last time they were together, and in turn she had hurt herself too. Eventually, she stopped torturing herself and nodded off into a nap.

Just before sunset another tropical squall blew in from the north. Wind gusts, and sheets of rain made driving difficult and slow. Alex pulled his Land Rover off the road and found a bit of shelter under a large spreading ceiba tree. They pulled in behind him, and Laurence went to see what was going on with Alex. He jogged back after a few minutes.

"Can you believe it? His wipers have stopped working." Laurence was drenched when he climbed back in. She dug out a towel from her duffel bag and handed it to him.

"Thanks." He dried his hair, while he talked. "Alex thinks it's a short, but it's a little difficult to work on right now as you can see." The wind and rain slammed against them, gently rocking the vehicle. He pulled out the roadmap from above the sun visor.

"We won't make it to the Usumacinta for hours at this rate." He coughed and said, "What do you think?"

"Since our wipers work, couldn't he follow us? We could turn on our lights."

"Yes. That might work, but what kind of speed would we make? We would have to go slowly, about twenty to twenty-five miles an hour or less."

"Right. And how far is the river?" Belinda leaned over to look at the map.

"Well we have two options, the best one is crossing via canoe at Agropecuaria, and it's a good fifty or sixty miles away." He pointed to it on the map. "But the closest crossing is here at Bonanza, twenty miles, but it will throw us to the south a bit. And the water is really fast there."

"In the event the river is up and we can't cross, do either of them have a place where we can stay over night?"

189

"Nothing in Bonanza, at the pecuaria there is a little agricultural technical school, a co-operative. Wait a minute. At Bonanza, I remember there are some nice hillside caves that hunters stay in. We can drive right up to them. We have plenty of camping equipment."

"Then considering that there's only a little daylight left, I think we should go to Bonanza. What's your vote?"

"I'm with you Belinda. I'll go tell Alex."

* * * * * * * * *

The rain intensified but the winds weakened. As the day darkened, the algae choked swamps glowed with green phosphorescence. All the way to Bonanza they crept along at twenty miles an hour with Alex staying as close as he could. They never got out of third gear. A couple of times Alex nearly rear-ended them, but the only thing he could see was their taillights. The road conditions were terrible, and later she found out Alex had been drinking rum all afternoon as well. It was a miracle that he didn't pile into them.

They got to Bonanza in the Usumacinta River gorge after dark, and drove down the muddy approach to the village. Water was cascading down the road, and they skidded a little before they stopped. In the headlights, the churning whitewater of the Usumacinta carried logs, stumps and branches as it boiled past. Laurence leaned against the wheel and had another coughing fit. "Looks like we camp Belinda. It'll probably subside tomorrow. Let's get up that hill." He turned the Rover around and they started bouncing their way up the ridge above the river, following a muddy rut that was just barely visible in the dark. On both sides thick vegetation grew in a tangled mass. They sideswiped a tree, and glanced off something, but kept moving so they wouldn't get stuck. A hole appeared in front of them and they hit it hard, and bounced up in the air, banging their heads on the roof.

Laurence downshifted, the gearbox whined, and they jumped forward again, slithered into a muddy bank, and were stuck. All four wheels were digging deep into the muck. Alex pulled up behind them, put his bumper against theirs, and pushed them out. They finally made it to a limestone ridge with an overhang that was so large; it covered both Land Rovers.

190

"Here we are. This looks like as good a place as we're going to find. Be careful getting out because it slopes down on your side."

She reached in the back and pulled out her duffel bag.

"Laurence that was some pretty impressive driving." She pulled up her hair and tucked it under her rain hat, then jammed it down tight.

He coughed, and said, "Let's hope there's some dry firewood in there. Got your flashlight?"

She took it out of the glove compartment, turned it on, and got out quickly. She stepped around the side of the Land Rover, a rock pivoted out from under her, and she twisted her ankle. She was thrown sideways into slimy vines and undergrowth. Falling and sliding about twenty feet, she lost her duffel bag in the darkness.

"Belinda. Where are you?" Laurence was scanning the slope with his flashlight.

"I'm over here. I think I twisted my ankle." The rain was pounding down hard on her, and the slope was muddy. She slipped, trying to get up.

"Hold on, I'm coming."

It was raining harder, she was getting soaked, and her foot was throbbing. She found her flashlight and started looking for the duffel bag. It was nowhere in sight. The rain was pounding down on her. Tree branches were snapping. She could hear Laurence crashing through the brush, and saw his flashlight bobbing in the dark. Then he was standing next to her, helping her up.

"How bad is your ankle? Can you walk?"

"It hurts like hell, but I can walk. I need to find my duffel bag."

"First we get you out of the rain. Then I find your duffel bag. Come on."

With Laurence holding her up, she limped back to the shelter of the overhang. Alex had a lantern going, and it was already attracting bugs.

The darkness of the overhang continued further back, suggesting a tunnel or cave.

"Is it a cave? Está es una cueva?" She asked Alex, who shrugged in answer, he was busy dragging tree limbs that had been stacked to one side, over to a dry place where someone had left a ring of stones.

"I'm going to find your duffel bag. I'll be right back." Laurence left and she helped Alex with the firewood.

Soon they had enough, and Alex soaked the wood in kerosene before lighting it with the lighter Belinda offered to him. It blazed up to the roof instantly. He tossed her lighter back to her and kept playing with the kerosene, squeezing off jets into the fire, making it burn brighter, jumping back. Belinda realized he was very drunk.

Even with the fire blazing, the blackness continued back into the hillside. She walked back about thirty feet with her flashlight and the darkness continued further back still. She could make out the outline of a passage in the rocks ahead, and she could hear water dripping and echoing somewhere in its depths.

Laurence came in with her duffel bag, winded, and coughing badly. He had to go clear his throat and spit over by the Land Rover. Belinda started digging through the bag for dry clothes and her aspirin bottle. About half of her clothes were damp; the bag had just gotten too wet. When Laurence stopped coughing, he came back with two bottles of rum.

"You seem to have a limitless supply of rum." She commented sarcastically to him.

"We bought a case in Flores. It's for medicinal use only, I assure you." He laughed.

Finally, she found some dry clothes. "Well here's a sweatshirt, now if I could just find some pants…"

"Belinda. I've got a pair of sweatpants that will fit you, if worse comes to worse."

"I may have to take you up on that. But you need to change too. You'll get a chill, and that won't help your condition any."

"Yeah. I will. Just give me a minute, what's over there?" He motioned toward the back of the cliff.

"It looks like a fairly extensive cave. Goes back further than I could see."

"Hmm. Let's check it out in awhile."

Belinda took the sweat pants, and went between the Rovers to change clothes. Even though she could see Alex tending the fire, she felt like he was glancing over at her. Not that he could see anything. Laurence went to change next, and left Belinda with her own bottle of rum. She sipped a little to wash the aspirin down, and to take the chill off. It warmed her right up.

Laurence came back bringing a cooler and a wooden box for them to sit on. Alex sat on the ground far away, on the other side.

"So Belinda," Laurence said. "You still want to go through with this? Tomorrow we could just go back the way we came, knowing we gave it a good effort, but the river was impassable."

"It doesn't look too good does it?"

"Not at the moment but it could be down a lot by mid-morning tomorrow. Although, I kind of doubt it. We could try a little divination, if you like."

"What do you mean?"

"Foretell the future."

"Yeah. Sure. How?"

"I've got my Tarot cards with me."

"You're serious? You can't be."

"Sure I am. Look, I've been interested in what some people call the occult, ever since I've learned that it works more often than can be explained rationally. I don't know why it does, but it does." He rummaged about in his canvas bag and extracted a dog-eared cardboard box. "I don't use the term occult, because I recognize that there are other ways of knowing things." He carefully withdrew a deck of cards.

"I prefer the traditional Ryder-Waite deck of the early 1900s, these New Agey Aquarian decks are to me, weak and nebulous. You see, prophecy is no more than an alternative way of knowing. It's simple really, and it's been around a long time. Longer than the field of Anthropology." He smoothed out the canvas bag, and started shuffling the cards. "I believe that the universe is connected by invisible patterns and human events can be predicted based upon simple, repeated mathematical steps. I have empirical evidence to back it up, even though I barely understand it. Few people know that the tarot deck is mathematically structured and quite symmetrical. The face cards, numbered 1 to 21 concurrently with one unnumbered face card, are called the Greater Trumps or Arcana, and have been determined by specialists to represent in their symbolism the classic patterns present in all of creation."

"Laurence, I am amazed that you find the Tarot deck mathematically appealing. You don't really believe this?"

He continued to shuffle before responding. "I do, because it is." He became more animated and excited as he continued. "In almost all cultures the sum total of all things can be depicted by a circle, correct?"

"Yes, with a few minor exceptions."

"I'm not interested in exceptions. I'm interested in patterns. The circle can be presented by the relationship of pi (3.142. 1), with a circumference between 21 and 22 and a diameter of 7; so the tarot Greater Arcana of 22 symbols can be investigated numerically."

"How so?" Laurence was speaking rapidly, and Belinda was having trouble keeping up with him.

"Numerically you can refer to our states of awareness or consciousness by working with symbol-ordering methods. You with me?"

"For example?"

He started writing on the back of a well-worn notebook that he had extracted from his pack. "As (2 x 11); or (3 x 7) + 1; and (4 x 5) + 2; or by the permutations of 3 equals 7, and of 4 equals 15, so that the trumps are split into seven supreme Arcana, and fifteen Great Arcana of awareness. You see?"

Belinda was surprised and bewildered, because it was apparent that Laurence deeply believed in what he was saying.

He shuffled the cards with skill. "Actually it's always easier to read for a stranger than it is for a friend. But let's give it a try anyway. Select a card to represent yourself."

"I've had my Tarot read for me many times before Laurence. I always choose the High Priestess." Belinda sighed; thinking at least this would be an amusing way to pass the time.

"Really? When?" He withdrew the card and placed it before them face up.

"In boarding school, there was this Turkish girl there. She had a knack."

"A knack?"

"She was able to guess accurately, is what I think now, looking back." Belinda thought about "Dark Salma." That was her nickname, dark skin, dark eyes, and dark hair. "Spooky" was the other nickname they used to describe her.

"Looking back? And what did you think at the time? You were how old?" He placed the deck in front of her. "Cut the cards with your left hand please, and concentrate on your question." Laurence was very serious all of a sudden, business-like in his approach.

"I was fifteen. I believed she was a fortuneteller then. She claimed to be. She scared me a little. Scared us all a bit."

"Your mind was more open then, not closed like it is now." He tapped the top of the deck. "Are you ready? Clear your mind and concentrate on the question."

Belinda held Salma's image in her mind, all she could think to ask the cards was the same question she always asked Salma. "What will the next seven days bring?" She liked it because it was safe, no matter how ominous Salma's reading it would pass in seven days.

She cut the cards.

"I'm going to use the Celtic cross formation for you Belinda. But first let's consider your card. The priestess is gracious. She symbolizes education, knowledge, and intuition. Spirituality and psychic awareness are other characteristics. She symbolizes considerable mystical power. She should represent you. Look, the letter B is on the left pillar behind her, could that stand for Belinda, I wonder? You chose well."

"I've always picked that card." Belinda shrugged.

"You know, the origins of the Tarot are obscure, although most scholars agree that they are probably of Eastern origin, the oldest specimens are around 1440 AD..." He dealt out the cards in a cruciform shape face down. "The 19th century Jewish scholar-magician, Eliphas Levi also known as Alphonse Louis Constant, claimed the Tarot came to the west through us Hebrews, and that the gypsies later compromised it. Still it is all rather vague. Shrouded in mystery, as you would expect it to be if you understood it as I do." He turned over the first card, it was:

"The Queen of Swords. This card covers the priestess, covers you, it represents the general atmosphere around you."

"That's it huh?" said Belinda, "Well at least she's got a sword."

"The Queen of Swords is not a symbol of power dear, quite the contrary. Here, in her upright position she suggests familiarity with sadness, mourning, and separation from all those you love and hold dear."

"That's pretty accurate." In spite of herself Belinda found she was getting intrigued.

"Of course it is. I know what I'm doing. Okay, let's continue. The next card symbolizes opposing elements good or evil surrounding your query." He turned it over. "The King of Cups reversed." He rubbed his beard absently, and didn't say anything.

"Well?"

"I don't like this card in this context very much." He sighed. "In the reversed position it signifies a dishonest man, deceit, scandal, and considerable loss."

"And that's what is opposing me now?"

Laurence nodded and said, "Afraid so. Well, lets look at the next card which represents the basis of your query; this is something already a part of your experience. He turned it over. "The Hanged Man." He paused before continuing. "In this context it is a powerful card, since it is a major trump. Here, I take it to mean that your life is in suspension, hanging if you will, awaiting the outcome of very powerful forces at play. It means that a mystery surrounds you, but on the positive side it means a good outcome is possible. The fourth card, the card behind, represents an element that has just passed."

He turned it over. "The Queen of Cups. Not good in this context. It would seem to indicate that you are, or have recently been, a vain, overly emotional woman. The Queen of Cups' intentions may be good, but she is unreliable, untrustworthy, and probably unfaithful. Sorry. Remember that I'm talking about her, in the abstract, not you. She is much affected by surrounding influences, therefore more dependent than most other cards on good or ill dignity. She also may indicate dishonesty or weaknesses."

"That's hitting a little too close to home." Belinda shivered at the accuracy.

"How so? You don't have to tell me." Laurence sat back on his heels, with his arms around his knees, looking intently at her.

"Before I broke up with Phil, just a few weeks before I left, I had an affair. I cheated on him." She pushed her hair back. "It had a lot to do with why…"

197

"Hey. That's okay. I'm not your confessor."

"No but it's been on my mind. I haven't told anyone."

Neither of them spoke for a moment.

"So are you still seeing this guy?"

"Off and on. He's married. I'm so stupid. Your reading is just a little too accurate for me right now. He's someone you know, and I probably shouldn't tell you..."

"Then don't. Let's go on. It's none of my business anyway. The next card, the card that crowns, represents a possible aspect of the future. This is not a card of certainty." He turned it over.

"Death."

Belinda felt cold and icy. "Laurence maybe we should stop now. This is giving me the creeps."

"Once you unleash these forces you have to play it through my dear. Now the death card understandably frightens people. The mysterious skeletal horseman, bearing a black banner. It's a powerful symbol, but the banner also contains the mystic rose, which symbolizes life, in this case I believe it represents transformation. I take it to mean that some alterations in your life are at work, whether you like it or not. It doesn't mean you are going to die." He cracked his knuckles and said, "Let's keep going. We're almost to the end."

"Wait. Please. Couldn't we just forget about all this?" Belinda grabbed Laurence's wrist as it hovered above the next card.

"No. I told you..." he removed her fingers from his wrist and turned it over.

"The Fool." He shook his head. "Lot of Major Trumps out there. Powerful forces indeed are at work tonight. This one is easy though; he signifies the journey outward. See? He's happily about to walk off the edge of the earth but he knows the angels will catch him. The Fool is one of my favorite cards; in fact I always select him to represent myself. Of course this could mean, that your fortune and mine are now bound together, and that would also hold for the question you posed of the cards. Interesting. I can hardly wait for the next card, which illuminates the deeper aspects of your situation. This card represents your fears, negative feelings or other uncertainties."

He turned over the card. "The Three of cups reversed. Hmm. It may indicate that you know that you have a weakness toward overindulgence, or satisfaction from sensual and sexual pleasures without any sense of love. Like sport sex?"

Belinda took a deep breath, and exhaled. "You haven't missed a beat yet Laurence."

"Hey. Nothing wrong with sport sex. I'm fond of it myself." He chuckled. "Belinda. Lighten up. These cards are only indicators. Only a guide. Okay? Now the next card represents your family or close friends' influence or opinions. Think of this as very close external forces."

He turned over the card. "The Hermit. Damn. Another major trump, what are the odds... I think this card indicates the need for you to withdraw from current events for a period of reevaluation and accumulating inner strength. A definite need for understanding. It could also indicate a wise man who will offer knowing guidance."

"Would that be you? Could that be this reading?"

"I'm The Fool, remember? Okay. The next to last card represents your hopes and desires. The forces you are currently adding whether conscious or otherwise." He paused. "And it is - The Six of Swords, symbolizing science. I get this card all the time. Good card. It indicates intelligence that has realized its goal. Healing. Labor. Work. Passage from difficulty. Journey by water. There is an open passageway that leads away from troublesome situations, but the destination is unknown."

"Finally a good card. Let's stop now. Okay?"

Laurence ignored her. "The final card symbolizes the possible outcome of all of this."

He turned it over.

"The Devil."

"Great. Thanks Laurence. Just when I thought things were looking up."

"Belinda, you know as well as I do that one of the archetypal symbols imbedded in our psyche is that of the monster. The monster symbolizes all that hurts us, and all that we use to hurt ourselves and others. The red-eyed monster within. Alternatively, evil is symbolized in this image of the prince of hell. And just as with Maya underworld symbolism, also in the Tarot, the devil has bat wings to suggest his nocturnal, cave-dwelling habitat. He also has a long-eared, horned head, and the torso of a beast to demonstrate his sub-human demeanor. Charming fellow isn't he?"

"And this is my possible outcome? Right here while I just happen to be in a cave? Wonderful. Thank you so much."

"I'll tell you what I think the whole thing means. You really need to examine your weaknesses, particularly in how they relate to your ideas of who you are, and your sense of security. It all suggests to me that you might be blinded by illusions that you think are real, but in fact, are not. Self-centered. It suggests that your life will change dramatically in the very near future. Either that, or you're going to get a bad haircut."

He saw that she didn't laugh. "Hey. I'm joking; don't take it all so seriously."

"So now we can stop?" Belinda asked feeling like someone had walked over her grave.

"Well it's traditional for me to ask if there is anything that needs clarification, if so we could select another card."

"No thank you. I've had enough of card games for one night." Belinda shivered.

"Are you cold? I could get you a blanket."

Thunder blasted from out of nowhere, causing Belinda to jump as rocks fell from the roof of the cave. One rock landed on the deck and flipped over a card, The Magician. Laurence scooped up the cards and put them away. Neither of them spoke for a few seconds.

Belinda felt anxious, and wished they had never opened the damned Tarot cards.

"Look, I'm sorry I dragged you and Alex along on this. I mean you could be staying in a dry, warm hotel tonight."

"We came of our own free will." He looked over at Alex sitting away from them. "Well. At least I did."

"He's not very friendly is he?" Belinda asked eager to direct the subject away from the Tarot cards.

"No. His social skills are even more impaired than mine."

"I don't know why you say that Laurence. You've always got on well with me and Delia."

"That's true." He stretched his legs toward the fire, and steam rose off his wet boots. "But I've always got along better with women, than men. My therapist says it stems from my relationship with my father."

"Which was?"

"Horrible."

"I'm sorry."

"Oh. Pay no attention to me. I'm getting drunk. Again. Got to put the beef worms to sleep, you know." He took another large gulp of rum.

"Well. I get along better with men, so we must have had similar experiences. I have always been competitive with other women. Nothing too unusual about that. Sadly, a lot of us are like that. But with me it was both of my parents. They were...careerists. Still are for that matter. They packed me off to boarding school when I was nine. Summers I would be sent to various camps. I knew kids whose parents were divorced Laurence, who saw them more often than mine saw me."

"So it's our parents' faults that we became archaeologists? Us poor little rich kids?" He was smiling down at the fire; Belinda couldn't see his eyes.

"Yes." Belinda laughed. "Let's blame everything on them. It's a hell of a lot easier than facing up to the consequences of our own actions." They both started laughing.

"You know Belinda; I got into archaeology for two reasons. One, I was very intrigued by it, and two, it really pissed off my father. He wanted me to go to law school. He used to say 'digging in the dirt is no way for a man to make a living.'"

Laurence started chuckling. "I showed him. Look at me now!"

Wet, bedraggled, and muddy, they both looked like a couple of homeless people. They laughed until their sides hurt.

On the other side of the fire, Alex got up muttering and cursing, and took a flashlight into the cave. They watched the light disappear into the darkness.

Belinda said, "He's obviously feeling antisocial."

"He's in a pissy mood." Laurence observed. "Maybe he'll fall into a hole. Find Xibalba, or better yet, maybe one of the Nine Lords will eat him. You know they're out tonight. In force."

Belinda nodded. "Like Lord *Cuhuma Quic,* the Blood Gatherer. He's one of my favorites."

"Yes Belinda. Good to see you're up on your Maya mythology, and what else do you remember about *Cuhuma Quic*? For a free bottle of rum, in twenty-five words or less?"

"Well, like most of the lords he could take human form. Shape shifters. They could be someone alive or dead. Ghosts. Spirits. They could take any form and hunt you at night. This is why the Maya to this day don't like to go out at night alone. They might run into *Sukunkyum* the chief Lord of the Night. Or possibly *Lord Kisin*, god of death, you never know whom you might encounter. I have always found that intriguing."

"What? How so?" Laurence threw the empty rum bottle into the fire.

"What if it were true? What if these lords really seemed to be able to do that? Maybe it was the Maya way to explain sociopaths." Belinda realized she wasn't explaining it very well.

"Gods taking human form? I'm not sure I'm getting this." Laurence got up to warm his back by the fire.

"I don't mean I really believe it could happen. But, if everyone else believes it. Let me try to explain it another way, from the Maya, from the perspective of their belief systems. I'm trying to grapple with this in my dissertation. I have often felt that the thin veneer of Christianity that overlays native Maya religion, is very thin indeed. You know, sometimes it feels that we are far from the Judaeo-Christian God down here."

"Yes. I know what you mean. We always see the results of the Maya beliefs, in the sites we excavate, the child sacrifices, torture, beheadings. These are the things that stand out. No there's no question to me that the Judaeo-Christian God was far away in those days."

"And what if He still is? What if this is an area that He doesn't pay much attention to? This is one of the things that I have been thinking about since I started my thesis work. Belief is so strong. If all the people in an area believe that something exists, or that you should do something one way as opposed to another. Then it really doesn't matter."

"If it is true? Or real? Or perceived to be real? So now we're getting into two of my favorite ambiguities. Perception and reality." Laurence was shadowboxing against the cliff wall. The fire made his shadow ten feet tall.

"Exactly." Belinda said. "All that's necessary is for everyone to believe it."

"Because the power of belief is such that the system operates as if it were true? Kind of existential isn't it?"

Laurence knew exactly what she was talking about, she thought.

"Right. Truth, *per se*, becomes moot, because by believing it, people make it true. At least to them. This is how religions evolved." Belinda reached for the rum.

"And cults." Laurence added.

"Religions start out as cults, but then they get bigger." Belinda took a big drink.

"The famous quote of Marx: "If God did not exist, it would have been necessary to invent Him? Did I get that right?" Laurence scratched his head "I think I'm a little drunk."

"And then He does exist." Saying these things made Belinda feel a little creepy. Like something was watching her, and not with approval. God?

"You know the thing about God that's always puzzled me Belinda?"

"What?"

"See, we humans are created in his image right?"

"According to the Book of Genesis, yes."

"And we're all flawed, everyone has a dark side, wouldn't you say?"

"Yes."

"So perhaps God is the same as us? Since we were supposedly created in his image."

"How so?"

"He has a dark side too. He's also the Devil; Yin and Yang, the monster from the Tarot deck. The devil is inside of Him, part of Him, half of Him. That would explain a lot, wouldn't it? Hatred, pain, war, disease. Genocide. The way these poor Maya Indians have suffered and continue to suffer down here."

"So you are suggesting that the duality of life is present in God?"

"God is life, because He is everywhere, and you can't see Him; another invisible pattern." Laurence put a log on the fire, and stood, holding his hands in the smoke. "Think about the difference between the Old Testament fire and brimstone God of us Hebrews, versus the New Testament 'blessed are the meek' God of Jesus. They are like split personalities. What if God isn't a perfect being? What if he's a schizophrenic? We are born with cancer genes, what if God has a dark malignancy inside of Him? When I die if it turns out that that's the way God is? I won't be surprised."

"Laurence, you are talking total nonsense." He was scaring her.

"Am I?" He shrugged his shoulders. "Well maybe I am, I think I am a little drunk actually, now that you mention it. Still it's something I've often wondered about." He walked back from the fire and sat down beside her.

"Maybe the Maya gods still exist in some form or other, I mean to the people down here? It's a fact that they do, according to everything I've read," she responded, feeling uneasy.

"Perhaps even in the Underworld?" Laurence arched an eyebrow.

"Especially in the Underworld." The creepy feeling would not go away.

"The Nine Lords of the Night. You know Belinda, I know of a fellow who was initiated into a highland Maya jaguar cult, an American anthropologist. A scholar. He was initiated as a shaman, a priest. He came to believe in their religion more than that of his own culture. Immersed himself totally."

"Ha, yes, the old 'going native' routine. Maybe he's just really impressionable."

Belinda really wanted to talk about something else.

Laurence laughed. "That may well be. Okay. So what else do you know about *Lord Cuhuma Quic*?"

"Let's see. He sits at the head of the banquet table in the night world of Xibalba. The other lords like Crunching Jaguar, Blood Woman, Skull Owl, and the rest of the gang, bring together all the human blood that has been lost by violence or illness, since their last banquet and they drink it all together. It's a big feast; they're all such party animals. Animals like bats, vultures, spiders, snakes, monsters, fun guys like that." She was trying hard to lighten the mood.

"Good job. Gross bunch, the lords of the underworld. The Nine Lords. Alex would fit right in. Maybe they'll keep him."

"You act like you're stuck with him. What's his official title with the institute?"

"Alex is with an affiliate. I was forced to..." They heard footsteps and saw his flashlight reappear. "We'll talk about that later." Laurence looked worried, but maybe it was just the rum.

Belinda really needed to go to the bathroom, and walked down the slope until she was behind the Land Rovers, leaving Laurence and Alex talking by the fire with their backs to her. On the way back to the cave, she stopped by Laurence's vehicle to get another bottle of rum. Maybe getting really drunk would alleviate the growing feeling of dread, of being watched.

She opened the rear passenger door and pulled up a sleeping bag that covered a large cardboard box. Inside were carefully wrapped objects. Through the newspaper, they felt like artifacts not rum bottles. Her archaeological instinct took over and she began to grope around. One piece felt like a stone mask and she unwrapped it.

It was startling, a beautiful jade carving, a life-sized funeral mask, a jaguar's face with red coral inlays around the mouth and eyes. They glowed and glistened in the reflected firelight. It was in the Early Classic style. Two columns of glyphs were carved on the inside and Belinda half-felt, half-read the first four glyphs, "Upon the death of Lord Night Jaguar, of Chanul Tzuk," a glyph she didn't recognize, then "...in the katun-ending..."

Laurence startled her from behind. "What have you got there Belinda?" He whispered drunkenly.

"Laurence this mask is from Chanul Tzuk. How did you get it?"

"Is it? Is that what the glyphs say? You know I'm not an epigrapher. Well anyway, Alex and I, um, we were..."

Alex came around from the other side of the Rover, extended his hand and flexed it. "Aqui!" He said to Belinda through clenched teeth and looking angrily at Laurence.

She gave him the mask. He grabbed it with his left hand, and he slapped her hard with the back of his right hand. She fell down on her side, hitting a large limestone rock.

Belinda was too stunned to say anything. She could smell blood in her nose and feel it running to the side. Tears streamed down her face, and she tried to wipe them off.

"Hey! There's no need!" Laurence was caught off-guard as Alex slapped him too. Alex started back toward the fire, cursing under his breath.

"Can we all go back to the fire? Please Belinda." Laurence helped her get up.

"I am so sorry. You okay?" He stopped and gave her a bandana for her nose.

As she walked back with them it was clear how the atmosphere had changed. Alex was in charge now. Laurence was scared. His fear was contagious. Something bad was about to happen, and she wondered how she was going to get out of there. Her heart was pounding as she walked back. At the campfire Alex handed the mask to Laurence, who simply stood and stared at it. His face was ashen, and apprehensive.

Alex went back to the Land Rover, and they could hear him digging about, metal things were clanking and sliding around. Laurence glanced over, and whispered to her, "Belinda you'd better get out of here!"

"Where? She motioned toward the dark jungle slope and the rain falling in torrents. She was trapped.

"Just go!" She looked over toward the Land Rover and saw the firelight glinting on a gun barrel as Alex started back towards them.

"Help me Laurence!" She screamed.

"I can't save you. I can't even save myself. But I will try to run him over."

Belinda picked up her flashlight and ran into the cave.

* * * * * * * *

Outside she heard Alex shouting at Laurence, and the sound of one of the Land Rovers starting up. She ran farther into the cave as the floor became sandy and loose. She was overpowered by an ammonia-like smell, it made her want to throw up, and she realized she was running through powdery bat guano, on a floor that sloped down. She slipped, fell, and looked over her shoulder and saw Alex at the cave entrance - raise his gun up and aim towards her.

She turned off the flashlight and moved slowly through the dark on her shaking hands and trembling knees, feeling her way against the wall.

Gunshots exploded into the cave and sprayed somewhere above her head. Rocks and sand fell on her. He had some kind of automatic. Hundreds of batwings fluttered and roared at once, and she fell forward, staying down with her arms over her head, trying to protect herself from thousands of panicking bats that were flitting around in the cave bumping, and falling, disoriented by the gunshots. Feeling the beat of their wings, she heard the

Land Rover engine screaming and saw the headlights swerve across the cave wall. It seemed that Laurence was trying to stop Alex.

Belinda crawled slowly down deeper into the passage, which was getting rockier and felt her way forward, further into the cave as bats continued to bounce off her back, head and arms. She lost control of her bladder, soaking her pants. Now she was at least fifty yards from the entrance. Her eyes were adjusting to the darkness and behind her; in the faint light from the campfire, she was able to see the edges of the passage, the fissures in the ceiling, and boulders on the floor. Ahead it was black, and she could not see anything. Her heart was pounding and she was in danger of hyperventilating, and having a panic attack. She was almost frozen with terror. Whatever happened at the front of the cave, something was resolved, because she heard one of the Land Rovers drive off.

Had they left? She stopped moving for a minute and listened, trying to control her trembling. Nothing. Maybe they had both left. She waited, shivering uncontrollably. Belinda was starting to feel hopeful, when a flashlight came on, and Alex entered the cave.

She was afraid to turn hers on, and present him with a target, but if she didn't move quickly he was going to kill her anyway.

Her adrenaline was pumping as she steeled herself to plunge deeper into the cave. She turned on the flashlight and took off running.

The explosions were deafening. Bullets sprayed behind her.

She ran for her life. Jumping, leaping, darting behind boulders, the passage continued to slope down and she stayed with it as a fissure opened to the left, but she kept running forward. The passage made a hard curve to the right, and she knew he couldn't see her, so she ran harder. The pain in her ankle was excruciating and felt like it was locking up, but she continued to run, favoring her left foot. She splashed into a cold stream, slipped and fell, but held onto her flashlight. The stream was in the passage now, and she continued splashing through it, hoping that he wasn't close enough to hear her.

For about 150 feet she moved down the stream, it got deeper, above her ankles, then above her knees, and although the passage was narrow here, the flashlight showed a tall, narrow cavity rising about thirty feet above her. She couldn't see Alex's light but she could hear him. He wasn't running, and it was clear he was tracking her. Belinda's heart felt like it would explode. Her body was shaking and shivering when she stopped to catch her breath.

She heard water splashing over rocks ahead, and wondered what the stream was coming to. Now the floor of the cave was a narrow sluice, a channel like a water slide of rock sloping down and the water was up to her waist, pulling her forward. She decided to go with it, and half-floated, half glided down the sluice, holding the flashlight up and ahead of her with both hands. She kicked off her boots, to be more buoyant. At least this way she was moving faster than he was. Drowning was a terrifying possibility, but he was going to kill her anyway.

The water was roaring up ahead and starting to foam, and the sluice was widening out. She was in an underground river now, and side stroked to the edge, pulling herself out onto a large platform, like a table of rock. She stopped to catch her breath.

Trying hard to gather her wits, Belinda limped across the shelf and headed toward the sound of the waterfall. After five minutes she came to it, and scanned the cavern with her flashlight. The sluice she was in had turned right, like a horseshoe, and it encircled the platform before it dropped into a ten-foot waterfall. Then it formed into another sluice, and blasted over yet another waterfall, which fell about twenty feet. At the bottom was a cauldron of foaming water and a whirlpool of waves crashing into the wall immediately below her. Her flashlight could not penetrate the gloom beyond the turbulence.

Trapped with nowhere to go, she stood rooted to the spot, staring at the water. There was no way out, unless she headed back the way she came, right into Alex.

Belinda turned off the flashlight and sat down on the smooth limestone, shivering, waiting to see if he had followed this far. Most people would give up, she thought.

But not Alex. She heard him get out of the sluice on the far side of the platform, water dripping from his clothes splashing onto the limestone. He was about 50 yards away, and if she was going to do anything the time was now. All she had for weapons were her flashlight, and the loose rocks.

He turned his flashlight on, and scanned the area to her left. She moved as quietly as she could in the opposite direction, the cold smooth stone under her feet, trying to outflank him, wanting to head back toward the entrance. She was about thirty feet from him, flashlight in one hand, and a rock in the other. The river was right beside her. She was going to make it.

Suddenly he spun around and she was caught in the light as he opened fire.

Belinda jumped into the water as bullets ripped into the rocks around her. Something burned into her shoulder and she was spun around forward, and pulled down into the first waterfall. Thrashing and kicking she could still hear him blasting away as she fell into the second waterfall.

* * * * * * * *

She went underwater for a while, and although she was an excellent swimmer, her lungs nearly exploded before the current tossed her to the surface and up to an air pocket in the underground river. Her left shoulder burned and throbbed, she screamed every time she was thrown against the rocks. There was no light anywhere; she was past the point of panicking in the blackness.

Weakening from blood loss, she could only use her right arm to guide her through the foaming water. She swallowed a lot of river. A cold stinging numbness spread over her from her hands and feet as she floated on her back and gasped for air.

Ahead she could hear roaring water in the darkness and it had to be another large waterfall. Too weak too swim, she went over it falling, plunging into space in the dark, terrified and numb. She knew she was dead.

36 Christopher Columbus Park

The late model Jaguar XJ6, pearl white, with white leather interior, was parked on Atlantic Avenue, next to Christopher Columbus Park. Although this was the North End of Boston, and an area of very low-crime, since the Mafia controlled it, the Jaguar was still an expensive car to leave isolated on the road, and unlocked. Boston Police Patrolman Vincent Saccetti shined his flashlight inside and around the car. It had been parked there from four to five a.m. He punched in the license number on his link to the Directory of Motor Vehicles computer, and while he waited for it to come up, stepped outside and lit a cigarette.

Looking over toward the deserted park, he saw something glinting by the statue of Columbus, and walked toward it. Behind a series of low hedges, a corpse was stretched out on his back. The gun glinting next to it was a Smith and Wesson 38 Special Revolver, stainless steel. A three hundred-dollar pistol, Vince thought, the stiff couldn't have been here long, and in this neighborhood someone would snag a gun like that. Fancy Italian suit, fine Italian shoes, shiny pistol, and a big bloody hole in the head. Suicide?

He went back to his patrol car and called it in.

37 Lord Night Star

She opened her eyes and felt the cold presence of a sheltering wall of limestone in the darkness of the cave. The wall was white. Her eyes adjusted slowly to the weak light and she saw she was in an immense dome-like chamber. Large crystals of flowstone sparkled in the faint light that leaked in from a hole in the roof far above her. The light dappled across the stalactites, and she saw her left leg dangling in a river of clear turquoise. Waves lapped rhythmically against the rock walls. On the other side of the river, the water over the course of millennia had piled rounded boulders and sand, against the cave wall. More fallen rock was stacked on top of the boulders, reaching to the top of the chamber. Strips of green and gray fungus glowed in facets; bands of minerals glistened and flexed. Large crystals and rounded rock columns contributed to the dark, strange beauty of the cavern.

She was lying on her back, and had been there awhile because her clothes were almost dry. Directly in front of her was a gigantic stalagmite; a pillar of stone that was at least thirty feet high and sixty feet in circumference. Ashes, charred pine bundles of pitch, and ceramic vessels were in a jumble around the formation. The Maya had worshipped here.

In spite of the burning pain in her shoulder, she was excited. She slowly rolled over, crawled to a pitch bundle and lit it with her lighter. Leaning up on her left elbow, she saw the cave walls immediately leap out of the darkness in sharp definition, and she saw that they were painted in blood red hieroglyphic panels. She started reading them. Lord Night Jaguar of Chanul Tzuk had been initiated here. His son, Lord Night Star was depicted as separated from his father by *Kisin*, the Lord of Death. This god was truly sinister looking, a vulture-like corpse with bones sticking out, vomiting blood. His penis was perforated with six stingray spines and bleeding into a fire made of crossed long bones.

The next part of the text she read out loud: "Lord Night Star was taken into the underworld in his twenty third year, by the betrayal of Lady Evening Star, a royal princess of Yaxchilan. His bones lie here. He is protected by *Itzamna* and will return, and…"

Limestone secretions obscured the next passage. She held the torch higher but could not see any more text; she caught her breath and realized she was weak, and dizzy.

Still, it was an amazing discovery. The burial chamber of Lord Night Star, she had found it in perfect condition. No one had been here in a thousand years.

If I don't get out of here soon it will be my burial chamber too. She thought, as darkness swam over her again and she passed out.

38 Final Manuscript

Martin sat in an office in the North End's precinct house. Before him was a laptop computer recovered from the trunk of Samuel Thomas's Jaguar. It was turned on. Only one text file was stored on it, and it had been opened. He read it:

"This of course is Laurence Eikelmann's famous missing computer. He gave it to me the night he died. That's right died, not murdered; he drank the black drink and took his own life. I am the one who attended him, and conducted the proper rituals that prepared his way into the next world. The strangulation was done at the climax when he requested it."

"I am the one who purged this hard drive so you can't find anything usable except for this, my exit statement, my suicide note. My final manuscript. (Not to be referenced without author's permission, get it?). I assisted in the genital mutilation, which was done while he was still alive, although heavily drugged. I removed his heart, and I ritually buried him. I forgot about the two pots that he had hidden in the ceiling."

"And that of course is why I'm following him now, that and because I am a walking dead man. But we all die a little every day. Laurence had wanted to leave this sphere for quite some time. He was ready to approach the divine. Believe it or not he was very spiritual, and religious, as am I. If you have ever experienced divine awareness from peyote, mescaline, psilocybin, fasting, if you ever experienced it, you would know what I am talking about. We all find God in our own way."

"Although, we both did some things that we are not proud of."

"I was the one that drew him into smuggling artifacts out of the museum. When you think about it, as Phil Ward used to say, they were stolen from Central America to begin with. Legally stolen with permits from governments, but without the permission of the cultures they belonged to. Is it wrong to steal something that has already been stolen? But that of course, is a separate issue. My contacts in the art world drew us all in."

"I knew my medical treatment would require hundreds of thousands of dollars. This of course was back when I thought of fighting. We hid our tracks extremely well, Laurence crafted the virus in the mainframe and it was thorough in its ability. Your information is lost, totally destroyed."

"Phil Ward helped us out occasionally, and I think he knows where Belinda Boothe is. I had one other partner in this. He is a major art and antiquities broker on Long Island with excellent international connections. I won't reveal him to you. I want this whole thing to end with me. He and his group wanted this computer too, because of Laurence's brilliant predictive model of royal Maya precincts. It was quite effective in locating tombs. His own karma will take care of him, but he won't get the program because I have destroyed all of its copies and versions. Other than that, there is little more to say. I hope for obvious reasons, that this can be kept quiet, but am I sorry? Not really. Everything I did, I did because I believed in it." "See you in the next world (and don't be late)."

Samuel Thomas

Martin sat at the desk staring at the screen, looking at the words, and thinking about the man who had written them. An inside job, an art smuggling ring penetrating to the heart of Harvard. Was that what this was all about? And what disease was he referring to?

39 Under World

Belinda awoke in burning pain, screaming. Water lifted her body, and roared all around her. She was quickly engulfed by the rapids. Her legs were crushed against the rocks, searing her body in bone-aching, white-hot agony. A huge wave swallowed her and she numbly felt herself floating free of the bank, and moving swiftly out into a channel. "Oh my God!" She screamed again as she was washed into a large boulder, water filled her mouth and she went down into total blackness.

40 Gloria Hurukan

In the thick green jungle, clouds of vapor floated through slender tree limbs and vines that arched over the campsite. Glittering neon blue butterflies skipped in the mottled light, and disappeared into the dense undergrowth. The rainforest had an eternal feeling. It felt to Jesse like it had always been there, and always would be. But he knew it was vanishing all around him, in the far distance he could hear a chainsaw starting up.

Early afternoon sunlight barely filtered down through the jungle canopy. The ground was covered in dense, dripping green moss. A heavy undergrowth of ferns, and thick flourishing bushes, made walking almost impossible. The damp earth sank lightly beneath his feet as Jesse tripped and fell over a ropy vine, and was immediately soaked from the neck down. The plants and ground were drenched, and a light rainy mist filled the air. The fog and the thick jungle vegetation allowed fifty feet of visibility at best.

The men of the EZLN were trying to make a fire, but with limited success. So far they had produced a great deal of smoke and very little heat. Everything was saturated and waterlogged. Jesse decided to look down slope for any possible dry wood.

He carefully picked his way down a steep incline, covered in ferns.

Ahead, he could hear rapidly moving water washing through rocks and gravel.

Something about the place was familiar. Had he been here before? He started cutting his way through the thick green mass, and was soon soaked to his skin, shivering. A heavy mass of vines and tree trunks barred his way.

He moved laterally and slipped. Losing his footing, he tumbled down a steep slope. Wet thorns lacerated his face and hands. He had lost his machete again, and crawled, pushed, and wrestled through the tangled vines and ferns toward the sound of the river. Finally, he thrashed and flailed his way through to a large flat boulder, and could hear the river roaring not far below him. His knee burned with pain, and he massaged it gently.

He lay on the rock gasping for breath, and looked at the sky. Large holes appeared in the boiling clouds, rays of sunlight started to filter through. It was much warmer than up in the jungle.

Below him he could see the river mist boiling up from a wide limestone gorge.

It cleared for a few seconds, and he knew where he was, on the Usumacinta River, somewhere between Yaxchilan and Piedras Negras.

He retrieved his machete and climbed down on to the large flat yellow boulders.

Eventually he reached the edge of the riverbank. Whitewater cascaded over the rocks next to him like a series of interlocking miniature waterfalls. This was the place where they had taken the rafts out, the portage back in 1992 when he first worked on the Chanul Tzuk Survey project.

He stripped off his clothes and dove into a crystal pool. The water was fresh, and the temperature was perfect.

When he emerged from the pool, he spread his clothes out on the rocks so they would dry quickly, then he stretched out on a smooth rock, warmed by the sun, and dried out. He lay on his back, like a big dog sunning himself. He almost went to sleep, but he heard something faintly over the rapids roaring.

From a distance, he heard a woman singing:

"Dale a tu' cuerpo alegria Macarena.
Que tu cuerpo es pa' darle alegria y cosas buenos…

As he put his clothes back on he saw they were steaming in the sunlight. He jogged down and up, and jumped between the stones on the shore, trying to find her. There she was in a bend in the river, bathing in a pool hollowed out in the limestone bedrock. She was wearing a silver crucifix and nothing else. Shaking her long wet hair back in one graceful arc, catching his eye, and smiling as she sang.

Jesse stopped about twenty yards from her and held up his right hand. "Hola."

"I know who you are. You are the Texan the Professor told me about."
She nonchalantly wrapped a towel around her body and stepped lithely out
of the pool. She was Maya by her accent, and her face could have come
from one of the Classic royal portraits of Palenque; high forehead, aquiline
nose, almond shaped eyes. As he watched her comb the water out of her
hair, Jesse thought she was the most beautiful woman he had ever seen.
He walked over the stones between them until he was standing in front of
her.

"You have me at a disadvantage. I don't know you, but my name is Jesse.
Jesse Salazar. He found himself bowing, like his grandfather.

I never bow. What the hell am I doing?

She extended her hand. "My name is Gloria Hurukan, pleased to meet
you."

"How come I haven't seen you before?"

"Because I'm on my way to meet the professor, I wanted to clean up first."
She gestured at her backpack, guitar case, clothes, and makeup kit on the
riverbank.

"You're carrying all that with you? Isn't it difficult?"

"Not really. I came up by boat from Frontera Corozal this morning."

"How did you know where to meet us?"

"It's a secret."

41 Magical Realism

Hera's Song was four days out of Key West making good time, and
romping toward the coast of Belize, under roller furling jib and Genoa.
The wind pushed her steadily. She was gliding across the Caribbean. In
front of the cabin, Delia was sunning herself, Madeline was asleep in the

salon and Phil and Patty were at the wheel under a canvas awning. Patty took the wheel from Phil and she opened a bottle of Red Stripe Beer.

"So you're thinking about?" She squinted over the wheel at him.

"Viet Nam."

"You think a lot about Viet Nam?"

"Trying not to. Lately it's been kind of tough though."

"Phil I can't imagine what you went through over there."

"You know something? It wasn't all bad. I enjoyed being a soldier, sometimes, actually often, I wish I still was." He unrolled a chart on the fold-down table.

"You were a good one. I remember when you came back from your first tour…"

"Let's talk about something else, okay? No offense but that first tour is something I don't want to think about right now."

"Okay. Then what happened at Harvard really? I'm having a hard time accepting it."

"So am I. God, I don't know. It felt like it was choreographed. Like I was following a script."

"How?"

"I'm not sure yet. I'm still trying to work it out." Phil looked at the chart, while Patty reached for the sunscreen. There was something else she wanted to address with her brother, and she could think of no other way, except to plunge right in.

"You know Phillip, I think it's terrible the way you've been treating Delia."

"What do you mean?" He was surprised by the change of subject, but Patty often did that to him.

"You know what I mean. The way you seem to avoid talking to her, and when you do it's in brief, little bullet sentences. Don't you like her?" Patty smiled quizzically.

"Like her? Sure. She's a good kid. I'm just a little preoccupied with other matters, plotting courses, planning ahead. Then there's the whole unresolved issue of Belinda." Phil shrugged. "By the way, this is one sweet sailing yacht, I've always liked Island Packets, and the cream colored gel paint is easy on your eyes out here. Really cuts down on the glare."

"Thanks, I'm rather fond of her myself."

"And this raised seat here just aft of the wheel gives you great visibility to port and starboard."

"We were talking about Delia, nice deflection attempt though." Patty grinned at him.

"You were talking about Delia. I'm talking and thinking about the mission, our course, and our provisions. Just trying to be prepared."

"Really? You know I've sailed these waters seven or eight times, and of course I appreciate your help, I really do…"

"Am I getting in your way?" Phil squinted at his sister.

"No. Well, yes a bit, but I don't mind, I think you're over planning a little, maybe."

"Proper planning prevents poor performance. That was the motto of Charlie Company, and I believe in it." Phil shrugged and downed about half of his beer.

"There is something about going to sea. A little bit of discipline, self-discipline and humility are required." Patty smiled and adjusted the wheel. "Prince Andrew, the Duke of York, said that."

"Friend of yours?" Phil grinned at his sister.

"An acquaintance. I met him last year at a high-toned fund-raiser at The Breakers, in West Palm Beach."

"So your message to me is?"

"Take a break, go forward, and talk to Delia. She's a good person."

"Aye. Aye Skipper." Phil chuckled and made his way forward.

Patty watched him, and was half-tempted to swerve the bow, and make him fall down, but resisted the temptation. I'm almost fifty years old, she thought, and I still like to mess with my little brother. Guess I'll never grow up.

Delia was wearing a modest white two-piece bathing suit, reclining on a beach towel against the front of the cabin, near the bowsprit. When she saw Phil approaching she put her book down, and smiled up at him. Phil sat down next to her, picked up the book and read the title.

"The Dark Romance of Diane Fossey. How is it?"

"Intriguing. I see something of myself in her."

"How so?"

"Oh, I'm also a bit obsessed with my work, my career. Lately like her, I've been something of a recluse."

"Really?" Phil felt awkward all of a sudden.

"It's no big deal." Delia shrugged and looked off at the horizon.

Phil sat down next to her, and put the book down. "You know I read somewhere that Fossey preferred the company of the mountain gorillas to that of humans."

Delia moved over so Phil could have room to lean back. "Can you blame her?"

"Not at all. There are a lot of people who aren't as well behaved as gorillas. Did you ever want to be a primatologist?"

"When I was an undergraduate at Yale, there was a woman there, a primatologist; she studied langurs in India."

"Sarah Hrdy?"

"Well yes as a matter of fact. She almost converted me."

"Like Jane Goodall. You're a lot better looking though."

Delia couldn't help but laugh. "Thank you. Yes I considered it, but I was turned by the force of archaeology."

"Thank God." Phil chuckled. "Or else you might be running around with a bunch of apes right now. Oh, you kind of, um…"

"Are?"

"Exactly."

Delia smiled and stretched out. Neither of them said anything for several minutes. They just listened to the ocean whispering underneath the bow and the wind billow the sails. It was a timeless moment.

"That was really nice." Delia said softly.

"Not talking?" Phil whispered.

"Yes." She sighed. "Most people think silences are awkward."

"But not us." Phil nodded, as the ocean spray whipped up off the bow.

"Not us." Delia nodded. They felt the wind building and the boat picking up speed. "God Phil, it's like we're skating across the water. I didn't know sailing could be so soothing. This is fantastic."

"Patty's got her in the groove now. My sister is a hell of a sailor. Listen."

The bow knifed through the water hissing softly. The balance between wind and water was perfect.

Tears welled in Delia's eyes. Phil noticed goose bumps on her skin. She shivered.

"Delia, are you okay?"

"Oh Phil. It's all just so beautiful." She sighed.

Phil gently put his arm around her shoulder and held her tight.

They sat there like that for a long time.

At the helm, Patty smiled to herself.

* * * * * * * *

It was midnight; Phil was at the helm as his watch began. Everyone else was asleep below. The wind stayed steady, and the boat hummed across the sea. He saw a light come on and go out in the main salon. Delia came out of the cabin passageway.

"I couldn't sleep. Want some company?"

"Sure. Pull up a chair."

Delia sat across from him, on a bench against the bulkhead. She looked up at the night sky. "God. Look at all the stars. The Pleiades are in close tonight."

"Just a beautiful night, all around."

"The sky is really black out here. Look. Scorpio is starting its crawl across the Milky Way." Delia stretched and yawned.

"The Cosmic Serpent of the Maya. The moon will be up in a bit."

"Can you see okay? I mean ahead of us?"

"You mean can I keep us from hitting something?" Phil grinned at her.

"Well now that you mention it."

"Nothing much out there from here to Ambergris Cay. Although you never know." He knocked on the wooden wheel.

"So you're not worried then." She shrugged and stretched her arms out, yawning. "Well if you're not going to worry than I won't."

"What I worry about are the things I can't see. That I know could be out there."

"Such as?"

"Probably the biggest danger is a loose container. You could be romping along like we are now, and just slam right in to one. One of the racing yachts hit one a few years ago, and she sank quickly. Ripped her bow off."

"A container?"

"Yes. Those ocean going, corrugated steel trailers? Eighteen wheelers and trains haul them on land. On the sea, they stack them up on container ships, on the deck after they fill up the hold. These containers occasionally break off in a storm, and go overboard. Then they float below the water's surface. More and more often boats plow into them, and sink."

"I wouldn't think there would be that many of them out there."

"They're estimated to number in the thousands."

"How can that be?"

"Think about the thousands of container ships at sea at any given time, more every year. How many containers have to fall off each year, say over the last thirty years?"

"I see. It's not something I want to think about right now."

"Sorry. You know it's just another symptom of a much larger problem."

"What?" Delia visualized an ocean full of lurking containers floating just below the water line.

"There's just too damned many people on the planet. They've torn up the land and fouled the seas. And no one really seems to give a damn."

Delia knew she had stumbled on to a topic that Phil felt passionate about, but it made her uneasy to hear him speak so harshly. Still, she wanted to get to know him better, so she said, "Well you and I both know what evolutionary ecology has shown about what happens to a species that overtaxes its own environment."

"Certain population adjustments, downward adjustments occur, as other natural systems respond. In other words, the species dies off in large numbers, until it reaches an evolutionary stable state, or expires."

"Do you think that will happen to us?"

"Good question. I used to think so. I was involved in a major downward population adjustment in Southeast Asia twenty four years ago." Pausing to adjust a line, Phil cranked it up taut.

"You never talk about that."

"Lately I've been thinking about it more. You don't really want to know what that was like. There's no way I could explain it anyway. No useful purpose in trying."

He could feel the old memories stirring, and consciously fought to repress them, because they scared him, the cold terrors of his youth.

"But you carry it around forever." She said softly.

225

In spite of his best efforts to suppress them, death and violence were creeping in from the edge of his memory. Picking up the weapons a couple of weeks ago had done it probably, opened up some of the old memory channels he had blocked off years ago. He didn't hear what Delia was saying. He needed to concentrate on being here now, in the present.

"What Delia?"

"I said I've only read about it, I was born during those years, 1967. I've read about it, seen movies, documentaries, but it seems so long ago..."

"It was long ago, over the hills and far away..."

They both were silent and listened to the night wind high in the sails. Delia spoke first. "You know the police Lieutenant read one of your Navy Cross citations to us."

Phil looked over at her abruptly, "What? He did? To who else besides you?"

"Madeline. I could tell the lieutenant admired and respected what you did. He said as much, but..."

"I wish he hadn't done that."

"Why Phil? It's nothing to be ashamed of."

"Hell I'm not ashamed of it. It's more complicated than that. That's a separate life; it happened to a different person and it's permanently closed. A different world. It's just really hard to explain."

"What you did was very brave, it..."

"No. What I did was survive." His voice had a hard edge. "I survived by turning off some switches inside of me and turning other ones on."

His voice softened, and Delia could tell he was remembering it. She was a little frightened by his mood shift.

"I'll tell you something I've never told anyone else." He sighed and took a deep breath, whispering now. "Pointless random death and violence, brutality, and the unbelievable horror that I saw in the first few months I was there, it all became mundane to me. Routine. I could see things that would terrify and paralyze a civilized man, and it wouldn't even faze me. I would feel nothing. I came up on three dead people in a car wreck, a few years ago down in Mexico. Same thing. When I drove through the slums of Vera Cruz last year, the suffering didn't faze me at all. Seen worse." His voice trailed off.

The paradox that he resented feeling numbed by the world proved to her that he wasn't completely numb. She did not know what to say and offered a pathetic observation, "Well people cope in different ways Phil." He was showing her the side he kept hidden from the world. She was astonished and touched at the same time.

"No. You don't understand. That's what I mean by turning off some switches. Problem is once you turn some of them off; you can't ever turn them back on again. They are gone. Early on, by the time I was in Quang Tri Province, it had all become very complicated and the enemy was nebulous. It got harder and harder to identify the enemy. But see, I came to realize that it really didn't matter." He took another deep breath. "We simplified it. I fought for my friends and they fought for me. No one else gave a damn about us." He turned the wheel slightly to starboard. But gradually they picked us off, by the end of my tour, only me and eight other guys from my original platoon made it back home in one piece."

"Why did you go back a second time, with the Special Operations Group?"

"The lieutenant did go into detail, didn't he?" Phil lit up a thin cigar before answering. "I went back for a little justice. I wanted to pay some folks back. Even up the score a bit."

"And did you?"

"Revenge is definitely a two-way street." He watched the moon emerge on the sea's dark horizon.

227

"Meaning?" Delia now saw that it was a different Phil Ward she was talking to, this one stood straighter, looked bigger, and seemed even more distant than the one she was talking to just ten minutes ago. He seemed transformed in the early moonlight.

"Meaning observe the moon rise, it is magical, and yet it's real." He pointed toward the horizon.

It was beautiful. The scattered puffy white clouds were backlit and glowing around a moon that seemed to lift itself out of the ocean. The wake streaming behind them was phosphorescent as the wind increased.

"You don't want to talk about it anymore. I understand." Delia wanted to lean over and hug him.

"I'll tell you one other thing. Something I rarely admit even to myself. Because it really doesn't matter anymore. But I wish it had all never happened. Viet Nam was a wasteland for everyone involved." He whispered. "Up until then I was just a kid in Kentucky, driving around the Bluegrass in my convertible, chasing those southern belles…" He sighed deeply.

"Would you have chased me?" Delia whispered, surprising herself as she felt his mood relax, and shift again.

Phil paused, and flicked his cigar over the side. He looked at Delia, about six feet away, her hair blowing straight back off her face, leaning against the cabin, with her breasts pushing forward against her sweatshirt, smiling shyly.

"What was the question?" He grinned at her.

Without a word she surprised herself again, by walking over and embracing him.

His skin felt warm against hers, as she placed her forehead against his chest. She reached up and touched his cheek, at this he turned toward her, her face was moving slowly upward, lips parted, eyes almost closed.

He tilted her head up so he could look into her eyes, and wrapped his arms around her. He kissed her with everything he had. As the kiss expanded, he felt her arms slide by his neck and shoulders, and his hands gripped her firmly below her waist.

Surprise gave way to a warm happiness, and then flamed into an inevitable excitement.

42 Brujo

Belinda's memory was a blur and she was sure she had suffered a very severe head injury. It's like my brain went though a Cuisinart and then a blender, I must have had a concussion, she thought as she sat on a plank bench in the hamlet of Santa Theresa. It was composed of nine thatched huts in an acre of partially cleared jungle. The continuous insect hum was electric. She had been there for three weeks. She didn't know exactly where the village was, and had never heard of it before, but this was where the Tzeltal women had brought her when they found her on the rocks by the river.

Her broken legs were stretched out in front of her. They had been smeared with a greasy, white salve, splinted with saplings and bound with string. Only two people in the village spoke Spanish, everyone else spoke Maya. Fortunately for her Domingo Xicaret, the village shaman who preferred to be called a brujo was one of the Spanish speakers. He had been treating her, and explaining his methods as he went. He was doing a good job, because her legs were straight and the bones were setting well.

The bullet wound in her left shoulder was healing up nicely too. Luckily, it had passed through without hitting her clavicle or scapula. The medications he had given her for pain were exceptional, she just felt dull throbbing pains now; nothing like the excruciating hell she had felt when the women had fished her out of the river. Insects had eaten her arms and face while she had been unconscious, but the lotions provided by the brujo were working well. If she lived through this, she would have a major ethno pharmacological study to publish based on what she had learned from Domingo. He had been very interested in teaching her his knowledge of the old Maya ways.

She had given Domingo her stainless steel Rolex watch, for taking care of her. It was all that she had left. Although he had tried several times to refuse it, finally he had accepted it and had offered care, protection, and when it was safe, promised he would get her out of Mexico. For now he was convinced that the gods had delivered her to him, and he would continue to look after her.

To keep her mind sharp, and to leave a record in case she didn't make it, she had acquired a pad of lined paper and some pencils, and was recording what she had learned from the Shaman. Because of her intense headaches, she believed she had not fully recovered from the concussion. Images came back in fragments, out of sequence. Sometimes her mind just blanked out and she knew that some time had passed, but she had no idea just how much time, it was very disconcerting.

Still, she thought, it's a miracle that I'm alive. She prayed every day now, thanking God for saving her.

Putting her notes down, Belinda thought hard, and tried to remember how long she had lain there on the riverbank. She remembered looking up into the eyes of a vulture, but that might have been a dream. She was told that she had been found unconscious on the riverbank by the Maya women, and brought to Santa Theresa, on a litter. Xicaret said that when he saw her that first morning, she was in the hands of *Kisin*, the Lord of Death, and if no one had found her she would certainly have died within a few hours. Belinda figured she had been found one or two days after Alex had shot her, but had no memory of anything until she regained consciousness that evening in Santa Theresa. Looking at her notes, she remembered how afraid she had been, and shuddered. The other thing that frightened her was that Xicaret said some rough-looking men were in the area looking for her all last week. Their leader's name was Alex and Domingo said he was a powerful brujo.

43 San Cristóbal

Jesse and Gloria lunched together, sitting on a log outside of San Cristóbal de Las Casas, while Garcia and other EZLN leaders met with several local Maya chiefs. It was an important meeting Jesse gathered, because the

Professor had seemed preoccupied and worried in the days leading up to it. The men were running out of food and supplies. Jesse had planned on leaving the group, and would have already left, but Gloria asked him to stay around a little longer.

"It's not like you eat very much, and you don't take up that much space." She shrugged.

Jesse chuckled, and cleared his throat. "I think I should leave anyway."

"It's up to you. I want you to stay." She smiled. "The Professor likes having you around too."

"I don't know why. I really don't contribute much."

"You work your share. You are the professor's witness."

"Witness?"

"Someone from El Norte who might understand what he sees."

"I understand that this revolution, movement, crusade, whatever it is, is seriously under funded, and underfed. I don't know how the professor keeps it all together. Membership in this group is very fluid, people arrive and leave constantly."

"It's not the only group."

"I gathered."

"Very good. You are being a good witness."

"One thing I don't understand is why the Maya have chosen Emiliano Zapata to be their patron saint. I mean the Mexican army assassinated him in 1919, and as far as I know he operated in the north, mostly in Morelos. He never set foot in Chiapas."

"As far as you know." She said smiling.

231

Jesse shook his head; he was starting to think that Gloria reveled in being an enigma. For the past week, he had made very little progress in getting to know her.

Gloria laughed. "Zapata is important because his demands, the demands of the Zapatista army in 1915 were land to work and democracy. *Tierra y Libertad*. These are the same things we want."

"So how did you get involved with all of this?"

"I studied under the professor at the University..." She halted abruptly.

"What university was that?' Jesse asked.

"I think I'll let the professor tell you. If he wants you to know he will tell you."

Jesse knew he had run into a brick wall, and decided to try another course. "How old were you when you left for school?"

"Eighteen. Why do you always ask so many questions?" She flipped her hair back and drank deeply from her canteen.

"Gloria, I'm just interested in getting to know you. Sorry." Jesse felt his face flush.

She put the canteen down between her legs and seemed to be evaluating him, staring at him with her enormous almond eyes. "Okay. I will give you the short version. My family was forced to move into the Selva Lacandona when I was four. We used to live in Las Margaritas. A rich mapache family, mestizo, ladino whatever you want to call them, to us they were rich landowners; they gradually took everything my parents had, because my parents were in debt to them. They took a piece of land here, a bit there, eventually they had everything. This happens all the time to all the Indians. Nothing very special about it."

"So we moved deeper into the valley, my parents, me and my two little brothers. The only way you could get there was on foot or horseback. No roads went there in those days. But we needed money, so my father, like so many other fathers went to El Norte to get work. He found a job in San

Antonio, working as a mechanic, and began to send money back to my mother. This went on for about a year, and then nothing. Nothing. My mother was afraid he had taken up with another woman, but it was much worse than that." She took a deep breath and looked up at the sky before continuing.

"He was found dead in an alley off South Zarzamora Street. No money. No identification. He had been robbed and stabbed three times. It took them weeks to find out who he was. Of course the San Antonio police never found out who did it. Just another dead mojado as far as they were concerned. But he was my father."

Jesse absorbed her story, stunned, thinking about the gulf between them. He knew exactly where Zarzamora Street was. He had two cousins on the San Antonio police force, and another first cousin who was county court clerk, but he was not going to tell Gloria she was wrong. He knew she was right. The American inside of him was ashamed and sorry. The Mexican inside of him was angry. He said nothing as his two selves strangled each other.

"So after that we moved back to Las Margaritas. My mother got a job as a servant for the richest family in town. My brothers and I helped her with the laundry, carrying wood, clearing land. And my mother became his mistress, although he had a wife already, but..." her voice trailed off, and she began picking up the remains of their lunch, orange peels, egg shells, and corn husks. She was looking down at the ground as she spoke.

"Anyway, when I was fourteen, I became his mistress too." She paused and looked at him with her eyes narrowed. "In secret. If I told my mother, he would kick us all out on the street. So I told no one. I got very good at keeping secrets. He taught me English and made me go to school. He was a very educated man, an engineer."

She idly dug a trench in the dirt with the heel of her shoe.

"But when I was almost sixteen I became pregnant. So there could be no more secrets. We left with what we could carry and moved back to the valley. My brothers were big enough to help in the fields by then." In a rush, she finished her story. "And I went to the university and met the

Professor, and the rest you know. That's it. All done." She looked up and stared at him blankly.

"And the baby?" Jesse was afraid to ask.

"I lost the baby on the trail to the valley. Miscarriage."

"I'm sorry Gloria."

"I'm not."

44 Moonlight

The moonlight on the water was sensuous. Phil caressed her softly and gently, prolonging her anticipation, which was almost unbearable. He lightly raked his fingers down the small of her back, and there was a tingling in the pit of her stomach. He radiated a vitality that drew her in like a magnet. She shuddered as he removed her bathing suit, and she was naked.

They made love on the deck, against the bulkhead, on the captain's chair against the wheel, and after Madeline came to take over her watch, they went downstairs and made love again on Phil's bed. They had broken a lamp on Phil's nightstand. Now resting in his bed, her back against his chest, with his arm around her belly, they were like spoons.

Happy and a little sore, Delia felt changed. Her feelings toward Phil were conflicted and swimming off in all directions. She couldn't believe she had unprotected sex, not just once, but three times in about four hours. She did not do things like that, what if she got pregnant? Simultaneously, she was excited about how things had developed, but felt guilty because Belinda was her best friend. And how did he feel? Did Phil just want to get laid? And what about Belinda? Things had become very complicated.

Phil's arm tightened gently around her waist and he whispered. "Don't worry you've done nothing wrong."

"How did you know what I was thinking?" Delia whispered back relaxing against the weight of his body.

"I could feel it for a minute. Tension. Everything is all right. It's great to be alive. I'm just floating here. It would be okay to die right now, that's how good I feel."

Delia smiled and relaxed some more. Then the anxiety came clawing back up.

"But what about Belinda, I mean, I know at least I think it's possible that you're still a little in love with her. Are you?"

Phil paused before answering. "Am I? I don't know for sure. Like I told you though, it's over between us. She ended it."

"But if, when, you see her again?"

"You don't have anything to worry about." He gently stroked her hair, it felt good.

"Why? Why don't I have anything to worry about?" Delia realized she was very anxious.

He swung her into the circle of his arms, and kissed her neck. "Because Delia, you are fine, and at least you seem to want me."

She rolled over, locked eyes with him and said. "I've always wanted you."

In seconds they were at it again.

45 Causal Generators

"Theories of a disgruntled student, an occult fanatic, a homosexual lover, a smuggling deal gone sideways, we looked at them all during the course of this investigation." Martin was saying to Mamett as they ate dinner at the Faculty Club.

"And?" Mamett asked as he lifted his glass of Merlot.

"And…" Martin shook his head. "And there are still some aspects of this case that I don't like."

"Such as?"

"Well you know I've got this nice and tidy suicide confession on a laptop computer. That is something new. I've never had one of those before. The alleged perpetrator of the murder of Laurence Eikelmann has confessed, and is dead. Things have died with him. The police departments in four different jurisdictions are satisfied. The whole story has moved out of the newspapers, now that it's been what? Two weeks since they cremated Professor Thomas? I've got a backlog of cases I'm catching up on. No more archaeologists have vanished or died. It's safe to walk the streets of Harvard Square again. The pressure is off, I should be happy." He folded up his napkin, and pushed away his plate.

"You are going somewhere with this." Mamett smiled.

"Where I'm going is this. Anyone could have typed that letter on that computer. Thomas could have been shot in the head at very close range, and the whole thing could have been a homicide staged to look like a suicide, and the trouble is, there's no way to prove it one way or the other."

"Forensics? Powder burns?"

"Inconclusive. But get this. The combined departmental press releases tell the public that everything is cut and dried. Crime is solved. Nothing to worry about anymore. It seems like all the departments, in Somerville, Cambridge, Boston and Harvard want to forget the whole thing, which is fine with me. But Kathryn Haden vanished from the face of the earth. She's still missing. Belinda Boothe is still a missing person, with the Cambridge police plodding along in their investigation." He snorted before continuing. "Some Mexican guy tried to kill Professor Prefontaine. Who was he? What about the art smuggling ring? Phil Ward is apparently a fugitive. And Delia's gone."

"Well she's on an authorized leave of absence, a vacation. I thought you knew?"

"I heard that. But have you talked to her lately?"

"No. I missed her phone call. But other people have talked to her."

"Okay, so everything should be wrapped up nice and neat."

"But?" Mamett could see the obvious confusion and frustration in Martin's face.

"But I can't let it go." Martin crossed his arms over his chest, and looked down at the remains of his dinner. "There are a lot of loose ends. Hell. It could be the whole thing is just one big ball of loose ends. It could be that nothing has been solved."

"Why do you think these other cases are related?" Mamett asked and signaled for another bottle of wine.

"Why do you think they aren't?" Martin responded.

"Let me clarify my position. Causal relationships are what we constantly seek when we conduct archaeological research. Why did the Maya civilization collapse? Why did it rise to begin with? What are the primary and secondary causal generators? I'm playing devil's advocate with you, the same as I would with a fellow archaeologist who has a pet theory."

"So continue your advocating. Identify some causal generators." Martin said and refilled his wineglass.

"Okay. I'll try. Allow me to approach it as an archaeological problem, chronologically. First, Kathryn Haden disappears at Chanul Tzuk, towards the end of August. A month or so later Phil Ward leaves Cambridge to go where?"

"He was last reported in Fort Lauderdale. Three weeks ago. Nothing since."

"Okay. So how could those two events be linked? I can see no obvious connection. Ward's termination from our graduate program is in no way linked to Haden's disappearance. As for Belinda, I still think she's just out of pocket somewhere in the Peten. Phones are few and far between down there. She'll be checking in soon I suspect."

"Well there are some things you don't know Professor."

"Such as?"

"I suppose I can tell you now that the case is officially suspended. But keep it to yourself please."

Mamett nodded his assent.

"One. There is evidence that places Ward in Mexico at the time of Haden's disappearance."

"I can't believe that. What evidence?" Mamett put his wine glass down.

"Circumstantial at best. The other things are well…you know about the ceramic pots checked out on his ID, in Eikelmann's ceiling, but what you don't know is that he was implicated in the suicide note."

"Samuel Thomas implicated Phil Ward? I didn't read that in the papers."

"If Thomas wrote that note. Yeah. We kept that out of the papers. Another thing we kept out was he said he was suffering from a disease. The autopsy results were negative, they checked for everything from AIDS to cirrhosis of the liver. Nothing turned up."

"Something psychological, neurological?"

"There's no evidence. Nothing in his medical records either. That may not be true at all, because he may not have written the note. Of course there's the possibility that he may have had another doctor that we don't know about, but…"

"Interesting." Mamett said and stroked his beard. "Then if the note is fraudulent?"

"Someone would obviously be trying to frame Ward."

"And if the note is genuine?"

"Ward's up to his eyeballs in it."

Neither of them spoke for a minute. Martin watched Mamett consider what he had just told him. He had really come to appreciate the Professor as one of the smartest men he had ever met.

Mamett broke his reverie and reached for his wine. "I begin to see why you are not satisfied. Let's consider Samuel, if he was involved in stealing artifacts from the museum, he was totally mad. But he never exhibited any behavior indicative of that."

"Possibly Laurence was the instigator?" Martin asked.

"Possibly. But why?" Mamett took a sip of water.

"If he was of the hacker mentality, he may not have had any other motive than thumbing his nose at Harvard." Martin suggested. "What about money? If they were making big money their bank accounts show no evidence of it. Of course they may have had secret accounts offshore. I'm still looking into that. But I've heard all kinds of estimates about how much those pots could be worth."

"A round figure of fifty thousand dollars per pot is a conservative estimate."

"So say one hundred thousand dollars. Have you found any other artifacts or pots missing? I mean besides the blood letter?"

"Well you know that is an interesting problem, what with the computer dead, we've had to move slowly, but so far, no other thefts have been detected. We're certain also, that the blood letter itself, is not from our collections."

"So where did it come from?"

"I have no idea. It may have been looted for all we can tell now. It certainly hasn't been reported or described in the literature, or I would have remembered it."

"Looted, huh? Then how did it wind up stuck in Laurence?"

"Well, in the circles they were supposedly traveling in, the art collectors are only two degrees of separation from the looters." Mamett pushed his plate over to one side.

"So I gather that with that much money at stake, looting is a really big problem, huh?"

"It is estimated to be a ten million dollar a month market just in Guatemala alone and it gets worse every year. Sergio Avendano had a shoot-out with some looters just last month."

"Really? He's back in Mexico now?"

"Yes. He went back a couple of days ago. He's going to be helping me take over Chanul Tzuk."

"So looters are violent, like drug smugglers? Because of the money?"

Mamett nodded. "Many museum collections are suspect. And even within archaeology there is a deep philosophical schism as to whether we should even study artifacts of questionable provenience. It's a complex problem."

"Come again?"

"Looted artifacts. Say the Boston Museum of Fine Arts 'acquires' a beautiful ceramic vessel from Chanul Tzuk. Let's say it's 'donated' by a trustee. I know before I even see it that it was smuggled out of Chiapas, because only the Carnegie Museum, and the University of Oregon, have ever had excavation permits for that site. They obviously could not have donated it, because according to the excavation permits, all artifacts ultimately belong to the Mexican government."

"So there are a lot of looted artifacts in American museums?"

"Thousands. And thousands more are floating around in art galleries, and private collections."

"So why would you want to study looted artifacts, isn't that like aiding and abetting the enemy?" Martin leaned back in his chair.

"That's one point of view Lieutenant. One I tend to agree with in principle, but it's not always that simple. Some Mayanists would argue that all data, no matter what their source, have value."

"How?"

"Glyphic texts are often preserved on looted artifacts. In my opinion, all hieroglyphic data regardless of context are valuable. And I have studied such artifacts in art collections here and in Europe. Certain breakthroughs in our understanding of Maya iconography, and mythology would not have been possible without studying looted artifacts. Take the case of the Grolier Codex for example." Mamett refilled their glasses.

"What's a codex?"

"An illustrated manuscript, made from bark paper, only four are known to have survived the Spanish conquest."

"How much would one of those be worth?"

"Name your price. Hundreds of thousands of dollars, probably a lot more, I have never really thought about it. In any event, in 1966 a Dr. Saenz, who was a wealthy Mexican collector, was informed through clandestine channels that he needed to take a trip to Villahermosa. He was met at the airport and then taken on a small private airplane deep into highland Chiapas. They landed on a dirt airstrip in the middle of the jungle, and a group of huecheros brought an assortment of artifacts to him that they had dug out of a cave. Among them was the codex."

"What's a huechero?"

"Pardon me. It's slang for looter. It's derived from the Maya word for armadillo, because the looters paw through the dirt sometimes with their bare hands."

"So the codex?"

"It was very controversial. Initially, a lot of Mayanists considered it a fake. But radiocarbon dating has proven it genuine, from the early 1200s. It's too important to ignore. It has to be studied. But therein lies the rub, if an archaeologist studies a looted artifact..."

"He helps legitimize looting. It is a complex problem isn't it?" Martin pushed his chair further back and stretched.

"Indeed. Still I can't believe Thomas was... Really, I don't understand any of this. It's all been very difficult for me to accept."

"Yeah. My gut instincts tell me that I don't have anything. But I know what I've got to do. I've got to talk to Ward. I have an Interpol all points bulletin and a federal A.P.B. out on him as well. He's wanted as an accessory, on several different charges. Most of which I trumped up." Martin shrugged.

"You really think he is involved, do you?"

"I don't know. Either he is, or someone is trying very hard to make me believe he is. Either way he needs to be questioned."

"You think he may have left the country?"

"It's possible. Actually it's probable. His sister and her boat are no longer in Fort Lauderdale. He seems to have been one step ahead of the investigation, from the beginning."

"So he could be?"

"Anywhere. If this guy doesn't want to be found. It's going to be tough."

"Why?"

"He's ex-USMC, S.O.G."

"I knew about the Marine part, but what is S.O.G.?"

"Special Operations Group. Specialists in covert operations. If he doesn't want us to find him, we won't."

46 Coast of Belize

There were many shallow areas, reefs, and sandbars to be avoided. The coast of Belize was a very tricky place to navigate which was why it had been a pirate's haven in the seventeenth and eighteenth centuries.

Phil was in the main salon checking the nautical charts of the coast and the cays. And of course, he thought, there are the government boats and checkpoints to be considered. Need to make sure we're nowhere near Mexican waters that would only compound the risk. The best approach would be at sunset. Phil selected a cove north of San Pedro that he had fished years ago, Thompson's Cove. That was where he would get off.

The challenges would be convincing Delia to stay on the boat and then getting ashore alone without attracting any attention from the authorities. He knew she wanted to go with him but that was impossible. The best way for him to infiltrate would be to hail a fishing boat and sneak into the country with the evening's catch. If they failed to encounter any fishing boats then getting into Thompson's Cove would be Plan B. After the tricky part of clearing the reef, it was a good anchorage. It was usually deserted too.

He could go ashore and Patty could go down to San Pedro the next day and clear customs. As he studied the chart, he thought again about his old friend Paul Trevino, who was a fishing guide in San Pedro. If he could get in touch with him, he could line up everything he would need to make it to the mainland and on to Guatemala. Paul knew everyone and every back road, creek, and river, between San Pedro and Melchor de Mencos on the Guatemalan border.

He rolled the chart up as Delia entered the cabin.

"Plotting again?" She sat on his lap, and hugged him.

"In more ways than one Delia."

"What do you mean?"

"I mean we're going to be off the coast of Belize tomorrow and…" This was going to be hard he thought. He had been putting it off for a couple of days now.

"And what?" She looked intently into his eyes.

"And that's when we'll have to split up."

"Like hell we will." She punched him lightly on his chest.

"Delia there's an old Marine Corps saying; 'Life is tough, but it's tougher when you're stupid.'"

"Meaning?"

"Meaning it would be stupid on both our parts to expose you to unnecessary risks."

"Really? Well I have an old saying for you: "Whether thou goest I will go." So forget about it."

"No really. I do this kind of work alone. I travel light and I travel fast, and it could be real dangerous because I can't go through the usual legal channels."

"I'll travel the same way." She put one hand on each side of his face and looked deep into his eyes. "Now listen to me. We're going together Phil. I'm coming with you."

He felt his resolve wavering, as she moved her breasts closer to his chest, and whispered in his ear.

"There are so many ways I could be an asset to you." Now she sat astride him and started kissing his neck. "Don't you think you could use me?"

Phil sighed and pulled her closer. "Right now I don't want to think about anything but this."

He carried her to his cabin and kicked the door closed behind him.

47 Heart Attack

The pain in his left side started out as a light tearing feeling. Martin thought it was either a pulled muscle, or just part of the normal aches and pains he got from being forty seven years old and twenty pounds over weight. Or it could just be heartburn from the Beef Wellington he had eaten for dinner, that and two bottles of wine he and Mamett had put away. Truth was he felt a little light headed and uncomfortable since he didn't drink that much anymore.

"Or maybe it's being stuck in this friggin traffic here on Mass Ave. At this rate I won't get home until midnight." He realized he was breathing heavily. "Calm down Sal. Remember stress is not your friend." He rolled down the window and inhaled the late October evening air. It smelled of burned leaves. He realized that he was hot and sweaty, as the pain stabbed him again sharply and deep inside the left side of his chest this time. He doubled over it hurt so much. Simultaneously his left arm started tingling, as a swiftly spreading numbness climbed up from his fingers to his elbow. The pain in his chest was burning and expanding now, and his eyes watered. He couldn't breathe without it hurting, and now he was panting. Then it dawned on him.

"Jesus Christ. I'm having a heart attack." He turned on the siren and the red lights under his grill, barely able to hold onto the steering wheel. He watched the cars part in front of him and accelerated up Massachusetts Avenue.

Mount Auburn Hospital was three miles away.

48 Ambergris Caye

Hera's Song sailed with the wind off the shore of Ambergris Caye. A low swell took them past the reef and into the shallow waters of the cove.

Patty had handled the situation masterfully. They furled the sails as they entered the cove in silence.

"We'll drop the hook here." Patty said to Phil, who in turn released the anchor.

They felt the anchor catch and *Hera's Song* came to a stop, bobbing gently in the shallow swells. Phil quickly had the zodiac raft over the port side, and loaded his backpack and gun bag onto it. He was focused, and intent on leaving quickly. He and Patty went over the checklist one last time, phone numbers and contact points.

Delia came up from below with a large bag slung over each shoulder. She placed them by the rail, in preparation for lowering them down into the raft.

"Let the record show ladies, that I offered Delia one final opportunity to reconsider going on this part of the trip with me." Phil said in resignation.

"And let the record show that I refused it for the tenth, and final time." Delia replied with great satisfaction.

Madeline and Patty laughed at Phil's discomfort. "I would like to observe that if you didn't take her with you, serious consequences would have resulted." Patty said still laughing.

"Such as?" Phil asked.

"Better that we not discuss them at this time."

"Okay. But remember Delia, the other part of our agreement?" Phil became very serious. "If I think that the situation could potentially put you at risk, you will return to the boat immediately, or make arrangements to be picked up. Right?"

"Right, and without any argument." Delia nodded.

"Okay then." Madeline said, as she helped Delia put her bags in the raft. "Time to get you two ashore."

Phil hugged his sister, who whispered in his ear. "I'll pray for you Phillip, but I know you'll be careful." Phil kissed her on the cheek, then turned and climbed down into the raft. Madeline already had the outboard started. Patty tossed them the bowline, and they turned and headed for the shore.

49 Orange Bleeds into Red

Martin weakly pushed the gearshift lever up into park. He turned off the siren, and slumped down into his seat. The pain was numbing him in his arms and legs. He was so tired; maybe he could just lie down here and rest. He fell over on his right side, and faintly felt hands on his arms and legs. He was being lifted onto a gurney, someone put an oxygen mask to his face, but he knew it was too late.

So this is how it feels to die, he thought.

I'm floating, it's all right, and there's my body down there. My skin is getting darker. Kind of blue. The doctor is injecting Narcan, and it won't work. The defibrillator won't work either. I'm getting lighter. The leaves on the trees are so beautiful in the last light of the day…the way the green fades into orange, the way orange bleeds into red.

50 Palenque

Jesse, Gloria, and Garcia emerged from the forest and walked to the shoulder of the road. They were a few miles outside of New Palestine, an evangelical settlement. Garcia laughed at the name and said, "For years now, Chiapas has been infested with chingos missionaries and anthropologists. I think it's a terminal disease. I've run into a half dozen anthropologists this year alone. God knows how many missionaries."

"Anyone I know?" Jesse asked.

"Do you know anyone at Harvard?"

"A couple of grad students."

"Well you may know them, but I doubt that they would want their names mentioned anymore than you would."

"They were helping you too?"

"Let's just say I prefer anthropologists to missionaries."

"Is that why we're all posing as American anthropologists today?" Jesse looked at them both, wearing T-shirts he had lent them, and wanted to laugh. Gloria's green shirt had the University of Oregon's crest and insignia on it in raised yellow letters. *Mens Agitat Molem*. Wisdom moves mountains. Garcia had selected a black Ralph Lauren Polo knit. They both look American all right, Jesse thought, and so do I, especially carrying this backpack.

"Well don't you think it would have been harder for us to pass as missionaries?"

Gloria laughed.

"Or we could tell people the truth, and say we are subversivos dedicated to overthrowing the establishment?" Garcia added.

"Anthropologist is fine. At least it's true in my case."

"Well you're one of the good ones. An archaeologist at least hires people, pays them a fair wage, and doesn't patronize them." Gloria said.

"Well no offense but archaeology has been bad too." Garcia said as they walked down the shoulder of the road. "True story. On top of the volcano San Martin Pajapan, an Olmec sculpture of the Maize God stood for three thousand years." Garcia wiped his forehead, in the humid morning heat. "In 1968 it was removed and taken to a museum in Vera Cruz. Ever since its removal rains have fallen off, the land has dried up, and crops are a

248

fraction of what they were. Of course the cattle ranchers moved in and the Indians moved out."

"And you think this happened because some archaeologists moved a statue?" Jesse asked in disbelief.

"It does not matter what I think. The Nahua villagers believe it is why they lost their milpas. They do not think archaeologists are their friends."

"The old gods should be left alone." Gloria was saying as a truck came over a hill, and they waved at it. Covered in dust and mud, with a huge painting of Our Lady of Guadeloupe half covering the hood, it drove a little past them and stopped.

Jesse jogged up to the window. Inside the ancient F150 were three Indian teenagers. They were headed for San Cristobal and were agreeable to providing the anthropologists a ride to Palenque. They climbed into the truck bed, as Jesse nodded towards the hood.

"Wherever I go I see the Virgin of Guadeloupe, from San Antonio to Chiapas. She is one popular lady. It's like seeing a piece of home down here."

"A lot of people down here call her Tonantzin, after the place where Diego had his vision." Gloria said. "But my people call her Ix Chel."

Jesse nodded and said, "The Goddess of the moon and water."

Gloria grinned, "You are very smart for an archaeologist."

"Anthropologist. He's very smart for an anthropologist." Garcia joked. They all laughed as the truck slowly negotiated the deep ruts, potholes and boulders in the road. Soon the forests on both sides were replaced, by burnt and barren stretches of black stumps and shattered trees. A dirty beige powder covered the grasses, logs and stumps for over a hundred yards on both sides of the road.

"What happened?" Jesse asked Gloria.

"After the government built this logging road, which is now called *La Ruta Maya*, the Indians came in to plant their crops. They burned the fields in the spring, which is traditionally just before the wet season starts, but a few years ago the wet season started late. Very late. The fires got out of control."

The truck accelerated and threw up so much dust, it choked them. Garcia pulled his shirt up to cover his mouth and nose. Jesse and Gloria followed his example. Villages surrounded by dead cornfields punctuated the desolate landscape. They all looked alike and had similar names, Nuevo Monterey, Nuevo Tampico. A mélange of tin roofs, corrugated plastic roofs, plank walls, and dirt floors passed by. One large ranch estate went along both sides of the road; cattle grazed in expansive pastures, a security fence and guardhouse flanked the entrance.

Garcia nodded toward the well-maintained estate. "A rich cacique. Why do some men have so much, when others have so little?"

A group of Lacandón Maya walked quickly into the forest, as the truck approached. Their distinctive white tunics faded from view. Jesse nodded toward them. "Lacandónes."

"Without question, the most anthropologically documented Maya in existence." Garcia said. "Do you know there are only two hundred or so of them left, but because of the public relations campaign carried out by American anthropologists, they have acquired exclusive timber rights here in the Montes Azules bioreserve?" He said resentfully. "They have displaced the colonias of campesinos and Tzeltal Maya that were already here. They all have satellite television now." He shook his head. "Another brilliant government policy."

More forests, and more ejidos and milpas went by. The smell of human waste, urine, diesel and gasoline permeated the air, as the truck stopped at a tienda in Nuevo Guerrero, and everyone got out. Several trucks were in a jumble on the barren ground in front of it. "Watch yourself around here." Garcia whispered before they climbed out.

Jesse was surprised to hear Tejano music playing from inside. It was a woman's voice, a singer he recognized from San Antonio, Lydia Mendoza.

"Esté amor apasionadoanda todo alborotado por volver;"

"That is my mother's favorite song." Gloria sang softly along with Lydia Mendoza.

She was surprised when Jesse joined in.

...a tus brazos otra vez,
quiero volver, volver, volver.

A sign in faded white letters, La Sepultura hung above the door next to a crude Coca-Cola sign. "I see we have a bartender with a morbid sense of humor," Jesse whispered to Gloria.

She smiled and said, "Does that mean the name of this place is "The Grave of Coca Cola?"

"Maybe they only have Pepsi?"

"How appropriate." Garcia observed. "Since tomorrow is Halloween, and the next day is Todos Santos. Sunday is El Dia de los Muertos."

The bar was decorated in paper mache skeletons, skulls, and coffins, which were crammed into every available space. The three of them bought a round of cokes, while the driver and his compadres ordered beers.

"We'll probably be in Palenque by noon. Excuse me for a minute." Garcia got up and walked out into the parking lot. They saw him go out to the right, and disappear from view.

Jesse looked over at Gloria who was finishing her coke. "He seems preoccupied this morning." He nodded toward Garcia.

"He is. We have very important business in Palenque this afternoon."

"Can I help in anyway?"

"It is possible." She smiled at him.

"I have got to call my father as soon as I can find a telephone. He's going to be really pissed off, because I haven't checked in, in awhile."

Gloria laughed. "So what are you going to tell him? Sorry dad, I've been running around in the jungle with Indians, trying to start a revolution, and I lost all track of time?"

"Now that's an original approach. Maybe I'll try it." They both laughed.

"You know Jesse; you're really starting to fit in down here. Sometimes I forget you are from Texas."

"I'll take that as a compliment."

"It's meant as one."

"Still, I can't forget it. I'm constantly reminded of my otherness. Wherever I go it seems like everyone is looking at me too."

Gloria laughed. "You don't know why?"

"No. What's so funny about that?"

"Hombre. You are one of the biggest Mexicans I've ever seen. How tall are you?"

"Almost six foot four."

"Wow. Anyone else in your family that big?"

"My father is about six three. Why?"

"No reason. Like you said, just trying to get to know you. So how long has your family lived in San Antonio?"

"My mother's side goes back to the mission days, the 1700's."

"Indios?"

"Yes. Coahuilteca, but later mixed with Canary Islanders. Salazar is originally Moorish. So we've always been outsiders."

"And your father?"

"His family came up from Monterey in 1915."

"Fleeing the revolution."

"Yes."

"And now here you are in the middle of another one."

"Well. Like I said, it doesn't look like much of a revolution to me."

"It will, before too long." She became solemn and quiet.

Garcia came back and sat down next to them, picked up his coke and drained it.

"I saw someone in the parking lot I know. He just came from Palenque. I may need to change my plans this afternoon. Jesse, I wonder if I could ask you to pick up a package for me at the Hotel Ruinas? We could meet afterwards at the main entrance to the site."

"Sure. Just pick up a package that's it?"

"Yes. They'll have it at the desk under my name."

"No problem."

"It is very important to me; I would very much appreciate it if you could do it, although our plans could change again."

The driver and his companions stood up, and nodded toward the truck.

Garcia stood and said, "Vámonos, my fellow anthropologists. Palenque awaits us."

* * * * * * * *

Another hotel was being built on the outskirts of Palenque, and the construction vehicles had torn up the road even worse. Jesse thought about how sad it was that the great Maya capitol was fast becoming a major tourist attraction. To him, Palenque in its remote setting on a hilltop overlooking the coastal plain was synonymous with solitude and spirituality. Now it was endangered.

Jesse walked up the street to the Hotel Ruinas to pick up the package. He entered the lobby, and noticed the cracked tiles on the floor, water stains on the wall, and threadbare furniture. It smelled of mildew, in conflict with ammonia. He walked over to the concierge, who leaned against the elevated mahogany desk, reading a magazine.

"Buenos Dias Señor."

"Buenos Dias. Can I help you?" He put the magazine down.

"I am here to pick up a package for Professor Garcia."

"Just a minute please." He walked into a closet behind the desk. Jesse could hear him moving boxes around. He felt like he was being watched, and surveyed the lobby behind him. It was completely empty.

"Here Señor." The concierge emerged from the closet. "It has been here for over a week, that's why I had to dig it out." He placed it on the desk in front of Jesse. It was a cardboard box, wrapped in duct tape. "Garcia" had been written in red felt ink, in the lower right corner. A business card was taped to the upper left corner.

"Thank you. Do I have to sign a receipt or anything?"

"No, the instructions were that someone would come to claim it, and that I should give it to whoever showed up."

"Gracias."

"Adios."

On the steps in front of the hotel, Jesse stopped to read the business card. It read Bianci Imports, Ltd, 3069 Avenida de Guerrrero, Villahermosa, and Tabasco. Bianci also had offices in New York, Houston and Los Angeles. No postage, so it had been handled privately.

Wonder what's in here? He thought. It feels fairly bulky, books? Probably books. The sun was an excruciating blaze out in the open street, and the humidity was heavy. He sat the box down on the sidewalk, and dug out his beat up A&M baseball cap from his backpack. After he put his hat on he continued up the street toward the ruins. From an alley beside the hotel he heard footsteps echo. He glanced over his shoulder and saw three medium sized men, and their larger, more powerfully built leader, coming up the street behind him. They were all wearing white Guyabera shirts, khakis and mirrored sunglasses, like a uniform. To see if they were following him, he quickly crossed the street, and two of them crossed over, hanging back about a block.

Now that he knew he was being followed, he tried to stay calm, and think of how he could elude them.

Casually he set the box down; kneeling to retie his shoe laces, and tighten the shoulder straps on his backpack. The two men on his side of the street suddenly seemed to be interested in a Volkswagen parked in front of a tienda. The two on the other side of the street continued to close the gap.

Jesse stood slowly, stretched his arms, bent down to scoop up the box, and tucking it under his arm like a football, ran full speed straight up the street toward Palenque. There were few people out in the sun, and he had a reasonably clear path. The ruins were about a mile away.

He glanced back over his shoulder, and saw that the two men on his side of the street were walking quickly, chasing him, while trying not to look like they were. There was no sign of their partners. He had a big lead, and concentrated on running as hard as he could, just to leave them behind. He stretched out his legs, and breathed deeply and evenly, knowing that they could not catch him. He was outside of the town now and spotted a path to his left heading off into the trees. He took it. In less than a minute he was in primary forest. He ran deep into it and came to a low limestone retaining wall.

Soaked in sweat and stopping to catch his breath, he looked back down the forest path.

No one was coming.

He jogged deeper into the woods until he was in the archaeological site. Looming up in a clearing ahead of him was one of the numerous unexcavated pyramids that ringed Palenque's periphery. About fifty yards further ahead he could see four of the mounds belonging to the North Group. He would have to backtrack through the west side of the site to meet up with Garcia and Gloria. Emerging from the vegetation near the North Group, he joined a line of tourists and walked through the plaza with them, using them as a screen to see if he was still being followed. No one came out of the woods. As they approached The Palace with its graceful lattices of stucco and limestone, he broke off and looped back toward the main entrance wishing he had time to see the site properly.

The path to the entrance was a narrow swath through the forest that curved and followed a dry streambed for about two hundred yards. He was alone as he walked through the forest, no tourists anywhere. The insect hum was like a jolt it was so loud. This was where all of the insects came to escape the mid day sun. Gnats and mosquitoes swarmed around his face, and he waved his hands to ward them off. He could feel them landing on his shoulders and swatted them with his hat. His shirt was soaked through with sweat and seemed to be attracting larger portions of the insect population. The further he went down the path the worse the insects got, which is why he didn't see or hear his pursuer until it was too late.

"Alto. Stop right there." The voice was behind him, a hoarse whisper, to the right. "Don't move until I tell you." He was wheezing trying to catch his breath. "I have a gun... pointed at your head."

Jesse froze in midstep.

"Very good. If you can continue to follow instructions, maybe I won't have to kill you. Now, turn to your right, and walk into the forest."

Jesse recognized one of the men from the street; he held a pistol in his right hand. He was still gasping for breath.

"Vámonos. Keep moving. I'll tell you when to stop."

Jesse walked carefully through the weeds and brush, further back into the forest. He could still hear the guy panting. Apparently, I almost ran his legs off, Jesse thought, now what do I do?

Jesse tripped over a fallen tree trunk, and stopped to gain his balance.

"Keep moving I said." They were closer now.

"It's hard to keep my balance, and hold this box."

"Shut up! Sit the box down, and move away from it, slowly."

Jesse moved his feet wide apart and bent over like a football center to sit the box down, which is when the idea came to him. He looked between his legs and saw that the guy was less than ten feet behind him, and in one continuous motion hiked the box through his legs, and pivoted around to his right.

Knocked off balance, his attacker was down on his side. The pistol was digging a hole in the ground, as he tried to get up. Jesse jumped on him, and wrenched the gun out of his hand. He heard a rip, as a knife appeared in his attacker's left hand, and the man slashed a hole in Jesse's backpack. Without thinking, Jesse hit him hard in the face with the pistol. He heard a cracking sound, and the man went limp.

Shaking and shivering from the adrenaline pumping through his blood, Jesse slowly stood up, wondering if he had killed him. He picked up the pistol; a brand new Glock 9.0 millimeter. He set the safety, idly cleared dirt out of the barrel, and studied his attacker, who was still breathing, but out cold. His nose was disjointed and bleeding. Jesse stuck the pistol in his belt, bent down, and scooped up the knife; a wicked looking hunter's knife with a straight six-inch blade set in a bone handle. He kept the knife in his right hand, and rolled the man over on his stomach. He was like Jell-O. He wouldn't wake up for a long time.

Jesse took the man's wallet from his back pocket, and started back the way he came. Idly rummaging through it, he felt something hard and metallic;

a police badge. His attacker was named Jaime Ortega; a Judicial Federal police officer from Chiapas.

Jesse had broken a federale's nose and knocked him out.

* * * * * * * *

Garcia and Gloria were waiting in the shade, sitting on a bench by the entrance hut and drinking cokes when Jesse walked up behind them. They didn't see him approach because they expected him to come through the entrance. He set the box down on the bench, and said.

"Sorry I'm late. I ran into a little trouble." He rotated his shoulders and stretched his arms.

"Are you okay?" Gloria asked.

"I'm fine, but there's a man back there about two hundred yards with a hell of a head ache." Garcia's eyes widened. "I took this off of him." Jesse opened his hand and showed them the police badge. "Professor. You want to tell me what's going on? What kind of crap am I in now?"

"I will Jesse. Are there any more of these men around?"

"There's at least three more, between here and town."

"So they are all to the west and north?"

"Right."

"Then we'll head south and east. Let's go."

"First tell me one thing. What's in the box?"

"Aside from a bunch of old paperbacks, twenty thousand U.S. dollars. Now let's move."

* * * * * * *

"Mira. Look. Our enemies have weapons. We have to have weapons. Weapons cost money. This money came from a new source in El Norte, from Long Island, New York. Somewhere along the line, somehow, our enemies learned of it. That is a big problem now." Garcia said as they made their way down the slopes of Palenque back toward La Ruta Maya.

"Where does the money come from?"

"Various sources. This one was from a new sympathizer. I know very little about him. He's a referral, and none of us use our real names."

"Is that why you sent me to pick up the box?"

"Yes. I had to know if we had been compromised. And we have been." Garcia said ruefully.

"So I was a guinea pig, a sacrifice?"

"Jesse. Let's say you had been caught. What would have happened? You would have been held, interrogated, and released because you know nothing. With me passing out a little more money here and there our friends may have released you very quickly. You said you wanted to do more to help? You have done that now. Are you having second thoughts?"

"I think you could have told me what I was walking into."

"I did not know exactly what you were walking into, and if I had voiced my suspicions you would not have acted like an innocent man."

"I'll keep the pistol."

"And the knife. Pretty knife too. I would say you earned them."

"So where do the weapons come from?" Jesse tucked the pistol in his waist.

"Three places. We get a few from our people buying the odd piece here and there. And we do not get many that way. We also buy them from the

259

hired gunmen that work on the ranches. But our best source is the police and the army."

"The police, so that guy I fought..."

"Must be in the network. Right. I have already considered that. You see when the police or the army arrest narcotraficantes, they confiscate their weapons. But they only turn in a few of them. The rest they sell on the black market. That's how we get the good stuff, AK-47s and M-16s. They think we are just another gang of drug traffickers, so they expect to get the weapons back anyway."

"So where to now?"

"Villahermosa. We need to abandon this plan and come up with a new one. We also need to do some shopping."

51 Trevino

Paul Trevino's house outside San Pedro was built out of cement blocks and stucco, with a roof of thatched palm and painted a light orange on the north side, and half of the west wall. The rest was unpainted. He had either run out of paint or interest or both. It was overgrown in wild tangles of bougainvillea and banana trees. An ancient rusted and dented Land Rover was up on blocks in the driveway. It had been there awhile because vegetation was flourishing in the space where the engine used to be. A generic Central American dog was asleep across the doorway, a complex mix of Chihuahua, Beagle, and whatever else was passing through. Delia thought that this one looked as if a blonde Labrador had been involved somewhere, because of the color and the webbed toes. It was very well fed and sleeping soundly. They approached within six feet of it and it still didn't stir.

"Should we wake her?" Delia asked.

"I don't want to step over her. Is she drugged or what?" Phil said chuckling softly.

At the sound of their voices, the dog cocked a floppy ear and opened her eyes. Stretching and tail wagging, she yawned and extended an extremely long pink tongue, speckled with black spots. She offered a friendly "Woof."

"Who is there?" A deep voice from within the house asked. "Nutmeg? Check them out."

Nutmeg came over and gave Delia a cursory sniff, tail wagging the whole time. She ignored Phil.

"Pablo. It's Phil Ward. This is a hell of a mean dog you got here."

"She's only mean to mean people. Phillip Ward! Two years since I saw you last man." He pronounced it "mon". "And who is the pretty lady? Hold on while I get dressed. I'll be right out. Come on in. The screen door is open."

They entered the living room, which was immaculately clean. The concrete floor had straw mats and throw rugs covering it. A wicker couch and chairs were arranged around a Maya rug from Honduras. The back wall was dominated by an enormous blue sailfish, one of the largest Delia had ever seen. The other walls were covered in photographs of people with fish, on boats, and standing beside large sailfish, marlins, and tarpon at the San Pedro pier. A painting of Bob Marley seemed out of place in their midst.

Paul came in wearing just a pair of wrinkled and faded khakis. He was almost six feet tall and blacker than any man she had ever seen. His head was completely shaved and he was powerfully built. He reminded Delia of a heavyweight boxer.

"Excuse me. I've got to find my glasses. We were drinking rum last night and they got away from me." Paul squinted around the living room. Came over and hugged Phil. "Feel the love man. It is all around you. How are you man?"

"I'm great. Paul Trevino, Delia Bell."

Paul bowed and kissed her hand like a courtier. Delia liked him immediately.

"Pleased to meet you." He said softly. "Would you like some coffee?"

"That would be wonderful."

The square house had a kitchen just off the living room and a bedroom to the right.

Delia gathered the bathroom was outside. "Is there somewhere I can wash up?" She asked.

"Sure, the sink is on the back patio and the facility is in the back yard."

"Here they are." Paul fished his steel rim glasses from under a boating magazine on the kitchen table. She heard him and Phil talking about his fishing business as she went out back to the patio.

A large white porcelain sink sat atop two stacks of cement blocks. It was open on the bottom and drained straight onto a gravel pad. It was all very clean. She saw that a plastic wash tub hung from a nail on the outside wall, and she put it in the sink. A large water jug was the rest of the plumbing. Delia started washing up as she heard a radio come on inside.

".... The sugar cane industry remains strong said the Prime Minister. More news on the hour. This is Radio Belize in the heart of the Caribbean basin. Happy All Saints Day to all you ghosts and spirits out there. I hope you didn't get in trouble on Halloween. The local time is eight thirty. Today is November first, and no one is awake yet to hear me. Perhaps the parrots are listening. Perhaps not. The temperature at Belize International Airport is a comfortable sixty-nine degrees Fahrenheit. Sixty-nine degrees. My favorite temperature. This is Alvin Gastineau and in honor of this splendid temperature, here's a little something from marvelous Marvin Gaye, Sexual Healing:"

"Baby I woke up this morning..."

Delia started washing her face, and she felt a tongue on her leg, interrupting her reverie. Nutmeg was licking her calf. She heard Phil say: "Knock knock. Would you like your coffee? Can we come out?"

"Sure. I'm finished. Nutmeg is washing my leg for me."

Phil and Paul came out with coffee mugs. Phil gave one to her. "I had forgotten it was Halloween last night. Paul went to a party in San Pedro, which is why he's moving a little slowly this morning."

Paul grinned at her. His glasses made him look scholarly. He was wearing a new dark blue University of Kentucky T-shirt over his khakis now. He kept pulling it out and looking at it obviously pleased with Phil's gift.

"Was it a costume party?" Delia asked.

"Oh yes."

"What did you go as?"

"A pirate. What else? My ancestors were pirates you know."

A young woman lithe and petite, with long black hair interrupted them. She wore the remains of a mermaid costume as she stumbled through the doorway. She glanced at Phil, mumbled at Paul, smiled shyly at Delia and walked toward the outhouse.

Phil raised his eyebrows, and whispered. "Who is that?"

"She is the light of my life. That is Esmeralda. Esmeralda Quan. I think she is still a little drunk." Paul grinned at them over his cup of coffee.

"She is very pretty." Delia said.

"She is half Maya, half Chinese, and half crazy too." Paul laughed.

"Is she even old enough to drink?" Phil asked.

"Oh that's cold man. She'll be twenty-one on Christmas Eve. She just looks like a baby. I can't believe you man." He chuckled.

"Kind of young for you isn't she Pablo? You're about what? Thirty six?"

"Thirty one man." Paul shook his head, and sat down on a rusted out ice chest.

He grinned up at Phil who was leaning against the doorway. "But you're getting up there now. You turn fifty yet? About time for the nursing home isn't it?"

"Forty two. Bastard." They were both laughing.

"And Delia is probably only what twenty two? You cradle robber."

Delia flushed and said, "I'm twenty six actually."

"Old enough to know better than hang around with this guy." Paul pointed at Phil. "God only knows what he's up to now."

"Well that's what I need to talk to you about Pablo." Phil said.

IV

52 Feast of Death

"Yes I'm sorry. I know it's been over three weeks but I haven't been near any phones."

"I already called the University of Oregon. They didn't know where you were either. You decide to drop out of college and you don't even tell your father!"

"I didn't drop out of school dad. I'm just sitting out a semester."

Jesse's father continued as if he didn't hear him. "I even went downtown to the Mexican Embassy. Those bastards could care less." Mario Salazar was famous for his temper. Someone had flipped him off in traffic on Broadway once, and he had followed them to Brackenridge Park, got out and proceeded to beat their car with a crow bar. It had made the ten o'clock news, Jesse always thought about it when his father got mad.

"I'm sorry dad." That made around ten apologies so far. It was about what Jesse had expected. "It's hard to phone down here."

"I don't care about that. Why haven't you come back? Mario broke into Spanish and went off like a rocket. Jesse decided to let him vent, and said nothing. The tirade continued for another ten minutes. Gloria stood next to him in the lobby of the Hotel Cencali, smiling at him, at his discomfort.

Finally his father asked, "Are you healthy? Do you have enough money?"

265

"I'm fine. I don't need anything. Really."

"How is your money holding out? How much do you have?"

"A couple hundred. But I don't need…"

"I'll wire you five hundred. Where can I wire you money?"

"Dad I don't know. I don't need any."

"Listen to me. You find a bank, and call me back. We'll do it this morning within the hour. Okay?"

"Okay."

After he hung up, Jesse thought about his father, and he knew he wouldn't call him back. His father had asked if he was still looking for Kathryn and Jesse had lied and said yes. The truth bothered him. For some time now, he had not been looking for her. Instead he had been drawn deeper and deeper into Garcia's hidden world, to the point now that a federal police officer was probably looking for him.

"What are you thinking?" Gloria asked.

"That I should go home to San Antonio and see my father."

"Are you going to?"

"Maybe. Hell. I don't know."

"Well I hope you stay," she said squeezing his arm.

"Really? Why?"

"I like having you around."

"Why?" They were outside in front of the hotel. Gloria signaled for a cab.

"Because you are a very nice man. I only know one other."

They climbed into the back of the Volkswagen Taxi. Gloria told the driver, "Take us to the University por favor."

* * * * * * * * *

"Ah." Garcia said as Gloria sat down in a big leather chair behind a desk in an office in the Economics Department, at the Universidad Autonoma de Villahermosa. Garcia stood next to her, reading a sociology journal. "It was good of my colleague to loan me the use of his office this afternoon. I have a lot of catching up to do." He turned the computer on.

Jesse watched Gloria log on to AztecNet. "So the EZLN uses the web for communication." He observed.

"The greatest tool a revolutionary could ask for." Garcia said, as he stretched and cracked his knuckles.

"You have forty-five messages, Professor." Gloria said, raising an eyebrow.

"Jesus. What is the oldest one?" Garcia walked behind her, and looked down at the screen.

"September 9th from Elena Mink."

"That's our Long Island connection I believe. Let me read it."

Jesse studied the office. According to the various diplomas and awards it belonged to a Professor Guillermo Joaquin Vargas -Valdes. His bachelor's degree in Sociology was from UNAM in 1969. He had then gone to Paris. There was a graduate degree, a Deuxième Cycle from the Sorbonne in Economics in 1977, and a D. Phil. From the London School of Economics dated 1980. Two rows of his bookshelf held books he had either written, co-authored, or edited. All but two of the edited volumes were in Spanish. The other two were in French.

"Where is your colleague?" Jesse asked.

"Sabbatical semester in Europe. He's at the University of Bordeaux." Garcia muttered as he typed on the keyboard.

"Too bad. Judging from his office, it would have been nice to have met him."

"Well we are staying at his house tonight. You could write him a note and perhaps meet him when he comes home next month. I just read some email from him."

"If I am still here."

Garcia looked up. "Oh? And where are you going?"

"I might go home to San Antonio for awhile."

"Really? There might be a very large favor you could do for us there."

"Like what?"

"Like what you did at Palenque. Only on a much larger scale."

"I could possibly be interested."

"We need to talk as soon as I get a better idea of what our enemies are up to."

* * * * * *

La casa de Vargas-Valdes was enormous, a three-story mansion located on a tree-lined boulevard flanking the Rio Grijalva. Jesse was impressed that it had eighteen rooms. The white stucco walls and red tile roof graced an extensive lawn that was beautifully landscaped in lush tropical flowering plants, and palms. They were sitting by the pool, which was composed of two levels; an upper shallow pool fed the Olympic-sized pool by a miniature waterfall. Everyone was drinking iced-tea provided by Vargas-Valdes servants.

"Before you ask Jesse, I'll tell you. Yes, he obviously is wealthy, and he has always been wealthy. We were classmates at UNAM in the late '60s, and he is one of my oldest and truest friends. No, he does not know much about what I do with the EZLN, but what he does know he approves of. His hidalgo ancestors made their money off the backs of the Indians,

268

logging mahogany, planting coffee, and sugarcane, and now he is interested in atonement. We will leave it there for now."

"Does he still own much land?"

"Not as much as his father, but it is still substantial." Garcia rose and stretched.

"Since we are going out this evening, I will take a siesta until about five. I am exhausted. If I sleep past then will you wake me?"

Jesse nodded; Gloria raised her tea, and smiled.

"Good. Excuse me until then."

Gloria reclined her chair back and clasped her hands over her flat belly. "This is nice." She said. In her black two piece swimsuit, flowing black hair, against glistening, deep brown skin, she was very alluring. But her body language said she wanted to be alone, so Jesse decided to swim a few laps in the lower pool.

After about six passes he swam over to the waterfall, went under it, and surfaced behind the water curtain. The sound of the waterfall soothed him, and he turned around, extended his feet back and let the water massage his legs, as he relaxed.

He felt guilty he realized about not being home with his father, although he knew that was exactly the way his father wanted him to feel. He would have to return home for awhile, that was all there was to it. Maybe by then his altercation with the policeman would be forgotten.

He was startled from his reverie by a hand gripping his calf and another one tickling his ribs. Gloria surfaced next to him laughing.

"I got you good." She said as she flipped her hair back.

"Yes. I jumped out of my skin." He felt her breast brush against his arm. Was it accidental? He wondered.

She rubbed her eyes, and smiled at him, put a hand on each shoulder and floated against him.

"I thought you had left, but you were hiding under here."

"Water relaxes me. I've always loved it." She is so beautiful, he thought.

She caressed his neck and looked into his eyes.

Jesse kissed her lightly on the lips.

She kissed back harder.

He put his arms around her and pulled her to him. She is like a mermaid, he thought, as she unfastened her top.

53 Positive Vibrations II

The boat engines idled as Paul and Phil handed down a cooler to Delia and Esmeralda. They were tied up at the pier in front of the Paradise Resort Hotel, where Paul kept his boat. Paul was excited about helping Phil and refused any money that Phil offered, but finally relented and allowed Phil to pay for gas for the trip to the mainland.

Paul's boat *Positive Vibrations II* was a Bertram thirty footer that he had salvaged off a reef a few years back, rebuilt, and refitted her as a serious sports fishing boat. "Canadian man was drunk coming out of San Pedro one night, and ripped her bottom off on the reef. But now she is happy in the service of Trevino." He gave Esmeralda a hug, and took over the wheel. "You ready to cast off Phillip?"

Phil nodded and untied the lines from the cleats on the pier. Nutmeg hopped up and stretched out near the bow, happy to be on the boat.

"Then let's go to Orange Walk Town." Paul knew people all over Belize and Guatemala, and after hearing Phil's story he had considered the best way to get them into Guatemala. They headed north up the windward side of Ambergris Caye toward the border. Just before entering Mexican waters, they would take the narrow channel cut at Xcalak and turn west.

"Happy Dia de los Muertos, everyone." Esmeralda said passing out cokes to Delia and Phil.

Paul crossed himself. "Esmeralda is coming with us to see her uncle in Orange Walk. He's an important person there."

"Oh? What does he do?" Delia asked.

"He owns a restaurant." Esmeralda sat down in a deck chair and started putting her hair up in a ponytail.

"He is a very well-connected man." Paul said. "He may be able to help us get some of what we need for Guatemala."

"Us? Who said you were coming Paul?" Phil asked.

"Who said I wasn't?"

Delia watched a brilliant turquoise lagoon pass by on the port side, a flock of seagulls circled above it. "So how long have you two known each other?" She asked Paul.

"Four years. Phillip hired me as a fishing guide, and wound up helping me salvage this boat." Paul laughed. "He worked pretty hard for a white boy."

Delia looked over at Phil who was getting ready to throw a line out. She noticed how tan he was getting, he looked leaner too. The scars on his shoulder and back intrigued her, but she still hadn't asked about them. They would get around to it.

He grinned at her. "Going to catch me a grouper."

"Paul was telling me how you two met." She said loudly trying to be heard over the wind and the engine's roar. Paul had the throttles all the way open. They skipped over the waves near the reef.

"Did he tell you he conned me into helping him get this boat off that reef?" Phil pointed to the breakers on the port side.

Delia nodded. "How did you ever find time to do that?"

Phil frowned at the memory. "It was after the Montebello project. It ended a week early, and my ticket was non-refundable, couldn't change it so I came out here to do some fishing. Ran into Pablo, stayed until it was time to leave."

"That's unusual for a project to end early." Delia said. "It's never happened on any that I've been involved with. Had a few go into overtime, but none of them ever ended early."

"That was an unusual project all the way around." Phil said, casting out his line.

"How so?"

"Not worth mentioning."

"What are you not telling me Phil? I'm just interested." He was doing it again she thought, going into one of his compartments.

"Ancient history."

"Oh come on. Now you've really got me curious."

"I'll tell you some other time. Right now I just want to fish."

Delia was starting to realize that Phil kept a lot of things compartmentalized, and she wasn't sure she liked it.

54 Dia de los Muertos

Jesse and Gloria had a perfect day and they anticipated a perfect evening. After making love they had showered, changed, and gone shopping in the boutiques at Plaza Juarez. Jesse enjoyed the way Gloria modeled her dresses, flouncing, spinning around, showing off her beautiful legs, and clearly enjoying the trappings of civilization after being so long in the jungle.

Now they were going out to eat at a fancy restaurant. It was Garcia's treat. He was excited about it because it was one of the finest French restaurants in Mexico, Restaurant Million, overlooking the Grijalva River. It had been a French restaurant since the days of Emperor Maximilian. Gloria sat between Garcia and Jesse in the back seat of the cab. Jesse admired her clothing selection. She looked very cosmopolitan he thought, with her hair in a French braid, and wearing a simple, black, off the shoulder dress.

He realized he was in love with her. Totally. Now what was he going to do?

Their cab drove past a cemetery that was overflowing with people, flowers, and offerings to the ancestors. The cemetery extended all the way to the riverbank and through its oak groves the Rio Grijalva was a silver ribbon in the early evening light. It was dusk and people were intent on getting the graves neat and well decorated. In the store windows, skulls and skeletons, altars and candles were readied.

"Death is as natural as life itself." Jesse thought out loud.

"That's true, as natural as sex. Tonight some of the ancestors might get lucky." Garcia responded.

Jesse wondered if he knew about him and Gloria, if he was referring to the fantastic afternoon they had just experienced.

"So is El Dia de los Muertos a big fiesta in San Antonio?" Gloria asked.

"In some neighborhoods, not so much in mine." Jesse answered. They were stopped at a red light and he was looking at a vendor selling sugar skulls on the street. "There are places on the south side where they still eat in the cemeteries with the dead. Do they still dine with the ancestors here?"

Garcia nodded. "Very much so. Until about eight o'clock. What part of San Antonio does your family live in?" He asked.

"Monte Vista, close to downtown." He paused before adding. "And, I'm thinking of flying back there next week." Jesse said.

"Gloria going with you?"

Jesse was too stunned to reply. "I haven't asked, I thought she needed to help you down here."

Gloria had a half-smile on her face.

"Well why don't you ask her?" Garcia said.

Jesse was a little surprised and off-balance. "Gloria? You want to go with me?"

"I have always wanted to go to Texas." She said demurely.

"Excellent." Garcia said. "You both will have a wonderful time. And you can help me simultaneously."

"How so?" Jesse asked.

"Later." Garcia said, nodding toward the cab driver.

* * * * * * * *

La Casa de Million was once a beautiful French provincial home. Now it was an elegant restaurant with a large open deck extending over the Rio Grijalva. Tables with white linen cloths, and candles created a nice ambience. The nine-course dinner had been superb, and Garcia had been a fine host. Telling humorous stories about his grad school days at UCLA, choosing an excellent Bordeaux wine, and generally just being his clever self. Close to eleven o'clock and toward the end of dessert, he excused himself to use the phone.

Gloria folded her napkin and smiled at Jesse. "Do you really want me to come to Texas with you?"

"God. God yes." He stuttered, and caught himself. "I mean of course."

"And meet your family? How many brothers and sisters do you have?"

"Four. Two brothers and two sisters. I am the youngest." He reached for his water glass, excited and anxious at the possibilities. "I wonder how my father will react. He will insist we sleep in separate rooms..."

"Is he like you?"

"Not really. I mean he left school in the eighth grade, worked like a dog his entire life. Built his restaurant and bar with his own hands. Everything he has he owns. Does not believe in debt."

"You admire him."

"Very much."

"How does he like Indians?"

Jesse was surprised by the question. "Fine. I guess... it's never really come up."

"Because in Mexico, I am a little "too Indian," too dark, for some Latino families. And forget about the hidalgos."

"That sounds like a bad experience. What happened?"

"It's just that… Oh. Here's the Professor."

Garcia sat down frowning. He finished his wine quietly.

"Something wrong?" Jesse asked.

"Could be. Not real sure. I have already paid the tab. Everyone ready?"

They nodded.

"Let us depart." He looked around the deck, as if he expected to see someone, Jesse noticed.

* * * * * *

Under magnificent oaks dripping with Spanish moss, they waited for a cab. Garcia had them stand in the shadows, away from the well-lit driveway.

"You care to tell us what's going on?" Jesse asked quietly.

"We may have to leave for Vera Cruz in the morning, a slight change in plans."

Jesse knew from experience that there was no point in pushing Garcia. As he always said, he would tell him whatever he thought he needed to know whenever he needed to know it.

A Chevrolet Corsica taxicab pulled up and they all got in. As they settled into their seats Garcia gave an address, a few blocks from the Valdes-Vargas villa, and whispered to Gloria, "Our unit in Ocosingo may have been compromised."

"Your phone call?"

"Yes. They may know about my colleague as well."

"They know where we are? Where we are staying?" Gloria asked worriedly.

"Possibly. Jesse those items you took in Palenque? You still have them with you?"

Jesse felt his adrenaline kick in. Garcia's voice had a faint hint of fear in it. Something he had not heard before.

"Yes sir."

"Are they accessible?"

Jesse nodded, touching the pistol in his waistband. The knife was in his pocket. He had been carrying them ever since Palenque.

"Good. I am similarly equipped. Gloria?"

"I have a little something in my handbag."

"Okay. When we get back to the house? I need you to be ready to leave in fifteen minutes." He turned his head suddenly. "Why are we slowing down here driver?" The cab was pulling into the cemetery gates they had passed earlier.

"I asked you a question pendejo." Garcia was reaching behind his back, as the driver opened the door and jumped out of the cab.

They rolled on for a hundred feet at about twenty miles an hour. Jesse grabbed for the wheel but it was too late. They ran straight into a crypt with a heavy jolt.

"Get the lights. Turn off the engine." Garcia said quietly, noticing that Jesse had already done it. "Let's get out of here. Stay low."

Jesse opened his door slowly, and got out on all fours with the pistol in his right hand. Garcia got out on the other side.

"Gloria, wait a second while we check it out." Jesse saw that she had a small .22 target pistol in her hand. She lay prone on the back seat.

He rolled over to get behind a large granite tombstone that had a cross chiseled on it.

A Chevrolet Suburban entered the gates and drove too fast toward them.

"Gloria - get out of the car!" Jesse shouted. She jumped out and was quickly beside him.

The Suburban's doors opened. No one got out. The engine stopped and the lights went out. Everything was frozen in the cemetery. Jesse was aware of the dimly lit candles flickering on the nearby graves, the tombstones in their neat rows, cicadas chirping, and Gloria's rapid breathing next to him.

He put his arm around her, and pulled her in closer. He heard his heart pounding.

"Is that you Professor Garcia?" A voice called out.

There was no reply.

Jesse realized he didn't know exactly where Garcia was.

"Oh come on professor. We know all about you. Your money. The girl. The big American Tejano. We don't know who he is yet, but we will find out. Your little visits to Palenque. We have informers everywhere. It is not nice to break a policeman's nose and take all of his belongings."

Jesse heard laughter from the Suburban. Someone else cursed, and the laughter stopped.

"I do not understand why an educated man like you would still support communism. It is bankrupt everywhere. I know you wanted us to believe you were narcotics traffickers, but you were a little too polished for me to believe that. Subversivos, that's what I suspect you are."

Gloria nudged Jesse, and started backing away on all fours toward the river, which was at least one hundred yards behind them.

"And do you know what I do with subversivos?"

The only sounds now were the cars on the boulevard, the cicadas, and the wind in the oaks. Jesse and Gloria continued to back away through the graveyard.

"No? Want to guess?"

Boots crunched on gravel. Heavy steps moved in their direction. Jesse could make out five men in the darkness. Where was their cab driver, he wondered.

"But maybe if you give me the money, I let you go. What do you think of that?"

"You might want to stop right there." It was Garcia's voice. Jesse could not see him, but his voice was coming from the far left, near a large mausoleum. "I could probably shoot at least two of you, before you could react." The men dropped to the ground. "I said stop!" Jesse saw the gun flash briefly beside the mausoleum.

One of the men screamed and was immediately silent.

The men returned fire aggressively. Bullets chipped stone off the mausoleum. A blue haze of gun smoke floated around the Suburban.

Gloria grabbed Jesse's arm and pulled him toward the river away from the firing. They sprinted fifty yards, and heard a shot buzz over their heads. They immediately dropped down on top of an old sunken grave. Jesse looked up and saw a plaster angel, half covered in moss, looking down on him. He was feeling his heart pound, as he extended his pistol with both hands, propped up on his elbows. He thought about the looters shooting at him and Avendano a few weeks back. Is it some weird planetary alignment, or am I just traveling with a bad crowd, he wondered.

Gloria fired with her .22. They heard it ricochet off stone. "Someone's coming! Right over there!" She whispered.

"What if it's Garcia?" he asked, not able to see who she was pointing at.

"It's not." She fired again, and they heard a body hit the ground, and a man moaned loudly "I got him!" She was excited, and started crawling forward. Jesse tried to catch her but she moved too quickly. Other shots were exchanged off to his left, moving away from the mausoleum. Garcia was alive and still fighting.

Six shots in rapid succession slammed into and around the angel. A stone splinter shattered from it, and it burrowed deep into Jesse's cheek, lodging next to his teeth. "God damn." He said as his mouth filled with blood. He couldn't see Gloria but he heard her .22 go off up ahead. Three shots. He spat out a clump of blood, and slowly crawled toward her. He tensed himself waiting for the shots, but none came.

A man lay face up in a little alleyway between two low crypts. Blood seeped from a hole in his forehead. Gloria knelt next to him, her back against the nearest crypt, took his gun and tossed her .22 over to Jesse. "Put this somewhere. I like his nine-millimeter better. He won't need it any more."

Jesse stuck the .22 in his crotch, too shocked to say anything. More shots were exchanged over by the mausoleum. "We had better circle back and see if we can help the Professor. Are you all right?" She touched the hole in his cheek.

"A stone splinter." He said absently looking at the dead man. He realized he was shaking. This was all wrong.

"A little higher and you would have lost your right eye." She hiked up her dress, and tore at her slip. "Do you have your knife?"

He silently handed it to her. The dead man looked to be Jesse's age. His expression was one of total surprise. His eyes were wide open and looking at Jesse, who felt nauseated.

Gloria tied the makeshift bandage around his head, and saw he was still staring at the dead man. "Hey. You never saw a dead body before?" She asked.

Jesse realized the cemetery was quiet. Gravel crunched nearby. They spun around.

Too late.

"Drop the guns." A voice said from the darkness to the right. It sounded vaguely familiar. A gun went off and a bullet hit between Jesse's legs. "The next one takes off your huevos. Drop it."

Another shot went by Gloria's head. This one came from behind them. "You too puta. Drop the gun." Jesse recognized the voice. It was the man who called them subversivos, the one who wanted the money.

Gloria looked at him helplessly, and dropped the gun. Jesse pitched his toward the crypt. Now he knew real terror.

A short powerfully built man emerged from behind the crypt. He was a swarthy Indian. He wore a black Guyabera shirt and black pants. His body odor was strong.

Two more men encircled them from the left and right, similarly dressed.

"Where is the other one? Where's Garcia?" The stocky man asked.

"Antonio chased him to the boulevard. I think he is still following him." It was their former cab driver, Jesse noticed. They had us marked for awhile, he thought.

"You think? Well I think you had better go find out. Get moving! Ortega. Cover me." He walked over and looked at the dead man. "Poor Manuel. Too bad. I never liked him much. He was something of a hoto. Really liked to frisk the boys.

So which of you killed him?" He pointed his gun first at Gloria then at Jesse. "Not talking? That's okay, plenty of time for that. Ortega, handcuff the American and then the little bitch." He held his gun steady, pointed at Jesse.

"Just so you know who killed you, my name is Alex Sanchez." He bowed sarcastically.

Jesse put his arms out in front of him. He shivered with fear, but tried not to show it. He knew his only hope was to keep them from finding the .22. in the crotch of his pants. So he held his hands out low in front of it, and then recognized Ortega, who had a bruised and crooked nose and a furious look in his eyes. After he handcuffed him, Ortega stood back and looked Jesse up and down. He frisked him as he talked, but stayed away from his crotch. The comments about hotos had perhaps influenced him.

"Big old Tejano. Took my gun and my knife. Broke my nose. Now I have my gun. Where is my knife?"

"Here Ortega." Alex had handcuffed and grinned as he felt up Gloria. She didn't make a sound or meet Jesse's eye. Alex tossed Ortega the knife.

Ortega smiled and opened it. "Now I get to be El Castrador. You better hope you kept my knife sharp hoto! You broke my nose but I'm going to cut your balls off."

Alex laughed, and said, "First let's take a walk down to the river. It will be less messy down there, and no one will be able to hear them scream."

Jesse felt the .22 next to his skin. The hard steel was his only chance.

* * * * * * * *

Gloria never made a sound. She was handcuffed to a low branch of an enormous oak tree, in an old part of the cemetery. Her hands were over her head. Jesse sat twenty feet away on a bench by the river, handcuffed and holding his hands between his knees. He had faced mind-chilling terror and swallowed it whole. Now he only wanted to live long enough to kill them. By using his elbows, he had maneuvered the .22 to where it was below the waist of his pants. It was all he wanted in the world, all he wanted to think about, getting the gun and using it before he died.

He visualized everything he would do before he did it. And if they killed him, so what? They were going to kill him anyway. His brain was like ice.

They were getting ready to rape her when he made his move.

He stood up and the pistol grip moved near his waistband. He grabbed it with both hands and squeezed off a shot that hit Sanchez in his gun arm, above his wrist.

Sanchez dropped his gun, and spun around with his pants down around his ankles, thrashing, trying to straighten up. He looked ludicrous.

Simultaneously, Gloria moved, kicking her foot back hard, and hit Sanchez directly in his testicles. He went down on his side holding his crotch. Ortega was flailing at her, screaming as she ground her teeth down on his arm, and shot his gun off next to her ear, but somehow it missed her and grazed Sanchez in the leg. She jerked her head back hard, and pulled with her teeth, jaws still locked on. Ortega dropped the gun, and grabbed at his bloody arm, screaming louder, hysterically. Sanchez groaned and scuttled around the trunk of the oak tree.

Jesse took careful aim, and calmly shot Ortega in the heart, silencing his high pitched scream forever. He slumped back twitching against a tombstone, before he gurgled and died. Gloria spat something meaty and fleshy out of her mouth, and gave a great heave, breaking off the oak branch and falling next to Ortega's body. She tried to sit up. Jesse was quickly beside her.

"Don't worry about me." She said in a painful hoarse whisper, her mouth a grisly red smeared with Ortega's arterial blood "Just kill the other one."

Sanchez had gone behind the tree. When Jesse rushed around it, no one was there. A trail of shiny blood led off among the tombstones.

"We need to move quickly, in case more of them show up." Gloria said.

They took Ortega's key, unlocked the handcuffs and collected the guns. Now they had four guns between them. Three nine millimeters, and Gloria's little .22 that had saved their lives.

"We saved the EZLN some money." Gloria smiled grimly. Blood was still smeared on her chin.

Ortega looked obscene lying there dead with his pants around his blood spattered knees, a bullet hole in his heart, and his jaws wide open in a permanent rictus scream.

They rolled his body into the river, and watched it float away.

"Are you sure you are all right?" Jesse asked. He felt totally drained, and shaken, but he was worried about Gloria.

They were walking north along the riverbank and had already left the cemetery behind them. Gloria stopped in her tracks, and straightened up, as she looked him in the eyes. Her face was still smeared with blood.

"You mean the attempted rape?"

Jesse nodded.

Gloria smiled grimly, before answering.

"I think I lost an ear drum when his pistol went off, but you know they really made a mistake. They were dumb."

"What do you mean?"

"They should have killed me, and they really should have killed you, but they wanted to make you watch, los pendejos machos."

"I wish I could have got to the pistol quicker, before..."

Gloria put her arms around him.

She held him close, and whispered, sobbing. "You saved my life. They paid for it. You saved my life. I love you so much Jesse."

And then she was crying.

55 Orange Walk Town

They had taken Paul's boat all the way up the New River, and two days out of San Pedro; arrived in Orange Walk Town. *Positive Vibrations II* was tied up at the dock on Riverside Street. They took adjoining rooms at Jane's Guest House on Market Lane.

It was a simple two-story clapboard house, in need of a paint job. The rooms were twelve U.S. dollars a night and quite comfortable.

Nutmeg was sleeping against the door and guarding Delia, as she undressed. The two of them were bonded now, and Delia made sure that Nutmeg always got an adequate supply of table scraps. So far, from fish to fowl, there had been nothing that the dog would not eat. She was a true omnivore.

Delia luxuriated in taking the longest shower of her life, and looked forward to using the phone to check in with Madeline and Patty on Ambergris, everyone in Boston and her folks in Ohio.

Well, she thought, I should have a nice calling card bill next month. She unpacked and started taking stock of what she had and what she would need, because from here, Phil said it was going to get primitive for awhile.

* * * * * * * * *

Phil, Esmeralda and Paul were at the *Hong Kong* Restaurant meeting with Zeng Quan, Esmeralda's uncle. The restaurant consisted of one large room, with small tables scattered about with mismatched chairs, a cracked concrete floor that was polished and gleaming, and a long bar with a mirror that ran the length of the back wall.

"I can get you all the materials on this list within two days, with two exceptions." Quan said. He looked up from the list, removed his glasses and put them away in a pocket of his white cotton Guyabera shirt.

"What two items?" Phil asked, sipping on an ice cold Belikin beer.

"The raft and the ammunition." Quan leaned forward and whispered, "Why you need so many bullets? You go to start a war with Guatemala?"

"Just going to do some hunting is all." Phil smiled.

Quan snorted. "Hunt with an AK-47 or M-16? You think I do not know what gun this 7.62 millimeter is for?"

Phil shrugged, and took another drink. He really didn't care what Quan thought as long as he could get the bullets.

"Then the other ammunition request is interesting, this 9 x 18. It reminds me of the 9 x 18 Makarov. A very reliable pistol made in Russia and built on a Walther PPK style blowback design. In size and power, cartridge is between the popular 9mm Luger and the .380, which the Europeans refer to as 9 millimeter short. Strange selection for hunting. Unless you are hunting something on two legs."

285

No one said anything. Phil stared idly at Mr. Quan.

"I can get the 9 x 18 ammunition." Quan said.

"Phillip, you may not know this, but Orange Walk is the center of the marijuana trade in northern Belize." Paul signaled for another round. "The marijuanista weapon of choice is the AK-47."

"Then it should be possible to get the ammo." Phil observed.

"Demand is high. Supply is low." Paul shrugged.

"I didn't say was not possible. I said can't do it in two days. Can't get drum magazines. Those come here from China. Can get the steel jackets." Quan leaned back in his chair and reached for his ice water. He said something in Chinese to Esmeralda, who shrugged in response.

"How long then?" Phil asked.

"Three days."

"And the raft?"

"Same."

"And how much for everything?"

Quan got out his calculator from another pocket, put his glasses back on, and started totaling everything up. After a few minutes he squinted at Phil and said, "Three thousand nine hundred sixty three dollars and seventy two cents. U.S. dollars."

"All I can give you is thirty six hundred."

"Then you may not get all the ammunition you want."

Phil decided he could live with that. "Okay. I'm willing to compromise there. But what about my Belizean passport and the Land Rover rental for two months, delivered to the place of my choosing?"

"Fake passport no problem. Best possible replica. Where you want this Rover exactly?"

Phil grinned, and pulled a map out of his back pocket. "Let me show you Mr. Quan."

He pointed to a spot west of the Guatemalan border town of Melchor de Mencos.

Quan squinted at the map.

"Guatemalan side of border?"

"Guatemalan side."

"That costs another five hundred."

Paul pushed his chair back; he was out of beer again. "I'll take it across Phil." Paul said. "No charge. I'll take us all across. No problem."

"Not my niece you don't." Quan said firmly. He spoke to Esmeralda in Chinese again. This time she sighed, crossed her arms and stared at the ceiling.

"Why uncle?" Paul asked.

"Don't call me that." He nodded curtly at Phil. "Because this one is a very dangerous man. I've seen his type before. In Shanghai."

Phil grinned and shook his head. "You might be able to help me with another problem Mr. Quan. I need to get the hunting equipment into Guatemala; it won't clear customs no matter who drives the Rover across..."

Quan had his calculator ready.

* * * * * * * *

"So you can be at Chanul Tzuk by no later than December 29th Delia?"

"Yes. I'll just stay down here I guess."

"So exactly what are you doing in Belize?" Mamett asked.

"I'm on my way to Guatemala. I'm going to see if I can find Belinda." Delia answered; she had already decided she wouldn't mention Phil. She didn't want it to get back to Lieutenant Martin.

"By yourself?"

"No Madeline is with me." She was amazed by how easily the lie came out.

"Well that's good. She's a very capable woman. Resourceful. Tough. But I've got a surprise for you."

"What?"

"Well I think I've located Belinda. I've sent word to her and I believe she'll be with us at Chanul Tzuk too." It was hard to hear him, there was so much static, and it sounded like he was in the next solar system, instead of Cambridge. Delia was calling from the public telephone building across from the police station. Phil sat outside the booth studying a map.

Delia gasped. "Well that's incredible news. Where is she?"

"Pretty much as I thought. Out of pocket. Up in the Peten with Hector Obregon, miles from any phones, or other creature comforts. Working on her dissertation research while she helps them salvage a looted Early Classic site."

"Where exactly?"

"A newly discovered site. Macondo. It's about thirty or forty miles northwest of Uaxactun."

"Macondo huh? Someone must have read Gabriel Garcia Marquez. Hard to get to?"

"You know the Peten."

"Who told you?"

"A colleague of Sergio Avendano's was up there last week. He told Sergio he saw her."

"So who'll have directions?"

"Someone at the museum should know. The National Museum in Guatemala City. Try Maria Vega, she's the Assistant Curator."

"Fantastic. Will Belinda ever be surprised." Delia was grinning now. "So how's Carl?"

"Much better. He's still a little weak, but now he comes into the department once in awhile. He still seems very depressed by everything."

"Should I give him a call?"

"Absolutely, but he's hard to get a hold of."

"And how is Professor Thomas?"

Mamett paused so long she thought she had lost the connection. "Patrick, are you still there?"

"You've been gone longer than I remembered. Delia, you'd better sit down. Samuel Thomas killed himself."

"What?"

"And in his note he confessed to assisting Laurence in his act of ritual suicide, and antiquities smuggling. It's all quite horrible. And that's not all. They think Phil Ward may have been involved. You haven't heard from him lately have you?"

"No." Even though she had rehearsed the lie, it sounded timid to her own ears.

"Not since you left Cambridge? Not a word?"

"No. Nothing. What does Lieutenant Martin think?" Delia felt her heart speeding up, pounding in her ears.

"He passed away last week. Heart attack."

"You'd better start from the beginning." Delia felt all the air go out of her.

* * * * * * * * *

"And that's pretty much it." She said to Phil as they sat on a bench outside of the phone building.

"So Patty and Madeline are flying on to Guatemala City to check with the museum?" He said quietly. "That's a good plan. We can go to Flores or Tikal, call and get directions from them and drive on into Macondo. We could be there in four or five days."

"What about the rest of what he said?" She asked. "Aren't you worried?"

"No more than I already was."

"Why?"

"Because darling, it confirms my hypothesis about the opposing forces. I know I am innocent of their accusations, therefore since they are able to kill Thomas, make it look like a suicide, 'solve' Laurence's murder and implicate me, all in a nice tidy bundle, it proves they are very, very good. Which we already knew. I just wonder how many are in on it, and who is in on it." He stood up and stretched.

"Still, it's great that Belinda is okay isn't it?" Phil seemed aloof again, and Delia wondered if it was because of Belinda. She felt her insecurity returning, and realized she was becoming very attached to him.

"Yes. It is. But I don't understand why she sent her luggage back if she was planning on staying down here awhile. It doesn't track."

"Well I'm sure she had a good reason. And she'll tell us when we see her. Maybe she came back for a weekend, turned around and flew back to Guatemala?"

He paused, looked at the map one more time before putting it away. "Maybe so, but it still doesn't make any sense."

They headed out of the telephone building.

"So with poor Lieutenant Martin dead, do you think the authorities are still looking for you?"

"The APBs didn't die with him."

56 Hotel Bonampak

Tuxtla Gutierrez was one of Jesse's favorite towns in all of Mexico. The capitol of Chiapas, it always seemed well-off, modern, neat and clean. The wide paved streets were well maintained, and the lawns and plazas were full of mango trees, banana trees, African tulip trees and hundreds of tropical flowers.

Jesse sat in a lounge chair on their balcony at the Hotel Bonampak. It was on the outskirts north of town. This was where Garcia had said to meet him in the note he had left at the Vargas-Valdes house. A gauze pad was attached to his cheek, and it still ached constantly.

He thought back to that horrible evening five nights ago. How they walked through alleyways and back yards in case Sanchez and his men were looking for them. They made it back to the villa before dawn. Bloody streaks on an upstairs bathroom sink, and a note were the only traces Garcia left.

Jesse could almost remember the note verbatim:

Tear up this note and flush it when you finish. I am wounded in my left hand, and going to see someone I can trust about it. Most of the money is in the armoire in Jesse's room. The rest is with me. Take it and get out of town as quickly as possible. Go to the Hotel Bonampak in Tuxtla Gutierrez. If I am not there in six days, go see our people in San Cristobal. Gloria, you know who to contact. Stay away from Raxabe, Ocosingo, Oxchuc and Villahermosa.

Buena Suerte
G.

Gloria emerged from the steaming bathroom drying her hair, and wrapped in a white beach towel. They had not made love since the incident. She had been morose and shown no interest in it. Jesse understood why, and wanted to help her more. He just didn't know how. Both of them had avoided talking about the night in the cemetery.

"You look very comfortable with your feet propped up out here," she said, as she sat down next to him.

"I am. And you are going to use all of the hotel's hot water." He laughed.

"What does that make? Three showers today?"

"Yes." Gloria flashed a faint smile and put her hair up in a towel turban. She could still not hear out of her right ear.

She lapsed into one of her silences again; Jesse tried to think of what he had done to upset her this time. After a few minutes she spoke.

"I still feel their filth on me. I cannot feel clean. No matter how many showers I take." She sobbed quietly. "And I'm scared all the time."

He held out his arms and she came over and sat down in his lap. "I've noticed the nightmares." He said.

"Yes. I am even scared in my sleep."

"We don't have to talk about it."

"I want to go home. But I have no home to go to." She broke then and started crying uncontrollably.

Jesse held her and stroked her hair. "You can go home with me. We can still do that."

"Hold me please."

* * * * * * * *

The hotel cafe had a beautifully tiled patio, surrounded by a lush tropical garden. Jesse, Gloria and Garcia were eating breakfast, enjoying the cool morning light and the colorful flowers that surrounded them.

Garcia had showed up at eight thirty and said, "Let's have breakfast."

"So as I was saying. Not only do we need the obvious, but we also need the mundane, the basic commodities." Garcia said, and stuffed his corn tortilla with eggs, diced tomatoes, and chorizo.

"Such as?" Jesse asked.

"Ammunition. This is where your trip to San Antonio comes in. I'm putting the details together; the logistics, but if I can arrange things will you do it? Will you bring it back? You may have to drive a truck down, but I will have your way prepared."

"If I do, will I get a chance to kill Sanchez?" Jesse whispered coldly.

Gloria looked up at him, startled by his simple violence.

"You know what kind of dish revenge is according to the Spanish, Jesse." Garcia muttered under his breath.

"It will be served very cold by then Señor, maybe even with an ice pick."

57 Border Crossing

The Belizean border guards waved the Land Rover through. The toughest part was coming up Phil thought, as he saw the line of trucks and buses bunched up ahead at the Guatemalan checkpoint. The once paved road

293

was rutted, and had been pounded into dust by all the heavy trucks, busses and machinery. A thick layer of gray dust covered the trees that arched over the road. Sitting next to Paul Trevino, who was driving, Phil looked at the faded Belize sign as they drove into the DMZ between the two countries; Thank You For Visiting the Sovereign and Independent Nation of Belize!

The Guatemalan sign was even more faded, but a bit more malevolent; Belice Es Guatemala!

Phil thought back to when he had been an embassy guard in Guatemala City, their old claim on Belize. Guatemala's territorial claim to Belize had not been emphasized much, after the Falkland's war. The war seemed to have discouraged the Guatemalans, that, and the continued presence of British military units inside of Belize.

Phil had mixed feelings as he approached the checkpoint. He loved the people and the land of Guatemala, but he hated the various governments that had brutalized it for the past twenty years. They were corrupt, bloodthirsty, and deadly. Guatemala reminded him a lot of Viet Nam.

A space appeared on the left, and Paul pulled in next to a blue bus belching diesel fumes. Soon they were immersed in a greasy black cloud.

It was considered good form to converse in Spanish, the border guards appreciated it, and if they liked you they might wave you through with a cursory glance.

The guard was in freshly pressed khakis; clean and all business. More professional looking than guards Phil had encountered in the past.

"Passports please."

Phil handed over his newly made fake Belizean passport. Here comes the first real test, he thought.

"Your purpose for visiting Guatemala?"

"Business."

"What kind of business?" He thumbed through Phil's passport.

"Archaeology."

He looked up. "You are all archaeologists? You three?"

"I'm not." Paul said. "I am a guide."

"But you are Miss." He read her passport. "Cordelia Marie Bell?"

"Yes sir."

"And the dog?"

"Belizean national sir." Delia said, giving him her warmest smile.

He smiled, and shuffled the three passports in his hand. "And why is a nice American girl traveling with two Belizeans? We have many professional archaeologists here in Guatemala."

"I know. We are going to visit them. Maria Vega and Hector Obregon at the national museum..." She extended her hand implicitly suggesting he return her passport to her. He stamped it and gave it back. He stamped the other two as well. He gave Paul's to him, looked one more time at Phil's and then gave it back.

He handed out three tourist cards, and said. "The tax is five quetzals each." Phil looked at the card, it said in English and Spanish, "The cost of this document is one quetzal." Phil silently paid the fifteen quetzals.

"Obregon comes through here all the time." The guard said to Delia. "I think he has a sanchita in Belize."

They all laughed politely.

"He's a great archaeologist." Delia said.

"Of course. He's Guatemalan." The guard said, leaning in a little more to look at the closely packed interior. "Two archaeologists and only one shovel?"

"Someone has to be the director." Delia smiled.

The guard laughed in response, and looked at the gas cans tied to the back. He gave one of them a thump.

"Do you know of a new site called Macondo?" She asked.

"There is a village, was a village northwest of here by that name. No one lives there now."

"What happened?"

"The troubles." He shrugged. "They all left. Pacification."

"But no archaeology...?"

"I have never heard of any ruins." He pushed his hat back, and wiped his forehead on his sleeve. "I almost forgot; any firearms or liquor to declare?"

"No." Paul and Delia said in unison. Phil shook his head.

"I must advise you against driving at night in the Peten and Chichicastenango regions."

"Guerillas?" Paul asked.

"That's what they like to call themselves. But they are just bandits. Enjoy your stay in Guatemala." He slapped the hood and motioned them through.

Paul put the Land Rover in gear, and drove across the long concrete bridge. He turned right and headed up hill into the town. It was a gloomy settlement. They drove by a few stores, bordellos and bars, a dusty mercado and a gas station as they headed west.

"Welcome to bloody Guatemala." Paul said grimly.

* * * * * * * *

Five miles down the road Paul had to slow down to less than ten miles an hour to creep through the potholes that led up to a military checkpoint.

"We all need to be very polite and patient here." He whispered. "We all have to get out and documentarsé."

"I've been here before." Phil said quietly.

They were forced to assume the position as teenaged Guatemalan soldiers frisked them in a very professional manner. They did not grope Delia, probably because their commanding officer was in attendance. They searched each individual bag, one item at a time. Phil had removed all dark green and khaki clothing, compasses, and cameras, and placed them in Quan's care. Anything that might be useful to the guerillas would be confiscated, and could result in detention in a Guatemalan military jail. Satisfied, the guards ordered them back into the Rover.

The pole across the road lifted and Paul drove through. On the right *Infierno Kaibil* passed by, Phil read the faded sign, Aqui Se Forjan Los Mejores Combatientes de América! He wondered as always how these troops would fare against real soldiers instead of unarmed Maya Indians, and poorly armed guerillas. He figured one platoon of Marines could handle it.

"They've made some improvements to this place since I was here last." Phil pointed at the new steel watchtower going up next to its decrepit wooden predecessor.

Three new bunkers were being excavated and soldiers drilled on the dusty parade ground. Unconsciously Phil analyzed the terrain and planned his assault on it. Give me one hour and one platoon he thought.

Three more military checkpoints were negotiated, as they made their way slowly west on the deeply rutted road, but they weren't searched again. Only their identification was checked.

In the hamlet of Manantial they stopped at a tienda. It was a small thatched hut with a red and white Gallo Cerveza sign above the door.

"This has to be it." Paul said, and parked the Rover in a washed out area in front of the hut. "There isn't any other building around here."

"We're a half hour early." Phil said, looking around. Two skinny mongrel dogs lay by the door sleeping. A rooster crowed somewhere nearby. "Man I feel naked without my pieces."

"That's the third time you've said that this morning." Paul said. "Relax. They'll be here soon. Thank God we got across the border and through the checkpoints with no problems."

"Delia had a lot to do with that. I think that border guard liked her." Phil chuckled.

"She played him like a fish." Paul said.

"Most men are simple." Delia said, laughing with them.

"Oh really?" Paul and Phil said in unison.

"Present company excluded of course."

"I hear a truck coming." Paul said, opening the door.

A bright red Chevrolet Suburban pulled in next to them. Zeng Quan, Esmeralda, and two Chinese teenagers were inside.

"I have the rest of your order." Quan said from the driver's seat.

"And I have the rest of your money. You don't want to do it here?" Phil asked, he didn't like the setting, it was too exposed.

"No. We drive two miles west. You follow."

They slowly crept down a devastated and ruined section of road, the center was cratered. A track snaked into the jungle to their right and they had to drive over massive tree roots and around deep potholes.

"This road looks like it was bombed." Delia said.

"It was back in '82." Phil said quietly. "All the way from here on into Chiapas, the helicopters pounced on anything that moved."

"Guatemalan soldiers crossed into Mexico? I don't remember hearing anything like that."

"There are a lot of things that happen down here that no one hears about. You can bet the Mexican government was in on it."

"But why?" Delia asked.

"Because Guatemala and Mexico subscribe to an old American belief; the only good Indian is a dead Indian."

"It's still happening man. That's why so many of them have come to Belize." Paul said.

Ahead the Suburban pulled behind a thicket and stopped. Paul parked the Rover next to it. Esmeralda climbed out and hugged Paul. Quan frowned, and said, "Let's do this quickly."

* * * * * * * *

They were re-supplied and Phil was happy to have his weapons back. Plus, Quan had come up with more ammunition than he had expected. The zodiac raft and air compressor were brand new, Phil wondered where they came from, and Paul said they probably "fell off a truck."

As they closed the tailgate, and prepared to depart, they witnessed a fiery argument between Quan and Esmeralda, it was conducted in rapid fire and furious Chinese. It was clear that Quan wanted his niece to go back to Belize with him, and equally apparent that she wanted to stay with Paul. Eventually some sort of agreement was reached; Quan embraced his niece and drove off in the Suburban. She came over to Paul grinning.

"I get to come too." She threw a battered suitcase in the back, and climbed in.

Paul sat down next to her.

"On to Tikal." Paul said. "Phil you want to drive?"

"Absolutely."

"I think her uncle doesn't like me." Paul said.

"Can't imagine why. You're such a wonderful fellow." Phil grinned.

"Maybe it's because I'm not Chinese."

"You're not? Really? I would never have guessed." They drove slowly down the road laughing.

58 Recruited

"So it's settled?" Mamett asked. "You will be responsible for the settlement pattern study at Chanul Tzuk? And you will consider driving down a project truck with supplies and equipment?"

"Well as I said Professor Mamett..."

"Just call me Patrick."

"Patrick. Well, that had been my understanding with Dr. Bennett, that I would do the settlement pattern study."

"And I am honoring all of his commitments. What about driving a truck down for us? I mean you're right in San Antonio, closer than anyone else."

Jesse and Gloria had only been in San Antonio a few hours before Mamett's phone call had taken him by surprise. "I would say there's a good chance I could do it. When do you want me to go?"

"Anytime after the second week of December."

"That's less than a month from now. Will everything be ready?"

"Everything will be ready before that, a week before."

"What about Christmas?"

"As long as you are ready to start work by December thirty first, I am completely flexible. You can ignore the call from Avendano; he was trying to help me find you, in the event you were still in Mexico."

"Can I bring a friend with me?"

"Yes. Of course. Another archaeologist?"

"Yes." Jesse lied without hesitation. This might be a way to get Garcia his ammunition, he thought.

"Absolutely."

"Can I have a few days to think it over?"

"Certainly. But I do hope you'll do it. Right now you are it. I have no other option and I need to get that truck and equipment down there intact."

59 The Jaguar Inn

The Jaguar Inn at Tikal was their base of operations. Phil and Paul were checking with the locals, to see if anyone had seen Belinda, if they knew where Macondo was, or if there were any "troubles" going on in the area. Phil paid for Paul and Esmeralda's room over their objections. He still wanted Paul to return, because he knew the crazy Belizean was losing money by not being in San Pedro.

"It's not tourist season man. I'm not missing anything. Besides, Esmeralda's never been to Tikal before. She loves it here. What have you found out?"

"Here's the story so far." Phil said, as they sat in a coconut grove outside the cafe bar. "Belinda did stay here the nights of August 23rd and 24th."

"That's what?" Delia asked. "Almost three months ago."

Phil nodded. "She hasn't been back here since then. Let's see, what else? Everyone says not to drive in the Peten at night. People have disappeared lately, and whether the military or someone else is responsible is unclear. So she could have run into trouble somewhere." He paused and took a long drink from his beer. "As for Macondo, there was a village about thirty kilometers north of here, by that name. It's been deserted since '82. No one knows of any ruins. No one's heard of any excavations."

"Of course if the site has been looted, and just recently discovered, the Department of Archaeology would not publicize it." Delia observed.

"True. That's why when Patty and Madeline get into Guatemala City tomorrow, the directions they get from the museum will be critical. The concierge informs me that the road is a pure bitch to get through. After you get to Uaxactun it's often impassable. Even for a Land Rover. Or so he says."

"Only one way to find out." Paul said and poured another Margarita out of the pitcher for Esmeralda.

"That's also true." Phil said, and took a breath before continuing. "Now comes the really funny part. The part that's not true. According to the guest book, I stayed here the same nights as Belinda. Paid cash too. Ran up a hell of dinner tab on the twenty fourth. Only trouble is I wasn't here. I was in Cambridge studying for my orals."

* * * * * * * *

They were strolling in the forest that loomed on both sides of the path to the excavations at Tikal's El Mundo Perdido. Up ahead workmen were chopping the underbrush with machetes, clearing the path. Monkeys chattered somewhere above them in the canopy. Delia reached for Phil's hand and held it as they walked. He seemed aloof and awkward to her.

"You know Tikal has always been my favorite Maya site." He shook his head regretfully. "So many things have happened since the first time I came here."

"Was that back when you were stationed at the embassy?"

"Yes. And Tikal is what made me want to be an archaeologist. It is so magnificent." He shook his head. "How did everything get so screwed up? I just wanted a new life, to be an archaeologist, and be left alone. I feel like I'm being pushed back, to a life I left behind."

His melancholy was disturbing. She decided to attack the problem and disperse it. "Okay. So someone came down here, met with Belinda and pretended to be you? So even in late August you were being set up?"

"Evidently. I guess it all ties in with the receipts the police found back in Cambridge. It may have been a cover story, a contingency plan that they would only use if something went wrong. Obviously, something happened down here and they used that contingency plan for a reason."

"But what?" Delia noticed that he held her hand more firmly now.

"In that letter from Belinda did she mention seeing anyone, any archaeologists we know?"

"Just Obregon."

"I can't believe he would be involved. I've known him for years. Okay. Let's go over it again. Until your recent conversation with Mamett, the last place that we could trace Belinda to was here at Tikal, the letter and the guest book confirm that."

"And a possible trip to Cambridge in September."

"I don't buy that. Never have. She would have called someone."

"So it's back to the elaborate deception?" Delia said thinking out loud.

Something stirred in her mind, and then she remembered it. She stopped and held both his hands. "Laurence Eikelmann. Laurence said she 'didn't deserve something', and that she 'wasn't supposed to be there', that night I came over to his apartment. He must have been referring to being down here with her? He must have pretended to be you."

Phil nodded. "Either him or Thomas, and it really was a contingency plan. In case something went wrong. And something did go wrong, because someone killed Eikelmann and Thomas, and that's why Belinda is missing. I don't believe either of them was a suicide, 'assisted' or otherwise."

They continued walking, no longer holding hands. Delia pushed her hair back, staring at the ground, trying to concentrate. It was like trying to reassemble a ceramic vessel, she had most of the pieces, but she was overlooking something. Ahead she saw something shiny and blue in the dirt, where the workmen had cleared the undergrowth.

She went over and picked it up. It was an earring made of turquoise, black coral, and seashell. She recognized it immediately because she had borrowed the earrings once.

"Belinda used to have a set like this." Delia said, showing it to Phil.

"I know. I bought them for her in the Bahamas two years ago. On Staniel Key. There's a necklace too."

"So she really was here." Delia handed it to Phil. "I mean right here on this path."

"And so was Laurence, and so was someone else." Phil said grimly.

"Phil, do you still love her?" Delia surprised herself, by asking.

"I feel something. But is it love? I don't use that word lightly. Obligated, concerned, these are some of the things I feel for sure." He pulled her in close, and looked into her eyes. "I feel the same way about you, only different. If that makes any sense." He shrugged.

Delia kissed him long, and slowly. Phil held her closely, and pulled her in tighter. The workmen stopped chopping with their machetes, and gestured.

She whispered in his ear. "They're probably thinking we should get a room."

"Isn't it nice that we already have one?"

60 Lord Ah Cacau

The University of Pennsylvania team found the skeleton of Lord Ah Cacau beneath Temple I at Tikal in the 1960s. Now he was stretched out on his back beneath his heavy jade necklaces in an exhibit in Guatemala City. Madeline and Patty stood beside it as the museum prepared to close, and they tried to count how many jade beads there were while they waited for Maria Vega the Assistant Curator of Archaeology of the National Museum.

"I count one hundred and twenty six." Madeline said.

"One hundred and seventeen." Patty countered.

"This place gives me the creeps." Madeline observed as lights were turned out in the rear exhibit halls.

"Kind of a Neo-Baroque pile, decaying away." Patty said. "Very European wouldn't be out of place in Bordeaux."

"You would think since so much of the museum is about the Maya, that they might have gone with a Maya architectural motif." Madeline said, turning, as she heard high heels clicking in the hall.

Maria Vega introduced herself, and led them to her office. "We haven't much time." She said, "The museum closes in fifteen minutes. Please sit down."

"Well we just need a few minutes of your time." Madeline implied she would not be hurried, by slowly taking a small notebook and pen from her purse.

"Yes. You asked about Macondo, in your phone call. Do you have a map with you?"

Madeline handed one over that she had bought in the museum gift shop.

Maria put on her glasses and smoothed the map out on her desk. "Alright, now where is Tikal? I always start at Tikal, and then go north to Uaxactun. It's a rough road; you would need four wheel drive, a winch, and probably chain saws. You cannot get in during the rainy season unless you are on horseback. From there you go northeast to El Ramonal, and then west to the ruins at Macondo. Do you want me to mark it on the map?"

"Please."

"Be sure to go with someone. There have been some incidents in the area the past few years and just recently." She folded up the map. "Okay. How else may I help you?" She seemed anxious to leave. Probably got a dinner date, Madeline thought.

"We're looking for a crew member, a young American woman named Belinda Boothe."

"Oh Belinda! I know her well. She studied here this summer for several weeks. Is she supposed to be up there with Obregon?"

"She's my niece. That's what her department at Harvard heard, in a round about way."

"She may well be. It's impossible to contact the project though, their radio has never worked. We sent them a replacement a few days ago."

"And when did you last see Belinda?"

"Oh let's see. Around the end of August, when I went on vacation."

"But not since?" Madeline wrote it all down.

"No. She was going to Tikal, and then on to Palenque I believe."

"But do you think she may be at Macondo?"

"It would make sense. It is a major Early Classic site on a scale equal to Rio Azul. That's what Belinda is studying you know? The Early Classic. She may be up there volunteering. She is such a free spirit, isn't she?"

61 Yaxchilan

Sunset backlit the ruins of Yaxchilan and gave them a rose colored glow, as the eastern sky darkened. At the foot of the Grand Stairway in the Main Plaza, Domingo Xicaret spread out his sacred bundle on Altar 10. Next to him, Belinda knelt by a moss-covered sculpture of a crocodile.

Domingo had erected his ka'an te' over the altar, thirteen gourds under an arch of green, leafy, saplings. The Maya zodiac appeared in the night sky above them, and Belinda sat respectfully, on a straw mat directly underneath the gourds. Domingo knelt beside her, moving things around, getting ready to begin.

"Tonight we go into the underworld." He said, neatly arranging candles, an obsidian blade, and small bark paper figures on the altar. "We commune with *Sukunkyum*, Lord of the Night. He may direct us to *Lord Kisin*, the god of death, and this could become very dangerous. Still we have no choice. Protect your pixan, your spirit double from Kisin, and be prepared as I taught you. Drink this." He handed her another pot of balche, and started burning the copal offering.

This makes seven balches, Belinda thought. I think I'm getting numb. She shifted her legs underneath her, they were almost completely healed but they still ached if she stayed in one position too long. She looked at the ceremonial vine with the obsidian barbs knotted in it, fearful of what she was about to do, and she placed the bark paper next to it.

"And now the night comes. And now the foretelling begins. *Sukunkyum* Lord of the Night, accept these offerings that we may belong here in your plaza. Accept our ch'ulel and mix it with yours. Here in your house."

He lit a match and the brazier flamed. The air was filled with copal incense. He removed his cotton shorts and sat naked from the waist down, deeply inhaling the incense. He held a pot of balche, offered it in turn to the four corners of the world and then he drank it. Chanting in his Mayan tongue he placed his penis on the smooth stone slab and picked up an obsidian blade. He brought the blade down and sliced the old scar tissue near the end, a deeper cut near the middle, and another one near the base. He sucked in his breath as the blood flowed freely. He cupped it in his hand and offered it to the lords before he scattered it on to bark paper. He placed the paper in the brazier and watched his offering turn to smoke as the gods accepted it.

Simultaneously, Belinda pulled the barbs through the tip of her tongue, her mouth filled with blood and she spat into her hand, scattered it on the paper and burned it. She was faint, ready to keel over.

"Now they will come." Xicaret mumbled. He exclaimed. "Do you see it? Do you see the gates of the underworld? I have shown it to you."

She gazed into the flames as the balche took hold and entered a trance state.

Something flickered; a vaguely human head started to take form.

Suddenly she saw Laurence's face in the flames, standing outside the entrance to the underworld. Eyes wide with terror.

"Belinda. I am so sorry. You okay?"

"I'm much better." She said dreamily, warmed by another pot of balche that numbed her tongue." How are you?"

"I am with *Lord Kisin* and I'm dead. You know, the really strange thing about death is the total absence of time." He laughed. "For an archaeologist that is almost beyond comprehension. This is not a nice place. And Kisin! What a scary bastard! Sometimes he's like the King Kong of vultures, enormous. Or when it suits him, he's a spider as big as the Milky Way. And Spider Man is always hungry." His form flickered out and then he coalesced again. "By the way, did I mention I was wrong about God?"

"Oh? How so?"

"He's not a schizophrenic."

"No?"

"No. It's worse than I thought. He suffers from multiple personality disorder."

He grinned in the flames, and his face flickered and became a death's head, skull and white teeth gleaming.

"I don't understand." She was in a stupor now, neither asleep, nor awake, somewhere in between.

"I don't expect you to. It's not important really. That you understand I mean. I understand that you slept around, that you've been loose with your morals. That's something else we have in common. Had in common."

It hit her like an electric shock, like being punched.

"Maybe. Maybe I was but I'm not anymore. How did you find that out?"

"All sorts of information floats around this place. Down here once something is known, it is never unknown. Kind of like the Internet." His face readjusted back into its fleshy form. "But I stray from my point. I'm trying to do one decent thing for you, even though it's a bit too late for me." He laughed. "But it's the least I can do considering the circumstances. Our brujo friend Alex is still looking for you. He won't rest until he finds you. I don't know how he knows, but he knows you are still

309

alive. So he's going to kill you. He's a good friend of *Lord Kisin*. They're real tight."

"What do I do?"

"What do you think? Either he is dead or you are dead. You have to kill him. Someone has to kill him."

62 Macondo

The road to Macondo was not really a road. It was sometimes two ruts, sometimes one rut, snaking through the jungle. It disappeared altogether, and then reappeared again. Someone with a chainsaw had passed through; tree trunks were down, and had recently been cut up. Green plastic bottles of chain saw oil were littered here and there. The Land Rover bogged down three times in the muddy swamps, and had to be winched out each time. Every time it happened it cost them an extra hour or two.

It had taken Patty and Madeline two days to make the trip from Guatemala City, to Tikal. Another two days had been lost in preparation. Now two days out of Tikal, Phil was frustrated, and worried that they might be off course. After leaving Uaxactun, the jungle became progressively thicker, and it was hard to tell if they were following a trail, or hallucinating one. He stopped the Land Rover and got out to look for traces.

"Where did it go?" Paul asked. "It was here a minute ago."

"Was it? Or were we just following someone's logging cut?" Phil unscrewed his water bottle and took a big drink. He looked in the back seats at Madeline, Esmeralda, Delia, the dog, and shook his head. What the hell was he doing out here? Leading a tour group?

"Glad you came Madeline? You could be in the lounge at the Jaguar Inn, having a cold Margarita with Patty about now."

Madeline smiled through the sweat on her lip. "Only one of us needed to stay back Phil, you know that. Besides, she's my niece and I want to see her." She stretched out her arms. "Is it four o'clock yet? Has the sun sunk below the yard arm?"

"I believe it has ma'am." Paul said, reaching under his seat for a small cooler that contained a bottle of rum, mixed with limejuice and water.

"God, it would be easy to disappear out here." Delia said. "Everything looks the same."

"They don't call it the lowlands for nothing." Phil said, feeling particularly low, and declining the rum concoction. He watched Nutmeg sniff around and head off to the left. "Now where is she going?"

"She's picked up the scent of something that's for sure." Paul said and walked around the hood. "We've got less than an hour left of daylight, you want to set up camp here?"

"Good as place as any." Phil said absently. A feeling, an almost recognizable memory of something distracted him. What was it?

* * * * * * * * *

Nutmeg smelled the men and their food, one man in particular smelled strong, his scent dominated all others. She followed it over a low hill, beside a watery bog, across a giant mahogany stump, and down beside a swamp, and there they were. Nine men eating around the back of a truck.

One man raised a shotgun when he saw her and fired. Something stung her back and she yelped, as she ran away.

* * * * * * * * *

"Shotgun." Phil said. "Pretty close. Could be hunters." He had the Ak-47 in his hands in seconds, and stuffed the Makarov into his pants pocket. The nagging feeling was turning more troublesome. Delia and Esmeralda looked up from the tent they were unpacking, and stood still. Madeline was in the Land Rover, stood up, and tried to see up ahead.

"What are they shooting at?" Paul instinctively reached for his shotgun. "I haven't seen any sign of game."

311

"Where's Nutmeg?" Delia asked. A wave of fear shivered her.

Phil recognized the feeling now; it was straight out of Viet Nam, and moving rapidly through his blood. "Paul, give the extra shotgun to Madeline."

"Esmeralda, could you please bring me some shells over here?" Paul moved out in front of the vehicle and stood by a large tree stump, as he peered into the darkening jungle.

"Delia to me." Phil said, crouching low next to a massive fallen ceiba tree.

"What is it?" Esmeralda asked.

Nutmeg dashed into the camp whimpering, tail between her legs, and ran over to Delia and Phil. Blood spotted the blonde fur on her flanks.

"She's been shot." Delia said, and stroked the trembling dog, trying to calm her down.

"Bastards. Stupid bastards." Paul waded into the jungle thicket, and became invisible in the gloom.

"Everyone be quiet." Phil whispered loudly, listening to the forest. Madeline came over to them, shotgun in one hand, and a box of shells in the other.

Phil thought he heard voices but wanted to get closer. He kept his voice down. "Paul. Madeline. I'm going forward…check things out. Keep alert, if anyone comes near, use your own judgment."

He was gone. Running silently through the trees, the people behind him were forgotten. He concentrated on what was in front of him, on every line and form in the jungle ahead, every sound, sensing for anything that was out of place. It was all too familiar.

His view ahead was blocked by a low hill, and he crept up to it carefully. He lay down on his side and looked over into a shallow swale. Phil realized he was on a Maya house mound, so a site was nearby somewhere, maybe they were in the outskirts of Macondo. Nothing but a marsh to his

312

left and jungle as far as the eye could see. But he heard a sound like a slap coming from his right. Then another slap. He headed that way.

* * * * * * * *

Paul stood watch on the left and Madeline on the right, while Delia and Esmeralda made the area easier to defend. They parked the Land Rover sideways, and unwound the winch cable and hook. Then they stretched out the cable, and hooked it around a cohune palm.

Paul liked it. It was Delia's idea, and it would definitely surprise anyone trying to flank them from that side, because in the increasing darkness, the hanging cable was almost invisible.

They stacked the stove, boxes, and other odd equipment around the tires to protect them. Having completed these duties, Delia returned to Madeline with another box of shells. Esmeralda crouched near Paul.

Delia took a pair of tweezers and started plucking buckshot from Nutmeg's flank, trying not to think about how frightened she was.

The forest was eerie. Silent. The sunlight was almost gone as they waited.

* * * * * * * *

Seven armed men in military style clothing, stood in front of a Ford F-350, 4 X 4. Half of them had M-16s and the rest held shotguns. They watched two other men; a very Indian-looking fellow had taken a cane and was beating the hell out of a smaller, younger man. Phil hid behind an enormous mahogany stump, watched and listened. He could not flank them on the left because the swamp extended as far as he could see in that direction. The right side was a possibility, but the cover wasn't that good.

Suddenly he experienced it all over again. All of the old symptoms of fear. He fought to control them, the knots in his stomach, the dry mouth, the muscle spasming in his neck. He choked it down, decided to stay put, and see what he could learn. Were they bandits, guerillas, paramilitaries? The smaller man was down on his knees, head lolling and bloody. The larger one limped, favored his left leg and leaned on his cane. He also had a cast on his right arm, but it didn't seem to bother him that much. He started talking quietly. It was very hard to hear him.

"Stealth. I told you. Stealth. So of course you shoot at a dog. Pendejo!" He kicked him in the head, and the man sprawled flat. "Help me understand what you were thinking. Were you going to eat it? Skin it? Stuff it?" He kicked him in the ribs, and then in the head again.

Phil thought they might kill the smaller guy, and shifted his AK-47, sighting in on the larger man's ear. I could drop him right now, he thought. He realized that the old switches were coming back on, like turning on an old machine, and a wave of emotion swept over him, shivering him. He tried to shake it off.

He watched the larger man wipe the blood off his cane on his fatigue pants. "I should do the same to you. Skin you and stuff you. But you are already stuffed. Stuffed full of shit."

Two men laughed and he turned on them.

"Did I say you could laugh?" He walked over to the truck, and extracted an M-16 from the bed. Phil strained to listen to him. "Pay attention. I have already explained this once. I will not explain it again. They were seen leaving Tikal yesterday morning. They could be very close. Stealth. No one shoots anything without my permission. Is that clear? That could have been their dog. Now they could be warned. Now they could be ready for us."

Phil was faced with a dilemma. Stay here and thin them out? Or go back and warn the others? He wanted the leader alive if possible. What the hell, he thought, and he squeezed the trigger.

* * * * * * * * *

They heard shots and Paul said. "That's an AK. That would be Phil."

A crescendo of shots answered in response.

314

"Shotguns and M-16s. We've got trouble now for sure. Okay, Esmeralda, Delia, I want you to crawl under the Land Rover and stay there. Madeline, get ready. Listen, you'll hear them before you see them."

Madeline nodded and stretched out in the classic prone position.

"Ever shoot anything with a shot gun?" He asked her.

"Just skeet."

"Men are easier to hit. Bigger you know."

"I know. I shot one in Cambridge with a pistol."

"Damn. I was three years in the BDF and I never shot at anyone. Damn."

Madeline grinned nervously, and flinched as many more shots were exchanged. They seemed closer.

* * * * * * * *

Phil dropped the leader, putting a round into his lame leg. He had time to wing another one before they pounded the stump with bullets. They were still blowing it away while he retreated back to the low hill. He could hear them moving to his right, but it was dark now and he couldn't see anything. The adrenaline was running and the fear was going away. His senses were acute. He could smell their scent. He heard everything clearly.

And they sure made a lot of noise; one was crashing through the jungle, very close now. The man was so close that Phil could see his boots and his shotgun. Phil tackled him, with his forearm and pulled him over, placing the barrel of the AK-47 against the young man's chin.

"If you shout you are dead." He pushed the gun deeper into his jaw. "Who are you?" Phil whispered.

"Pedro Cantu. Please don't kill me."

"How old are you?"

"Twenty. Please senor, I beg you don't kill me."

"Your accent is not Guatemalan."

"I am from Chiapas. Please don't kill me." The boy was shaking. Phil could smell urine.

"Did you wet yourself Pedro? Did you know that if I cough, this gun could blow your head off? Did you know that?"

He nodded and started sobbing.

"Who do you work for?"

"I am a policeman." He whimpered.

Phil almost let go of him, he was so surprised.

"What are you doing here?"

Phil heard Nutmeg barking and gunfire erupted behind him.

He had been flanked.

* * * * * * * *

Nutmeg was lying beside Madeline, licking her wounds when she stiffened, rose up and started barking.

Bullets filled the air above her, and Madeline could see the guns flashing no more than thirty feet away. She fired both barrels, pumped, and fired again. Bullets pounded the ground around her, Nutmeg cried out, and something hard and hot burned into her arm, another one clipped her shoulder, spinning her around, and another one blew a hole in her side. White-hot pain seared her and the darkness rushed in.

From the other side Paul fired three volleys, and a shower of bullets hammered the earth around him, stinging his leg. "Oh man. We've got problems now." He said rolling toward the Land Rover, feeling the blood seeping into his boot.

Delia saw that Madeline was not firing. She felt the temptation to sink into the earth under the vehicle, and hide, but she left Esmeralda and crawled toward Madeline.

"God please don't be dead Madeline. Please don't be dead."

* * * * * * * *

Phil had neutralized Pedro. He wouldn't wake up for awhile. He ran toward the fighting with the Makarov in his left hand, and the AK-47 in his right. No time to watch, no time to do anything but run and fire. Run and fire at an M16 flashing as it blasted the camp to his left. The blood frenzy was inside of him now, the sounds of battle screaming in his ears, he did not hear the bullets whipping around him, the cries, or the curses. Chanting his war cry, he fired again, spraying the area with lead, and kept running and firing. The gunfire to his left was dense; M-16s versus shotguns. Another one shot at him, but he was faster and fired back. He heard a death rattle nearby.

Someone was shooting into the camp, and Phil sprayed him too, running and firing and shooting another one who barely missed him with his volley. Someone else was screaming ahead, was it Delia? He could see a shotgun flash about thirty feet away, and realized he was almost back to the camp. "Delia?" he yelled out, and someone else was shooting at him.

Delia knelt beside Madeline. She was dying. Delia screamed, ignoring the bullets ripping the wind around her. She howled in agony and fury, and picked up Madeline's shotgun. Crying, bawling and screaming, she loaded shells into it. Insanity was in the night, beating its bat wings against the treetops. Someone was firing at her, and she pumped the shotgun dry in reply. A male voice moaned. They were firing all around her and had surrounded the camp. Someone else screamed in Spanish and she heard Paul firing back at him. From behind her she heard Esmeralda sigh and moan.

Phil was yelling in the trees, yelling and firing. Something burned near the Land Rover, and the smoke was spreading. She was out of ammunition.

Then it was quiet and she heard steps running behind her near the vehicle. Paul fired, and missed, and the man hit the cable at full speed and went sprawling onto the ground, a few feet away from Delia. Not bothering to reload, she only had time to club him with the shotgun and club him she did, repeatedly, as he struggled to bring around his weapon. A shotgun discharged next to her head, hot blood splattered across her face, and the world went silent, as her attacker fell limp. Paul stood next to her, the barrel of his shotgun smoking.

Two hundred feet from Paul, a man was fleeing back toward the truck. Phil was determined to catch him. He ran after him and fired in the direction of the noise crashing through the undergrowth.

The man hit the ground and was firing back at Phil. From his left, in the direction of the Ford another M-16 opened up. Now who the hell is that? Phil thought. Couldn't be Pedro. Must be the guy with the cane. I've blundered into a crossfire. Good job man. They had him pinned down.

* * * * * * * *

Paul cradled Esmeralda in his arms. "Come on baby wake up. Wake up." He felt blood on her ribs, plastered to her shirt. Was it buckshot? He couldn't tell if she was breathing. The bleeding seemed to have stopped. He heard two M-16s firing at an Ak-47 in the distance. He knew what he had to do. He made a silent prayer over Esmeralda, and gently lowered her head. He reloaded the magazine to his old Winchester Model 12. He ignored the burning tent. Now he was ready.

"Watch the fort Delia." He said and slipped into the jungle.

Delia did not reply. She was too busy trying to bind Madeline's stomach wound.

* * * * * * * *

Bullets buzzed over Phil's head and stitched the ground around him. I could die here, he thought, in this swampy night, in the middle of madness, but I'm not giving up yet. Someone's going to have to reload, and when they do, I make my move. He held his pistol up and fired at the man near the truck, to keep him honest. Bullets thrummed the air above Phil's head, and he flattened himself again. I could die here all right. One hell of a mess.

Paul saw the flashes of the M-16s. It looked like two of them had Phil pinned down. He saw Phil's pistol fire, and rushed the one on the right The M-16 fired again, the white blaze stabbing through the smoke blowing from the camp.

His victim never saw him. Paul kept firing until the magazine tube was empty. In the gun flashes he could see that he was obliterating the man's head, and yet he kept shooting.

Phil heard Paul blasting away to his right and ran for the slope, rolling and firing toward the last place he had seen the M-16 fire. He heard the truck start up, and saw it reversing quickly, with no lights. Phil had time to fire a burst as it turned and sped away, and then everything was quiet.

Paul came over to him, and said, "Madeline, Esmeralda, and Nutmeg were all hit. We need to get back."

Phil jogged toward the camp, the adrenaline still pumping. Paul trailed behind him, and went to Esmeralda. Phil knelt next to Madeline and Delia.

"She's dying Phil. I've bound her wounds, but she's lost a lot of blood." Delia tried to think of what else could be done for Madeline.

"Where all has she been hit?"

"Right arm, left shoulder, left side."

"Stomach wound?" Phil hoped she wasn't gut shot.

"Close to the stomach. That's for sure."

"Paul? Esmeralda?"

"She's still breathing, but she's hurt bad." Paul was carrying her to the Land Rover.

"Okay. Let's very carefully get everyone in the vehicle and try to find Macondo. They'll have better medical supplies than what we've got in the first aid kit."

"What about Nutmeg?" Delia asked.

"Is she?"

"She'll probably be okay."

"I'll get her. If it hadn't been for her we would have been ambushed and we'd all be dead right now."

"What about the fire?"

"Let it burn."

* * * * * * * *

They followed the truck's tracks. Phil drove slowly, thankful that the women were unconscious and couldn't feel the bumps and jolts. Delia held Madeline, and Paul held Esmeralda. Phil was worried that they were lost, and that two women would die because he had not come alone. And in his first time in combat in twenty years, he had let himself get flanked, and caught in a crossfire.

It seemed like they had been driving in the dark for hours, but it had barely been one hour, when Phil saw lights looming in the darkness ahead. He stopped the vehicle, turned off the engine and listened. A gasoline powered electrical generator was purring faintly in the distance.

"What do you think?" Paul asked. "It's about where it ought to be."

"I think we found Macondo."

* * * * * * * * *

They were nearing the lights when a soldier stepped out of a thicket to their left.

He held up a hand and said "Alto."

Phil stopped the vehicle, and whispered to Paul and Delia. "Cover up the weapons." He saw a jaguar patch on the soldier's shoulder and thought; well at least they're not from Kaibil.

"This is a restricted archaeological zone, and it is closed to the public, by order of the government of Guatemala." The soldier said.

"We are archaeologists and we need help. Bandits attacked us. These two women are dying." The soldier climbed quickly on to the running board, and said. "The infirmary is right over there. Let's go."

* * * * * * * *

Madeline and Esmeralda were lying next to each other on some rough plank tables inside a thatched hut. The Guatemalan Army corpsman, Sergeant Padilla, was very good. Gunshots were his specialty. He had trained at Fort Sam Houston in San Antonio, he told them, while he worked on Madeline, who was in critical condition. Paul never let go of Esmeralda's hand as Delia and Phil cleaned her wounds.

"Whoever bound these wounds knew what they were doing." Padilla observed.

"Delia did it." Phil said.

"You probably saved her life." He worked quietly and quickly, injecting her with antibiotics, and morphine. As he cut away the skin around the wound, he made a clucking sound. "Well she's lucky that it missed her stomach, but there is a hole in the intestine, a large one. And the bullet passed all the way through, carried in a lot of dirt and clothing. Have to clean and suction it immediately. She's hemorrhaging. A lot of dark blood in the intestines. See? The wall is discolored." He wiped the blood away, and started suctioning. "We've got a bleeder here spurting blood, that is the main problem." He worked quickly and was silent for awhile.

A shotgun blast at close range had hit Esmeralda in the left side near her ribs. She was weak from loss of blood, when she woke up. "Pablo?" Her eyes fluttered open.

"Right here baby. Try not to move."

321

"Where are we?" Her eyes blinked rapidly.

"A doctor is going to fix you up in just a bit." Paul smoothed her hair back off of her forehead.

"Okay." She passed out again.

Phil noticed blood leaking from Paul's boot. "Hey man. You were hit!"

"No big deal. It looks worse than it is."

"Sit down Paul and let me check it." Delia went to work on Paul's leg.

* * * * * * * *

Phil was watching the orange glow of dawn brighten over the jungle, when Delia found him.

"Madeline is going to have to be evacuated as soon as we can get a helicopter in here. Padilla is talking it over with his Captain."

"And how is Madeline?" Phil was afraid Madeline would not make it.

"She's stable. He did a good job, cleaned the wound, stopped the bleeding, and gave her plasma. But she needs an illiostomy as soon as possible. Somehow we're going to have to get her to a good hospital today. They'll have to repair her colon in a real operating room, and soon."

"If the army can get a helicopter in here, then we'll need to get an air ambulance in to Flores." He shook his head. "It'll be hard, but I think it's doable. Are you okay Delia?" She looked pale and drawn.

"Just sleepy. Maybe a little worried. Correction. I'm scared."

"Want to go curl up with me?"

"I thought you'd never ask."

They started walking toward their tent. "And where's Paul?" Phil still seemed keyed up, and was restlessly looking around.

"Next to Esmeralda. Asleep. His wound was fairly superficial. Esmeralda should bounce back pretty well too; most of the buckshot didn't penetrate very far."

"And Belinda's never even been here." Phil asked. "Somehow I'm not surprised." They walked under a sheltering ceiba tree.

"Three of the crew members are from the museum in G.C., and they know her well. No one has seen her, or heard from her since she went to Tikal back in August."

Phil put his arm around her and hugged her. "I'm glad you're all right. This whole thing has been a disaster. A wild goose chase. And it was Mamett who told you Belinda was here."

"Well actually, he said Sergio Avendano told him she was here." Delia hugged him back, just being with him made her happy. They had not been able to share any moments together, since they had left Tikal.

"I guess I need to pay a visit to Chiapas and talk to Avendano."

Delia was so emotionally drained, she could hardly think. Phil in contrast seemed to be running on pure adrenaline. He stopped suddenly. "Wait a minute. You said a newspaper story about Haden's disappearance in Chiapas was in her luggage?"

"Yes." Delia saw his expression light up.

"Don't you see? That's where she went. She went to Chiapas to help the search party out, to volunteer." He cracked his knuckles and rubbed his hands together.

"That sounds like something she would do." Delia mused.

"Any honorable archaeologist would do it if they were close enough to Chanul Tzuk, and from Tikal she wasn't that far away. Two days or three at the most." Phil was pulling his folded and tattered map out of his back pocket. "I can't believe it never occurred to me before. Don't you see that's what happened?"

"Well we'll just have to go check." Delia said.

"So how soon will Obregon get back? We need to find out if he knows anything that will help us find her." Phil asked.

"He returns from Tintal tomorrow."

"Still I know that's what she did. She went to Chanul Tzuk." Phil yawned, and stretched. "God. All of a sudden I feel worn out."

"Well we haven't slept much for two days." He sounded curt, distracted. Was there something more that he was keeping from her? "So do you think they were looters or do you think we were setup?"

"I think our opponents are tying up loose ends, which is why they hit us last night. Perhaps that's what Eikelmann was to begin with, a loose end, maybe that's how all this got started."

"Then Belinda is?"

"Exactly."

63 Just Give Me the Truth

The man's ropy guts were strung out in the tall weeds. They had turned blackish blue in the mid morning heat. The air smelled of blood, burned meat and gunpowder.

Vultures hopped about on the ground plucking at bloody scraps and more circled above them. The smell was old and familiar to Phil, sweet and foul, sticking in his nostrils like a mist, the smell of dead men rotting in the sun.

Phil had joined Captain Macias, the platoon commander, and three of his men to search the area looking for survivors.

"Look at this." Macias stood by the swamp and gestured Phil over. He pointed to a bloody trail made by something with squat feet and long claws, leading down the slope and into the swamp.

"Crocodile?" Phil asked.

"Probably took the body to his nest." He looked across the silent swamp and back up the slope. "And you counted nine last night?"

"One definitely got away."

"One is in the swamp so that leaves seven. Let's keep looking."

The Captain was in his late 20s and of a suspicious mind. Without saying anything, he let Phil know he was skeptical of his story, starting with his Belizean passport. "And all you had were two shotguns?"

"Yes."

"They are not recorded on your passports."

"I know."

"And they had M-16s and shotguns, and there were nine of them." He shook his head walking over the low platform mound.

He doesn't believe a word of it, Phil thought.

"So two of them are unaccounted for?" Macias lit a cigarette. His men were stacking the weapons they had picked up in the back of the jeep. They would come back and bury the bodies on the next trip.

"Yes. One that I knocked out around here somewhere and one got away."

"One that you knocked out. I see. So that one was probably taken by the crocodile." He strolled over with his hands in his pockets and exhaled. "Okay." He said in perfect English. "You want to cut the bullshit now?" He had a thin smile under his well-trimmed mustache.

"What do you mean?"

Macias pulled an empty steel magazine out of his pocket and held it up to Phil.

"Unless I am severely mistaken this fits an AK-47. You want to tell me where it is?"

"I have it." Phil shrugged, no use trying to bluff anymore.

"I will have to confiscate it of course."

"I understand." Oh well, he thought, at least I still have the Makarov.

"And the shotguns."

"I understand."

"And you are not a Belizean are you?"

"No. I'm an American."

"Ex-military?"

"Yes."

The Captain took a deep draw on his cigarette. He smiled again as he exhaled.

"I can't congratulate myself too much. It was rather obvious, and the remains of the firefight proved it."

Phil didn't reply. He wanted to see where the Captain was going.

"So you were special forces?"

"S.O.G. USMC."

"Haven't lost your edge have you?" The Captain raised an eyebrow. "It looks like your AK-47 killed four of them. I count only two that were killed by shotguns. A shotgun pulverized one of them. Very messy. I would say you still have your talents hombre."

"I wouldn't."

"Why?" Macias pushed his hat back.

"I drove into an ambush. I was flanked, and I was caught in a crossfire. Hell of a good job." Phil shook his head in disgust.

The captain laughed so loud that some of the vultures nearby were startled and took flight.

"But you are alive hombre. Your people are alive and they are not!" He pointed in the direction of the vultures, and slapped Phil on the shoulder. "Now suppose you tell me what you are really doing in Guatemala?"

"You want the long or the short version?"

"Just the give me the truth."

* * * * * * * *

Phil told his story while they drove back to the camp, and concluded it in the captain's old-fashioned garrison tent. "Okay. So you are searching for a woman you love? That I can accept. But what about this woman Delia? What is the story there?"

"Well like I said. She and Belinda are friends."

"Come on. I mean what is the story with her? She seems to be your girl friend too."

Phil didn't know what to say so he shrugged, and this caused Macias to start laughing again. "So she's your sanchita. I understand. Okay. Two more questions. You were in Viet Nam?"

"Yes. Two tours."

"Fascinating. Clearly you saw some combat."

Phil nodded. His expression signaled that he would rather not talk about it, and the captain understood.

"Why do you speak Spanish like you are from Guatemala City?"

"I was an Embassy Guard there for two years."

"Ah. Marine Corps that makes sense." He leaned back on his campstool. "Okay. The question before me is what do I do with you? You are either telling the truth or you are CIA. You killed seven or eight Mexican nationals in my country last night." He shook his head.

"But it was in self defense. And they were really bad hombres." Phil shrugged.

"That is true and they, like you, were in my country illegally."

"Also true." Phil nodded.

"What do you think I should do?" He said, and lit a cigarette.

"Let us go?" Phil smiled; he thought he had the captain deciphered.

"And why would I do that?"

"Say I made a donation to the soldier's fund?"

"How about instead, a donation to the officers funds? A generous donation?"

"How generous?"

"One thousand US dollars?"

Phil paused, and decided now was not the time to bargain. "Consider it done. Will some of it go to Corpsman Padilla?"

"I'll see that he's taken care of. We can work out the details later."

They shook hands. Phil accepted one of the Captain's cigarettes. Maybe I should start smoking again, he thought.

"A couple of other things." Phil asked, and lit his cigarette.

"Yes?"

"I appreciate the effort you made to have a helicopter sent up here for Madeline. Can the rest of my people stay here under your protection until they are well enough to travel? Without shall we say, any 'official' problems?"

"Yes of course, and?"

"And why is a platoon of elite Guatemalan soldiers out here?"

"You want the long or the short version?"

They both laughed.

The Captain explained that looting in the northeastern Peten had reached critical levels. Five days previously a Guatemalan archaeological survey team had happened upon a large group of looters at the site of Tintal.

"There were only three of them. Unarmed. They never had a chance."

"Who were the attackers?"

"Who knows? Maybe they were the same men who attacked you last night. I realize one of them said they were police. Maybe he lied. None of them were carrying police identification. But that does not mean anything. One of them had five hundred US dollars in a money clip."

"For the officer's fund?" Phil raised an eyebrow.

"Probably." Macias shrugged. "So were they drug runners? Mexican guerillas? Guatemalan guerillas? All of the above? None of the above? It is all very frustrating. The huechero profession is getting more complex every day. I just know that I am supposed to protect this archaeological field camp, and gather intelligence for the next few weeks" He stood up and walked Phil out of the tent. "You may have done me a big favor by thinning out the opposition last night. This is why I am more kindly disposed toward you than I would be under most conditions."

* * * * * * * * *

Madeline was drinking soup broth when Phil entered. Esmeralda was napping.

"Good morning. Glad to see you awake. How are you feeling?"

"Glad to be seen. I'm not sure how I'm feeling." She was heavily bandaged and very pale. "I feel thoroughly drugged."

"Do you think if we got a helicopter in here this afternoon you would be well enough to travel?" Phil sat down on a wooden footlocker beside the bed. Seeing her like this made him wish the helicopter were already there.

"I think so. Padilla's repaired my insides fairly well, but I understand I need an illiostomy immediately, which obviously he can't do out here. I'm just glad he was able to accomplish as much as he did."

"Padilla's a good man. So is the Captain. Macias has offered us the use of an army helicopter. And we should try for this afternoon because there is a weak tropical depression coming in tonight." The last place Phil would have expected help from in an emergency, was the Guatemalan army, but Macias was old school.

"So where will they take me?" Her features became more animated.

"Flores. There's an airport there, and we are trying to get an air ambulance to fly down from Texas or New Orleans."

"And I could be back in the states in a hospital by tonight?"

"That's the plan." He realized how much he would miss Madeline.

330

"That would be wonderful. Who will be coming with me?"

"Delia." He hesitated, wondering how he was going to convince her.

"She won't like that. But then she is the obvious choice."

"I'm going to need your help." Phil mopped his brow. It was starting to get very humid.

"What about Belinda? We're not giving up on her are we?"

"I'll continue to look for her. Alone."

"Delia won't like that either." Madeline smiled faintly.

"I guess I'm going to need a lot of help from you then." He could tell that this much conversation was an effort for her, and that he needed to leave and let her rest. He stood up.

"You can count on it Phillip. Did I ever tell you, how much I appreciate you?"

Phil held up his hand. "The best thing you can do for me Madeline is just get better."

* * * * * * * * *

They had taken showers, and now totally exhausted Delia and Phil climbed into their tent.

Delia stretched out on top of her sleeping bag. "Madeline says we're flying out this afternoon. But you're not going to go with us?" She found herself agonizing over it.

"Don't you think that's probably best?"

"No. I want you to come with me."

"I have to continue this mission." He put his arm around her. "You asked me the other day if I still loved Belinda. I realize now the answer is no. But I still want to find her. I don't want to quit right in the middle..."

"But what if something happens to you? You could disappear too."

"I won't. I'll be in occasional communication with Patty and she'll be with Paul and Esmeralda on Ambergris Caye. Delia, honey listen to me. I think it's clear that the rest of the answers are in Chiapas. I'm going to make my way down the Usumacinta, and see if anyone has seen her. Pay a visit to Avendano as well. You are supposed to be in San Cristobal on December 29th right?"

"Right."

"Hell or high water, I'll meet you then." He propped himself up on his elbow and looked at her.

His eyes showed that he was totally honest, so she asked the question that she was most afraid of.

"Phillip. Promise me you won't do anything with Belinda?" She looked up at him, disoriented.

"You mean like sleep with her?" He didn't blink.

"Yes."

"I promise Delia. You have my word."

"What will you do when you see her?"

"Baby. Let me try to explain it. I know she's in trouble and I want to help her. But it's more complicated than that. See I gave her my heart. She gave it back, but she kept some of the pieces. I want to get them back."

"Then what?"

"Then I'll give it all to you."

She pulled him down close to her.

* * * * * * * *

The helicopter swooped in over the camp and made one low-level pass before touching down in the landing zone. Hearing a Huey come in over the jungle canopy gave Phil cold chills. At one time that had been an everyday sound in his life. Soldiers carried Madeline on a stretcher and carefully placed her inside. Others loaded the luggage. Delia and Phil stood a little away from the group of Padilla, Macias, and Paul.

"Phil, promise me that you will be all right." Delia asked in a small voice.

"I promise." He wrapped his arms around her and whispered in her ear.

"Promise me I'll see you in San Cristobal."

"You will."

She hugged him hard, and he kissed her deeply, honestly. It felt right. He walked her to the helicopter. They ducked under the blade's backwash. Just before she climbed in he leaned close to her ear, so close his lips brushed her skin.

"And Delia?" He held her arms; she could feel the helicopter starting to move.

"Yes?"

"I love you."

The turbines whined, and the helicopter lifted up - blowing the grass flat, and taking them somewhere in the direction of Flores. Phil stood and watched until it disappeared over the horizon.

* * * * * * * *

The next morning it started to rain hard and a looter trench in the main plaza at Macondo caved in. Obregon's crew cleaned off the walls and mapped the features. The site had been ravaged. Over fifty huechero trenches had been found so far.

Phil and Paul joined in the salvage excavation, while they waited for Esmeralda to recover, and get well enough to travel. It was proper archaeological etiquette to pitch in, but this time Phil needed the physical labor to keep him from thinking about the ambush, all the killing, and his fear when he was pinned down. The work provided distance from his torment. He threw himself into it like a demon, doing most of the coarse pick and shovel work. Paul sat on a stool to save his wounded leg and sifted through the debris on a mounted screen nearby.

Obregon returned by mid morning and was glad to have their help. He was short, and rotund, and his jolly demeanor camouflaged a sharp archaeological mind. He and Phil had known each other for years.

On the fourth day of their visit, Phil was on the stairway of the main pyramid, clearing rubble with three of the archaeologists from Guatemala City. Suddenly, his pick hit something hard and hollow. He heard a faint echo when he tapped the stone under the rubble.

The Guatemalan archaeologists stopped what they were doing to listen. Phil tapped again.

"Think we got a capstone here."

"I will go tell Professor Obregon." Said Santiago, a young curatorial aide, on his first excavation.

"Bring some more shovels over here." Phil and the others got to work trying to expose the surface of the capstone. The crewmembers responded quickly. They looked to him as a leader. News of what they had done against the bandits had made them all instant celebrities in the camp, particularly Phil, who tried to shrug it all off.

After three hours they had exposed a large limestone cap rock, with the dimensions of a parking space. Obregon and Santiago moved in to document it, while Phil and the rest of the crew took a break.

As he watched Santiago and Obregon set up the transit, Phil went over his mental countdown. From now on, he would be going alone, like he should have done to begin with.

* * * * * * * *

It was time to remove the slab, which was broken in several places. The largest fragment probably weighed about two hundred pounds, Phil thought. Captain Macias brought a squad of soldiers over to assist in the removal. After an hour the fragments were stacked neatly beside the excavation unit.

"What do you think?" Obregon asked Phil, as he examined a red ceramic fragment.

"It is starting to look like a *katun* ending event. I mean it's been inserted into an Early Classic stairway. But the fragments in the sand are predominantly Terminal Classic."

"Right. 900 AD. The last known occupation of Macondo."

"It will be interesting to see what's under the sand."

"Any bets?"

"The usual. Offerings. Sacrifices."

They put up a grid and began removing the sandy layer. About twenty centimeters down Phil hit the first skull. He brushed it off, and let Santiago finish the detail work with a dental pick. Santiago encountered another skull underneath the first one. And then Phil found another one. None of the skulls so far, were attached to bodies.

By the time the light was fading they had exposed a pit with twenty-seven skulls jumbled up in its center. Many of the teeth had jade inlays, which indicated that they were members of the aristocracy. As they continued working under lanterns, Phil noticed something else.

"I count nine children. The rest are adults."

"So we have eighteen adults, nine children?" Obregon asked.

"That's how it looks." He dusted his hands off on his pants.

"All of them sacrificed, and thrown into a pit in the center of the main stairway."

"So that you would have to walk on them, every time you went up the stairs. I'll bet that we have nine female adults and nine males too." Phil picked up a clipboard and wrote down his comments.

"Royal families of Macondo?"

"Nine families for the Nine Lords? Executed and humiliated for eternity as offerings to the lords of the night." Phil remembered other occurrences like it from the literature. "Hester's team from the University of Texas found a very similar feature at Colha, and Mamett had one at Kichpanha in Northern Belize."

"Invasion? Outsiders taking over?" Obregon bent down and picked up another ceramic fragment.

"Either that or an internal rebellion?" Phil dusted off his jeans. "It seems very personal doesn't it?"

"Reminds me of the pacification program." Obregon shook his head

* * * * * * * * *

For two more days they worked at Macondo, mostly in the lab because a tropical wave rained down incessantly. Late in the afternoon Macias asked Phil to meet him in his tent.

"That Esmeralda sure is something. I cannot believe how quickly she has healed." Macias lit a cigar and offered one to Phil.

"And I can't believe what a good host you have been." Phil accepted the cigar and trimmed it with his knife.

"Well it has been a beneficial meeting. Even fortuitous. In my report I said my platoon killed the huecheros. You understand why of course?"

Phil nodded. "It works out better for all of us that way, but I sure could have done without it."

"What do you mean? I would have thought…"

"It's hard to explain, but just understand that killing people diminishes you. It makes it that much harder…" Phil trailed off; he couldn't put it into words.

"The next time?"

"The fear, the guilt…" Phil halted. Neither of them spoke for a minute.

"Indeed." Macias puffed away on his cigar. The rain hammered on the canvas.

"I understand you are going to keep looking for the damsel in distress? Such a noble quest." His eyes twinkled.

Phil smiled, relieved to change the subject. "Yes. But I'll be out of your hair. I'm going to Chiapas."

"If I hear about a revolution, I will know who started it." He chuckled. "I might be able to escort you to the border. I think it might even be my duty to do so."

"That would make things a lot easier for me." Phil savored the cigar. "You know Captain; you are not at all what I expected."

"What did you expect?" He propped his feet upon a footlocker and exhaled a cloud of smoke around his face.

"The Kaibil Regiment." Phil shrugged.

"Those animals. I regret that they are even in my army." Macias spat a piece of tobacco out on the floor.

337

"How long have you been in?"

"Since 1989."

"You weren't part of the 'pacification' program." Phil was relieved.

"Before my time. Thank God. Thus far in my career, I have never fired a shot in anger." Macias shrugged.

"I hope you never have to. So the army is improving?"

"Healing slowly, just like the rest of the country." Macias seemed uncomfortable talking politics, and came to the point. "Here is what I will do for you, and see if it fits in your plans. When the rain lifts in a couple of days, I will detach one squad and two jeeps, and escort you, Paul and Esmeralda back to Tikal. There they can pick up your sister and return to Belize through Melchor."

"Sounds good."

"I personally will ride with you from Tikal to Flores and from there to the border, to the river, where you can put your raft in the Usumacinta. And then you are on your own and out of my country. Just promise me you will always sleep on the Mexican side. Okay?"

Phil laughed and slapped his leg. "Captain, I appreciate your generosity."

"Truly Mr. Ward, it has been an experience to remember."

* * * * * * * * *

It always comes back to Tikal, Phil thought, while he watched Patty, Paul and Esmeralda packing up the Land Rover in front of the Jaguar Inn. Esmeralda was doing a lot better, laughing and happy to be going back to Belize, and Nutmeg looked like she had gained weight. Patty was acting like she disapproved of the plan, but resigned herself to it.

"I consent to wait in San Pedro Phillip, but we will have to have an agreed time reference."

"What do you mean?" He helped her with a duffel bag.

"If I don't hear from you within two weeks I will be in Chiapas looking for you."

She tied a red scarf around her hair, and smiled at him. "This is what you wanted anyway isn't it? To go in solo?"

"It is. Now I'm just responsible for me."

"Well take care of yourself. Remember you did the right thing. I hate it that you are going without me." She hugged him and kissed him on the cheek. Paul came around the vehicle and waited his turn.

Phil offered his hand but Paul gave him a big hug too.

"Feel the love man. It is all around you." He grinned, and slapped Phil on the shoulder.

"Pablo you be careful. Look after my sister."

"I'll do that." He whispered so that only Phil could hear him. "Get those other bastards for me Phillip. And get back in one piece."

"It will be my endeavor Pablo."

He watched them drive out followed by the military jeep, splashing through the puddles in the parking lot. Macias came over, impeccably dressed in a well-starched olive drab uniform.

"Mr. Ward shall we depart for the river?"

Phil nodded. "Looks like it's about that time." He climbed into the jeep, and they headed out. He would continue the mission.

* * * * * * * *

The road ended at the Bonanza Cooperative. A muddy slope was flanked on the left by a high limestone ridge. On the right a cluster of thatched dwellings huddled against the massive ledge. In front of them the

Usumacinta swept past, dark green, with currents fast and deep. Across the river the limestone gorge cliffs were three hundred feet high and higher. Thick vegetation, ferns, and banyans climbed up the slopes in an emerald mosaic. The villagers were lighting fires and lamps as the late afternoon shadows loomed across the gorge.

A group of villagers came out of their huts to stare at the soldiers. The soldiers stared back and waved. The villagers did not wave back.

"Well it's too late for us to start back to Flores, so I guess we camp with you tonight." Macias observed.

"What's up there?" Phil gestured to the slope. "See those ruts? Vehicles have gone up to that ledge."

"Let's check it out." They climbed back in the jeep and bounced up the slope. In a few minutes they emerged under an enormous limestone overhang. The sunlight was fading fast as they unpacked their gear.

"This will do fine." Macias said. "We will not need our tents. I like it."

"Looks like a cave back there." This place reminds me of Copperhead Rock shelter, Phil thought, as he walked toward the cave. I'm getting the strongest feeling of deja vu.

"This was guerilla country not too long ago. The Fuerzas Armadas Rebeldes, the FAR used to operate out of this area. I think I'll post a guard." Macias said, looking for his cigars.

Phil noticed four empty rum bottles lying by an old campfire ring of burnt stones. Something glinted near the cave entrance. He walked to it and found a scatter of what could have been Uzi shells. He picked one up. It was fairly dusty, and had been laying there awhile.

"Did the FAR have Uzis?" Phil asked Macias.

"Not that I ever heard of. That's a weapon favored by narcotraficantes."

Phil went to his pack and dug out his flashlight. "I'm going to check inside the cave."

"I'll come with you."

* * * * * * * *

"So someone chased someone else into the cave with an Uzi." Macias said as they sat by the campfire.

"But only one set of tracks came back out." Phil observed, thinking about the footprints he had seen in the cave. Were they Belinda's?

"You think this is the way she came?" Macias stretched out on top of his sleeping bag. It was a humid night and moths were starting to discover their fire. Phil lit mosquito coils, and sprayed Deet on his clothes.

"It's possible. It's the way I would have come if I were her."

"Still, those tracks could be a year old."

"They could be. But it really doesn't matter." Phil felt fatigue overtaking him as he stretched out.

"Why?"

"Because whether she was here months ago, or not, she's not here now."

* * * * * * * *

A group of villagers watched Phil remove the raft and the compressor from the back of the jeep. Two of Macias' men unloaded the rest of his gear. The Zodiac raft was able to hold four people comfortably, and was about ten feet long. It came with a foot pump, spray skirt; paddles and a carrying bag. As they pushed it into the river, Phil noticed it was extremely stable. He held the tether rope as Macias handed him the last of his gear.

"Well hombre that's it." Macias extended his hand, and Phil shook it.

"Captain, thanks again for all of your help."

"Oh yes. I almost forgot. One other thing." Macias grinned and waved one of his men over, he was carrying Phil's gun bag. "I am returning your weapon. I think you might need it." He shrugged and addressed the soldier. "Set it inside the raft." He turned back to Phil. "Give me your word that you will not stop on the Guatemalan side."

"You have my word. Unless I have no other option." Phil was stunned.

"Then take care of yourself and good luck."

Phil saluted the Captain and pushed off into the Usumacinta.

64 San Antonio

Gloria looked at the auto repair shops with signs in Spanish, the botanicas, the pharmacias, checked out the taco and raspa vendors, and saw all the small frame houses, decorated with Christmas lights. People were going out dressed in their best clothes for Saturday night. "This could be Mexico." She said. "I can see why my father lived here. It was like home to him."

Jesse smiled and said, "You could argue that Mexico starts on the south side of San Antonio. Once you cross Commerce Street you're there."

"Tell me again how you know these people we are meeting?" She asked.

"Delia Bell is an archaeology graduate student like me. She goes to Harvard. I've met her at professional meetings, and we know a lot of the same people. Patrick Mamett is her professor. He is taking over Chanul Tzuk from my advisor. I have never met him before, although I know him by reputation."

"Which is?"

"He's a major player, definitely on the rise."

They pulled into the restaurant parking lot. From the restaurant, Mariachi music carried out into the late November night:
"La musica Mexicana es más bonita..."

Gloria hooked her arm with Jesse's and they entered Karam's Restaurant. Inside the place was packed, with a waiting line standing near the entrance. They had reservations and the maitre d' took them through the boisterous dining area out to the sculpture garden in the back.

"Look at this." Gloria was delighted. "It's fantastic. It reminds me of Olmec Park in Villahermosa."

Scattered in a tropical landscape with subdued lighting were replicas of Olmec and Maya sculptures; colossal heads, Maya lords, a Toltec fountain. Sitting at a small table in the back, next to an Olmec head, were Patrick Mamett and Delia Bell.

Introductions were exchanged and everyone sat down.

"An excellent selection Jesse." Mamett was halfway through a Margarita. "If the food matches the decor, we are in for a feast."

"The food is great here." A waiter came over and they ordered a pitcher of Margaritas.

"I was sorry to hear about your friend, how is she doing?" Jesse asked Delia.

"Madeline's recovering well. The past two weeks have gone by quickly. She may be able to go home in a week. The University of Texas Hospital here has done a superb job." Delia sipped some water.

"And what of Belinda Boothe?" Jesse asked.

"Back to square one I'm afraid. She's missing we think, somewhere in Chiapas. She was reportedly seen at Macondo, where we were attacked by bandits. I've never been so scared in my life." Delia reached for her drink. "Phil thinks Belinda went to Chiapas to help look for Kathryn Haden, and got sidetracked somewhere."

"Well like I said on the phone. I never saw her in Chiapas, and I think I would have. I was all over the place looking for Kathryn. How is Phil anyway? I met him when he worked at Montebello."

"He's somewhere on the Usumacinta, doing okay I guess. No one's heard from him since last week when he was in Frontera Corozal. But then, it's not like there are a lot of phones on the river."

"No. That's true. So the looting is getting bad in Guatemala too? I can tell you it's horrible in Chiapas."

Delia nodded. "You should have seen what happened at Macondo. And I guess you heard about the killings at Tintal?"

Jesse nodded. Mamett cleared his throat. "These incidents are why I have arranged through my colleague Sergio Avendano, to have an army detachment stationed at Chanul Tzuk. He is sorry for the mix-up about Belinda at Macondo, and Sergio sends his regards too, by the way Jesse." Mamett continued. "He speaks very highly of you."

"Avendano is one of the most knowledgeable Mayanists I know." Jesse looked up as the waiter arrived to take their order.

* * * * * * * * *

After dinner and three pitchers of Margaritas, everyone was in a buoyant mood. The Mariachis were in the garden serenading the customers. Mamett rekindled the conversation.

"Before I get too borracho let me tell you how the schedule looks. I have a new GMC Suburban that the project has purchased, here at a dealership in northwest San Antonio ready for delivery. I finished the paperwork this afternoon. Jesse I want you to go with me tomorrow to pick it up, and drive it for awhile, to see if it has any bugs."

"Great."

"In two weeks all of the equipment will be ready to load. So will you and Gloria be able to drive it all down?" Mamett smiled. "Gloria you don't say much do you?"

"I am too borracha, Señor." She held her chin up with both hands and giggled.

Everyone laughed. Jesse replied, "Sure we can do it. Delia, are you going to come with us?"

"Probably not. I'm either going home for the holidays, or staying with Madeline, and I think I'll fly down a few days after Christmas."

The Mariachis came over and asked Jesse if he had any requests, before he could say anything, Gloria asked, "Do you know Volver, Volver?"

In reply the trumpets, guitars, and violins started up and Gloria sang with them in her beautiful soprano voice…

Sitting across the garden near the Toltec fountain, Garcia watched. He paid his tab in cash, and left a nice tip. He knew there was no point in trying to make contact tonight, they were too far-gone.

65 Smoking Water

The really odd thing about the Usumacinta was that it flowed north. During his first two weeks on the river, Phil often felt disoriented. The other problem was the density of jungle; it was as thick as anything he had ever seen. It surpassed a good portion of Viet Nam, and it was impossible to see any landmarks. He kept wondering if his compass was working correctly. He had been going down the river slowly, stopping at settlements, showing Belinda's picture, asking questions, getting nowhere. His anxiety ebbed and flowed with the river.

Phil had last rafted the Usumacinta in 1990, when he worked on the Montebello Project. He had a healthy respect for it, and knew that when he got down below Frontera Corozal, there were stretches like Chicozapote Falls, and Smoking Water, where his best bet would be to get out and portage around the hazards, if there was time.

The forest canopy was abundant, and the upper portions of the Usumacinta were nearly untouched. He saw the occasional thatched hut here and there, but actual settlements were scarce. At one time in the mid 80s, refugee camps were spread up and down the river. Most of these were abandoned and overgrown now.

Snakes moved off rotting logs as he passed. Caymans and crocodiles sunned themselves on the riverbanks wherever the sunlight penetrated. Neon green parrots and Scarlet macaws squawked in the red cedar and ceiba treetops. Luminous white orchids grew in thick bunches in the emerald background. He could sense a village before he saw one, because he saw fewer animals as he neared the settlements.

He would occasionally pass other river traffic; Indians in dugout canoes, Ladinos in fiberglass boats, but overall the upper Usumacinta was swift and sparsely populated. He mentally noted the different animals he saw; spider monkeys, toucans and peccaries. He fished and caught a few robalo; they made a good supplement to his daily fare of boxed and canned foods. Most of all he enjoyed the solitude.

Whenever the river widened out, it slowed, and the horizon became visible. He could see the green ruggedness of the mountains of the Sierra del Lacandon. On the Guatemalan side he passed several burned out lumber camps, relics of the "troubles" of the 1980s.

He thought of Delia often, and knew he was lucky. There was something with Delia that he had never known. With Belinda, it had been a contest of wills, but Delia seemed so natural to be with. He guessed he had lived long enough now to appreciate a woman like Delia, but he did not feel that he really deserved her, not yet. Above all he wanted to preserve and defend what he had with her, but there was still the unfinished business with Belinda. Once that was cleared up he could be with Delia without any baggage.

After two weeks on the river he started to think that the whole thing was absurd, and he would never find Belinda. The men he had killed in Guatemala, and the men he had killed in Viet Nam, the spattered gore of his memory, started haunting his mind at night. He rolled those thoughts up and put them in a deep frozen spot inside of him. The freezer was getting full.

346

Eventually he reached the dismal town of Frontera Corozal. He spent two days in a primitive hotel and got one phone call out to Patty back in San Pedro. He had her relay a message to Delia who was still in San Antonio with Madeline.

The next day he passed a grass airstrip, and hauled out at Yaxchilan at around noon. The ruins were deserted except for the caretaker at the entrance. Phil paid the entry fee and made his way around the Main Plaza to the hieroglyphic stairway in front of Structure 33. He remembered that one of the kings of Yaxchilan, Bird Jaguar IV, had erected this and twelve other buildings during his reign in the middle 700s. But Structure 33 was constructed to face the summer solstice, probably to exhibit the king's relationship with the sun. He thought too, about Tatiana Prouskouriakoff, the Russian émigré who had conclusively proven that the monuments at Yaxchilan, and Piedras Negras did not depict gods and priests, as previously thought, but were actually commemorating historical figures and historical events. She created a new era in epigraphic studies, one of the biggest breakthroughs in Maya archaeology. He listened to the wind in the trees, and felt the spirituality of the place, and decided that he would stay with archaeology a while longer yet. How could he possibly ever think of giving it up? At last, he thought, my brain is clearing and I'm thinking lucidly again.

On an impulse, as he was leaving, he showed the caretaker Belinda's picture, and saw a fleeting glimpse of recognition flash across his face.

"You have seen her?" Phil tried not to get his hopes up.

"I think so. Maybe. Does she travel with a brujo?"

He seemed sincere. Phil opened his wallet and selected a handful of the larger denomination pesos. "I would be very grateful for anything you might think of, or recall."

"This woman and the brujo came here one night a few weeks ago. He comes two or three times a year. This was the first time I ever saw him with a gringa. That's why I remember it."

"The brujo's name?" Phil fought to contain his excitement.

"Domingo. I believe."

"Did they come by land, or by river?" Phil peeled off a few more notes and gave them to the caretaker.

"Gracias Señor. By the river, in a canoe."

"Which direction did they go?" He was anxious to get started.

"Down river." The caretaker extended his left arm.

Phil thanked him. He jogged back to the raft, thinking that after all this time, he finally had a lead. He would stop at every habitation and look for Belinda and a brujo named Domingo.

66 River Walk

They sipped beers at an outside table on San Antonio's River Walk. The trees along the banks were festooned with multicolored lights. Hordes of tourists were out shopping for Christmas. A number of them were from Mexico.

"You have a project vehicle to drive, and all of the official permits to bring archaeological equipment into Mexico?" Garcia smiled. "It is the perfect cover. Perfect."

"Yes, that new green Suburban." Jesse pointed to it parked on the street above them. "It's meant to be. We're scheduled to leave next week."

"Good." Garcia squinted at his beer. "Do you know though, that if you are caught with high caliber ammunition at the border or anytime you are in Mexico, that it could result in a thirty year prison sentence?" Garcia whispered.

Jesse rubbed his jaw; he knew what was coming. "No I didn't know that. I didn't know it was that stiff."

"Do you still want to do it Jesse?"

"Yes." He nodded, and realized he was fully committed now. He felt his stomach twist.

"Gloria?"

"Of course." She replied indignantly.

Garcia paused to sip his beer, before continuing. "Good. I hoped you had not changed your mind." He put a key on the table. "This is a key to a storage unit on Austin Highway. Number C-18." He handed them a card. "This is the address and the access code to the gate. The ammunition is packed in standard, plain storage boxes; you can label them however you choose. Put them in first and then cover them with your archaeological supplies."

"I think we can handle it." Jesse drained his beer.

"Finally, here is a diagram of Mexican customs in Matamoros. Cross the border between midnight and three a.m. on the morning of December 19th, and you should have no trouble. Go to Lane 3. Give the guard a fifty-dollar bill; have it mixed in with your papers. I can't guarantee it but…" He paused and sipped his beer.

"I'm still in." Jesse signaled for another beer, and thought about it all. What have I got myself into? Can't get out of it, what would Gloria think?

"When you get to San Cristobal, here's what I want you to do..."

67 Dreaming in a Dream

He was about twenty miles down river from Yaxchilan. The Usumacinta brought Phil through a series of narrow jagged passages. It was exhilarating. The raft kept picking up speed and bounded through the rapids. The white water roared and the current veered him into a whirlpool. He paddled hard to break free of its pull, and escaped it.

Exhausted, and drained, he let the river run him through Chicozapote Falls, too tired to care, and by a miracle he cleared it and came to a long stretch of slower open water. He took time out to thank God for not drowning him and beached the raft so he could recover his senses, and dump out the water he had taken on.

Around noon, as he drifted in the slower and wider stretches, he saw the remains of a mule carcass rotting in branches twenty feet above him, and fragments of an old shattered boat, evidence of the river's power and volatility.

Late in the afternoon, while a blue heron screeched above him and forest shadows stretched across the river, he recognized the black rocks on a beach up ahead.

A series of low hills next to the river marked the approach to the great Classic site of Piedras Negras. He remembered his promise to Macias about not camping in Guatemala, but there was no other place to stop nearby.

He pitched his tent where the beach met the jungle. After eating a dinner of canned ham and crackers, he stretched out on top of his sleeping bag so exhausted that he went to sleep in seconds. He dreamed he rafted down the Usumacinta, got caught in the whirlpool, and was swept through the falls. It was a complete replay of the day he had just experienced. He lay down on his sleeping bag, fell asleep in his tent, and started to dream. Belinda was walking down the river's edge toward him, dressed in a blue embroidered Maya skirt, and a simple white blouse. She stopped a few feet from the tent and whispered. "Phillip." It echoed in his mind.

"Phillip?"

He wanted to wake up but he was confused. First he thought he had to wake up in the first dream within this dream.

"Phillip?"

He struggled; it was like trying to swim through Jell-O. He could not wake up. The plastic zipper was unzipped; he distinctly heard the sound in his dream. She shook his shoulder.

"Phillip. It's me. Wake up!"

She shook him hard and he woke up slowly and realized he was not dreaming.

Belinda was squeezing his shoulder, sitting in his tent.

"Is it really you?" he rubbed his eyes, and tried to shake the cobwebs out of his brain.

"Yes. And it's really you too." She smiled her incredible smile, and hugged him.

"I can't believe it." He was totally stunned, and at a loss for words.

"Believe it. I prayed to the gods to send you to me, and they did!"

She put her arms around him, and her mouth covered his hungrily.

68 Matamoros

Ten minutes after midnight on December 19th, Jesse and Gloria were in Lane 3 at the border crossing in Matamoros. The whole area was bathed in high intensity incandescent light. He looked behind his seat at the fully loaded interior. The ammunition boxes were marked as "Excavation Forms."

He tried not to show his nervousness as they pulled up one space. The Suburban would be checked next. All necessary entry papers, his tourist card, Gloria's passport, car papers, a manifest listing all of the equipment in Spanish and English, and a crisp fifty dollar bill were stuck on a clipboard in Gloria's lap.

They pulled up and the guard asked for their papers. Gloria passed the clipboard to Jesse and he gave it to the guard.

"Gracias." The man seemed subdued and polite, maybe a little sleepy. He walked around the truck peering in to the windows. Jesse realized his hands were sweating, and sticking to the steering wheel. His stomach contorted.

The guard walked over to Gloria's side of the truck, and gave her the clipboard back. He handed her an orange Tourista sticker and said "Put this up on your windshield."

Gloria stuck it on the inside right corner.

The guard smiled and said, "Enjoy your stay in Mexico."

They drove through the dark empty streets of Matamoros, looking for a hotel.

Gloria kissed him on the cheek and whispered, "We did it!"

69 Shamanic Soul Travel

Belinda was kissing him erotically, and trying to get his shirt off. She had some kind of bump on the end of her tongue and Phil was rather aroused, but slowly he came to his senses. His promise to Delia came back to him, and how much he cared for her. He still cared for Belinda too and that was what was confusing. Realizing he had better get control of the situation, he broke off, and pulled her arms down.

"Wait. Hold on." His heart pounded an erratic rhythm, and he tugged his shirt back down.

"What's the matter?" She colored deeply.

Phil struggled to catch his breath. "We need to talk."

"I know, there's a lot I have to tell you, but it can wait." She shook her head vehemently.

"What I've got to tell you can't wait."

She took a deep breath and said, "Then tell me."

"Belinda, I'm involved with Delia now." He tried to catch his breath.

"What?"

"Let's go outside and walk on the beach." He made for the tent door, and stood up, and helped pull her up as she crawled out. "For me, everything changed when I flunked my orals, but events were set in motion way before that..."

* * * * * * * *

The new moon and Venus glowed in the night sky as they walked along the narrow black beach. Finally, Phil finished his account. Belinda was silent for a moment, as she considered all he had told her.

"God, poor Laurence. You know I had a vision where he told me he was dead? I really liked him even though I know he was caught up in something horrible." She took a deep breath. "And Professor Thomas killed himself? That is so hard to believe."

"I have my doubts." Phil put his hands behind his back, and stared up at the stars. Part of him wanted to put his arms around her, but another part kept thinking about Delia. This is going to be so hard, he thought, being with Belinda is like being in a dream. I think I still love her.

"And Prefontaine, and Madeline, will they be all right?"

"They both should recover."

"My God. There's more to it than I thought. Phillip, I think I know who killed Kathryn Haden."

Phil looked directly into her eyes. "Who?"

"A man named Alex Sanchez; I think he is a major looter. He tried to kill me. He still wants me dead. I need you to help protect me from him. Let me tell you what happened back in August when I started out for Chanul Tzuk. And one other thing Phillip?" She leaned forward and caressed his neck, as their eyes locked.

"What?"

"After I'm done I want you to look me in the eye and tell me you don't love me anymore? Like I believe that? You and Delia for God's sake! I'm surprised with both of you." She shook her head. "Although I shouldn't be. Delia's had a crush on you from day one." She took a deep breath before continuing. "So anyway, I pulled into Tikal with a blown water pump, and who should park next to me..."

* * * * * * * *

They walked back to the campfire while Belinda told her story. She got to the part about the cave, and Phil interrupted her.

"I knew it; I knew you had been there."

"And then I entered the underworld. I almost died. Let me tell you about the tomb of Lord Night Jaguar..."

Phil revived the dying fire while she talked. It was as exciting as it ever was to be around her. She became more and more animated and enthusiastic in her narrative, particularly about her studies with Domingo Xicaret, cutting her tongue, the bloodletting ritual.

"That explains the bump on your tongue. I knew you felt different."

She smiled mockingly and said, "You did not put up much of a fight there at the beginning Phillip."

He nodded. "Well I was half asleep and dreaming of you. So I was confused."

"Dreaming of me? I have had a lot of dreams about you too, tried to reach you in them. I've felt at times that I did reach you and I think you know I did. How do you think you found me? Who do you think entered your subconscious?"

"I did feel something. There was this one dream I had in Kentucky that was unreal." Phil nodded.

"Phillip, I think I have learned the secret of shamanic soul travel, among other secrets of the world. I can send my soul to travel in dreams. And I think you know you are my soul mate. You do know that don't you?" She locked eyes with him, her incredible eyes.

There was something beautiful and yet unnerving about her. She was hypnotic. Belinda had changed dramatically, transformed into something powerful. Manipulative. Phil felt very unsure about her. An element of danger, something almost irresistible, the attraction was strong, and he felt his resolve wavering. Then it came to him.

"Belinda did you put some kind of spell on me?" He looked away, at the moon and stars.

"Maybe. What's wrong with a little enchantment? Do you believe in magic?"

"That's cheating." He threw another piece of wood on the fire and tried to avoid her gaze.

"So?" She posed like that time in Kentucky, in the Red River Gorge. Her hand on her hip, eyes sparkling, defiantly sexy, almost impossible to resist.

"So cut it out. I'm not going for it." He shook his head and took a deep breath.

"Well you're no fun."

* * * * * * * * *

Downstream from Piedras Negras they approached San Jose canyon in the early morning light. The river was rocky, huge waves were starting to break and the raft was picking up speed. Belinda was forward paddling on either side, as needed. The spray soaked her blouse and revealed her free-swinging breasts; her skirt was hiked up around her knees exposing her long tanned and graceful legs. She's not giving up, Phil thought ruefully.

355

I've always thought of her as one of the most beautiful and alluring women I have ever seen - wonder how long I can hold out? He shook his head, and mentally slapped himself. As long as it takes. Damn it.

They had put the raft in as the jungle sky lightened earlier that morning, after talking through the rest of the night. An awkward truce had been agreed to, although it was clear that Belinda resented his resistance to her charms. She still needed him for protection.

"And what of your shaman, your brujo?" Phil asked as the river turned to foam.

"I'll be going back to study with Domingo one day when the time is right, but for now I'll go back to civilization with you, let Madeline and my family know I'm all right, and watch out for Sanchez. I feel safer with you around." She smiled at him, and put both her hands on her hips. "I knew you would find me."

"Pick up a paddle; it's getting a little bumpy."

* * * * * * * *

They resumed their conversation on the other side of the rapids.

"Do you know how to use a pistol Belinda?" She seemed to be returning to normal, Phil thought. Although "normal" was not a word he would ever associate with Belinda.

"No, but I'm sure you can teach me. Explain to me again why you want to go to San Javier, and talk to Avendano?" She stretched out leisurely against the bow, and displayed a lot of bare thigh.

"To find out if he set us up for an ambush. It's possible he didn't, but I want to satisfy my curiosity. If Laurence was involved in the antiquities trade, and he helped loot Chanul Tzuk, who knows who else could be involved? And you think it was this Alex fellow that killed Kathryn Haden? Why not Laurence?"

"Are you serious? Can you picture him killing anyone? Really?" Belinda seemed certain.

"Yeah but he was an accessory, at the very least." Phil felt like they were starting to figure out what happened, but that there was more that he still needed to understand.

"I think when he realized the enormity of what he had done, that his soul died."

She spoke softly. "He was so sad and he was so lost, the occult offered something to him. When I met up with him, it was like he was empty. Like he didn't give a damn about much of anything."

"Why did he do it? That's the part I don't understand." Phil shook his head.

"Who knows?" Belinda flipped her hair back, and put it up in a ponytail. "He once said though that money is all the reason anyone needs to do anything. He was always so circumspect. But I believe that he was drawn in gradually through the occult, and through mysticism. Eventually, he was in too deep to get out. No way to get back."

"I always thought his moral compass didn't work all that well. What do you think they did with Haden's body?" He felt anguished thinking about Kathryn, she must have been at the wrong place at exactly the wrong time.

"I suppose she's somewhere at Chanul Tzuk... It's all so horrible." Belinda paused. "I need to call Mamett and get his views on all of this."

"Well when we get to Tenosique, there will be telephones. I'm sure you've got a lot of catching up to do."

"I wonder what Delia will think when she learns we're traveling together." She laughed.

"I'll just jump off that bridge, when we come to it."

* * * * * * * *

The river widened out, and the current slowed, on both banks the jungle cascaded right down to the water. Belinda squinted at him. "God what I

357

would give for a pair of sunglasses. Of everything I lost I miss my Ray bans the most."

Phil took his pair off and extended them to her. She shook her head. "Go on take them Bel."

She smiled and put them on. "Thank you Phillip. You are the last of the real gentlemen." She patted his leg. "That's the first time you've called me Bel in months."

"Did I?" He smiled at her. "Don't make a big deal out of it. I'm just glad to find you in one piece."

Belinda frowned. "There for awhile I was in several pieces. And my head. I still get these really weird bone crunching head aches. Phillip I'm worried that something is wrong with me."

"Soon as we get a chance we'll get you to a real doctor."

"Well let me tell you, my brujo friend Domingo flat out saved my life. I owe him everything." She thought again of the eye of the vulture looking at her as she lay on the river bank. It made her shiver.

"You okay?" Phil stopped paddling, and leaned toward her.

She put her hand on his wrist and squeezed hard. "I'm afraid that something..."

He put his hand over hers and held it. "What? What is it?"

"Phillip I've done some terrible things to you. To myself. I've been messed up and I want a chance to atone for it all, but…" She put her head against his shoulder.

"Look Belinda, you don't have to do this." He held her firmly in his arms.

She started crying quietly as she shuddered. "Death. Phil. I dream of death every night. My death. Laurence's. Death has got inside me and has made himself at home. I can't shake him. And I'm afraid that…"

"What?" He stroked her hair, and felt the old warmth for her come back into his heart.

"I'm afraid that I'll die, before I make things right with you." She wrapped her arms around him and held tighter.

"Belinda. You don't have to worry about that. You're not going to die either. I won't let anything happen to you, and baby whatever you may have done, I forgive you."

"Do you still love me?" She nuzzled his chest.

"It's not that simple Bel." He heard a splash and looked at the riverbank.

A cayuco, a dug-out canoe pushed off from the near shore. Two young Maya men were poling it toward them. Phil broke out of her embrace and watched them approach. As they closed on the raft, Belinda waved. "I know them. It's the twins, Angel and Miguel. They're from Santa Theresa."

The cayuco pulled in close to the raft and they drifted together. The twins began talking excitedly in Maya as Belinda listened. Phil only understood a few words of it.

Belinda listened and nodded, and then she flinched like she had been hit.

"Santa Theresa was raided this morning by men with guns." She took a deep breath. "They were looking for me. They killed two people and took Domingo down river, about four hours ago. They were in two boats."

"Any idea who they were?" Phil pulled the gun bag over next to his feet. Belinda stuttered as she asked the question in Maya.

"They were in the area months ago looking for me. God, I'm afraid it sounds like Alex Sanchez. What can we do? Domingo saved my life." Her face was white.

"We continue down river and hope. But with a four hour jump on us? It doesn't look good. How many men were there?"

Belinda talked with the twins for a few more minutes and then they pushed off and headed back toward the shore. She took a deep breath and shook her head.

"Six men that they are sure about. Maybe more." She rubbed her eyes; Phil could tell she was trying not to cry. "They're going back to Santa Theresa to help move the village deeper into the jungle. I told them we would look for Domingo. They think he's already dead…"

Phil paddled the raft back out into the main current. "I think now is a good time for that pistol lesson Belinda."

* * * * * * * *

The sun cast long shadows across the river when Phil spotted the tracks. Overlapping muddy ruts showed where someone had pulled a boat trailer up the left bank. He steered toward it and nudged the raft in against a low overhanging coconut palm. Belinda went forward and tied the raft to the tree.

"Now what?" She climbed back and sat next to him.

"I want you to wait here with the pistol. If anything looks wrong fire two warning shots, and I'll run back here. I'm going to follow those tracks a bit. I won't be long." He unpacked the AK-47 and slipped over the side.

"Phil, can't I come with you?" He heard the fear in her voice, and patted her leg, and squeezed her arm.

"Bel, I won't be far and I need you to watch the raft and our supplies." He started wading ashore, the water only came up to his knees.

"Okay. Two shots right?" Belinda held the Makarov with both hands.

"Right, and if you hear me fire two shots then get in the river and get the hell out of here." He started up the muddy slope.

"Don't be long."

"Can't. We've only got about an hour of sunlight left." Phil disappeared into the forest gloom.

* * * * * * * *

The track up from the river was heavily rutted in places and widened out around some of the longer and deeper muddy ditches. Phil glided silently through the lengthening shadows. The smell of wood smoke was coming from somewhere nearby, so humans weren't too far away, but there were no sounds or signs on the trail, except for an empty rum bottle that someone had tossed recently. He thought the tire tracks were very similar to ones he had seen outside Macondo three weeks before, and it made him run faster. The burning wood smell intensified as he moved inland and the trail seemed to be taking him right to it.

In the deepening gloom he could make out smoke drifting across a clear area up ahead. Phil guessed he was about two miles from the river. He approached the clearing from the jungle to his right, intent on not making a sound, as the last rays of sunlight stabbed down through the trees.

Another smell drifted from the clearing, a strong odor of dead, rotting flesh, and blood. He could hear thousands of flies humming. A thatched hut was open on all sides in the center of the clearing. A fire burned out behind it. Behind the fire a headless corpse was stretched across a black stone altar. Walking slowly toward the altar Phil saw it was carved in the shape of a vulture, *Lord Kisin*.

He approached the area cautiously. The bare ground was stained black with blood. Clouds of flies formed in the hut, and Phil gave it a wide berth. The butchered body of the dead man had words carved deep into his gaping bloody torso.

Brujo

No Mas

"Domingo." Phil whispered. Domingo's heart had been cut out, and his stomach and legs were sheeted in blood. Something was under the cloud of flies in the hut, but in the fading light Phil could not tell what it was. He was conscious that he was switching off again, not letting the full impact of this horror affect him, as he tried to stay calm and fight down his revulsion. But a part of his mind, his soul was screaming deep inside of him, because twenty four years ago he had seen things like this. Now he knew what he was up against, and it made him feel depleted and worn out. He could not match his opponent's ruthlessness.

Phil picked up a fallen branch and lit it off the smoldering fire. He walked into the hut and waved it through the clouds of flies, burning and singeing hundreds of them in the air. The flies thinned out and he could see what they had been feasting on. A wooden bench held eight decomposing human heads. Four of them were gleaming white skulls, picked completely clean. Two had maggots squirming and pulsing all over them. The one on the end had to be Domingo's. His filmy gray eyes gaped at Phil from blood crusted sockets.

"God damn you!" He yelled, loathing the men who had done this.

The forest became silent in response. In a rage he kicked one of the hut's support poles and felt it loosen. He knew what to do.

Carefully, as if he might hurt him, he took down Domingo's body and placed it on its' back on the floor of the hut. He put the defiled head back on Domingo's shoulders. As he worked in silence, tears streamed from his eyes, and soon he was sobbing, silently crying for Domingo and all the wasted lives he had ever known. He kicked down the poles of the thatched hut and was satisfied by the way it covered Domingo's remains. He picked up the burning branch and touched the pile of dried thatch. It ignited like gasoline, and soon the funeral pyre blazed in the early twilight. A cloud of vultures flew out of the treetops, into the silvery sky, flapping their wings heavily as they circled.

Phil tried to think of something to say. "God, please accept this man into your house. I never knew him, but I hear he was a good man, a healer, a saver of lives. Let him sleep in peace." Phil took a deep breath and watched the ashes and sparks float up into the twilight sky. From somewhere he remembered a line from Hamlet.

"For in that sleep of death what dreams may come when we have shuffled off this mortal coil?" It was all he could remember, he added, "And God

362

help me find the men who did this, and give me the strength I need. For I will show them no mercy. Let me be your instrument. Amen."

* * * * * * * *

Silver streaks of fading sunlight reflected off the river when Phil made it back to Belinda. He hugged her, and untied the raft. He sat down, and all the air went out of him. Belinda saw his blood streaked clothes but did not say anything until they were moving out into the current.

"He's dead." She took a deep breath.

Phil nodded and picked up his paddle.

"You don't want to talk about it." She touched his arm.

"I know something I didn't know until now. If it was Sanchez, and I think it was, then he must have led the group that fought us at Macondo, and he definitely killed Eikelmann. And…"

"And what?"

"And he really needs to die. The world needs to be rid of him." He stopped paddling as the current caught them. "I wonder…"

"What?"

"If I've got what it takes to do it."

70 Out of the EZLN

Gloria and Jesse waited in San Cristobal de Las Casas on Christmas morning. They were parked in front of a closed leather shop on Avenue Crescencio Rosa. The streets of the city were adorned with Christmas decorations, and completely deserted. Even the street orphans were gone. Jesse thought about how San Cristobal had become a major city of over one hundred thousand people, most of them living in misery. As recently

363

as ten years ago it had been half that size. Now you could buy anything here that you could in San Antonio; from computers to satellite dishes.

Sometime during the next thirty minutes, a flatbed truck was supposed to pull up next to them, and they were supposed to follow it. While they waited, Jesse presented a small gift wrapped present to Gloria. Inside was a pair of jade earrings.

"Oh they are so beautiful. Thank you." She immediately started putting them on. "Reach under your seat Jesse."

A flat box wrapped in blue paper, was under his seat. Inside was a Suunto compass, encased in stainless steel. "Where did you find one of these?"

"Here in town when we were shopping yesterday. I remember when you told me what the pendejos took away from you at Raxabe; the thing you seemed most upset about was losing your compass." She smiled as she hung it around his neck.

He leaned over and kissed her, and heard a truck coming up the street. Sitting in the cab of a beat up flatbed truck, was Garcia. He rolled his window down. "Merry Christmas you two. Do you have my presents?"

"Yes. Our trip was uneventful." Jesse started up the Suburban. "Thank God."

Garcia and Gloria began transferring the boxes of ammunition, while Jesse kept watch. When they had loaded the last box, Garcia shook Jesse's hand and said, "Well things will start to get a little more exciting real soon." He grinned.

"How soon?" Jesse asked.

"A matter of days, but I think you have done more than your part."

"What are you saying?

"You have done more than enough. This is as far as it goes for you."

"What do you mean?" Jesse felt used.

"That your service with the EZLN has come to an end." He shrugged his shoulders. "Please understand I do it to protect us both. In the end, you will be better off if you distance yourself from us."

Before getting in the truck to leave Gloria said, "I do not approve of this Jesse, but I will find you soon, please believe me."

71 What Remains Hidden

The Villahermosa airport was busy four days after Christmas, and lines were backed up everywhere. Phil and Belinda waited by the gate for Delia to disembark. Belinda was dressed like an American again in blue jeans and a T-shirt. Phil had helped replenish her wardrobe and makeup kit for Christmas. But Phil seemed different to Belinda, almost if he was preparing himself for war. He constantly cleaned his weapons, sharpened his knife and withdrew deeper into himself.

They spoke no more about Domingo; Belinda was still hurting from the loss. Other times when they were alone at night he would hold her and stroke her forehead, and they would just be together in silence. It comforted her like it always did. Sex was no longer an issue. He had made it clear that he had given his word to Delia, and Belinda knew Phil would keep it, regrettably.

Still, she had not completely given up on the idea getting him back. She would have to try a different approach. Standing next to Phil, she thought about how it was now necessary to neutralize Delia. Friendship was one thing, but she felt she still had a claim on him, and that she could extract Delia somehow. After all he had loved her first, he had loved her longer and eventually he would realize that he still loved her. Even though Belinda knew she had betrayed him, and rejected him, she still wanted him back. His resistance only made her want him more. Logic, she thought, has nothing to do with it.

Delia emerged from the line of holiday travelers, and hugged Phil, who took her carry-on bag from her. Delia hugged Belinda.

"God Belinda. It's so good to see you. You've lost too much weight."

Belinda laughed, "Well it wasn't exactly a stress-free diet."

They walked toward baggage claim and Phil asked Delia, "Were you ever able to get hold of Mamett or Avendano?"

Delia shrugged, "Actually no. But you know how the holidays are. I've played phone tag with Patrick, but he said he would be landing here on this same flight tomorrow morning."

"Well I've learned that Avendano will be back at the museum in San Javier tomorrow on the 30th. I'll be paying him a visit then, or Friday. I've known him since the Montebello Project and I really hope he's not involved." Phil watched the crowds around the baggage carousels, looking to see if anyone was watching them.

"So you spent the holidays getting Madeline back home to Beacon Hill?" Belinda lightly touched Delia's shoulder. "That was very kind of you."

"It was the least I could do, considering all she's done for me. She really appreciated all the calls you made this past week." They had reached the conveyor belt and waited for the bags to come up. "You lifted Madeline's spirits quite a lot, but she doesn't understand why you won't come home." Delia collected her bags, and Phil carried them.

"I won't be safe until Alex Sanchez is taken care of."

"Whoever this guy is, I'll get my point across to him." Phil said. They walked toward the parking lot to the rented VW. "It's a matter of flushing him out."

* * * * * * * * * *

The Hotel Diego de Mazariegos incorporated two enormous mansions that were built in 1528, not long after the founding of San Cristobal de las Casas. Two patios paved with stone slabs and flanked by four corridors of wooden columns connected the mansions. Adobe walls and red tile roofs completed the colonial ambience. Although it was awkward for all concerned, Phil, Delia and Belinda shared a suite. Belinda simply did not

366

want to be left alone. In light of all she had been through they understood her fear and anxiety.

Phil went jogging early the next morning and left Belinda and Delia alone together. They were waiting for Jesse Salazar, who was scheduled to show up with the project equipment around mid-morning.

Not after Phil left to work out, the tension between the two women broke. Delia was combing her hair in front of the dresser as Belinda emerged from the shower. A red puckered scar on Belinda's shoulder caught Delia's eye.

"Phil's got a couple of scars like that." Delia noticed.

"I know. Actually he has three of them. Two up here." Belinda pointed to her left shoulder. "And one above his left knee on his inner thigh."

Something about the way Belinda said "inner thigh" annoyed Delia, but she tried to overlook it. She combed her hair in fierce silence.

"Something on your mind Delia?" Belinda seemed smug. "Something you want to ask me?"

Delia placed the comb on the dresser. "Yes Belinda, there is, since you seem to be in a confrontational mood." She took a deep breath and plunged in. "When was the last time you slept with Phil?"

Belinda smiled as she toweled off her hair. "That's not the issue here. The real question is am I going to continue to sleep with him?"

"What?" Delia felt her stomach sink, and her heart race.

"And the answer is I haven't decided yet." She wrapped a towel around her, and sat down on the edge of the bed.

"You're saying it's all up to you?" Delia hugged her stomach.

"Yes." Belinda unfastened a new bottle of blue nail polish, and coolly started working on her nails. "Yes. I would say so." She finished painting her nails while Delia furiously picked up the room in silence.

The phone rang and Belinda answered. "Great. We'll come right down." She pulled on a pair of jeans and said to Delia, "Jesse Salazar is here."

* * * * * * * *

Phil was still in his jogging sweats when he joined everyone on the patio, and Belinda was relieved when he came back. Whenever he was out of her sight she worried until he returned. Jesse and Delia were busy talking about the upcoming project.

Jesse turned toward her, "Belinda you've been very quiet, are you going to work with us at Chanul Tzuk?"

"I haven't decided yet. It depends on what Phil wants to do. For now, he makes my decisions." She said distractedly, "I just want to put all the pieces together. Lately, I feel fragile, as if my mind might slip away from me. It's hard to understand I know, and it is even harder to explain."

Phil took a long drink of water. "I'm staying here until I figure out what the hell's been going on, and who's been trying to frame me. I want to know how all of this happened. And then I want to get myself un-framed."

"Speaking of that Belinda, I hear from Delia that you've got quite a story to tell, concerning the late Laurence Eikelmann?" Jesse asked quietly.

"But I don't comprehend it all completely." The other thing she was feeling, was impending disaster that would not go away. Something terrible was about to happen. Belinda could feel it coming.

"Well?" Jesse gestured impatiently.

"Well what?" The feeling that she was being watched came over her again, as she looked about the patio.

"Let's hear it. I am very interested."

"Wait." Belinda held up her hand as she tried to focus her thoughts. "Okay. I was at the Jaguar Inn at Tikal, in late August. He pulled up with his friend, or affiliate, a horrible smelly man named Alex Sanchez."

Jesse and Gloria looked like they had been punched. Gloria's eyes narrowed.

"Did you say Alex Sanchez?" Jesse asked. His voice was like ice.

* * * * * * * *

"And then I met Phil, and we hooked up with Delia, and here we all are." Belinda had told it all very quickly, and felt drained afterwards.

"Belinda, this Alex Sanchez, did you say he smelled badly?" Delia asked.

"Oh God yes. He had a horrible stench. He reeked. Almost like spoiled meat." She made a face at the memory of it. "He's the scariest man I've ever met. It's almost like he's inhuman."

"That sounds a lot like the same man who attacked me at the Peabody Museum." Delia whispered.

"And we happen to know a policeman by that name." Jesse sipped his coffee.

"Renegade police from Chiapas attacked us at Macondo, and I suspect Sanchez led them. He tortured and killed Belinda's friend Domingo too." Phil leaned forward and put down his empty water glass. "Okay. We have most of the missing pieces now that we can finally compare notes. Sanchez is a Mexican cop, and a killer. He's at the center of it all. Think back, what happened first?"

Belinda felt an overwhelming wave of despair come over her, but she tried to fight it off. "From the moment I found that mask in the back of Laurence's Land Rover, I've known as sure as I know anything, that Kathryn Haden probably interrupted Sanchez and Laurence while they were looting a tomb at Chanul Tzuk. Sanchez must have killed her. He did something with the body, and then they fled into Guatemala, staying ahead of the search parties, until I ran into them. Sanchez tried to kill me too. He almost succeeded, and Laurence fled." Belinda paused. "I'm sure about that much. Where did Laurence run to?" She started biting the polish off her fingernails.

369

Delia answered. "Laurence flew back to Boston with your luggage and tried to make it look like you had returned, so people would not look for you down here. It was the first attempt at misdirection and confusion. It also worked for awhile." Delia was speaking rapidly; Belinda could tell she had been thinking about it all for a long time. It was like a dam had broken inside of her. "Sanchez must have followed him back to Boston, probably unsure about him since he had panicked that night at the cave?"

"Who knows?" Belinda shrugged. "Trying to figure out why Sanchez does anything is probably fruitless. He looked down the river for me for a couple of weeks, and then I heard no more about him until last week when they raided Santa Theresa and killed Domingo." Belinda shuddered. "The man is an animal."

"So like an animal, he follows Laurence his prey, back to Cambridge, and for whatever reason, sacrifices him." Delia paused before continuing. "But Sanchez wasn't finished because he needed Laurence's computer, which must have contained incriminating evidence? It had something important on it. And he needed to know if Laurence had revealed anything to me, the night I had him taken to the ER. That's why he was following me." She took a deep breath, and looked around the table. "Does that make sense to you all? I mean so far?"

"It's like an archaeological excavation, we can see the outlines of it, but we can't tell how far it goes, or what remains hidden." Phil said momentarily interrupting Delia.

"All along their second misdirection contingency plan was to frame you Phil, in case everything blew up, and they did a very good job of that. They almost had me convinced. Finally, to shut down the police investigation, Sanchez killed Professor Thomas, and tried to make it look like he committed suicide. Now with Thomas dead, and identified as the mastermind behind it all, Sanchez again implicates you, just for good measure?"

"And Laurence apparently had resorted to stealing from the museum collections, and he also tried to frame me." Phil pushed his chair back. "But why? Was it easier to rip-off the museum, than it was to loot sites?"

370

Belinda squeezed his hand. "A lot of money was involved, hundred of thousands…but why did they pick you? It seems personal doesn't it Phillip? They probably hoped that you would try to fight your way out of it (which you in fact did), and…that something would happen to you as a result?"

"Well Phil and Laurence weren't exactly close." Delia looked at Phil. "What am I overlooking?"

"I feel like it's right here in front of us, but we just can't see it." Belinda winced. One of her old migraine headaches was coming back on.

"Okay wait. I think I can follow this line." Delia put her elbows on the table, and massaged the bridge of her nose. "Let's take a look at the hypothesis that Avendano told Patrick that Belinda was at Macondo, which we all know now was a lie. She was never there."

"I don't even know where it is." Belinda noticed that she had completely gnawed and stripped the polish off one of her nails.

"According to Patrick, Avendano's story is that a friend of Sergio's told him you were there, and that sounds suspicious doesn't it?" Delia looked around the table.

Phil cracked his knuckles. "Either Avendano or Mamett, or possibly both of them are lying. Jesse, that's why you and I need to start with Avendano."

"You are not suggesting that Sergio Avendano is mixed up in this?" Jesse interrupted. "I can accept everything that's been said here this morning, but I can't accept that. It's preposterous."

"If it's not him, it's his so-called, unidentified, colleague." Delia said firmly.

"Let's not lose sight of the fact that the big problem is still Sanchez." Phil interjected. "He probably led the attack at Macondo, and later tortured and killed Domingo. The obvious motive is he's tying up loose ends. And that means all of us sitting here are loose ends. And that means…"

371

"He'll try again." Delia whispered.

"Exactly. And we are all at risk because he's going to be very hard to stop. There is really nothing that he won't do. The man is capable of anything. Please keep that in mind for all of our sakes."

72 Reconnaissance

"Jesse it is good to see you." Avendano embraced him. "And Phil Ward. It has been a long time." They shook hands. "I heard you were terminated at Harvard? I am very sorry to hear that…even Harvard makes mistakes regrettably." Avendano said, as they entered his office. He moved two stacks of books out of chairs so Phil and Jesse could sit down. "What are your plans now? You know the institute could use you, if you are interested in moving to Mexico."

"Sergio, I might be interested in such an opportunity since I am going to keep doing archaeology. I just haven't decided in what capacity yet. Let's set up some time to talk about that. I appreciate it very much. Thank you." Phil smiled, trying to think of how to raise the next question; he had known Avendano a long time. He even liked and respected him, but he also knew someone had set them up. Phil decided to flank the subject. "Did I tell you I found Belinda Boothe, or rather she found me?"

Avendano smiled and nodded. "Really? Patrick will be glad to hear that. He was getting quite concerned. Have you told him?"

"Not yet. He's gone away for the holidays. But he'll be here tomorrow to start up Chanul Tzuk." Phil watched Avendano idly pick his keys up off the desk.

"I know. I'm going to be lending some assistance to the project. You and I will be working together again Jesse."

Jesse nodded. "I'm looking forward to it."

Avendano put the keys down again. "Well that's fantastic Phil. And how is Belinda?"

"She's doing quite well, considering. Funny thing though, she wasn't at Macondo like you said." Phil waited for Avendano's reaction.

"Like I said? You and I have not talked." Avendano frowned. "Oh you mean like I told Patrick? Well someone told me that. I have never even been to Macondo."

"So who told you?" Phil asked with a quiet firmness.

Avendano paused before answering and glanced at the ceiling. "I believe it was...Carlos Valdez. He's an affiliate."

"Where can we talk to him?" Jesse asked.

"He's at the museum in San Cristobal. Is it important? Shall I call him?" Avendano seemed like he genuinely wanted to be helpful.

"No it's a short drive back. We'll look him up this afternoon. It's not all that important. Probably a simple case of mistaken identity." Phil stood up to go, and then asked, "There's someone else I'm looking for. Do you know a huechero by the name of Alex Sanchez?"

Jesse stared at Avendano, as he stood up next to Phil. Avendano rubbed his jaw and paused again before answering, "It's a fairly common name. I am sure I do not know any huecheros by that name. There is a policeman in San Cristobal, named Alejandro Sanchez."

Phil looked at him hard. "A policeman? What kind of policeman?"

"Judicial Federal. He's the regional chief."

* * * * * * * * *

"Well?" Phil asked Jesse as they sat in their rental VW down the street from the institute.

"I don't know. I can't believe he admits he knows who Sanchez is, but that by itself doesn't prove anything."

"He did seem distracted though didn't he?" Phil put the keys in the ignition but didn't start the car.

"Honestly, Phil I thought he seemed normal."

"Yeah…well, I thought he acted a little slippery." Phil leaned back in the car seat and put his sunglasses on.

Jesse stared down the tree-lined boulevard. From a side door to the institute Avendano emerged, and walked to his Mercedes.

"Now where's he going?" Phil asked.

Jesse looked at his watch. "Siesta?"

"Just for fun, let's follow him. We have time."

* * * * * * * * *

On the south side of San Javier they drove through a maze of train yards and warehouses. Avendano parked behind an eighteen wheeler and entered a long gray warehouse. Phil and Jesse parked two blocks down.

"So?" Jesse asked.

"Let's wait a minute and see if he comes out." Phil turned off the engine.

After a minute, Phil opened the door and got out. "Want to take a walk with me?"

"I'm going to be awfully embarrassed if I run into him."

"You might be much worse than that." Phil whispered.

They walked down the right side of the street using the parked eighteen wheelers as a screen and approached the warehouse. When they got to Avendano's Mercedes, Phil looked in, and saw nothing out of the ordinary. He walked across the gravel and peered into the first grimy window.

"Nothing. Just a bunch of boxes."

"Phil. I don't like this. What if we run into Avendano? What am I going to say to him?" Jesse stayed at the corner of the warehouse with his arms crossed.

"Say we're doing some archaeological reconnaissance work?" Phil grinned at Jesse as he started walking down the side of the building.

"Very funny."

Jesse watched Phil go around the corner of the building, and hesitated before following him. When he rounded the corner, Phil motioned Jesse over. He was standing on a large water pipe looking in a window.

"Take a look at this Jesse." He whispered. "It turns out that we really are doing archaeological recon."

Through the dirt and grime Jesse saw the warehouse floor, and several freshly made wooden crates. To the right, under a flight of stairs was a table with Maya ceramic pots laid out on top of it. Next to the table a large square stone object was covered with a dusty gray piece of canvas.

"Okay. So maybe the institute has rented some auxiliary lab space?" Jesse asked.

"You don't really believe that do you? I know it's hard to accept that Avendano is mixed up in this but…" Phil pushed Jesse down and whispered, "Someone's coming down the stairs!"

They listened to unintelligible voices speaking quietly, and a motor started up inside the warehouse.

"Stay down." Phil warned him.

"But I have to look." Jesse shrugged, and turned his head sideways peering over the dirty window ledge. Phil looked with him. "Oh my God, they have the altar."

The canvas was pulled off to one side, and a forklift maneuvered under the stone altar. It had an Olmec were-jaguar face framed by Maya glyphs carved on it. The men pushing the pallet toward the forklift wore leather belts with guns and handcuffs attached. They were unmistakably policemen.

Phil and Jesse backed silently away and jogged back to their car. When Phil had safely backed the car out and turned around, he finally spoke. "Sometimes it sucks to be right."

"Okay. So Avendano and the Federal police are in on it together. What do we do now?" Jesse felt ill. He had always trusted Avendano.

"Well I think we should assume for our own protection that many of the government archaeologists and police in this area are probably in on it, so we'll have to go outside of Chiapas for help."

Phil sped out of the warehouse district and turned on the road that would take them up into the mountains.

"Where can we go?" Jesse watched the slums go by.

"Hell I don't know. Mexico City? The National Museum? We're basically screwed as far as I can tell. Since we're up against federal authorities…I think we should just get the hell out of Mexico. We are in way over our heads man. Time to withdraw. We should all leave the country right now. Today."

"I still want Sanchez." Jesse said coldly.

"I do too Jesse, but he's not going to roll over for us. And it's going too be really hard. Unless…"

"Unless what?"

"Maybe we could lure him into an ambush? That would be the best way. Then we could all leave Mexico knowing we had improved the world a bit by his removal from it?" Phil shifted into third gear as they hit a long incline, and thought about his time as a sniper. "I hate leaving him around to do more damage to people. There's nothing to keep him from coming after us."

"Are you talking about cold blooded murder? I can't agree to that man."

"Tell me Jesse. You think Sanchez wouldn't do the same to us?"

* * * * * * * *

Later in the afternoon, they were half way back to San Cristobal de las Casas, driving the VW slowly through a forested mountain pass.

"Strange, I know Avendano is an antiquities smuggler and has been lying to me from day one, but I still can't believe it." Jesse looked out the window at the trees going by, and shook his head.

"Believe it. I think there's still more to this whole thing, but we're getting closer." Phil watched a black Ford Bronco go past. "The best plan is to poke and prod and pull the rest of the truth loose from the safety of the United States. We need to get back on our own turf. In the process maybe we can give Sanchez a little payback."

The Bronco turned around and came back toward them in the rear view mirror.

Red lights flashed inside the grill and it began to tail gate them. Three men were in it, and the passenger motioned for them to pull over. He held his hand outside the window so that Phil could see his badge.

The Makarov was in Phil's pocket, and if he were searched, it would mean heavy jail time. He slipped it under his seat and pulled over.

The police politely asked him to present his papers. Then they asked Phil and Jesse to get out of the car, and as soon as he got out, Phil was punched in the stomach, and clubbed with a baton. Phil passed out. His last thought before the blackness overtook him was; so they got us after all.

He regained consciousness in a filthy basement jail cell reeking of human waste. The walls were covered with graffiti and crude drawings. Jesse was in the cell next to him, and had been badly beaten up. Blood spotted his University of Oregon T-shirt and he looked like he was unconscious. Above Jesse was a fairly good rendition of Our Lady of Guadeloupe executed on the ceiling; Phil wondered how it had been done, since the roof was about fourteen feet high. He noticed that none of the cells around them were occupied. Probably an ominous sign.

It had to be late at night because the entire jail was quiet. He had a throbbing headache and checked the back of his head and felt a bloody crust. These cops were good. They had neutralized him professionally. Phil wondered what they wanted from them. There had to be a reason why they weren't dead already.

73 Kyrie Eleison

Belinda woke up cold and afraid. She felt despair sinking in and called out for Phil. Turning the bedside lamp on, she saw that it was midnight and Phil and Jesse still had not returned. Belinda had a cold stabbing pain in her head, and knew something was wrong. She felt a wretchedness she had never known before, as she climbed out of bed, and went to wake up Delia.

* * * * * * * *

The man with the cane and the limp entered Phil's cell and he recognized him immediately. It was the man he had shot at Macondo. It had to be Alex Sanchez. "Buenos Dias, Senor Ward. Happy New Year. It will be a very brief 1994 for you I fear." The man smelled badly enough to stink up a cell that already reeked.

"Alex Sanchez?" Phil looked at him, and thought about all of the people this man had killed.

"Si. We meet again, although we've never been properly introduced. Tell me. When you shot me in the leg," he pointed toward his cast, "did you miss?"

"I wanted you alive."

"And I want you dead. But first I need to know how much you know." Sanchez lit a cigarette.

"What about him?" Phil pointed at Jesse who was still passed out on the floor of the jail.

"Ah. The big old Tejano. Put up a hell of a fight I heard. Took three men to subdue him. He has to die too." Sanchez shrugged.

"I don't know anything." Phil knew he was on dangerous ground now; anything he said could affect Delia and Belinda. He would protect them with his life.

"Oh I doubt that. You're a smart fellow. Educated at Harvard. Smart hombre." He prodded Phil's foot with his cane. "What you don't know you can probably guess. You have talked to that bitch Belinda, yes?"

Phil looked at Sanchez and visualized sticking a knife in his throat and twisting it.

Sanchez continued, "I should have killed her. Oh well, I may get another chance." He walked over to the other side of the cell and leaned against the bars. "You need to talk to me. You know why?"

Phil stared at him. He knew what kind of man Sanchez was now and it didn't matter what he said to him. Sanchez held all the cards and there was no way out.

"You remember Eikelmann? You must know that I killed him. I enjoyed it. The last thing he saw was his heart beating in my hands, before I ripped it out. Later I ate it. It was very good." He paused to flick the ashes off his cigarette. "Domingo, the same way. That was fun too." He shrugged. "You could die that way. Or you could die more peacefully, say a bullet to the brain? Either way you are a dead man."

"Like the way you killed Samuel Thomas?" Phil asked quickly.

"Very good. See? I knew you were smart."

"Why Thomas?"

"I had to clean things up. He was available, and I needed him."

"So he wasn't involved?" Phil was relieved. He had always liked Thomas.

"No. Not at all. He had the computer. I needed it. I also needed a way to stop the police investigation, so improvised, and that worked out well." Sanchez frowned. "You are smart. You have me talking. Suppose you talk. Tell me who else you think is involved?"

"Based on what happened after our visit to him, I would have to say Avendano of course." Phil felt the back of his head carefully.

'Don Avendano. Thinks he is some kind of cacique. Still, you have to give him credit. He said from the beginning that you would be a problem."

"I've known him a long time. But not very well apparently." Phil shook his head. "Why did you kill Kathryn Haden?"

Sanchez shrugged. "She recognized me and Laurence. We had visited the site the day before. Laurence predicted they were going to hit a tomb, and they did. But we got to it first. And there she was. Bad luck. It was tough digging in that rain but it paid off. Business has been very good lately." Sanchez laughed quietly and stared at Phil.

"What did you do with her body?" Phil whispered.

"It's under the plaza, what better place to bury someone than in an archaeological excavation?" He laughed, "Hah - wait... I think you need to tell me something." He looked up at the ceiling and back at Phil. "Why do you think I killed Laurence?"

Phil massaged the back of his neck. "Hell. I don't know. He was always unstable."

"And a pain in the ass. So why did I kill him?" Sanchez prodded Phil in the chest with his cane.

"He was going to talk?"

"I think he would, because he was crazy and could not be trusted. Still, he knew how to find tombs with that computer of his. But he was a drug addict and a drunk, and he thought he was a brujo. He was killed by a real brujo." He raked the iron bars with his cane. "I killed him because he was stealing money from us, and sending it down here to the communists, to subversives. Can you believe that? He thought I was too stupid to find out. He cost me a lot of money."

Sanchez shook his head. "Just a dumb Mexican right?" He laughed again, speaking of dumb Mexicans..." He gestured at Jesse and laughed harshly, then was silent. "So you do know very little. Good." He opened the cell door.

"Why don't you just kill me now and be done with it?" Phil stood up and looked Sanchez in the eye. It was like looking into the eyes of a shark, black and opaque. Lifeless.

"I should, but too many witnesses. And I have something special planned for you. You have the ch'ulel of a warrior, when I kill you tomorrow morning I will take your power too. Just like I took Domingo's."

He tapped Phil on the head with his cane and left.

A little while later Jesse woke up groaning. From somewhere nearby Phil could hear cathedral bells chiming the hour. They echoed though the corridors of the jail. It was midnight, and mass was starting.

"What happened?" Jesse looked despondently about the cell.

"We're in jail in San Cristobal. I was formally introduced to Sanchez a little while ago, although we did meet once before." Phil felt like he had dragged Jesse into this mess. "Jesse I'm sorry."

Jesse stood up slowly. "I remember punching one of them in the nose, and I guess they whacked me on the back of my head."

"I know the feeling." Phil turned and showed Jesse his head wound.

"Well partner, at least we know we figured it all out. Not that it'll do us a hell of a lot of good. It was Sanchez and Avendano the whole time." Jesse stretched. "God I'm hungry. Think they'll feed us?"

"You mean before they kill us?" Phil laughed. "At least you keep things in perspective man."

"We're pretty much screwed aren't we?" Jesse whispered.

"It does look that way." Phil stood up and stretched, he felt pains from his head to his feet. Lost and trapped, he feared for their lives, and regretted everything he had done. "Jesus what a mess I've made of things. I had the arrogance to think I could handle this and now? Jesse I'm sorry I got you into this."

"Hell Phil. I got myself into it. We make a pretty good team man."

"I'm not so sure about that. I mean, look where we are."

From across the plaza they could hear the New Year's Eve mass. It echoed into the jail. Several hundred voices sang the litany: "Kyrie eleison, Kyrie eleison…"

"God I haven't been to mass in a long time." Jesse shook his head ruefully.

"Me either. This looks like our last chance too."

"Kyrie eleison. Christ have mercy." Jesse whispered.

"Lord have mercy." Phil responded.

"Amen."

* * * * * * * *

Steps echoed down the hall. Phil stood up trying to be ready for anything, but they were in Jesse's cell immediately, kicking and beating him.

Sanchez and four large men pounded Jesse with batons. Jesse was on his hands and knees. Somehow he stood up and lashed out with his elbows and arms yelling, whirling and flailing back at them.

One guard was knocked toward Phil and he quickly put him in a hammerlock and pulled the baton out of the man's hands. Jesse was covered in blood. He shouted and grabbed a baton of his own and laid a guard out. Phil pulled the baton against his guard's neck with his right hand and with his left hand tried to pull the gun out of the leather belt. Jesse kicked out, and his boot connected with someone's jaw and now another guard was down. Pistol shots rang out in rapid fire, and Jesse was on the cell floor holding his thigh, while blood poured out between his fingers. Sanchez turned and pointed the gun at Phil.

"Release him."

Phil let the guard go and saw the blood flowing freely from Jesse's leg. "Lift your leg up Jesse and tie your belt above the wound."

Jesse feebly tried to do it, but Sanchez lashed his cane out and struck Jesse's hand away. Simultaneously, Phil's guard thrust his baton through the bars and clipped him in the head. Phil reeled and blood flowed into his eyes. The other two guards had their pistols out and covered Phil and Jesse.

"Tejano boy, you just signed your death warrant." Sanchez walked quickly over to Jesse, a knife in his right hand. With his left hand he pulled Jesse up by his ear and cut it off. Jesse screamed, and fell back as blood flowed down his neck. Still screaming, he grabbed at his missing ear with his left hand. Sanchez held the bloody piece of flesh up to the light. "Oh. An appetizer." He put it in his mouth and ate it. "Needs something. Some salsa perhaps?"

He wiped his bloodstained hands off on the wall. In dazed horror and through a crimson film, the image was seared onto Phil's eyes; two unconscious guards, stretched out on the floor, Jesse's face covered in blood and Sanchez grinning. Jesse was whispering. "Hail Mary full of grace the Lord is with thee. Blessed art thou…"

Sanchez laughed. "Pray hard boy! The Lord is not with thee." He kicked Jesse's leg, directly in the bullet hole. Jesse moaned, and fell over onto his side. Sanchez knelt beside him and said. "I can't decide what to cut off next. Your balls? Your nose? One of your eyes perhaps?" He laughed and put the knife against Jesse's eyelid.

"You sure are a brave bastard when it's five on one." Phil shouted through clenched teeth. "Even so you couldn't handle him. Could you?"

Sanchez stood up and leered at Phil. "So you want to die too gringo? Shut the hell up or I'll cut your gringo tongue out and feed it to my dogs. I have important business with the Tejano." He stood up and prodded Jesse's gasping body with his cane. "So tell me where Garcia is, where the rest of the money is, and then maybe I'll let you die. Or more torture could be provided. That could be fun. It's up to you."

"What makes you think he knows anything?" Phil shouted. "Why don't you come over here and try that on me? One on one? You don't have the huevos for that though, do you?" Phil was beyond fear. He knew they were going to die. But he wanted to spare Jesse any further suffering. The best idea he could come up with was to provoke Sanchez to shoot them both, so they could avoid the fates of Laurence and Domingo.

Sanchez nodded at the guards and they left Jesse's cell and came into Phil's. They opened the door and Phil rushed them, ignoring the baton blows that rained down on him. He had his hands around a man's neck and was squeezing hard, when a baton crunched his temple and he fell into the rushing blackness.

* * * * * * * * *

Delia and Belinda loaded up the Suburban dejectedly. Phil and Jesse still had not shown up. Gloria had disappeared too. As Delia put the last bag in, she turned to Belinda.

"Look, we've got plenty of time before Patrick's flight lands. Let's go by San Javier first, and see if Avendano knows where Phil and Jesse are. It will only take an extra hour. I have a really bad feeling about all of this."

"So do I." Belinda hugged herself, she felt desolate. "I've been having premonitions since last night."

They drove slowly out of the hotel parking lot.

* * * * * * * *

Belinda saw their blue VW Jetta on the shoulder of the road. It was obviously abandoned. "I have the spare key. Maybe they had car trouble." Belinda got out and opened the VW. It started right up. She put her head against the steering wheel, took a deep breath, and asked in a low, tormented voice. "Okay. So they didn't have car trouble. What did happen?"

Delia kicked the gravel on the shoulder of the road. "So maybe we were right about Avendano? If we go there he'll just lie to us." She looked deflated.

"And if the police took Phil and Jesse, they're not going to help us." Belinda said. "So we can't go to the police."

"God. What do we do?" Delia looked up at the sky, as if expecting an answer.

Belinda got out of the VW, and locked it up. "Well it won't do any good. It never does, but all that's left for us is to contact the American Embassy, in Tuxtla Gutierrez. Too far to go today, and I hate to leave without Phil and Jesse."

Delia swallowed the despair in her throat and said. "Look, I know we suspect everyone, but after we pick up Patrick, maybe we should go back to Chanul Tzuk, as originally planned. Phil knows that's where we're supposed to be, and that's where he'll go if he's able to get there. When Mamett gets in, we'll check with him, and if Phil and Jesse are not here by tomorrow morning, we'll go to the embassy."

"It will be closed dear." Belinda said hopelessly. "Tomorrow is New Year's Day."

"We'll make them open it up. Do you have a better idea?"

"No."

* * * * * * * *

They reached the camp after dark. Jesse and Phil still had not arrived. Delia, Belinda, and Patrick unpacked equipment and listened to the insects humming across the hills. Bats flitted under the thatched roof while Belinda finished explaining their fears about Phil and Jesse to Mamett.

"Seems to be more bats than last year." Patrick watched a bat flop around in the thatch. He was exhausted from flying all day, and stretched his legs out in front of him. "In light of what happened to Kathryn Haden, it is obvious that we should be concerned about both of them. And I am." He took a deep breath and exhaled. "But Sergio will be here in the morning. If they still have not turned up, we'll have the police look for them, or the army, or both." He stood and stretched. "Those are two pretty big guys, and I think they can take care of themselves. I believe they will show up."

"Patrick, since some members of the police may be involved; I think we will have much better chances with the army." Belinda sat down heavily in a folding chair.

"Okay. And Sergio's bringing some soldiers over here in the morning to help with site security. So really, I believe Salazar and Ward will turn up tomorrow. They probably had car trouble; got a ride somewhere and you all just missed each other. You know how it is down here. Look, I'm going to go set up my cot and go to sleep. I'm fairly well jet-lagged, and I can address this whole thing better after I'm rested. Wake me up when they come in, or if anything else happens."

74 Zapatistas

The Municipal jail was silent, asleep on New Years Day. Phil at first thought he heard a car back fire, and another loud popping sound. A crescendo started up and he recognized the unmistakable sounds of pistols, shotguns, M-16s and AK- 47s firing in the streets of San Cristobal. People shouted, and glass was breaking. Startled into awareness, he heard the gun fire rapidly approaching the central plaza.

"What the hell's going on?" Phil's entire body ached as he woke up. He went to the door of his cell, and listened to the shooting. Jesse's body lay in a twisted bloody pile on the jail floor. Had Sanchez returned during the night while he was knocked out? "Jesse wake up. Something's happening."

Jesse did not move.

Car alarms and burglar alarms joined the sounds of battle. Phil paced his cell, his cage. He attempted to stick his head through the bars to look down the corridor, and also tried to reach Jesse through the bars, but he was just out of reach. Prisoners were yelling and screaming throughout the jail, in a jumbled mixture of Spanish and Maya.

He heard voices shouting from the offices, and a grenade went off outside. Something burned nearby. A guard came running down the corridor, running away from the action. When he was close enough, Phil extended his foot and his arm, grabbing him, and hit the guard's head against the iron bars. As the man went limp, Phil grappled with his unconscious body and eventually got the guard's key chain off his leather belt.

He let the guard down gently, and then opened his cell door. Damn, he thought, all hell is breaking loose. I've got to wake Jesse up and get him out of here. Then I've got to find him a doctor.

Another grenade went off, deafening Phil. In the smoke, people were suddenly in the corridors unlocking the jail cells. A petite woman with bandoleers over her brown shirt, a black ski mask, and green fatigues was holding a shotgun on one of the jailers, making him unlock each cell. When she reached Jesse and Phil she opened the door and said, "You are freed in the name of the Zapatista Army of National Liberation, Jesse Salazar. Excuse me Señor. I see you have already liberated yourself?"

"I appreciate the assistance." Phil bowed. "I am Phil Ward; do you know my fiend Jesse?"

"Very well. Let's wake him up and get him out of here."

"I couldn't agree more."

Jesse's body was cold and he would not wake up. He was not breathing, and did not have a pulse. Phil tried CPR, but to no avail. After about ten minutes he gave up, resigned, and close to tears.

"He didn't make it. They killed him during the night." He said to the woman in the ski mask.

She knelt down and hugged his lifeless body and began weeping.

****

Leaving the jail, Phil was stunned by the turn of events. From the stairs, he could see that the center of town was full of masked rebels in brown and green uniforms. They were treating crowds of startled tourists and civilians politely, while they rounded up government officials, and police. Clouds of papers and documents floated down like confetti from the government office windows. He followed Gloria, and helped her carry Jesse's body through the crowd of jubilant rebels.

"I will go find him a stretcher." Gloria said and disappeared into the crowd.

The town's been liberated, Phil thought, it truly was a miracle, but it was too late for Jesse. He watched the guerillas carry boxes and drawers of files and records, down the Palacio Municipal steps and throw them on a bonfire. I'm right in the middle of a revolution; he felt faint from the beatings and realized he was about ready to pass out.

"Here we go." Gloria said and they placed Jesse's body on a stretcher. They moved down the nearest alley; on a side street Phil saw a group of policemen in a pickup truck, trying to get out of town. They were attempting to make their way uphill, through a herd of goats scrambling toward them. From the main plaza people were cheering. San Cristobal de las Casas had fallen.

Gloria said, "Five centuries of suffering, and hopelessness have come apart right here in Chiapas. The revolution is here now, and I have lost the man I love," she sobbed.

"Where are we taking him?" Phil asked. He concentrated hard on not passing out, willing himself to stand up.

"To the morgue. After that I do not know. Somehow I have to tell his father in San Antonio," she said trying not to cry.

Phil made the Sign of the Cross and said, "He was a good man. I will miss him very much."

* * * * * * * * *

On New Years morning Delia, Belinda, and Mamett drank coffee, and listened to gunfire echoing sporadically across the hills. They were all on edge. Delia turned on the radio to the Ocosingo station XOECH.

"... Leaders like Villa and Zapata emerged, poor men just like us. We have been denied the most elemental education so that others can use us..." She turned the radio off.

"Looks like they've captured Ocosingo." Mamett observed.

"Who are they Patrick?" Delia looked out at the hills.

"I have no idea." Mamett shrugged and drained his coffee. "The latest in a long line of Maya rebellions?" He stood up, and looked down the road. "What's that?"

"Someone's coming." Belinda nervously watched a dust cloud approach. "I see one, no, a bunch of jeeps."

"Thank God." Mamett said. "It's Sergio and the army."

* * * * * * * * *

By early afternoon the rout of the government forces in San Cristobal was complete. An impromptu fiesta made it hard to move in the streets around the plaza. After running into heavy small arms fire on a side street, Phil made his way to an aid station that had been set up in the patio of the Hotel Diego de Mazariegos. The Zapatistas had draped a giant Mexican tricolor flanked by the blue and white banners of the EZLN in front of the

Palacio Municipal. Several speeches of liberation were being made over a public address system.

Phil listened to the celebration while the medics attended to him, but he was impatient to check on Delia and Belinda and get out to the camp. With all of the chaos going on in the middle of town, it was going to be difficult.

All I want now is just to get them out alive, he thought. To hell with everything else. No more losses.

The medics cleaned and bandaged Phil's wounds and he began to feel a little better. He refused painkillers, because they would put him to sleep. They gave Phil aspirin and he took a handful. He drank two liters of water and realized he was seriously dehydrated.

Gloria returned in a Jeep Cherokee. After borrowing some pillows and cushions from the hotel, and placing them in the passenger seat of the jeep, Phil got in. Gloria drove him out of town onto the main highway.

The EZLN had taken over a city of one hundred thousand inhabitants. Phil noticed that the guerillas were well-behaved and did not loot. The same could not be said for some of the locals who were smashing store windows on a side street. Abandoned cars and trucks were ransacked and some were burning. Just let me get them out of here in one piece, Phil thought, that's all I want. God, please let the girls be all right.

* * * * * * * *

Avendano finished talking. Everyone was quiet, absorbing it. Delia spoke first.

"So, now we know for sure that Phil and Jesse disappeared after they left your office. What do we do?"

Avendano stood up. "I recommend we do nothing for now. We stay right here. This is where we are supposed to be and it is a site that is easily defended. Just as it was in antiquity. There is only one approach, only one road in. We have a platoon of soldiers deployed in a perimeter around us, and we can expect reinforcements. As soon as Federal forces liberate the area, we will look for Jesse and Phil. Do you agree Patrick?"

"I'm very concerned about them but I really don't see how we have any other option. All that planning and hard work is out the window." He shook his head and stood up. "I would say the field season is likely aborted now. But you know what? I think I'm going to go take a bath. I feel greasy and filthy from traveling, and sleeping in my clothes. I'll think better when I'm clean." He started toward the door. "I'll be in the lagoon if anyone needs me."

Delia and Belinda left the hut together, and walked toward the site. When they were far enough away that no one could hear them. Belinda said. "This whole thing stinks."

"I know Avendano is lying." Delia whispered.

"And what about Mamett?"

"Meaning?" Delia pulled her hair back.

"Meaning I'm not sure that I trust either one of them. And you know what else? I don't feel like I'm being protected, I feel like we're prisoners."

"I trust Patrick but he's friends with Avendano so maybe we should tell him... What are you going to do?" Delia put a barrette around her pony tail, and glanced around to see if anyone was watching them.

"I'm getting the hell out of here at the earliest opportunity." Belinda said firmly. You are coming with me?"

Delia paused before answering. "I think so. But let's go get Phil's gun bag and a few other things first."

* * * * * * * *

Phil and Gloria reached the final checkpoint, a flatbed trailer turned on its side. A tractor was parked next to it. A squad of hooded rebels, signaled for them to stop.

"It's around here somewhere." Gloria said, and got out of the jeep.

"Wait. I know where it is. I should go on foot the rest of the way." Phil got out after her. They were less than a mile from Chanul Tzuk, he was anxious to get there.

"Gloria." A friendly voice called out to her.

"Professor?" She saw Garcia walking toward them from the flatbed.

"What do you think of our revolution now?" Garcia had a wide grin.

"It's wonderful. It looks you pulled it off." Gloria embraced him.

"Not quite, but we're getting there. Where is Jesse?"

"He…he did not make it. The police killed him." She began weeping again.

"Tell me what happened." Garcia embraced her.

* * * * * * * *

Gloria introduced Garcia to Phil. They stood on a hill at the edge of the jungle, and Phil looked at the land between him and Chanul Tzuk. The EZLN field hospital where they stood was made up of three large canvas tents, situated on a long stony ridge. The ridge sloped gradually down to the lagoon and swamps that encircled the ruins. From where they were, Phil estimated the main pyramid was four miles away.

The EZLN checkpoint was erected where the paved road changed to gravel. A few miles to the northwest he could see smoke drifting out of a hole in the jungle, and he figured that was where the archaeological field camp was set up. A cold feeling, an overwhelming dread came over him, and he knew death was in the air. He wondered if he could face it one more time.

"So where are you going next?" Garcia offered Phil a canteen.

"To Chanul Tzuk." Phil pointed up the road.

"The army has a platoon up there, and they'll probably reinforce it. It's a strategic point. It commands the road between San Javier and San Cristobal, and with the lagoon and swamps around it, it's easily defended." Garcia pointed toward the swamp and seemed worried. "Do you really have to go? Why not stay with us?"

"I have to go." Phil laced up his hiking boots.

"I see." Garcia paused before continuing. He seemed to have reached a decision. "Maybe you can help us out. Or we could help you out?"

"How?" Phil stood up wearily.

"I know we have to take control of Chanul Tzuk before it is reinforced. I've just been avoiding admitting it. You could help us get in. I'll accompany you with some of my troops?"

"You've got what? Maybe twenty men here?"

Garcia nodded. "But I'll bring them all."

"Count me in. I need all of the help I can get."

* * * * * * * *

Belinda and Delia knelt behind a thicket of bushes, and watched a black Ford Bronco approach the camp. Belinda wished she knew how to use the AK-47 she held in the gun bag. The Bronco stopped, and Alex Sanchez got out. He walked on his cane about a hundred feet and started relieving himself, on the edge of the parking area.

"Check this out." Belinda said and pointed to Avendano, who was walking toward Sanchez. "It's him. We've got to get the hell out of here now."

They turned in the opposite direction and headed toward the lagoon.

* * * * * * * *

"Don't move. Remain absolutely still. Put your gun down slowly on the ground." Phil whispered.

The soldier did as he was told. Phil put his arm around the man's neck and chopped him hard on the side of the head. Garcia pulled the body into the tall grass.

"Did you kill him?" Gloria whispered.

"No. I just put him out for awhile. Tie him up. I don't want to kill any more people if I can avoid it. I've had enough of death and killing." He picked up the soldier's weapon. "I do prefer his M-16 to this single shot shotgun that your friends gave me. No offense Garcia."

"None taken." Garcia signaled for his men to come forward.

"How long you been involved with the Zapatistas anyway?" Phil asked Gloria as he picked up the ammunition magazines.

"Two years. You don't approve?"

"Gloria it's your business. And it was Jesse's too, I gather. I approve of anyone who fights for what they believe in."

"And you? What do you believe in?" Garcia motioned his men to disperse.

"Right now I believe in this M-16, and I believe that all I want to do is get Delia and Belinda out of here alive. I also believe it's going to be dark soon and that means we don't have much time left to finish infiltrating their picket line."

"I couldn't agree more. Let's move out." Garcia directed his men to fan out on both sides of the path. He disappeared into the tall grass after them.

* * * * * * * *

No boats or canoes were on the shore so there was no way to get across the lagoon. Belinda and Delia turned around and made their way west, jogging and running. They reached the edge of the cenote, as the sun started to sink behind the mountains.

"What's up that arroyo?" Belinda breathed raggedly.

"If I remember the maps correctly, it's a dirt road that gets out to the main highway." Delia paused to catch her breath. They had been running for a half hour. She had a burning pain in her ribs.

"Good. We've almost made it." Belinda hugged Delia around her shoulders.

"Delia in case something happens, I need to tell you something."

"What?"

"You remember in the hotel you asked me about sleeping with Phil?"

"Yeah." Delia noticed Belinda was blushing.

"I was just messing with you. I was deliberately ambiguous. I haven't slept with him since we broke up. Bless his heart, he wouldn't go for it. And now that I know what kind of man I lost..." She paused and squeezed Delia's shoulder. "Anyway, I just wanted you to know."

"Thanks. I hoped it was something like that." She hugged Belinda back.

"Alto ladies. Where do you think you are going?" A soldier emerged from the jungle and pointed his gun at them.

* * * * * * * *

Phil and Gloria were thirty meters out of the camp and in deep woods. Garcia and his men were off to their left. They watched Alex Sanchez, Sergio Avendano, and four soldiers walk into a hut talking and gesturing, but they could not hear what they were saying.

Gloria moved in closer, focusing her eyes on Sanchez. Phil wanted her to wait, but they were too close to the camp for him to say anything.

Sanchez left the hut and started walking out toward the site. Gloria stalked him.

Phil went after her, his heart pounding, hoping he could find Delia and Belinda before it all broke loose.

* * * * * * * *

"No ladies, you cannot leave the camp. It is not safe." The soldier turned on his portable radio and said, "I'm at position 18, I have two gringas trying to leave the camp, headed for the main highway."

A voice Belinda didn't recognize said, "Someone will be right there. Hold your position."

Belinda sat down next to the gun bag and unzipped it while he talked. When he turned the radio off to put it on his belt, she pointed the AK-47 at him. "Give me your gun."

The soldier handed it over.

"Thank you. Now you will remain here. Please do not cause any trouble. Delia, let's leave now."

* * * * * * * *

Gloria nudged Sanchez hard in the back.

"You are not moving as fast as the last time I saw you."

"The little puta Maya. We meet again. How did you get here?"

"We're going for a walk Sanchez. Move!"

Sanchez seemed to accentuate his limp, but he made his way slowly, deeper into the woods. Gloria wedged the barrel of her gun between his shoulder blades.

* * * * * * * *

Avendano rubbed his chin. "Do you want me to go get Belinda and Delia? And where did Sanchez go?"

"Sure. Go get them. Or I could go?" Mamett stood up. "Hell. Let's both go. I wonder where they thought they were going. Your soldiers had better treat them with respect."

"We'll take two of the men with us." Avendano turned to the soldiers outside the hut and said, "Guillermo, Juan accompany us por favor."

In the darkness of the jungle Phil listened and watched them come out.

* * * * * * * * *

"Get down on the ground, and put your hands over your head." They were standing next to the ancient ball court. Placing his cane on the ground first, Sanchez obeyed Gloria's orders.

"I think I'll send you to hell now." Gloria took a step back and lowered her weapon.

As quick as a snake Sanchez grabbed his cane and whipped it around hard, knocking the shotgun out of Gloria's hands. He kicked out his foot, and connected with Gloria's ankle. She fell hard. He swung the cane again and brought it down quickly on the back of her head, and watched Gloria sink into the soft earth.

Sanchez stood up breathing hard. "Puta. Too bad there is no time to kill you properly, to gut you like a fish and pull out your heart." He untwisted the handle of his cane and withdrew a rapier blade from the cylinder. "But I can try out my new cane on you." He raised both hands to plunge the blade into Gloria's back.

* * * * * * * * *

"Delia. Belinda. Where are you? Come out; come out, wherever you are."

Mamett led Avendano and the soldiers around the cenote. He stopped and put his hands on his hips. "You are probably wondering why I called this meeting of the Harvard Club of Chanul Tzuk. Come on girls give me a break."

He smiled as he saw Delia walk into the clearing. "Delia where's Belinda?"

"Oh we were just out for a little stroll, and we were wondering why we can't leave the camp." She said quietly, and stood with her arms crossed.

"Because it's not safe dear." Mamett motioned the soldiers to stay put. "One would think that would be obvious."

"See Patrick, that's not what we think at all. We think they intend to kill every one of us. We're the only loose ends left, aren't we? I mean along with Phillip and Jesse. And Sergio's friends have probably taken care of them." She felt queasy, like she might throw up at any second.

"Now you baffle me Delia. I have no idea what you are talking about." Avendano's voice was a whisper.

"I'm confused too. We're only concerned about your safety. What the hell is wrong with you?" Mamett called out louder. "Belinda. Come on out. I know you can hear me. We need to get moving."

"Guillermo bring the senorita back." Avendano pointed at Delia.

* * * * * * * * *

Phil's M-16 blasted once and Sanchez grabbed his chest as he fell. Phil fired again missing him completely, as a ceiba tree dissolved in a green haze. Sanchez tried to crawl away into the darkness. Phil shot him one more time, and he stopped moving.

Gloria stood up shaking. She checked Sanchez for a pulse.

"Anything?" Phil asked.

Gloria shook her head. "Thank God you killed him. Mira, you go after your friends. I will make sure he is dead." Phil noticed she had a knife in her hand.

"Okay. But please be careful. It's still very dangerous out here."

398

* * * * * * * *

"Who the hell is firing that M-16?" Avendano shouted over the gun shots. "The guerrillas are here. Vámonos! Come on out Belinda we need to get going. Quit messing around."

"Sergio since this soldier has his gun in my ribs, I was wondering am I being rescued or taken prisoner? It is all rather confusing."

"We need to get moving, it's not safe out here." Avendano gestured at the soldier and Delia felt a hand on her elbow pushing her toward Sergio.

Belinda emerged from the darkness. She stood behind Mamett with the AK-47. "Why don't you tell me what's going on Patrick? Why don't you just tell me?"

"Belinda we all need to get out of here." Mamett gestured towards the camp.

Avendano nodded and Juan fired and hit Belinda's leg. She dropped her weapon and went down. Delia ran to her side.

"What are you doing?" Mamett turned toward Avendano.

"Sorry about that Belinda, but you were being so difficult. Now we can all get out of here." Sergio waved the soldiers forward. They picked up Belinda and pushed Delia forward.

"Not just yet." They heard Phil's voice from behind Mamett. "Put down all of your weapons." He fired a burst over their heads.

"Phil please wait." Belinda's voice cracked, now she felt it coming in the air. It was almost here. She had been expecting it…a black force pressing ever closer.

"My God, so Phil Ward is here too." Mamett turned toward Phil's voice. "Hey Phil. Hold on there's no reason for any more violence. It's just a communication problem."

"I'll make it easy for you all. Sergio, you release Delia and Belinda and we'll all forget the whole thing."

Avendano's eyes narrowed. "Why should I?"

"Because Sergio...I will kill you if you don't." Phil aimed directly at Avendano's head.

"I see." Avendano had a pistol in his hand. "Tell me. Who is going to save Delia and Belinda?" He laughed. "You? Because...before you can kill me, I will kill at least one of them. This is what is called a Mexican stand-off."

Belinda could feel her heart beating in her chest as if it had doubled in size, pounding and echoing in her eardrums. The dark thing she had felt coming for her was here now. She grabbed her guard's gun barrel and the M-16 went off in a burst. Mamett dove for the ground as shots whipped above his head. A gun fired nearby and more bullets spattered the ground in front of him. Phil entered the clearing and shot a soldier who was shooting at him. Belinda picked up an M-16 and shot at Juan. He fell next to Mamett.

Guillermo turned, aimed at Belinda and Phil dropped him. Phil saw Avendano aiming the pistol at him and turned to fire, but he knew he was too slow and wouldn't make it when Avendano pulled the trigger.

Belinda jumped in front of Avendano and Phil fired as he fired.

A red mist exploded out of her back and into Phil's eyes. She screamed and was slammed flat on her back.

Phil emptied the M-16 into Avendano, who was dead before he hit the ground.

All was silent.

Gun smoke drifted like a blue fog over the cenote. Phil, Delia and Mamett were the only ones moving. Phil cradled Belinda's head in his lap, rocking her gently. "Bel baby. Please don't die on me."

"I don't know… if I can do that… Phillip." She smiled up at him and blinked. "God. I'm so cold and it's so dark. So much I need to say to you and…no time now."

"Don't go Belinda please… Please?" He felt her coldness flowing into his hands up his arms, and into his heart.

"You are the only one who ever… really loved me. You really did love me didn't you?"

"Yes." Phil nodded, feeling the tears welling in his eyes. "Yes I did. I do still. Don't… please don't." he sobbed.

She coughed. "And in my way Phillip I always loved you…I hope you know that." Her eyes closed and she died.

"No." Phil howled in agony. A raw rage of grief consumed him.

From all around them the sounds of thousands of bat wings rent the stillness. They rose up from the trees, hills and ridges. It looked like every bat in the world took flight, blotting out the silvery sky, ascending into the twilight.

* * * * * * * *

Phil wept and watched his tears fall on Belinda's lifeless skin. He was in agony. I tried to save her but she died saving me. God I would trade places with her right now if I could.

Delia wept quietly behind him. "Poor Belinda after everything she's been through…" she whispered.

Mamett was in the bushes retching.

Phil gently rocked Belinda's body, and wiped the dust from her face.

A sharp metallic sound came from the bushes. Mamett stood on the edge of the clearing with a shotgun in his hands. He shivered and gripped the shotgun tighter with his finger on the trigger. Mamett's face was pale and sweat-streaked. He stared at them.

Phil realized they were both unarmed. The M-16 lay behind Delia.

"What are you doing Patrick?" Delia whispered.

"Sorry Delia. Really I am. But it has come down to this." He pointed the gun at them. "One or both of you would have figured it out. Too intelligent for your own good, regrettably."

"Belinda already suspected." Delia looked at Belinda's lifeless body and wiped her eyes with the back of her hand.

"And you see what it got her. These things happen during revolutions." Mamett shrugged and took a step toward them. "People just…disappear."

"Why Patrick?" Phil knew he was too far from the M-16 to do anything.

Mamett's eyes were wide as he bared his teeth. "Why Phillip? Because you were a half-wit looking for your better half! Belinda. You just had to go look for her. And then Laurence that incredible idiot…God, I really do hate students. As if any of this matters."

Speaking in a hoarse whisper, Mamett straightened up slowly. "But none of you will ever understand that I alone found the beast chained to its howling blasphemy unremembered and ignored." He shivered again. "Weeping tears that flow into the sewers and back to the sea from which we all crawled. We are all beasts roaming this earth knowing that we shall return to the earth."

He's completely insane, Phil thought. He heard Delia weeping next to him. They heard gun shots in the distance. The Zapatistas were still fighting the soldiers, too far off to help them.

"You haven't told us anything, you idiot bastard." Phil choked out a desperate laugh and stood up and looked Mamett in the eye. He moved to put his body between Delia and Mamett's shotgun. He will kill me, but maybe I can take him with me and save Delia, he thought.

"If I told you, you wouldn't begin to understand. Look, I have every right to do what I do, because I am a virtuoso, a practitioner of my art of archaeology. He sneered. "If that stupid bitch Kathryn Haden had not gone out… Oh well, all's well that ends, and this is where it all ends."

Mamett stepped closer to the edge of the cenote and glanced down. "And that cop couldn't leave well enough alone either. I even liked him. But I had to put a little something in his wine. A little something I learned from the Jaguar Cult. I am a member in good standing after all. So are Avendano and Sanchez. It's really too bad about Sergio."

"Really too bad about Sanchez too," Phil said.

"What?"

"I killed him a few minutes ago. I only wish I could have made him suffer more."

"No matter, more money for me is all you accomplished." Mamett shook his head and his face gleamed. "And finally we come down to you, Phillip the half-wit. It's been pure hell cleaning this mess up. Did I ever mention that I had a brief affair with the lovely Belinda? Hmm?"

"What?" Phil gasped.

"Good. I can see in your face that you didn't know. It is all quite regrettable really. I never meant for it to get this far. But I pulled all the strings from the very beginning." He aimed the shotgun at Phil.

"Put the gun down Patrick. It's your last chance to live." Phil said, and watched Mamett lower his head.

"I will do no such thing Phillip. You know I had to work hard to flunk you out at the orals. You put up a better defense than I had ever anticipated."

Phil leaped.

The shotgun went off at the same time that he landed heavily on Mamett. They rolled toward the cenote's edge. Phil felt a burning pain in his stomach. Bastard got me, he thought.

Phil lost his grip on the weapon and saw Mamett bring the barrel up. The edge of it sliced Phil above his eye, reopening his wound, and he could barely see, as blood flowed into the socket.

Delia aimed the M-16 toward Mamett but could not get a clear shot.

Mamett fought with the strength of madness. Phil could not get the upper hand. His wounds and exhaustion were slowing him down. Mamett was biting and thrashing; about to break loose. Now they were on the lip of the cenote. Phil kicked out as hard as he could and they rolled over, falling into the deep ancient pool.

In the black icy water he couldn't see anything at first, but he felt Mamett's arm clench around his neck as they sank. His grip was tightening, and Phil tried to get under the death lock with his hands, but his body moved sluggishly. He felt himself weakening, as they continued to descend, and the pressure in his lungs was building. He dug his fingers into Mamett's face and clawed at his eyes. He felt an eyeball in his grip, and tried to pull it out of the socket. Bubbles exploded from Mamett's nose, and he wrenched his head free.

Deeper they sank, slowly flailing away at each other, as his hands closed tight on Mamett's neck, Phil lost his breath in one agonizing gasp. Water poured into his nose, throat, and lungs. His body was wracked in spasms, and he felt icy fingers seep into every pore. His legs were like lead now. Mamett stopped moving and released his grip. Phil's hands remained locked on Mamett's neck.

I hope I killed him, because I will never make it out of here, he thought as his body continued to sink downward. Below him he could barely see Mamett floating motionlessly, and then he could see nothing, as he felt the darkness embrace him.

* * * * * * * *

"They are both still in the cenote Delia?" Garcia asked.

"Yes. I am diving in." She sobbed, and crawled to the ledge.

"No. You are in no condition. I will do it." Garcia took off his boots and slipped over the ledge.

75 Aftermath

The Zapatistas had driven the soldiers out of Chanul Tzuk and pursued them up the valley. Delia helped Garcia zip up Belinda's body in his sleeping bag and they gently placed her in the back of the Suburban. Garcia and Delia drove to the field camp where they reunited with Gloria. They all sat around Gloria's cot and listened to the running battle as it moved away from them and over the hills. The endless night finally grayed into dawn.

"Now I know who Jesse and Phil reminded me of…the Hero Twins." Delia said.

"What?" Gloria asked her.

"The Hero Twins from Maya mythology. They descended into the underworld, fought the Lords of Death, and finally defeated them?"

Gloria nodded sadly before answering. "I am so sorry about Phil and Belinda."

"I don't know what to do with myself Gloria. I am sorry about Jesse too...so many deaths, so many. I am afraid it will drive me crazy if I think about it too much." Delia tried not to start crying again.

Gloria said simply, "I know."

Garcia interrupted their reverie.

"We have formed a burial detail. Do you want us to… you know?" He ran out of words.

"Belinda?" Delia asked and the grief washed over her. She shuddered and felt tears forming again. "I don't know if I can…"

"We can bury her next to our own dead. Mark the grave. There will be a priest…" Garcia stood up. He looked exhausted standing next to Gloria.

"Sure. That would be fine. I'll try to help." Delia staggered to her feet.

* * * * * * * * *

Early the next morning they prepared to leave. "So neither Phil nor Mamett's body was recovered." Delia sighed, watching a squad of Zapatistas get into a captured Jeep. "I cannot believe that Phil, Belinda and Jesse are all…"

"The two bodies are still in the cenote." Gloria said. "But thank God Phil killed Sanchez. He was a truly evil man. We are going to burn his body." She watched Garcia walking toward them. The three of them stood in a loose circle next to the Suburban. No one had anything to say.

"Well, I guess this is goodbye." Delia climbed into the Suburban. On the passenger's seat was Sanchez's cane. "Thank you so much for helping me." She felt like she was sleepwalking. I guess this is what shock feels like, she thought.

Garcia clapped his hands. "We will escort you to the pass, until you clear our lines, and it should be pretty easy to get back to Tuxtla Gutierrez from there. I am very sorry about your losses."

"So am I. And I have no idea what to do now."

76 Convergence of Illusions

The visiting room at Rockview Hospital near Belize City was noisy and crowded. Under the slowly rotating ceiling fans and pulsing shadows, Paul Trevino gently pushed his way through the visitors and psychiatric patients.

Delia Bell sat in an old rocker near the kitchen. Paul sat down in an adjacent plastic chair, and clasped her hands in his. "Delia, how are you?"

406

"Heavily medicated Paul. I'm not really here" She smiled, and released his hands, adjusting the blue bathrobe around her knees.

"I brought you a book that I found on *Hera's Song*. Patty said you left it behind." He handed her *The Dark Romance of Diane Fossey*.

"Thank you. I guess I have plenty of time to finish it now."

"Delia. Are the doctors helping you at all?"

She stared at him blankly for a few seconds before answering. "There is nothing anyone can do for me Paul."

He nodded. "Okay, I don't know how to put this nicely so I'll just ask you straight out. Are you still suicidal? If they released you today, would you try it again?" He averted his eyes from her bandaged wrists.

"Probably...He set everything off you know, and C.S. Lewis was right by the way."

"He was right about what?" Paul was having difficulty tracking her elusive mental shifts.

"That grief feels so much like fear." A tear welled in her right eye.

"Who set everything off?" Paul asked and poured Delia a glass of water.

"Mamett," Delia mused. "I think his habit of studying artifacts in private collections and his ambition and greed provided fertile ground."

Paul was glad to have her talk about it. Maybe it would help her focus her mind. He had never seen anyone so haunted and fragile. "Then Mamett hooked up with Avendano, and Eikelmann...and Sanchez right?"

Delia nodded. "Like I was saying the last time you visited, their evil was a very mundane blend of immorality, ambition and avarice. They would sacrifice everything and everyone for a chance to get rich; or in Mamett's case...famous."

407

She stared at the floor. "In a way they sacrificed all of us, Kathryn Haden, Laurence, Professor Thomas, Jesse, Belinda, and Phil...Me." she sobbed.

"Mamett probably rationalized that the real owners of the artifacts were the ancient Maya, and the next thing you know they're all looting sites." Paul shook his head; maybe talking about it was a bad idea after all.

"But Laurence had second thoughts." Delia said softly, fighting back the tears.

Paul nodded. "And this is why Sanchez killed him."

"And that's how Laurence justified himself. He was aiding the revolutionaries." Delia leaned back and spread out her hands. "That's just how he was. He would skate out to the edge of the envelope and then go on across."

"On the other hand, Mamett liked to think of himself as a big-time Harvard archaeologist. He would let nothing stand in his way."

"A horrible convergence of illusions that killed a lot of people." Delia said, "But God I miss Phil, I was ready to build my world around him and now that world is gone." She sighed. "Sometimes though, I feel like, he's still here with me, and I don't think I will ever believe that he is really gone until his body is found."

"I know what you mean. Me too." He picked up her hand and held it. Her eyes darkened with pain and Paul kissed her on her forehead.

Delia frowned. "But you know something I just thought of? Not a shred of physical evidence links Mamett with his cohorts; just his actions at the cenote, so he could have possibly talked his way out of it." Delia picked up her water.

"Except that he was a sociopath." Paul added. "Who knows how long he could have maintained his act?"

"In the end, it got away from him. Out of his control." Delia looked vacantly at the people in the room as if she had just noticed their presence for the first time. "God Paul, I am so tired."

"But he hooked up with some bad hombres." Paul said. "And they couldn't be contained." He took a deep breath, before carefully saying, "I know it is difficult to think about, but where do you think the bodies are? Since that cenote is drained by an underground river…will they ever be found?"

"Honestly, I don't think either of them will ever be found." Delia stood up to leave, and wrapped her bath robe tighter. She shivered even though the room was hot and humid. "I fear they will always be with the Lords of the Night…and so I am afraid, will I, because I see them all the time. They are here right now."